SWEET SURRENDER

Hayden was too startled to offer an objection as he placed the engagement ring on her finger. She recognized many of the emotions that battled within her, such as fear, surprise, and confusion. She also recognized joy, but tried to ignore it was there. It shouldn't be.

Without warning, his large hand took her face and held it gently. As he cupped her chin, lifting her face to his, she felt a shiver of heat ripple through her. She knew what was coming next. She knew she had to prevent it.

Hayden opened her mouth slightly to protest, but before a word could come out, his lips were on hers. His kiss was slow and thoughtful, sending a warm surge through her. Hayden felt her body begin to melt as she gave herself freely to the passion of his tongue. Was this real, she asked herself.

Then, as fast as it began, his lips parted from hers.

''This is definitely one part of keeping up appearances I will enjoy,'' Cannon said with a heavy breath.

LOOK FOR THESE ARABESQUE ROMANCES

SWEET SURRENDER

Angela Winters

Pinnacle Books
Kensington Publishing Corp.
http://www.arabesquebooks.com

PINNACLE BOOKS are published by

Kensington Publishing Corp.
850 Third Avenue
New York, NY 10022

Pinnacle and the P logo Reg. U.S. Pat. & TM Off.

First Printing: March, 1998
10 9 8 7 6 5 4 3 2 1

Printed in the United States of America

This book is dedicated to my parents,
Matthew Winters and Merea Winters,
for their love and support.

Chapter One

"I've never been so frightened in my entire life," Elise Campbell said, as she gently placed her soft chocolate brown hands against her cheeks. She looked drained of energy as she concentrated on her husband, Tom, who was sleeping peacefully in their bed. She hadn't left his side since bringing him home from the hospital earlier that day.

"I wasn't frightened." Hayden Campbell squeezed her mother's shoulders in comfort while standing behind her. "I knew he'd come through. I never doubted it."

She recalled that dreadful day. She had been sitting at her office desk three weeks ago when she received a frantic call from her mother. Her father had suffered a heart attack and was being rushed to Evanston Hospital. Hayden had suddenly felt the world falling down around her. *Life without Daddy.* The memories of their treasured relationship had come rushing back to her, replaying in her mind. Even at twenty-seven, Hayden still needed her daddy and knew her mother would die inside without her lifelong mate. Elise Campbell had already suffered enough loss in her lifetime.

As Hayden had rushed to the hospital, located in the north

suburb of Chicago, she was scared out of her mind. *Life without Daddy.* Please, God, no.

Three weeks and a triple-bypass later, Tom Campbell was finally at home with his wife and daughter. It had been a hard three weeks for Hayden, who had wanted to fall apart from the sadness, frustration, and joy, but had to be strong for her father and her mother.

Both women stared affectionately as he rested. Life would never be the same, Hayden knew that, but at least he was still here.

Hayden had reassured her mother only to comfort her. She knew Elise saw nothing in this world except Tom. For years it had made her jealous. The truth was, between her father and her younger brother, Michael, Hayden felt she placed third on her mother's list of importance.

Hayden remembered most of her childhood consisting of her mother's attention centered on Michael and his accomplishments. He was so intelligent, incredibly charming for his age, and becoming such a handsome young man. He was going to go far. Possibly a doctor, a Wall Street whiz, or even a famous actor on account of his great looks and welcoming personality.

Then there was Hayden. She was a cute little thing, she'd been told often by her mother. She'd be pretty when she grew up. She'd marry a doctor, a Wall Street whiz, or even a famous actor with good looks and a welcoming personality. There were bits and pieces of praise from her mother, moments of affection that Hayden tore from her past and held onto. Few and far between and nothing like her father. No, Elise's heart held little room for anyone other than her husband and son. At least that was the impression Hayden had.

Hayden would be lying if she said she hadn't transferred some of her anger and hurt at her mother's lack of affection onto her brother. Although she loved him dearly, as a confused child and teenager desperate for attention, she held some animosity toward him, although he never threw his mother's love in his sister's face.

Hayden had transferred some of that anger and hurt to herself as well. She was seventeen when Michael was killed in an automobile accident at the tender age of sixteen. Mixed with her grief, Hayden felt guilt. It was a guilt that overwhelmed her for a year after his death, as she watched her father's heart break and her mother let go of life a little bit. Moments actually came when she wished it had been her who had died. She had actually believed at the time that it would have been easier that way. It wasn't until she went away to college that Hayden began to let go of her guilt and her grief and began to live again.

"You weren't worried, were you?" Elise gently pat Hayden's comforting hand, her eyes closing halfway in tender approval. "You're a strong girl, Hayden." She lifted her head to see her young daughter's coffee-colored face and smiled into her large, black eyes. "You don't need anybody to hold your hand. You've always been so strong."

"Yes, Mama." Hayden felt her heart drop at the sound of her mother's words. *No, Mama,* her heart screamed. *I need you to hold my hand sometimes. I'm not always so strong. I was scared and I still am.* "He's fine now and that's all that counts."

"Yes, it is." Elise stood up from the antique, cherry wood rocking chair placed next to the bed in their Evanston home. The pillow seat cushion she had made herself before Hayden was born was faded and used, but had never been replaced. Not much had been replaced in the quaint three-bedroom house. Its style and feel was southern comfort, which Elise had decorated with memories of her Tennessee upbringing. "I'm going to go make us some tea. Let me know if he wakes."

"Okay, Mama." Hayden took her mother's seat, smiling inside as she felt the woman's compassionate hand run over her long, thick dark brown hair. Her mother's touch, as seldom as it came, brought Hayden such warmth and security. It wasn't her mother's love for her she doubted. It was the amount.

Hayden looked at her father again. Tom Campbell was a very handsome man at sixty. With smooth, coffee colored skin like Hayden and an eggshell white head of hair and mustache, he was quite a picture. His features were strong and prominent, his eyes soft and understanding. Hayden had always been proud of how attractive both her parents were and adored how much they continued to remind each other of it.

As tender images focused in her memory, she could see her father taking her to Arlington Park to watch the horses race when she was a little girl. That was their event. No one, neither Mama nor Michael, could come along. Every time they went, Hayden had been so excited to go, only to burst into tears as soon as she'd seen the jockeys whip their horses to make them run faster.

"Make them stop, Daddy." Little Hayden had buried her face in her father's strong chest. "They're awful and cruel. The horses are running as fast as they can."

"There now, princess." As he always had, Tom Campbell rubbed his daughter's back with strong reassuring motions. "The horses will be alright."

"They're such beautiful and peaceful animals," she cried.

"They'll be alright, princess." He had handed her a chocolate bar with little crisps inside, as always. "The men love their horses. They wouldn't hurt them."

Hayden had taken the candy bar, and as always, returned to watching the race. She knew the jockeys did the same thing every time, but continued to come just for the pleasure of turning to Daddy. So reliable. So comforting.

Now she was twenty-seven and on her own, but she still needed Daddy to hold her when she cried and he had, whenever she called upon him. The thought of losing that frightened Hayden more than she cared to even admit to herself. She squeezed his hand.

"How is he doing?" Elise returned to the room, placing the tea set on the end table beside the small bed.

"He's still sleeping. He looks fine." Hayden stood up to pour tea for the both of them.

Elise recaptured her seat next to her husband, loving concern in her eyes. "He's been sleeping all day. Is that good? I'm afraid he won't wake up."

"Don't worry, Mama." She handed her mother a cup with

a reassuring smile. "The doctor said he needed lots of rest. He's breathing fine."

"I know." Elise sighed, her fingers tensed around the cup. "It's just that I don't know what I'd do if I lost both my men. First Michael, now—"

"Mama," Hayden interrupted, not wanting to relive old, painful memories. "Don't even think about that. Please, just let him sleep and don't upset yourself. Let's cherish the time we have with him."

"That's just it," Elise said, as she took a quick sip of her tea. "How much time is that? He needs me now and I don't know how long I can be with him like this."

"What do you mean?" Hayden faced her mother with confused eyes. "You get six weeks off don't you? We talked about this. That's what most companies give for sick leave."

"No, dear. That's what companies like yours give." Elise would not take her eyes off her husband as her brows centered in frustration. "Alan can't afford that."

"He can't afford it? What does that have to do with anything?" Hayden tried to keep her voice down, so she wouldn't wake her father.

Alan Graham was president and owner of AG Enterprises, a small marketing firm in Skokie where Elise Campbell had worked as a secretary for almost ten years.

"He can't afford to lose his only secretary," Elise explained. "I'm not just a secretary, I do the books, I do everything."

"He's not losing his secretary," Hayden answered quickly. "You'll be back, but Daddy needs you now. Nothing is more important than that."

"What can Alan do?"

"Mom, I know you care about your boss, but that isn't your concern. He can hire a temp. Everyone does it."

"He is hiring one for two weeks. He's giving me two weeks." Elise's eyes lowered her eyes to the tea cup. After a moment, she frowned as if deciding she no longer liked the taste and placed the cup back on the tray.

"I've never heard of a two-week sick leave," Hayden said with pursed lips.

"It's not sick leave." Elise paused with a heavyhearted sigh. "It's my vacation."

"Vacation!" She placed her cup on the tray, afraid she would spill on her green silk business suit. "You and Daddy were going to use your vacation to go on a cruise when he gets better. Alan can't get away with this. There are laws. Has Alan every heard of the Family and Medical Leave Act?"

"Of course he has." Elise appeared frustrated at the direction the conversation was taking. "Alan said his company is too small and that law doesn't apply to him."

"Well, we'll see about that." Hayden wasn't so sure her mother was right or wrong, but she was certain there was something she could do.

"Hayden, I don't want to talk about it anymore." Elise leaned across the bed and gently brushed her husband's arm. "I don't want to get into any legal issues. We need my job now more than ever."

"I'm sorry, Mama," Hayden said in a calmer voice. Leaning against the wall, she decided she wouldn't talk about it anymore today, but this was definitely not over.

"I have some good news," she said, wanting to change the subject herself.

"What is it, dear?" Elise briefly glanced in Hayden's direction, then returned her eyes to her husband.

"I've been awarded the Coverling Corporation account." She had received the good news four days ago from her boss, Roger Green, president of R&D Public Relations, the downtown Chicago firm she had been working at as an executive for five years.

Hayden had been hoping for the opportunity to head the account for a long time. A Fortune 200 company, Coverling was considered cream of the crop in its industry. These past few weeks it hadn't been Hayden's number one concern, which surprised her all the more when Roger awarded her charge of the account. He had to call her at the hospital, which was where she had practically lived for the past three weeks. Considered by those who knew her to have always been a *people person,* public relations was considered the *perfect* field for Hayden. Over the five years she had been with R&D, her hard work produced results and she was given more and more responsibility. Coverling was the opportunity that could send her career into warp speed. She had worked hard to get where she was today, only there was no one to share it with.

"That's nice, dear." Elise forced a smile, never turning from her husband. "That's very good for you."

Hayden wasn't at all surprised at her mother's indifference. She had become used to it. She could try to convince herself it was because her father was home from the hospital today, but the reaction would have been the same a year ago and would be the same a year from now. Elise Campbell loved her daughter, but her pride was in her son even though he was no longer here.

"They shape diamonds and precious jewels," Hayden continued although she knew it was useless. Her mother had never shown a great interest in her personal life or career. "They work with the finest jewelers from around the world."

"That's great." Elise gave a thoughtful smile, although her heart and mind were obviously elsewhere.

"Thanks." Hayden accepted the bone thrown to her. She gathered herself together, feeling exhausted through and through. "I really must go now. I have some preparation to do on the account."

"Alright, dear." Elise spoke in a whisper. "I'll call you if he wakes up."

"Thanks, Mama." Hayden glanced at her father once more before leaving the bedroom, then turned again to her mother. "If you want to do something about this sick leave, you know where I am."

"Around the corner, of course," Elise said. "Bye bye, dear."

Hayden wasn't literally around the corner, but she lived less than a ten-minute drive away on the north side of Evanston. Although she was in a financial position to live in a luxury apartment in the city, such as North Lake Shore Drive, she was unwilling to be so far from her parents. She adored them both and knew her foundation was rooted firmly in their love and guidance. There were other reasons to stay. After losing Michael ten years ago, Hayden knew she was all her parents had and she had to be as close as possible. More now than ever before, she was glad she would be, in case her father needed her.

Tom Campbell did wake up later that night and Hayden quickly returned to his side. She had already scheduled three more days off from work to be with him and help her mother care for him upon his return home, so getting sleep for herself wasn't a concern. What was a concern was that when he woke up, he was weak, tired and complained constantly.

"Daddy," Hayden said as she reached out to him. He was tossing and turning restlessly in the bed. "Don't move around so much. Calm down."

"I can't," he snapped. "No matter what position I lay in I'm uncomfortable. This is ridiculous."

Hayden looked across the bed at her mother, whose eyes seemed to strain to hold back tears. She knew two weeks would never be enough time for her mother to tend to him. "Mama, what about hiring a nurse?"

"A nurse?" she asked, seeming uncertain. "Hire a full-time nurse to stay here all day? We can't afford that."

"I'll pay for it," Hayden said. She had no idea what was involved in hiring home care, but was certain it wasn't too difficult. Money wasn't an issue.

"No," Tom said, as he lifted up from the bed, leaning against the pillows along the headboard

"Tom," Elise said, "please lie down and rest."

"I will not!" He shrugged with irritation. "I'm tired of lying down. I've been lying down for three weeks now, and I don't feel any better."

"What nurse would put up with that personality?" Elise asked Hayden. "He's constantly crabby and terribly difficult."

"They're used to it," Hayden said. "They can handle people worse than Daddy."

"Stop talking about me like I'm not here." Tom stubbornly pouted as he grabbed the covers and pulled them up to his neck. "It's cold in here."

"I'll turn the heat up." Elise quickly left her chair and headed for the heat thermostat in the hallway.

Hayden's worries grew as she knew it wasn't cold at all. This was an unusually warm day in March. What could be wrong? She wished he would lie down.

"You aren't paying for anything," Tom said to his daughter. He wasn't pouting now, but looking at her sternly. As sternly as a sixty-year-old sickly man could. "I know you gave your mother some money again yesterday and I've had enough of that. I won't have my child taking care of me."

"But, Daddy—"

"No." He held up his hand to silence her. "This is not up for discussion."

"Fine," Hayden said. She knew when her father had made the final decision, and this was one of those times. "What about health insurance? HMOs or PPOs. They pay for that kind of . . ."

"No nurse," he said, shaking his head. "I won't have some stranger in my home. Attending to me like an . . . like an . . ."

Hayden felt her heart drop as she saw realization hit her father. This man, this strong man, this man she adored. He had so much pride, enough for all of them. That pride was holding on to its last breath now. It tore her apart to see him begin to understand that.

"Maybe I can take a little longer off," Hayden said as Elise rejoined them and sat on the bed next to her husband. "When Mama has to go back, I'll take off and stay here. We have a sick leave policy that includes any family members."

"I thought you said you just started a new account," Elise said, as she placed another pillow behind her husband. "You said it was a big one, right? You can't take any more time off than you have."

"But I . . ."

"Hayden," Tom said in almost a whisper, as he looked tenderly into his daughter's eyes. "Baby, please. I know you mean well, but I'm a proud man, and at sixty, I'm just not ready to have my child do the things . . . well, you know."

"Yes, Daddy." The words came as almost a whimper as Hayden felt tears at her throat. "I understand."

"We'll think of something." Elise looked with eyes of devotion at Tom. "It will work out."

It had to, Hayden thought to herself. Her father's chances depended on it. The family's happiness depended on it.

Back at work, Hayden found it difficult to concentrate on planning a program for Coverling. She was working up the courage to call Alan Graham and demand he give her mother at least six weeks leave, but she didn't want to threaten her mother's job. After all, her father had no choice but to quit his job as a high school math teacher after the heart attack; the stress of dealing with a couple hundred teenagers a day was too high for an already high strung man. Her parents needed Elise's income. Hayden offered so many times to help them out, and when times were bad they allowed her to, but only then. They would have to let her help now.

"What are you daydreaming about?"

Hayden lifted her head from her work to see Donna Nouri, her best friend and coworker, in her office doorway. She looked sharp today as usual, her Mediterranean heritage gave her soft olive-colored skin and thick dark brown hair that fell straight down her back. Her eyes were a radiant blue, her nose small and fine. She was the quintessential business woman in her power suits. Today's selection was a mauve rayon pantsuit, possibly DKNY or Liz Claiborne, perfectly tailored to fit her svelte figure. Everything was perfectly in place. Donna loved to look in control.

"I'm not daydreaming. I'm agonizing over what we talked about yesterday. You know, about my mother and her job."

Hayden had told Donna everything. They had been friends for only four years, but to both it seemed like they'd known each other since childhood. Even when she tried to keep a secret, it was useless. Donna was extremely perceptive and knew how to get anything from anyone.

"I was thinking about you." Donna strolled into the office and sat her thin figure in the chair opposite Hayden's desk. She leaned back, placing a newspaper on her lap.

"I know." Hayden smiled appreciatively. "My mother and I really appreciate the food you sent to the house and the flowers and the . . ."

"Oh, that. You're welcome, but I meant I was thinking about your problem." She unfolded a copy of *Represent Chicago,* the city's leading African-American daily newspaper. Every black professional in the Chicago area read this paper, which was a mixture of news, business reports, arts and entertainment, as well as local gossip for and about African-Americans.

"What's this for?" Hayden asked.

"Have you ever heard of Cannon Factor?" Donna asked.

"The name sounds familiar." Hayden took the newspaper and began leafing through it. "A famous doctor. He's dead isn't he?"

"You're talking about Craig Factor," Donna said. "He's a world famous doctor. I'm talking about his son, Cannon. He's Cook County Health Commissioner. He used to be a doctor, too. Well, he still is, but he's not practicing anymore. He's loaded. His dad left him a ton of money and he's made quite a bit himself."

"Now that I think of it," Hayden said, "I do know of him. His name gets mentioned a lot on the social scene. Is that right?"

"If you actually went to a social event in the city you would have met him. You haven't partied in a long time."

"I go to association meetings," Hayden said defensively.

"To network for business," Donna said. "Doesn't count. Ever seen him?"

"Who, Cannon?" Hayden thought back. "Can't remember."

"Then you haven't, because if you had, you would definitely remember. He's absolutely gorgeous and only thirty-eight years old."

Hayden noticed Donna's eyes squinting as they usually did when she was plotting something. "What does he have to do with my father?"

"Maybe he can help your mom with her job situation. He's had a rep as a playboy off and on, but when it comes to helping other people, I think he delivers."

"How do you know?" Hayden leaned across the desk, interested in hearing more. Could this man help her?

"Remember, a year ago my uncle Eric finally admitted he was an alcoholic? He wanted to get into a clinic, but his company's insurance wouldn't pay for it. There was a whole bunch of red tape. Anyway, he wrote a complaint to Dr. Factor and the man bent over backward for my uncle. I'm not sure if he found a loop hole, pulled some strings, or called in a favor, but Uncle Eric has been on the straight and narrow ever since. It saved his marriage."

"So he does this often for people?" Hayden allowed a flicker of hope to light within her. Her mother's two weeks were almost up. "Does he work with health insurance problems?"

"I don't know what he does exactly, but he has connections across the city. The person who referred him to my uncle said Cannon had also done something great for her family." Her eyebrows raised suggestively. "I heard he does a lot of other stuff, too."

"Like what, playboy stuff?" Hayden knew this wasn't any of her business, but Donna was very good at gossip and it usually turned out that whatever gossip she told turned out to be true. "You know I don't keep up with the society scene."

"Yes." Donna pointed toward the paper on the desk. "I used to hear some rumors about him. You know, stuff like he's dated every woman in Chicago. He's a wham bam thank you ma'am. I haven't heard anything recently, but that's what made me think of him. I just read in an editorial in there he was seen leaving a downtown hotel with two women last night. Very young women.''

Hayden resumed leafing through the paper. ''Sounds like a yucky guy.'' She didn't like what she was hearing, but if he served the people well, should she judge him?

''I guess,'' Donna said. ''I know when he was a doctor, he had a huge practice in Northbrook and an even larger reputation with the ladies.''

''That's a shame.'' Hayden couldn't stand men who used women like arm pieces. She couldn't stand women who allowed them to. Most of all, she couldn't understand such irresponsible sexual habits in this day and age.

Finally she found the short article on Cannon Factor in the editorial section of the paper.

FACTOR SEEN IN COMPROMISING POSITION, AGAIN
Lee Sampson

Before reading anything else, Hayden noticed his picture in the center bottom of the page. She was drawn to it almost as if by force. Cannon Factor was a strikingly handsome man with an inherent strength in his face. His compelling light brown eyes showed a quiet, but determined man who needn't say anything to show his power. His sharp nose and generous mouth molded perfectly on his nut-brown-colored face. A thin, finely shaved goatee complimented a charming smile that, Hayden had to admit, would make any woman think twice about him. Better yet, think three times, maybe four. The picture only went to his shoulders, which appeared broad and expansive and Hayden caught herself wondering what he looked like below those shoulders.

''He's gorgeous isn't he?'' Donna asked, acknowledging Hayden's stare.

''Well . . . yes, I guess so.'' Hayden blinked before she reluctantly pulled her eyes from the paper to respond to her friend. ''An effective weapon, I'd think.''

"You got that right." Donna stood up, ready to leave. "Keep the paper. I've got to get back to work. What are you working on?"

"I'm putting together the six-month plan for Coverling Corporation." Hayden proudly held up their new client's annual report.

Donna had told her weeks ago she would head the account, being a constant source of encouragement. Despite being at the same level, there wasn't any unhealthy competition between the two. Hayden wanted the best for Donna as well, knowing how capable she was.

"Well," Donna said. "When you have time, give Factor's office a call or write him. But read the article first. You'll want to be prepared for his smooth lines when they come."

Hayden let out a sarcastic laugh. "I know I don't get out much anymore, but I'm sure I've heard them all. Besides, getting a new man is the last thing on my mind right now."

"That reminds me," Donna said as she swung around, standing in the doorway of the modernly designed office. "Have you talked to Alec recently?"

"No." Hayden felt a quick sting at her heart at the mention of Alec Gavin.

After dating the young electrical engineer for eight months, she was certain she was falling in love with him. They got along so well, both advancing in their careers, sharing each other's company as friends and lovers. Hayden's parents even liked him, which was new since Tom Campbell had never thought any man good enough for his daughter.

Then came that night out of the blue. She was stunned at first when he abruptly ended the relationship to move to Atlanta in response to a job offer. She hadn't expected him to stay, the opportunity was too good. She was almost certain she wouldn't have moved with him, because Chicago would always be her home as long as her parents were there and her career was just hitting stride, but that hadn't been a definite. She loved Alex and would have considered it if he had asked her. That was it.

He never bothered to ask her. He just told her he was leaving for Atlanta and the relationship was over.

"Do you know if he likes Atlanta?" Donna's lashes flickered sympathetically as she spoke with care. She had been there for Hayden when the breakup took its toll on her. "Maybe he hates it and misses you."

"I doubt," she replied, forcing a smile. "He's only been there two months and Atlanta is a great town."

"Just asking." Donna lowered her head, seeming to know from Hayden's expression that now was not the time to discuss Alec. "Well, if you ever want to talk about him or anything, you know where my office is."

"Bye, hon, and thanks." Hayden flashed a warm smile

"You're welcome." With a quick flip of her thick dark brown mane and a wink, Donna disappeared around the corner.

Hayden took a moment to look around her office in silence. It was a bit messy, with files and papers here and there. Her small window overlooking the scenic downtown skyscrapers looked as if it hadn't been washed in a while. She smiled bleakly to herself as she thought of the building cleaning service. She missed Petra, the young woman who came to her office every day around 6 P.M.

Alec Gavin. Her mind was trying to avoid that topic. She had dealt with this loss in its time, but new, more important problems had taken its place. There was still closure that was needed in regards to their love affair, but Hayden knew it would have to be at another time.

She threw Alec from her mind and returned her attention to the editorial, taking another moment to look at the impressive picture again before reading.

Cook County Health Commissioner Dr. Cannon Factor has been caught in another compromising position, yet again surrounding his personal life.

A source close to the commissioner reports he was seen leaving a fund-raiser for a local charity at The Hyatt

Regency Chicago on the evening of March 16 with two women, said to be only in their very low twenties.

This is the second time this month Factor's moral character has come into question. Before this, the only news about him was how impressive a job he's been doing as commissioner. He was seen earlier this month in what has been described as heated verbal *warfare* with a woman who accompanied him to a local sports event. The thirty-eight-year-old bachelor, admits a well-publicized wild life as a playboy and risk taker in his earlier years, causing a great deal of conflict between him and his famous father, Dr. Craig Factor, but Junior claims to have matured from that stage in his life, no longer involved in such unrespectable activities.

This reporter wonders, if so, why not tell us where you were on March 16? When questioned for comment, as before, Factor refused to respond.

No, Dr. Factor is not a married man and there is an argument for his personal choices being just that, but come on. Yes, Factor may be an effective health commissioner, but do the citizens of Chicago want their tax money to go to this man's salary? How do we know how he paid for that hotel room at The Hyatt?

With a speculative eyebrow raised, Hayden questioned whether or not she wanted anything to do with the man she was reading about, but she knew she wasn't full of choices and was running out of time. How many women he chose to sleep with was insignificant to the fact that he might be able to help her situation. Knowing she had to do something, Hayden decided to stop by the commissioner's office on her lunch hour.

The James R. Thompson Center State Building, named after a past mayor, was located in downtown Chicago, on Lake and LaSalle Streets. Hayden usually enjoyed walking around downtown, especially in the spring and summer, but to save time, she decided to take a cab. As she passed the usual group of protesters and entered the building famous for holding trials of mafia kingpins and crooked judges, she went straight to the directory.

HEALTH DEPARTMENT, 600

The sixth floor was committed entirely to the city's public health department and the workers were very busy when she entered. Watching the people running back and forth, yelling over the phones, piling files high on each desk, she assumed they should have their hands full with the extracurricular activities of Cannon Factor. Cover-up can take a great deal of time and cause extreme frustration. Nevertheless, she was grateful for the situation because as a result everyone ignored her arrival, giving her options besides being ushered to a chair to wait or fill out forms. She made the deduction that since everyone was on the left side of the floor, Dr. Factor's office must be on the right. After six years in the business world, she had learned when crisis management was at its highest, most executives stay as far away from the boss as possible.

Heading for the commissioner's office, Hayden cautiously halted around the corner at the sound of conversation close by. Peeking her head slightly forward, she noticed a young man in his late twenties in a Chicago Bulls T-shirt and blue jeans pleading with a State Building security guard for access to Dr. Factor's office.

"Just one question." The young man pushed his gold-rimmed glasses firmly on his face while lifting a reasoning finger in the air.

"Listen, Sampson." The security guard spoke with a deep monotone voice, showing the certainty he felt about what he had to say. "Take your little pad and pencil and hit the curb. The commissioner is busy."

Hayden took a good look at the young reporter. She assumed he was Lee Sampson, the writer of this morning's article on Dr. Factor. He was persistent, Hayden thought, as she saw the smaller man wasn't the least bit intimidated by the considerably larger guard.

"So much you know, buddy," Sampson said sarcastically. "In the 1990s we use tape recorders, not pen and paper." He reached into his baggy pants' pocket and brought out a miniature recorder, waving it in the air right in front of the guard's face.

"For a little guy, you sure got a big mouth." The security guard's voice was threatening as he leaned over.

Sampson wasn't actually little, Hayden decided, probably a little under six feet. It was just the guard was so big, looking at least 6 feet 4 inches and 250 pounds.

"Listen, buddy," Sampson said, "I just want to ask Factor about March 16. The rumors . . ."

In his attempt to return the recorder to its previous place, Sampson missed the open pocket and the recorder fell to the ground, shattering into pieces.

He cursed aloud as he dove for the batteries that were rolling under a nearby desk. Hayden laughed quietly, as he hit his head on the front of the desk, sending all the paper work on top flying. Now it was the guard's turn to curse and scramble. Sensing the opportunity, Hayden decided to go for it and headed for the glass office door marked CANNON FACTOR. Neither man noticed her as she quickly hid herself in the small wall crevice next to the door.

To her surprise, the door to Dr. Factor's office wasn't completely closed and she strained her limber body to an angle, allowing herself to look inside and see three people in heated conversation.

"Personally, I think we should get the police involved," an older man around his midfifties was yelling, his brick brown-colored forehead tensed with lines across it.

"No, Warren. No police," said another man with a resigned tone.

Hayden knew immediately the other man was Cannon Factor. He looked even more devastating in person now that she saw how tall and physically fit he was. His ruggedly handsome face was tamed with his well-groomed attire, a midnight blue, tailored business suit. As angry as he looked at the moment, the very confident way in which he stood, told anyone that this was an important man and Hayden had to acknowledge the quick tingle of excitement she felt at the sight of him.

"Fine, no police." The man Cannon called Warren ran a distressed hand over his head and blinked several times quickly. "Then a private investigator. Someone to find out who is doing this."

"Listen, Warren." An African-American woman in her forties, sitting on the edge of the desk with her back to Hayden spoke in a soft, calming tone. "Cannon says no, then no. We can handle this ourselves. Besides, could we get a private investigator to find out a reporter's source? Follow Lee Sampson? I don't think we want to go there. If we were found out, the damage to Cannon's career . . ."

At that moment, Hayden's heart jumped to her throat as she let out a gasp. Her arm was grabbed firmly from behind and she was swung around.

"Come with me, young lady." The security guard looked down at her with dangerous disapproval.

Hayden felt a quick shiver of panic run through her as everyone in the office turned their attention to her. Warren charged the door and swung it wide open.

"I thought you were manning the door?" the woman asked the guard sharply, with her angry face now in Hayden's sight.

"I'm sorry, Ms. Holly, I won't let it happen again," the guard said, sounding almost intimidated. "These reporters, you know."

"At least we have a good-looking one this time." Cannon's deep voice held a staid calmness as he quickly looked her up and down. The sight of the young woman struggling in the guard's grip would be comical if it weren't for the fact that he found her so attractive.

She's exquisite, a voice inside screamed to him. He was stricken by the beautiful, shiny texture of her skin, her large, playful eyes, and those long legs that seemed to go on for miles

past the midthigh black skirt. It was the most pleasant sight he
had witnessed all day.

Hayden jerked away from the security guard to no avail. He
had three times her strength.

"I'm not a reporter," she spat out stubbornly, "but I wonder
why you would make such a sexist comment, thinking that I
was. How would it help your . . . current situation if I reported
that?"

"You're very funny." Ms. Holly smirked at Hayden as she
lifted her chin. "We've all had a laugh. Now you can leave."

"Calm down, Maryann. Hold on." Cannon held up a cautious hand in the direction of the guard. He was more than
amused by how well this young woman stood up to the pressure
and was curious as to what she wanted. A voice inside said,
don't let this woman go without knowing who she is. "If you
aren't a reporter, then who are you?"

Hayden gave the disappointed security guard a victorious
smile as he let her arm go, turning her attention to Cannon.
"My name is Hayden Campbell and my mother's employer is
denying her sick leave to care for my father. He just had triple-
bypass surgery."

"We can't deal with this now," Warren said impatiently to
Cannon.

"Well, dear." Maryann Holly walked slowly toward Hayden, with condescending fake sympathy written all over her
face. "I'm very sorry for you and so is the commissioner, but
you need to file a formal complaint with the Department of
Labor, not us." She pointed to the door. "That office is on the
third floor."

Hayden looked directly into the woman's eyes, feeling
enough courage that she had gotten this far. She only needed
a little more to win this argument.

"Excuse me, but I don't have time to fill out a million
government red tape forms." She turned away from a half
stunned Maryann and looked earnestly at Cannon. "I need help
now."

"I said—" The woman's tone was tight as she tried to maintain her composure.

"Maryann, it's alright." Cannon silenced the woman with a quick look. He was intrigued by the gall this beautiful woman had. *You got her name,* the voice said, *you need more.* "Ms. Campbell, it may be unpleasant, but you *do* have to fill out some standard forms."

Hayden embarrassed herself by unwillingly responding to his charming smile with one of her own. She could tell that Maryann Holly was beyond impatience, but she was more disturbed by her own reaction to the handsome playboy who stood before her. She wished he wasn't so attractive.

"On the other hand," Cannon said, as he casually sat down in his saddle brown leather chair. "Let me hear what you have to say." No, he didn't have the time, but her face, lit up with sweet animation, told him to make time. *Keep Ms. Campbell in this office as long as you possibly can,* the voice urged.

Hayden beamed with accomplishment in response to the frowns on both Warren and Maryann's faces. "Thank you."

"Cannon, we really must deal with matters at hand," Warren said in a begrudging tone.

Cannon kept his eyes on the compelling young woman as she arranged herself on the comfortable chair across from his desk. The sight of her made him forget matters at hand and he wanted to do that for a moment longer. "Later, Warren. I would appreciate it if you and Maryann would go about your business now. I know you both have a lot to do."

Maryann sighed her disgust aloud as she gathered a stack of papers together and walked briskly out of the room. Hayden didn't look, but she knew the woman was staring intently at her the whole time.

Warren checked his watch. "I do have to be in court at two, so I should leave." He picked up a silver briefcase that looked like a large, rectangular soup can. "I want you to think about calling the police."

"Warren, that is out of the question." The finality in Cannon's tone prevented any further protest from the older man.

"Spreading rumors is not a crime. We don't need this kind of publicity."

As she watched Warren leave, Hayden couldn't help but be impressed with Cannon's control. People listened to this man. Maybe he could help her after all.

"I'm sorry to interrupt your meeting," Hayden said, unusually aware that they were alone now, "but this is important and needs to be resolved."

He leaned back in his chair, lifting his strong arms and joining his dark hands together behind his head. "You'll have to excuse Warren and Maryann. Warren is my lawyer and Maryann is my assistant. They're both very protective of my time."

"You're very fortunate," Hayden said flatly, although she wasn't concerned with his hierarchy of loyalty. It was in her nature to be friendly and open with people, even those she'd just met, but there was no time for that now. A serious situation called for serious behavior. Besides, Hayden hadn't forgotten that article this morning. A man like Cannon would probably interpret friendliness as an invitation.

"You now have my full attention." An easy smile played at the corners of his mouth as he took in her features. With little makeup, her face seemed to shine with natural beauty and kindness.

"Well, Mr. Factor, I—"

"Cannon, please," he said, interrupting. "You can call me Cannon. May I call you Hayden?"

"It really doesn't matter to me, sir." She spoke in irritation, not so much with him, but with herself for having to fight the smile that wanted to surface on her face. As she noticed the stubborn pout he was forming, she complied, "Alright."

"Hayden is a peculiar name." Cannon's eyebrows raised inquiringly. "Where did it come from?"

"My parents," she said, "which by the way is who I came to talk to you about."

Cannon grinned briefly at her attitude. Was it demeaning to refer to it as spunk? He wasn't sure what he could or couldn't say in these days of political correctness. Whatever the right way was to describe her attitude, he like it. "Alright, Hayden. What is the situation again?"

"My father," she began, "had a heart attack a month ago, which was followed by triple-bypass surgery."

"I'm sorry," Cannon interjected.

"Thank you." At least he was listening to her, Hayden thought as she held his vivid eyes with hers. "The doctors decided he should stay in bed for the next couple of months."

"How old is your father?" Cannon asked.

"Sixty," she answered. "My mother is a bookkeeper at AG Enterprises, a small marketing firm in Skokie, and her boss has refused her sick leave."

"How many people are employed at the firm?" Cannon was certain he knew what the problem was as he placed thoughts together in his mind.

"Six. There used to be eight, but they went through some hard times and he had to lay off two people a year ago." As she was speaking, Hayden looked directly into his eyes and noticed how, in their softness, they appeared brilliantly intelligent. It wasn't a wonder to her that someone so young, with such a questionable reputation, had gotten so far. He was probably some kind of genius in medicine. Having a well-placed father couldn't hurt either.

"If there are only six people," Cannon said, feeling a slight surge of excitement well up inside as the woman kept her eyes directly on him. He could tell she wasn't easily intimidated despite the soft appearance she put forward. "I can assume the firm is private?"

"Yes it is." She hesitated for a reaction, but he showed none, only responding to her stare with one of his own, so she continued. "Her boss, Alan Graham, says he can't afford to give her sick leave for six weeks because he's too small and she's the only person who keep the books and knows where all the files are. He's only offering her two weeks vacation, but this is unacceptable Mr., I mean, Cannon. What can you do?"

He rubbed at his neatly shaved goatee, never taking his eyes off her. In his two years as health commissioner, hundreds of women and men had come to him with problems that he either had no jurisdiction over, or did, but could not change the laws. It hurt him every time. He wanted to help everyone, that had always been his problem. Now he wanted to help Hayden Campbell.

"Hayden, I'll tell you right off the bat"—placing his hands firmly on the desk, he leaned over regarding her carefully— "he has a case. The Family and Medical Leave Act of 1993 decrees up to twelve weeks of unpaid leave, but there are two exceptions. First, a worker has to have worked for their employer for at least one year, which your mother has. The other is that the company must have fifty employees or more within a seventy-five miles radius, which doesn't apply in your case. Also, Mr. Graham can show, as you said, he's been going through rough times financially. It's possible he truly can't afford it."

"Every boss says that whenever they're pushed to give someone a raise or buy new equipment." She faced his challenge boldly although her courage was wavering.

"Yes, that's true," Cannon said, impressed with her determination. "But to give your mother six to twelve weeks of paid sick leave, which I assume is what she needs, while at the same time paying a replacement for six to twelve weeks is very expensive. The expenses double if there's extensive training involved."

"My mother has been a loyal bookkeeper for that man almost ten years now. He owes her this favor. I would go to him, but I don't want to put her job in jeopardy by upsetting him. If I have to I will, but I want to give my mother that chance. She can't afford to take unpaid leave because my father had to quit his job, but if it was all she could get we would take it. My father refuses a nurse. He's a stubborn man and . . ." Her voice bit with the anticipation of emotions that threatened to surface as she heard her own words. Was she begging? Had her life come to this that she needed to beg a stranger to save her family? "Isn't this your job? Isn't it your job to improve health care for people?"

"Yes, Hayden, it is my job to improve health conditions and care," Cannon said, "but I have to improve them for employers as well as employees. There are two sides to every health issue. Now you can try to sue for principal, but . . ."

"There's no time for that." She leaned forward to meet his stern gaze. "Why is this such a problem? Is it because this is a Skokie case and not Chicago? Let me guess, you don't deal personally with low-profile cases? Well, Mr. Factor, you are Cook County Health Commissioner and Skokie is in Cook County, so it is just as important as Chicago."

"I'm aware of that, Ms. Campbell." His voice was edgy, a little irritated by her accusation, but he remained calm. He knew she was angry for the right reasons and he admired that. "I am very busy and I can't attend to every situation personally."

She eyed the copy of today's *Represent Chicago* on the edge of his desk. "Apparently you spend your time wisely."

As Cannon quickly put together her connotation, his light eyes blazed with anger and his brows centered. "Those are all lies, blatant lies!"

"I don't care if they are or aren't." She felt herself becoming emotional and wanted to stop before she began to cry. "I just need you to help my mother. My father is a strong man, but there is no telling what could happen. You're a doctor, you know this. He needs her. These next six weeks are critical."

His expression of anger quickly calmed as he observed her in silence. Hayden felt terribly embarrassed for losing her composure and uncomfortable at his steady gaze. She ached for him to say something. Anything.

"I may be able to help you out," he answered after a short silence. "I can't promise you, but I'll make some calls. Why don't you give me your card and I'll get back to you."

Hayden felt herself deflate as she heard his words. Was there a book for all government employees giving that response as sufficient for all occasions?

"Of course," she responded flatly, as she avoided his outstretched hand and placed the card face down on the desk. "Thanks for your time, Commissioner." As she turned to walk out, he called after her.

"You're in public relations?" Curiosity made up his face as he looked at her card, then at her again. An idea came to him so quickly, he surprised himself.

"Yes." She wondered what that had to do with anything as she watched his eyes drift off for a moment. "So?"

"Nothing." He shrugged his thoughts away, thinking it was a ridiculous idea. "I will get back to you, Hayden."

"Mm-mm," she responded with an obvious lack of enthusiasm, and walked out of his office.

Ordering lunch at her desk outside Cannon's office, Maryann eyed Hayden suspiciously as she walked by. Hayden ignored her and walked past her and Lee Sampson who stood against the wall stairing her down. It didn't brother her. She was used to men staring at her. She always dressed on the conservative side for business, but her slim figure and beauty stood out, and attracted attention from men everywhere.

With a quick smirk she thought back for a moment about Cannon's reputation and figured she may have gotten more attention from Cannon Factor if she had undone a couple of the top buttons on her straw yellow silk blouse, disappointment took over as she realized she had gotten nowhere. Oblivious to everything around her and feeling an hour of her time wasted, she hastily approached the elevators and headed for the third floor.

As he held the lilac-colored card firmly in his hands, Cannon swung around in his chair. Hayden Campbell, Senior Account Executive, R&D Public Relations.

"Public relations." He murmured the words to himself. Could this be a blessing in disguise? On one of the worst days he could remember, was God being merciful? Was this a light at the end of the tunnel?

These rumors would not defeat him, he swore to himself as he pounded a strong, black fist on his desk. He wasn't about to let past indiscretions and present rumors deter him. He didn't care who was behind them. Whoever it was, they weren't stronger than his dreams, his goals, or his aspirations. When he had made his plans a month ago, he'd known it was the right thing to do. No one would stop him.

No one.

"Cannon." Maryann's voice over the intercom broke Cannon from his thoughts. "It's John Dannell on line one for you."

"Thanks, Maryann." Cannon smiled to himself as he picked up the phone. His mood slightly better than before after meeting the beautiful Hayden Campbell, the sound of his best friend's voice made him feel even better. "Hey, John. What's up, brother?"

"Read the paper this morning." John's usually raspy voice sounded sincerely concerned. "This is awful. Jesse and I feel for you, man."

"Thanks, John. I appreciate it." Cannon sighed and glanced at the card. "It doesn't look good, but I may have a solution."

"What solution?"

"You'll see," Cannon said. "I haven't thought it completely through, but I have a feeling things are looking up."

While at her parents' home that evening, Hayden chose not to tell them about her meeting with Cannon. Elise had no desire to discuss her sick leave situation because it made her so angry. Whenever Elise was angry, Tom got upset and Hayden couldn't allow that to happen. Holding onto some hope that Cannon Factor would come through, Hayden decided not to cause any more tension. So, as her mother washed the dinner dishes, Hayden quietly read the day's sports pages to her father.

"With hockey and basketball nearing their end and football

several months away, baseball is again on the minds of sports fans across the city and the Chicago Cubs . . .''

"No baseball.'' Tom Campbell moaned. Although he was never a complacent man, he was quickly taking on the personality of an eternal grouch. "I don't like baseball.''

"What are you talking about, Daddy?'' Hayden placed the paper on the bed next to her father and gave him an earnest stare. "Stop being difficult. You've been taking me to Cubs games for twenty years.''

"It was my duty.'' He folded his arms stubbornly across his chest. "If you're from the North Shore, you're a Cubs fan, so I went. Your mama wasn't interested, so I took you and Michael. Then he became a White Sox fan and . . . oh, the hell with it all.''

She looked at him squarely, prepared to argue, but decided against it. He tried to hide it, but she knew how much he hurt when remembering Michael. "You're being silly and if you keep cursing, I'm telling Mama. No matter what you say, when you get well we're going to Wrigley Field or even Comiskey Park for a change.''

"If I ever get well.'' His voice hardened.

"Daddy, don't say that.'' She grasped his hand tightly and pulled it to her lap as she scooted closer to him on the bed. She bit back her tears as the painful thought occurred to her. *Life without Daddy.* "You'll get well.''

"You sweet little girl.'' He smiled as his voice softened again.

It was a smile Hayden hadn't seen in a long time and missed terribly.

"You shouldn't be at your father's bedside,'' he said. "You have work to do and a life to live.''

"Daddy, please. There is no place else in this world I would rather be.'' She smiled, not wanting him to know how upset and uncertain she was. She wanted him to believe she had complete confidence that everything was going to be fine. She only wished she did.

"I'm only a burden on you and your mother,'' he said, his

eyes turning up to the ceiling in anguish. "I'm like a child who needs to be taken care of now. I'm interrupting everyone's work schedule and life schedule. What happened to me happened because I ate like a pig and sat on my rear all day. It way my fault. I should have died from that heart attack."

"Daddy, stop it now." A tear trailed her cheek. She fought back as hard as she could. "This is only for a little while. You know very well the doctor said with a few changes in your diet and exercise plan, after a few months you'll be able to carry on with your life basically as usual.

"They have to say that. They can't say the truth. They can't say that everyday could be my last or that nothing in my life will ever be the same. You know I'm right. At least if I had died your mother would have gotten my life insurance. Instead, here she is practically slaving for a boss who won't even let her stay home with me for a measly six weeks. All these bills. The HMOs don't want to pay a penny more than zero. You could live a lifestyle worthy of your salary if you didn't have to help us out so much." He stopped briefly, wincing in pain as he placed his hand to his chest.

"Are you alright, Daddy?" Hayden screamed in exasperation. She begged herself not to panic, but be a voice of reason and comfort. "The doctor said not to get yourself upset."

"I'm fine." He stubbornly pushed her reaching hand away. "You know I'm right. He said even getting upset could kill me. What kind of life can a person have and not get upset?"

"What's wrong?" Elise Campbell ran into the room, drying towel in hand. She ran to her husband, her eyes wide with concern. "Why is Hayden screaming?"

"Nothing, dear." Tom calmed his wife down by rubbing her hands gently and smiling lovingly into her eyes. "Hayden doesn't want to hear me say what's possible."

"Tom, you're scaring her." Elise sat on the bed opposite Hayden. "You're scaring me, too. The doctor said half your chances depend on willpower alone."

"Daddy, everything will work out," Hayden said.

She remembered the doctor also saying ·his recovery

depended on the love and support of family and friends. Something they couldn't give to the fullest if they weren't around him all day. "You aren't a burden, Daddy. This whole mess with Mama's job is a hassle, but I would prefer a million hassles a day forever to losing you. We both would."

He forced an apologetic smile, shaking his head in embarrassment. "I know, baby, I know. It's just so upsetting when you spend so long taking care of and providing for your family only to turn around and be useless."

"You are not useless, Thomas Campbell." Elise gently smacked his hand. "Providing an income is not what made you the head of this family. It's your strength, your courage, your love, and your leadership and you still have all of that."

Tom leaned up to kiss his wife, then turned to Hayden and kissed her tear-stained cheek. He looked at her with a hopeful glint in his amber brown eyes.

"Everything will be alright, baby girl." He spoke in a tone resembling the reassuring one he had used to sooth her for so many years now. "Wipe those tears away."

And, as she had for so many years now, Hayden did as he said and wiped her cheeks. It was difficult for her to see the man she had thought of as the strongest in the world in this vulnerable position. The most indestructible man ever was losing hope. He had always been the one to hold up when others doubted, if money was tight or family or friends passed away. He had kept this family together when Michael died in that car crash ten years ago.

Hayden looked upon her rock, her foundation, and knew she needed to hear from Cannon Factor soon. Her first and probably accurate impression of him may have been that he was a sexist playboy, but her family's future happiness just might be in his hands and that was all that mattered.

Chapter Two

Hayden felt exhausted by eleven the next morning. She had been up all night, first with her father, then at her own apartment, worrying about her mother's job situation. To make matters worse, upon arriving at work, she was faced with a crisis at Coverling Corporation. Yesterday, the executive vice president had resigned without warning and shareholders were blowing their tops over the company's stock price, which threatened to plummet. It was Hayden's responsibility to calm the press, a task she took on with distaste as there was really no such thing as a calm press.

"Niles Schultz was a valued member of Coverling," she said, checking her company notes, faxed over from her new client at eight that morning. Still new to the company, she was acutely aware of every word she said so as not to blow the account. "His departure was a disappointment, but the chief executive officer, chief financial officer, as well as the president are all abreast of every one of his tasks. The company was not left cold."

"Come on, Ms. Campbell." The seventh inquisitor of the morning was a *Chicago Tribune* business reporter. "You can't lead people to believe that this role left empty causes no upheaval within the company. The executive vice president of a fourteen-billion-dollar corporation is a very important person."

"Yes, he was important, but Senior Vice President Liza Kelly worked right alongside him and she has temporarily taken on his responsibilities. It is not an empty seat." She was growing tired of repeating the same thing over and over again.

The monotony was broken when Donna, with her ever-confident composure, entered the room with quick steps, waving a newspaper in the air. Astonishment was all over her young face. Hayden put a hand out to stop her from speaking and pointed to the phone. Biting her lip in frustration, Donna placed a copy of *Represent Chicago,* opened to page five, on the desk, sat firmly in the chair across from Hayden and stared.

"We need more answers than this, Ms. Campbell," the reporter said. His voice sounded as if he had smoked one hundred cigarettes a day for the last forty years. "The stock has dropped two dollars since trading opened this morning. Are Coverling stockholder's going to lose their money?"

"The stock is suffering slightly now, but if the shareholders stick with Coverling, as soon as Schultz is permanently replaced, we are fully confident . . ." Hayden suddenly realized what was on page five of the paper that lay in front of her. It was her picture!

"Excuse me, Ms. Campbell, I didn't get that," the voice persisted.

"We are . . . fully confident . . . things will return to normal." The heavy lashes that shadowed Hayden's cheek flew up as she slid the paper toward herself and read the headline.

FACTOR ENTERTAINING ON TAXPAYER'S TIME?
Lee Sampson

The shock hit her full force and she stammered for words. "We are confident the quality of Coverling stock is in good shape and will stay that way. Mr. Messinger, I hope I've answered your questions, because I must go now. I will contact the media as soon as new information is available and will certainly make you aware of any press conferences we plan. Goodbye.'' She swiftly replaced the receiver on the phone, still looking for the words to explain her surprise.

''What is this?'' Hayden's voice was choked.

''It's you, baby!'' Donna was almost laughing out of amazement. ''Read it. It's hilarious.''

Hayden quickly scanned the article.

This reporter does not find pleasure in reporting negative news about one of our own, but the truth must be told.

Who is the woman pictured left (name not known) seen leaving the office of Cannon Factor, Cook County Health Commissioner? She is not an employee of the city or county, as you can see. She is not wearing the required ID badge for all employees.

At risk of sounding like a crybaby, I must say I spent hours trying to get a comment out of Dr. Factor concerning last week's revelation of his evening at a downtown hotel with two young women. As a member of the press, I would assume clearing this issue up would be a priority, but it was made certain he was seeing no one.

I watched as the young and beautiful woman past by me and security, directly into the commissioner's office. Factor then dismissed all of his support staff and spent several moments alone with her.

What exactly is Mr. Factor doing while the public wonders about several allegations? Is the old playboy reputaton of the past making a return? Here's another one. Does he conduct personal business with one of his several lady friends on taxpayer's time?

A soft gasp escaped Hayden as she sat there, blank and amazed. Then suddenly, anger took over as she felt her face turning hot with rage. How dare he!

''Now calm down,'' Donna said cautiously. ''You know you

have a tendency toward a quick temper. You better slow it down and count to ten.''

"Count to ten, my . . .'' She caught herself before cursing. "I thought reporters were supposed to have all the facts before going to print! Whatever happened to objective reporting? This is filled with so many innuendos its ridiculous. How can he get away with this?''

"He can.'' Donna was serious now, unusually so for her. "We're both PR girls. We know journalists and as long as he doesn't specifically mention you or say this as a fact, it's legal. It's not ethical, but legal. Besides, even though Simpson is a reporter, he writes about Cannon for the editorial section. He can write whatever he thinks there.''

"Unbelievable.'' Hayden stood up and began pacing the room as she vented her anger. "This is a reputable newspaper. They never print this kind of tabloid stuff. How can they allow this?''

"It's not such a big deal, Hayden. Just call them and have them retract or—''

"Not a big deal?'' she retorted harshly, with a quick toss of her head causing her black mane to flip in the air. "Donna, my daddy reads this paper everyday!'' Hayden panicked at the thought of her father thinking she was involved with a man like Cannon Factor. "What will he do if he thinks I'm caught up in some scandal? Are you aware of his condition?''

Donna turned to the inside of the front page. "Call Lee Sampson. The number to the paper is right here. Call him and set him straight. Then run to your parents' house and steal the paper before they can read it. You know, like you used to do when a letter would come from your teacher in high school?''

Hayden's mouth curved into an unconscious smile as the muscles in her oval-shaped face softened. Donna's constant sense of humor could be infectious at times, even times as bad as now. Hayden had always wished she could see life through Donna's eyes. Nothing ever seemed that bad to her.

"You think all this is funny don't you?'' Hayden returned to her desk, pulling the phone toward her. "I'll have you know

I was a straight-A student at Evanston Township High School and never ever had to run home to hide letters from school.''

"Oh, I guess it was just me." Donna let go a quick giggle and a guilty shrug. "Tell the truth though. It's got to be a little exciting being part of a mini-scandal, isn't it?"

"No," Hayden said scornfully, as her long fingers dialed the numbers listed on the paper. "I'm not a part of any scandal. I'm an innocent bystander and I'm going to clear my name."

"Represent Chicago," said a voice over the phone. "May I help you?"

"Yes," Hayden said calmly, "Lee Sampson please."

"I'm sorry ma'am, Mr. Sampson is out of the newsroom at the moment. Is this call about today's story?"

"Yes, the one on Health Commissioner Factor. I would—"

"Well Ms.," the woman interrupted, "we've been getting several calls on that story and all we can tell you right now is that Mr. Factor has made no comment and no, we have not found out the woman's name, but Mr. Sampson does have several leads. If I can take a message, he will return—"

"I'm that woman!" Hayden yelled. Had the woman said they'd received several calls? From whom? she wondered. Someone from her church or her mother's card club? "That's me in the picture and I want to clear up everything. I am not one of—"

"I'm sorry, ma'am, but we've had more than a few women calling to identify themselves in that picture. One said she was a beauty queen. Another said she was a topless dancer who is carrying his baby. We can't simply take your word for it, we need proof, ma'am."

Hayden was amazed. She couldn't believe what she was hearing. All of this from only wanting to help her family? It wasn't fair.

"Listen, young lady." A silken thread of warning could be heard in her voice now. "I don't know when *Represent Chicago* began running tabloid stories, but you're not going to get away with it. Your paper is in for a serious law suit. I don't need proof. Apparently Mr. Sampson doesn't either."

"Please, ma'am." The woman's voice began showing signs of irritation. "If you leave your name and number . . ."

"How do I know he won't take it and print it all over Chicago?" Hayden waited for a response, but upon not getting one, decided against leaving the information. "I'll call again later. Goodbye." She hung up the phone, disappointed at getting nowhere.

"What did they say?" Donna's eyes brightened with curiosity.

"People have been calling them all morning. They've even had women saying they were me. One said she was pregnant with his baby!"

"Oh, my . . ." Donna clamped both hands over her mouth in surprise. "I guess that's not so funny."

"No, it isn't." Hayden forced herself to settle down, quickly trying to think of her next move. "I've got to do something about this."

"Ms. Campbell." The voice over the telephone speaker belonged to Marcy Poss, Hayden's assistant. "There's a Maryann Holly with Commissioner Factor's office on line two for you."

Remembering the less-than-friendly woman from Cannon's office, Hayden picked up the phone after telling Donna who Maryann was.

"Hello, Maryann," she began, "this is Hayden. I was extremely offended by today's—"

"We know, *Represent Chicago*. Cannon is disturbed as well." Maryann's voice sounded very unsympathetic. "This is why I suggested you go to the Department of Labor. You should . . . have . . . listened."

The choppy way her words were coming through made Hayden think someone was interrupting her. She was growing a little impatient with the short silence that followed until a voice came again over the receiver.

"Hayden?" It was a man's deep, strong voice that returned. "Hayden, it's Cannon Factor."

"Cannon, I'm very upset about this." She purposefully spoke

with a firm, unbroken voice, acknowledging the approving wink from Donna. "I have several family members and friends who read this paper."

"As well as I," he responded, his voice was rough with anxiety. "I have to deal with this constantly."

"You couldn't possibly be comparing the two of us. My lifestyle doesn't nearly—"

"Listen, Ms. Campbell, this isn't an issue of lifestyle." Cannon's tone was cold and exact. "This article was wrong. Period."

"It would not have been printed at all if your personal life wasn't under so much speculation again. Yes, Mr. Factor, I know about your past and how it seems to have reappeared, but I don't care about that. I care about this story and I want to know what you plan to do about it." She'd read that he hadn't responded to the previous allegations, but he would have to do something now, whether he wanted to or not.

"Ms. Campbell." Marcy's timid voice came again over the intercom. "Chuck Matton with the *Chicago Sun Times* is on line three. It's about Coverling."

Hayden bit her lip to keep from instructing Marcy to tell the *Sun Times* where to go. This was her job and she had to do it, despite the other mini-emergencies in her life.

Seeming to understanding the time for discussions was over, Donna pouted as she lifted her little figure from the chair and exited the office. Before leaving, she mouthed the words, *I'll be back.*

"Cannon," Hayden said, "I have to go, but I expect you to—"

"I can clear up everything," he said. "Sampson is right outside my office. I also have some information for you on your mother's situation."

Hayden quickly remembered how she'd gotten involved with Cannon in the first place and felt a sudden flicker of hope.

"Can we meet later today?" Cannon asked. "I would like to discuss this with you."

"I suppose." Reluctance slowed her response. She wanted

nothing to do with this man, but if he had news about her family situation, she knew she needed to speak with him.

"Meet me at the Metropolitan Club at six thirty tonight," he said smoothly. "I'll work everything out."

As she hung up the phone, Hayden felt no wonder as to why he was such a ladies' man. When he chose to make it so, his voice was extremely soothing and persuasive. At that moment, all the anxiety she'd been feeling had momentarily vanished.

Only momentarily. As she picked up line three, Hayden wondered if she had made the right decision. She wondered if it mattered what happened to her. After all, helping Mom and Dad was all that was important now, and Cannon Factor was beginning to look like the only way to go about doing that.

The Metropolitan Club was an old, private club located in the famous Sears Tower in the city's downtown area. Roger, R&D's president, held a membership to the club and Hayden occasionally came along as they used the club to entertain their most prestigious clients. They had several meetings with Coverling at the Metropolitan Club before sealing the account.

As she approached the front desk of the lavish location, she wondered if taxpayers were paying for Dr. Factor's membership. The club had a mixture of that *old money* feel with dashes of modern designs here and there. There were comfortable smoke leather chairs, cherry wood tables, and some of the most famous paintings in the world. Hayden was sure the dues were high.

She approached the attendant who stood at the entrance to the dining room. "Ms. Hayden Campbell. I'm meeting Cannon Factor."

"Oh, yes," the attendant said with a smile as wide as his face. He looked her up and down with approving black eyes as he ran one hand through his short, curly black hair and smoothed out his rose-colored uniform jacket with the other. "I should have known that."

"Excuse me?" Hayden asked, noting the rise in the man's left brow.

"Mr. Factor is a regular here." He stepped from behind his stand. "He always meets with a beautiful woman. He's a very lucky man."

Hayden rolled her eyes in disgust. Apparently everyone but her knew of Cannon's reputation and it only served to anger her more that she had now been falsely included in this man's harem.

The attendant escorted her through the main dining room where she observed several people, mostly men, making deals and partnerships over filet mignon. She was unfazed by the stares she received. She knew she looked spectacular in her two-piece, cherry red pantsuit with a thin satin trim tracing from her neck down her front to where the top stopped at the top of her small, but shapely hips. She wondered if some of the looks were of recognition from the morning's paper.

She was led down a hallway she had never been through, toward a much more private dining room, darker than the rest of dining area. Sitting patiently in the first booth was Cannon Factor, observing a portrait on the wall with his hands calmly laid across the table.

Hayden felt an unwelcome blush come to her cheeks at the sight of him and it startled her. As he sat there, devilishly handsome, she saw a masculine figure of a man that was alluring, big and powerful, yet soft and somewhat vulnerable. Only being the second time she had seen him face to face, Hayden wasn't sure how she could see so much from looking at him, but she could.

She felt her pulse race as he suddenly turned his head and met her eyes with his. An irresistibly devastating grin leaped to his face as he slid out of the cozy booth to meet her.

"Hello, Hayden. It's nice to see you again, even though it's under these unfortunate circumstances." At the sight of her, Cannon felt that same surge of energy he had when she'd walked into his office yesterday. Her slender, dark figure and fiery eyes were captivating. She was unique in her beauty and

it took a lot of determination on his part to remind himself this
was a business meeting.

"Hello, Cannon." Hayden accepted his outstretched hand
and shook it firmly. Feeling his iron grip, she couldn't ignore
a sudden sense of discomfort the touch caused her. As she
hastily drew her hand away, Hayden wished she wasn't so
preoccupied with his appearance.

Cannon kept his smile, despite noticing her withdrawal. It
disappointed him for more reasons than one. He realized his
plan would be more difficult if Ms. Campbell couldn't bear to
be near him as it seemed, but he wouldn't let her obvious
disdain for him deter him from what he wanted.

"You look lovely, Hayden," he said.

As his eyes assessed her quickly, Hayden hoped the semi-
darkness of their area hid her reaction to his apparent approval.
As she took her seat in the booth across from him, she had to
remind herself this man was a playboy who knew every look
and smile in the book to make a woman's knees go weak.

"I took the liberty of ordering for us." He watched her
intently while taking a sip of his cocktail. So much about her
was a mystery and that put him at a disadvantage. "I hope you
like chicken marsala. It's done very well here."

"I didn't know we were having dinner." A bit of apprehension swept through her at the thought of an evening with Cannon. She wasn't sure why, because she was certain she wasn't
in any danger of his charms. After Alec, romance of any kind
was the last thing on her mind.

"Well," he said, shrugging nonchalantly, "I figured we'd
be here for a while. We have a lot to discuss."

She took a sip of water, not realizing until now how dry her
throat felt. What was it that he said? *I figured we'd be here
for a while.* She smiled to herself, proud to detect his Casanova
moves.

"Listen, Cannon." She spoke with directness, while placing
her napkin across her lap. "I'm here to discuss two things.
How to clear up this . . . this mess with the paper and help my
mother's situation. That's it."

He raised an eyebrow in amusement as his mouth curved into a smile. She was definitely, a no-nonsense women and although it frustrated him, in many ways he liked that. He respected that and was attracted to it.

Hayden found that the goatee he sported gave him a even more manly aura, but it wasn't so much that she was intimidated. His eyes showed a tender side to the strength of his handsome square face. His dark skin was flawless, his dark curly hair was cut clean and short. Everything about this man showed self-confidence and attraction and she found it all entirely too distracting.

"Although I find you very attractive," Cannon said, "I have not set my sights on you, Hayden. That is one of the things I wanted to clear up." He paused a moment as the waiter brought their salads and asked Hayden for her drink order. She refused any and he quickly retreated.

"You see," he continued, "all of these things Lee Sampson is writing about me are false. None of them are true. At least not his perception or insinuation."

She eyed him suspiciously, taking a bite of her salad. "Cannon, you don't have to convince me of that. I'm not at all concerned with your lifestyle choices."

"That's just it, Hayden." His shoulders lowered as he sighed. "I'm not trying to convince you of anything. These rumors actually are lies. You can see that for yourself. This latest one involving you wasn't true."

"No it wasn't," she admitted. "But *Represent Chicago* is a reputable paper. Something must make them feel confident about their stance on your personal life. They wouldn't be able to make something out of nothing. It's coming from somewhere."

"Yes, it is." He paused, looking her intensely in the eye. It was suddenly of utmost importance to him that she believed him, for reasons other than the obvious. For reasons he chose to ignore. "Someone out there is trying to bring up my past and use it to smear my reputation. I'm not sure who, but they're

Lee Sampson's source for these articles. They're trying to destroy my career.''

The suggestion lit a spark of interest in Hayden. ''Why would they do that? From what I hear, your record as health commissioner is secularly spotless.''

''Yes, and they haven't had anything to say about my performance as commissioner, so they take on my moral character.'' He lowered his head a bit, observing the table. He felt suddenly embarrassed to tell her about this past. ''I admit I was a ladies' man in my younger days. Although I was always responsible, I did enjoy the company of women.''

''What does any of this have to do with me and my situation?'' Hayden knew she sounded selfish, but she felt extremely uncomfortable listening to him discuss his amorous tendencies of the past.

''You're right. It's not your concern.'' His voice was resigned. ''Not yet, at least.''

She shot him a cautious glance in response to his comments. She held back as the waiter came to serve dinner, but as soon as he left, she pushed Cannon to explain.

''You did clear everything up with Sampson today?'' she asked. ''There will be a retraction in the paper tomorrow, right?''

''Well.'' His eyes squinted in uncertainty as he frowned. ''I wanted to speak with you first. I thought we could work something out.''

Hayden leaned back in the booth, folding her arms across her chest. What game was he playing with her? ''What are you talking about, Cannon? And please, no bull. I'm not a reporter or one of your young girlfriends.''

''Straight forward and honest,'' he began. ''I need public relations advice and I need a lot. I need help in dealing with the media and preparing myself for interviewing. I know, being in government, I should have these skills, but I don't. I need a public way of combating these rumors without bringing more attention to them. My future career depends on it.''

"You want me to advise you?" she asked with a hint of sarcasm.

"In exchange for my help." At least she was listening, Cannon thought to himself.

"Help with what?" In her opinion, he wanted a miracle worker.

"Your mother's situation." Cannon felt a bit of a confidence boost as she unfolded her arms from their defensive cross in response to his words.

"What can you do?" She leaned forward, anxious to hear some good news.

"Do you know a man named Gary Hampton?" he asked.

"No," she responded anxiously, upon drawing a blank at the name.

"Gary Hampton is the man who loaned Alan Graham the money to keep his business going when it was in serious trouble a year ago."

"Yes, I remember that." Hayden remembered her mother was afraid she would lose her job. The company had lost three clients and Alan was difficult to be around. How did Cannon know so much about Alan Graham?

Expecting her confusion, Cannon explained. "For a big city, Chicago is a very small world. Gary Hampton was a friend of my late father, Craig Factor. I'm sure you've heard of him. He knew everyone in the city. He was a surgeon and once saved Gary's wife's life. Gary also helped me and my best friend, John, with financial consulting when we started our practice. I've helped him out a time or two. I called in a favor and, at my request, Gary promises to talk to Alan."

Hayden shook her head, amazed at where connections could get someone in this world. "I don't want Alan bullied. I'm mad at him for doing this to my mother, but if he's pushed he might fire her."

"Don't worry about a thing." He smiled a disarming smile. "Gary is perfection at this. He calls in favors all the time, and he uses the utmost tact. Your mother's job is as safe as it ever was."

"You'll have him do this in exchange for my advice?" Hayden found this hard to believe, but wanted to so badly. As she looked into his tempting eyes, something told her she could believe.

"Yes." He paused to place a forkful of food in his mouth and chew. "I'm just looking for some part-time consulting. A little advice here and there. I know you have a demanding career, so I don't expect a lot from you. It's just when I saw your card, something clicked. I made some calls and found out that you're about the best thing going at R&D. I think it's a good deal."

"I think something could be worked out." She wiped her mouth gently with her napkin, wanting to believe that everything at home could soon be alright. She wondered who he had called. "As long as you're aware that PR is not miracle work. When you're seen leaving a party of peers with two young women, there isn't anything I can do to fix that. I will not lie for you."

"Hayden, that story was slanted." He noticed her skepticism and knew he would have to explain everything. "A *male* friend of mine was visiting from college in Denver. His name is Benjamin Long. He has two daughters who live in the suburbs, twenty-one and twenty-two years old. He's staying at the Hyatt. It's just a coincidence I met him for a drink in the lobby and I promised I'd escort the girls to a cab on their way out to the nightclubs. While they were dressing, I returned to the fundraiser. When they were ready, they came and got me. I was pretty much done for the evening myself, so I joined them in the cab. After they were dropped off at a local bar, the cab took me home."

"Why not explain that?" Hayden chose to believe him for now. She could always find out later if he was lying.

"My friend is going through a messy divorce and if his wife knew his daughters were spending time with him, well . . ." He sighed heavily. "It's just that things are complicated enough for him right now. I don't even think the girls were supposed to be at the hotel. I get the impression they told their mom they were just going out for a night on the town. With all that, I didn't want to involve him in any of this. Besides, it's not as simple as telling the press the truth. Sometimes if you respond to a rumor, they twist your words and the situation gets even worse.''

''One word of advice, Cannon,'' Hayden said with a professional tone to her voice. ''You always respond. It may be unpleasant to involve friends, but your reputation and that of the mayor, who appointed you, is at stake. It doesn't matter if someone interprets what you say as hiding aliens in your basement, you respond.''

His eyes grew openly amused, a flash of humor crossed his face. This woman before him was a take-charge woman and she knew her stuff. This was just what he needed. She was just what he needed. ''Hiding aliens? You're a funny lady, Hayden Campbell. I guess I've sort of lost my sense of humor in all this.''

She was embarrassed by the shock of pleasure she felt in response to his appreciation, but quickly dismissed it from her mind and got back to business. ''The article mentioned that this last situation with the two women was the second incident in a month. What was the other?''

He waved a dismissing hand. ''Sampson reported that I was seen arguing in public with a woman at a Chicago Bulls game. It was my sister, Mavis. She came with me and my friend John and his wife. We always argue. I try to avoid it in public, but that's not always easy.''

''You have to find a way to make it easier, Cannon,'' she said. ''You're in the spotlight now.''

''Hayden, do we have a deal?'' Cannon felt now the question was moot, but wanted to make sure.

''Yes.'' The word came quick and without thought, which surprised Hayden. With Coverling, along with her other accounts, she was already overworked. When would she find the time?

''I'm going to tell you something in confidence.'' He cleared his throat, looking her directly in the eyes. ''If I tell you anything about me, it's that I care about people, all people. I want to contribute to society in the best way I can. First, it was as a doctor, then as health commissioner. Now, I'm ready for more. I'm planning to run for the United States Senate in the November elections.''

"You are?" She felt a quick sense of pride at the thought of another black congressman for her state. Illinois was proud of those who had come before him such as Senator Carol Moseley Braun and Representative Jesse Jackson, Jr. Everyone knew the current senator, Cliff Young, was retiring from office at the end of this term. A few names had been thrown around, but no one person had yet been picked to run in his place or oppose his successor. "Well then, you really do need a few public relations tips. I hope I can help you."

"I hope we can help each other." He held out his strong dark hand to her again.

Hayden hesitated, remembering how uncomfortable touching him earlier had made her feel, but accepted his gesture with a shake. Their hands were still entwined as a bright flash hit them. Unable to see at first, Hayden winced and blinked away the pain the intense light caused in her eyes. When her sight returned, there was no one was there.

Cannon cursed out loud as he slid out of the booth, heated anger bubbling within him. He had had enough of this.

"What was that?" Hayden asked.

"It was Sampson, taking another one of those damn pictures." He threw his napkin on the table and headed down the hallway after the man.

"Cannon, stop!" Hayden called after him with an outstretched hand.

He turned back to her. "I'm going to get that picture and set him straight once and for all."

"You can't." She gave him a stern look that matched her tone. "If you seriously want to run for senator in the near future, assaulting members of the press, provoked or not, is number one on the no-no list."

He stared at her for a moment, deciding whether or not to

accept her advice, then quietly regained his seat. "You're right. It would be especially unwise here. Some very influential people belong to this club. See how much I need you? You've just saved my career already."

Hayden was almost ashamed at the satisfaction she felt from his praise. She could only think to herself how dangerous a man this was who sat across from her. Attraction, intelligence, wealth, influence, charm, and the icing on the cake: humor.

The waiter courteously approached the table. "Please allow me to show you our deserts."

"Hayden, would you like desert?" Cannon passed her an allowing smile, hoping she would stay longer. Despite her obvious reserve for him, he thought she was a likeable and interesting person and found her more than pleasurable to look at.

Deciding she had spent enough time with Cannon Factor, Hayden refused desert.

"No, thank you," she said with a polite smile. She was already too aware of her attraction to him. Any longer and she wasn't so certain she could keep herself from falling under his spell as the smile he was giving her now already made her cheeks flush and sent a tingle to the pit of her stomach. He was far too dangerous. "It's getting late and the ride into the suburbs is a long one. I need to visit my father before I go home as well."

"How *is* your father, Hayden?" Cannon hid the disappointment he felt from his face.

"I don't know." The words came out of an emotional heart as low as a whisper. Hayden lowered her head, shaking it back and forth. "I'm worried. He used to be so strong. I just . . ."

"It's hard." With genuine concern, Cannon reached over and placed his hand over hers. Her beautiful brown skin felt wonderfully soft to the touch. "I know it's hard, but if you and your mother stick with it, you'll make him strong again."

She raised her head in response to his touch, feeling a tremor of heat slide from her hand, up her arm and to her chest. Her eyes connected with his and she saw the warmth. It touched her and frightened her at the same time. It was then she realized that she had let herself open up to a man she neither knew nor trusted. Suddenly, Hayden wanted nothing more than to be as far away from Cannon Factor as possible.

"Thank you," she said quickly, as she pulled her hand away and reached for her purse. "Good night, Cannon."

"Good night, Hayden."

As he watched her walk away, Cannon wanted desperately to understand all the emotions he felt now. All he wanted to understand was that he was happy he would be getting a great public relations professional to help him fulfill his dream of becoming a senator. Only there was more. This beautiful woman he barely knew made him feel something. A need to be understood maybe, or believed. Not by the public, but by her.

The next morning Hayden was hard at work planning a press conference for Coverling, but was unable to get last night's dinner with Cannon off her mind. She tried her best to concentrate on other things. She was at least happy she had succeeded in confiscating yesterday's copy of *Represent Chicago* before her father was able to read it. When he asked for it, she merely distracted him, discussing his favorite topic, sports.

This morning, she noticed today's issue of the paper in Donna's hand as she entered Hayden's office.

"Don't tell me." She met Donna's satirical gaze with a reserved one of her own. "A picture of Cannon and myself at the Met Club."

"Holding hands." She plopped down in the chair, sliding the paper across the table. "You told me this would happen when I called you last night and you were right."

Hayden opened the paper to page seven where Donna had creased it. There, was a small picture of herself and Cannon. It was taken when they had been shaking hands, consummating their agreement to help each other. Unfortunately, she had to admit it did look like they were holding hands instead of shaking them. Hayden was surprised at the contented smile on her face.

She looked genuinely happy and as if she was enjoying herself socially, not professionally.

"We aren't holding hands," she corrected Donna. "We're shaking hands."

"Whatever," Donna said with a roll of her eyes. "Just read it."

HEALTH COMMISSIONER SETTLING DOWN?
Lee Sampson

At the risk of sounding like a broken record, this reporter will not spend a lot of time on Cook County Health Commissioner Cannon Factor. I have received numerous calls to get off his back. Those loyal fans might be happy to read this.

I would simply like to mention Factor was seen at the Metropolitan Club, a club he frequents, with a young woman (pictured left) in what appears to be an intimate encounter. This is the same woman seen coming in and out of Factor's office yesterday, when no one was supposed to be allowed in to talk to the commissioner. This is the first time in a long time Factor has been seen with the same woman consecutively. Maybe he's decided to change, having second thoughts about returning to his past lifestyle, which has garnered so much negative publicity recently.

I cannot resist. Factor, tell us if we (the taxpayers) footed the bill for your private dinner.

Hayden shook her head in disgust. "This guy feeds off negativity. So much negative publicity. Yeah and all of it from him." She looked at Donna. "You want to know why people hate the media? Guys like this! I wonder what type of grudge he has against Cannon."

"Correct me if I'm wrong," Donna asked slowly, with a hint of confusion, "are you defending the same man today you called a jerk yesterday?"

"I'm not defending him." Hayden felt a little uncomfortable about her outburst in Cannon's favor. "It's just that this is wrong. I was there and we were only discussing my mother's situation. He agreed to help me in return for some professional consulting and we shook hands." She noticed Donna's disbelieving grin. "It's true!"

"What's he doing for Elise?" Donna asked.

"He's going to call in a favor." Hayden raised her hands in the air. "I don't want to explain it. I don't even know if it's legal."

"This man has you engaging in illegal activities?" Donna finished in a whisper.

"No." Frustration was settling in. Donna's curiosity sometimes touched a nerve in Hayden, but she knew there would be no rest until she answered. "I don't know. If it helps my father get well, I don't care."

"Professional consulting?" Skepticism invaded Donna's every word.

"Yes! Strictly professional. You know, I've had enough of your dirty mind this week. It's Friday, and I'm busy. I have to plan a news conference."

"You're busy? Damon wants you on the Coverling mishap exclusively so everyone else is carrying the rest of your accounts. We're swamped, too."

"Then what are you doing in my office gossiping?" She arched finely shaped eyebrows at Donna with a playful smile.

"You asked me to do you a favor last night, remember?" Donna placed her hands on hips.

"Oh, yeah," Hayden said. "You did it already?"

"Right away. My curiosity got the best of me. I called my ex, Bob Hansen. He's a good guy, for a cop. For a boyfriend, he was a dud."

"Let's skip the relationship review," Hayden said. "Did he call the Hyatt?"

"He sure did. He's friends with one of the managers. He's been known to canvas the hotel on weekend nights. Help out a bit. He called and asked, of course saying it was official police business, if a Benjamin Long had been a guest at the Hyatt on the night of March sixteenth or nights before.''

Hayden would never admit to Cannon she'd followed up on his explanation for the Hyatt rumor, but it nagged at her. After getting home last night. She called Donna, knowing she had a friend with the Chicago police department, and asked if he could find out if Benjamin Long from Denver had been at the hotel as Cannon had said.

"I got good news and bad news," Donna said. "Bad news, the hotel has no record of a Benjamin Long."

Hayden felt a certain and strong sense of disappointment at the news. She realized she'd been hoping for something else. Hoping more than she should have. "What's the good news?"

"Good news is an amazing coincidence. The woman he talked to distinctly remembered a man checking in on the fifteenth and paying in cash. She paid a little extra attention because usually celebrities do that. So, she asked where he was coming from. He said he was coming from Denver. He checked in under the name of Morgan Freeman. You know, the actor? Only this guy was definitely not Morgan Freeman."

"I guess I'll have to hope that was Benjamin Long's way of avoiding his wife finding out he was in Chicago." Hayden remembered Cannon saying it was an ugly divorce. She wanted to believe him, but without real evidence, how could she? After all, she wasn't one to believe in coincidences as easily as Donna.

"You never know." Donna shrugged her shoulders with a tilt of her head. "You sure do seem to care a lot."

"I care about getting my work done," Hayden said, feeling suddenly uncomfortable about Donna's suggestions. "Thanks a lot for your help. I'll take you to lunch soon, but right now I got to get back to work.

Donna started out of the chair. "Okay, I'm leaving. And you're welcome."

"Ms. Campbell?" It was Marcy on the intercom. "Mr. Factor is on line one for you."

As she noticed Donna return to the chair, hoping to listen

in on the conversation, Hayden quickly shoed her away before picking up the phone.

"Hello, Cannon." She spoke in a friendly and professional voice. "I take it you've read the paper this morning?"

"Yes." He spoke with laid-back and quiet emphasis. "Sampson said he tried to be positive, but he just isn't capable. Listen, Hayden, I need to speak with you. I'm being interviewed Monday and I need some advice."

"Is something wrong?"

"No, everything is fine right now." Cannon caught himself in an inch of a second believing she was genuinely concerned for him. "Can we get together this weekend?"

"I suppose so." She hesitated at the tone of his voice, which sounded more personal than professional. "Cannon, I would really prefer to limit my services until everything is cleared up with my mother."

"I keep my end of every deal I make, Ms. Campbell," he said harshly. "Can you come to my condo tomorrow or not?"

"Your apartment?" Hayden was very uncomfortable with that suggestion. Did she think he was a liar? "I don't know if that's . . ."

"Other people will be there if that's what you're worried about." He couldn't understand why her general mistrust angered him so much. She had agreed to help him. Why should he care? "I thought we had a deal."

"I know." She fought all her doubts, doing her best to remember that this was for her parents, not herself. She took down his address and agreed to meet him tomorrow afternoon.

Cannon's condominium was in Lake Point Towers, one of the finest buildings in the city overlooking Lake Michigan and the residential area, referred to as Chicago's Gold Coast because its residents were relatively wealthy people. As she rode the elevator to his floor, Hayden's doubts about coming continued as they had since she agreed to come. She was beginning to fear Lee Sampson and his ever-present camera. Both her parents had seen yesterday's paper with her and Cannon at the club, and bombarded Hayden with questions. With a little careful maneuvering, she explained it away as a business dinner, which was true, taken out of context. How could she explain being seen visiting his home on the weekend?

On warm spring weekends such as today, she usually dressed very casual and free, but she wasn't comfortable wearing a T-shirt and jeans shorts to Cannon's home. So, instead she chose a pink, cotton short-sleeved blouse and knee-length beige shorts. It was appropriate for the unusually warm seventy degree weather in late March, but not too revealing.

A gray-haired man greeted her at the door and she immediately recognized him as Warren, the older man in Cannon's office a few days ago. As they said their hellos, she noticed the frown on his raisin-colored face was a permanent fixture as it remained when he happily greeted her.

She made a quick observation of the apartment as Warren led her to Cannon's office. Either Cannon Factor had impeccable taste or the place was decorated by a professional. The apartment spoke in masculine tones with various shades of green, black, and blue circled with dabs of white all over. The large, floor-to-ceiling windows gave a scenic view of the lake. The furniture was Italian leather, the statues and art were crystal or silver, the carpet a deep plush white. It was obvious that money had been spent on this home and plenty of it. What caught Hayden's eye more than all else was a black and white marble statue of the universal symbol for medicine, which Warren told her used to belong to the famous Dr. Craig Factor. Over six feet tall, it stood out among the other objects as the sun shone brightly on it through the terrace doors.

"Hayden, it's nice to see you." Cannon took a quick look at his watch as she entered his office. "I'm not used to working with anyone who is on time."

"Hello, Cannon." Hayden gave a courteous smile, thoroughly annoyed at herself for immediately noticing his appearance. She found his tall strong form appealing in a Morehouse College T-shirt and blue jeans. Physically distracted by his dark curving muscles, she turned away, only to face the woman standing beside him as he sat at his desk. "Hello, Maryann."

"Good afternoon, Hayden." Maryann pasted on a brittle smile for her.

Hayden wasn't sure if it was just to herself or if Maryann was this rude to everyone. She only noticed that the woman obviously worshiped Cannon and seemed to exude pride from merely standing beside him.

"What can I help you with?" Hayden sat down on the black leather sofa near the window. The view from a distance was of Soldier Field, home of the Chicago Bears and football greats such as Walter Payton and Gale Sayers. Observing the office, Hayden found an appreciation for Cannon's selections. Add that to his list of bachelor attributes; good taste.

"I'm being interviewed on Tony Brown's Journal Monday for next Sunday's show on PBS." His demeanor was strong as always, but his soft eyes showed a hint of nervousness. He had to admit to himself that her beauty was a distraction from his every thought and he was already nervous enough. "I'd like your opinion on addressing any controversial questions he might ask me."

"Well as I said before," she answered, "you tell the truth. Explain the misunderstandings as you did to me at dinner the other night."

"Dinner?" The heavy lashes on Maryann's hard face lifted in surprise. "When did you have dinner?"

"Don't worry about that, Maryann," Cannon said curtly. "We had dinner last night to discuss our arrangement. Go on, Hayden."

"I understand your friend may be going through a messy divorce." She tried to ignore Maryann's look of disgust. "But, if you want to run for senator, the truth has . . ."

"Hayden! Cannon knows what he has to." Maryann was fuming now. She looked at Cannon and said, "Did you hire her for this? I could have told you this."

"Maryann, please!" There was an edge in his voice, showing

she had pushed him far enough. He stood up to face her, towering over her by at least half a foot.

"I thought she was a crisis management person." Maryann's tone didn't sound so much angry as it did hurt. "Someone who only came in for emergencies. Now she's your campaigner?"

"Maryann," Cannon said sternly and calmly. "I don't want you to take this the wrong way, but I think you should leave." Cannon spoke in a firm voice, not without compassion. "I'll take notes from my discussion with Hayden and you and I can go over them Monday."

Maryann gasped aloud in surprise at her dismissal. Completely silent, she took one quick contemptuous look at Hayden and stormed out of the office. Hayden wasn't sure she agreed with how Cannon handled the situation, but he definitely handled it and that in itself was impressive. He had an unquestionable quality of leadership about him.

"That wasn't necessary." With a blow of her lips, Hayden confidently blew back several straying strands of her thick hair that lay in her eyes. "She wasn't bothering me."

"She was bothering me," Warren said in an agitated tone. He folded his arms across his chest and leaned against the wall. "That woman is in an eternal bad mood."

"It's best that she leave." Cannon came across the room and sat beside Hayden on the sofa. He felt his heart begin to race at the thought of what he was about to do. "I want to talk to you about something I think it best she didn't know about."

Hayden looked cautiously at Cannon, then Warren and back to Cannon. "What is it?" she asked.

"Hayden." Cannon slid closer to her on the sofa and looked intently into her seductively dark eyes. "Hayden Campbell, will you marry me?"

Chapter Three

Startled and shocked, Hayden could only sit with her mouth wide open, unable to say a word. She stared blankly at Cannon. Had he just asked her to marry him? She must have been mistaken. This must be a joke.

"Wh-what?" Finally she found a word.

"I want you to be my wife." His eyes showed an uneasy caution. He knew this wouldn't be easy. What little he knew of Hayden Campbell worked against him being successful with this endeavor, but he had to try.

"Are you crazy? Are you joking?" Shock caused the words to wedge in her throat as she shot up off the sofa and stared down at him with wide eyes.

"Maybe I am crazy." He stood up, an uncertain smile on his face. "But I'm not joking. Please don't panic, Hayden, I can explain everything. Warren and I can."

"What does Warren . . . ?" She turned to the older man who was still leaning against the wall with a casual look on his face as if he was not at all surprised by Cannon's sudden proposal.

"Hayden, you may want to get comfortable in your seat."

Warren stepped closer to the both of them, his tone professional and precise. "This may take a while."

"I sincerely doubt that." She reclaimed her seat on the sofa, crossing her arms in defiance. She would listen for a second, but knew this was crazy. Marry? He had to be out of his mind.

Cannon returned to his desk and calmly leaned against it, an unmistakably serious look on his face. Here it goes, he thought. All or nothing.

"It all started yesterday," he began, "when I saw Sampson's article on us at the Metropolitan Club. I thought, hey, for once he sort of complimented me. Then I called him and we talked. He's a tabloid sort of guy, but not that bad once you get into a conversation with him. I was about to deny the rumor when, out of context, he told me today he'd been getting all these calls from people telling him to leave me alone especially now that I was with one woman and trying to settle down."

"Hold on," Hayden said, quickly catching on to where this was leading. "You want me to . . ."

"Just please listen." He held out a silencing hand to her, noticing her dislike of that motion. "Please. I started thinking, what could be better PR than to get married? Not just to combat this negative publicity, but also to help me win in my race for senator. Everyone knows the public likes their politicians settled and married with children."

"Have you lost your mind?" Intense astonishment was still on her beautiful brown face. "You want me to marry you to improve your image?"

He shrugged in partial agreement. "It's more complicated than that, but yes."

"Cannon, I'm ashamed of you." She looked at him with a motherly disapproval. Was this man so devoid of morality? "I would have assumed that the reason you've held out on marriage for as long as you have was because you realized it's an important emotional and spiritual commitment."

"Hayden, you're young." He rubbed his goatee with an amusing smile, trying to hide his nervous tension. "Marriage always has been and will always be an arrangement. For some it's love, for others it's money. You wouldn't believe how many people get married just to break free from their parents' controlling grip. Single parents many times marry someone they don't love themselves, but think will be a good father or mother to their kids.''

"Some people." Warren spoke after an observant silence. "Some people marry to advance their careers and some do it to help their parents in a time of need."

She gave him a respectful glance, noting his reference to her current situation. "Is that so, Warren?"

"When I was your age," Cannon continued, "I thought I would find this one woman who was perfect in everything. I would fall in love and live happily ever after. When you're twenty-five you think that way."

"Twenty-five?" She laughed in a cold manner, suggesting how unbelievable this all was. "You don't even know how old I am and you want to marry me? For your information, I'm twenty-seven and I may be young, Cannon, but I'm old enough to know that when I get married it will be under the arrangement of love and only that!"

She reached for her purse and turned to leave when Warren called after her.

"You haven't even asked what's in it for you," he said.

Her dark eyes were filling with rage as she swung around to face both men. "If there is no love, and trust me there is none, then there's nothing in it for me." She placed a haughty hand on her fine hip.

"Well, you never know." Cannon turned to Warren with a satirical smile and said, "Let's write love in as an option."

Fuming now, she approached his desk and leaned forward. Her eyes filled with icy contempt. "You think this is a joke? I shouldn't be surprised, a man of your character."

A serious look returned to his face as his dark eyebrows slanted in a frown. "I've explained to you that those rumors are not true."

"I'm supposed to take your word?" she asked sarcastically.

''The word of a man who would marry someone he knew nothing about to advance his career?''

''People do it all the time.'' His deep voice raised, but he kept his control. He knew he needed this and yelling at Hayden, no matter how frustrating she was, would not help.

''Not me!'' She met him with a defiant tone of her own.

''If you could both calm down,'' Warren interjected, lowering his hands in a silencing gesture, ''I can explain the terms of the agreement.''

''Listen to yourself, Warren,'' she pleaded. ''You sound like you're putting a business deal together. You're talking about marriage here.''

''A marriage that could be very beneficial to you.'' Warren stood behind Cannon's chair now, showing his support. ''In your family situation as well as your career and financial future.''

Still angry, but curious as to how he could make such a ridiculous idea sound reasonable, Hayden firmly placed her purse on Cannon's desk. ''I'm sure I'll regret asking this, but what do you mean?''

''Alright, now we're getting somewhere.'' Warren entwined his fingers, cracking his knuckles. ''Would you like to start, Cannon, or should I?''

''I will, Warren, thank you.'' Cannon returned his expression to one of careless charm. She had agreed to listen, that was all he had been doubtful about. Now that she was all ears, he would win. He was sure of it. ''Hayden, I realize your parents are the most important thing in this world to you. It's very admirable how you value your roots and stay close by. I've already promised to get your mother her six weeks sick leave in exchange for your professional advice and I will honor that.''

''You bet you will,'' she said with confidence. ''We have a deal.''

''I know.'' He smiled briefly at her strength, although, at the moment, it was his enemy. ''But I can offer you more. More for your parents and yourself.''

''I'm listening.'' She couldn't believe she was saying this, but it couldn't hurt to listen. She knew she'd end up turning him down anyway.

"Have you ever heard of a man named Michael Kent?"

"No," she answered after thinking a moment.

"Well if you've read anything on heart disease, heart attacks, and cardiology, he either wrote it or was quoted in it. Michael Kent is one of the top five cardiologists in the country and he practices in downtown Chicago."

"Wait a second." Suddenly she did remember the name. "We wanted him to look after Daddy, but he was too expensive. The insurance will only pay for care priced at the average and he was far above that. Dr. Kent wasn't on their plan."

"Yes, he is expensive, but well worth it." Cannon spoke in a tone showing his familiarity with the man. "Even if you had the money, he would've probably turned you down. He's extremely busy."

"Oh, Cannon, you take too long," Warren said impatiently. "It shows you've been working for the government. You don't know how to get to the point."

Hayden couldn't help but smile at Cannon's insulted expression, but she tried to put on a serious face as Warren began speaking to her.

"Cannon is good friends with Kent. Kent studied premed at Morehouse with his father, Craig. Cannon has already talked to Kent and he will be your father's doctor free of charge to you. Now that school is out, he won't be teaching his college course and has a bit more free time."

Hayden couldn't believe what she was hearing. The doctor they had now was alright, but he was young; only two years out of residency and Hayden was uncomfortable with his style and experience.

"That isn't all, Ms. Campbell," Warren said, sounding like to a salesman on a television infomercial. "As you may know by now, Cannon has several connections in the business world as well as the medical industry. His family's name has pull. Being married to him gives you immediate access to these people. It can increase your clientele as well as improve your importance and monetary value with your company. You could go into business for yourself even.''

''You could put yourself in a position where, financially, neither of your parents will have to work.'' Cannon continued to rub his goatee.

Hayden realized now this movement was a very cool attempt at controlling his nerves. She felt a certain sense of accomplishment at getting to know something vulnerable about this man.

''That along with your settlement after the divorce,'' Warren added.

''Divorce?'' Hayden hadn't thought of that. She had yet to fully grasp the idea of marriage, and now Warren was mentioning the divorce.

''Yes, divorce or annulment, whichever you prefer.'' Cannon spoke with a tone of uninvolvement, hoping she would understand how professional he meant this to be. ''The marriage would last until four months after my victory as senator.''

''You're extremely confident of victory for someone with a public relations problem.'' She smiled to herself as she noticed her comment made him momentarily lose his calm composure. ''That's almost a year from now.''

''So you're interested?'' His boldly handsome face showed mild anticipation. He knew all he needed was a maybe.

''I'm not saying that.'' She was taken off guard by his words and embarrassed because she couldn't help but be a little interested because of what she would get out of this for her family. ''It's still wrong to deceive the public. It's all wrong.''

''What are you holding onto?'' Cannon stood up, his patience wearing thin. ''Mr. Right isn't out there anywhere. Neither is Ms. Right. If you're old enough to know what you want, then you're old enough to know the reality of your chances at getting it.''

''Why don't you ask one of your girlfriends to do this?'' Hayden asked. ''You have several.''

''I do not have several.'' He mocked her with the last word. ''I wouldn't ask a personal acquaintance to join me in a temporary business arrangement. I'm not interested in marriage as you see it. It could get messy and involved if it got personal.''

"I can't believe how you mock an institution as sacred as this.'' She shook her head in disbelief.

"I can't believe you still live in some fairytale where a knight in shining armor will come for you. Even if you do, it's no big deal. This marriage will be over in less than a year. Your savior can come along then.''

"So you're saying, until then I should settle for less?'' She grabbed her purse, ready to leave. "Settle for you?''

Cannon's dark face transformed to an expression of intense anger. He couldn't help but be affected by her low opinion of him. "You're kind of a smart aleck aren't you?''

"You're just now figuring that out?'' She laughed sardonically. "I'm a little disappointed in you, Dr. Factor. I thought a man at your level of success would be a little quicker.''

Something intense flared through him in response to her sarcastic insults. This spitfire wasn't going to get the best of him. "I may not be as prim and proper as you, Ms. Campbell, but I am not less.''

She stared for a moment, speechless as she faced a man who would not allow anyone to put him down. "I didn't mean you were less. I just meant you aren't . . . this isn't for me.'' She was angry at herself for letting him rattle her, but she had.

Cannon turned his back to her and walked to the large window above the sofa. "The offer still stands. You might want to think about it.''

Hayden felt an odd twinge of disappointment at his physical rejection of her. She took a quick glance at Warren as his head lowered in disappointment. She was angry at them both for making her feel as if she was doing something wrong. How dare they?

With a loud sigh and a final glance at the strong back of Cannon Factor, Hayden turned and walked out of the room and out of the apartment.

*   *   *

For the rest of that day as well as Sunday, Hayden couldn't wipe Cannon's proposal from her mind. She thought herself crazy for even considering it, but she was.

It made her angry that she had to agree with him in the least. There was no knight in shining armor ready to take her away. After a couple of relationship disappointments, she thought she had found someone special in Alec Gavin. He was a young engineer with high hopes for a successful career. She found him handsome and charming. He made her laugh with the satirical slant he placed on every single thing. Alec had a happy-go-lucky attitude about life, like Hayden's friend Donna, and Hayden liked that. He made her laugh on her worst days. Despite this, she could share with him serious, personal feelings and she had thought he was listening. Alec was the first man she had dated with whom she felt comfortable talking with about Michael's death, even to the small extent she had.

As they grew closer, she came to truly care for him. She didn't want to admit it, but she had loved him. It wasn't a fire and ice kind of love like in the movies, but it was a comfortable and interesting love; one she was eager to explore and deepen. He had been her friend and her lover, or so she thought. She would have married him if he asked. Yet, he never asked.

With a pained heart, she remembered feeling very rejected and betrayed when he told her he was moving to Atlanta to take a job offered to him. It wasn't so much that he was leaving, but Hayden had felt lied to. She knew he had traveled to Atlanta for an engineering seminar, but he hadn't told her he'd set up some job interviews with area companies and he hadn't said anything to her about them upon returning to Chicago. She couldn't even remember him mentioning he was interested in moving to Atlanta, or anywhere else for the matter. When she asked him why he'd kept it all from her, he grew defensive and accused her of trying to cage him. After some brief discussion and empty accusations, the breakup was very civil. It was almost too civil for Hayden to stand. She remembered the words exactly.

"We continue to go over this, Hayden, and there is no middle ground." Alec lowered his head as he leaned over the balcony fence of Hayden's Evanston apartment. He was attractive, even when somber, in his form-fitting wool coat.

"How can we find a middle ground, Alec?" she asked, her heart sinking because of the fact that he could no longer look her in the eye. After eight months, it had come to this. They were out on the balcony although it was freezing. It was the place they usually went to discuss personal issues or disagreements. "I can't let go of the hurt I feel because you kept this from me. I feel like you lied. Then you come home and say *'I'm taking a job in Atlanta and I want to break up to keep things uncomplicated.'* That was the word you used, right? Uncomplicated? That's so cold, Alec."

"I don't see it that way." His dark, small eyes looked outward at the view of Dyche Stadium where Northwestern University played football games. "Long-distance relationships are too difficult. I can't concentrate on a new job and a new life in Atlanta and a relationship with you here in Chicago. Listen, it's how I feel, so I guess there isn't anything left to say. I don't want to continue going back and forth on this."

"Neither do I." Her heart heaved a heavy sigh as the words they spoke seemed so final. She doubted whether or not she had the desire to keep someone who would do what he had just done in her life at all.

"I'm leaving next Tuesday." He turned to her, only able to look at her deep purple wool coat.

"Goodbye." She felt so cold. Chicago winters were brutal.

"Goodbye." With that he turned and walked away.

Hayden hadn't seen or heard from him since.

More than losing him, it hurt to realize she had spent eight months of her life committing herself to someone who only thought of her as a temporary relationship. Someone who could let go of her so easily, so quickly.

No, knights in shining armor didn't exist; at least not for

her. She was old enough to accept that and she had accepted it after a month of crying and feeling sorry for herself with Donna at her side.

It still didn't mean she should settle for a business arrangement.

Then she thought about her father. How much better could his chances be if Michael Kent was his doctor? She loved her father with all her heart and couldn't imagine him not here. It wasn't just Daddy she worried about. Deep down inside she knew he was the link between her mother and herself. Their relationship was simple and quiet at best. How would things be between the two women if he was no longer around?

Dr. Michael Kent was one of the best cardiologist in the country. When Hayden returned home from her visit with Cannon she looked again at all the books and brochures she had purchased on the subject since her father's heart attack. Either a mention of Kent or a quote of his could be found in every index or footnote as Cannon had said.

Then there was the free-of-charge stipulation. Fortunately her father's insurance held him for eighteen months after leaving due to medical problems, but at only 80 percent. A full twenty 20 percent of any medical bill, especially involving the heart, was a lot of money. It was a financial strain on Hayden and her mother. Cannon said he would take care of all that with a phone call to a family friend. If only it where that simple, Hayden thought.

She hadn't considered using Cannon to develop business contacts, although it would be helpful to her career. She had been a straight-A student at the Northwestern University and worked very hard at her job. It was sobering to know, in the real world, despite all that, her chances of further success were not measured so much by what she did, but who she knew. Cannon knew everybody; she was sure of that, but with everything going on in her life now, networking was simply not a priority. Neither was any money she could get in a divorce settlement. What did he think, she was some kind of wife for hire? Monetary compensation would be degrading and demoralizing.

Speaking of demoralizing, what about his reputation? Who had Cannon Factor been and who was he now? Were the rumors being spread by a bitter person trying to ruin Cannon's career or were the consequences of leading a loose lifestyle finally catching up with him? Hayden always thought of herself as open-minded. Although she was careful about the company she kept, she never wanted to judge someone on their personal choices. She just couldn't see herself motivated to be so supportive to someone with such questionable moral character.

Thinking further in those terms, she wondered how close a marriage this would be? He meant strictly businesses, but exactly what did he expect from her? Only a pretty face, appearing as a supportive, loving wife behind the man. Could she live with herself from a moral standpoint? Could she lie to her parents? Could she lie to her friends? Would she have to? Would he humiliate her with his womanizing while they were married? How fast could a year go by? How long after the marriage would she be judged by it? Would she be deceiving the public into voting for a man undeserving of such a high political office? Hayden was getting a headache thinking about it all. It was impossible, she told herself. Impossible.

As she laid her head on her pillow Sunday night, she wanted to forget everything and anything for just a moment. The last thing she needed was a distressing phone call from her mother, but it was what she got less than a second after her eyes began to close.

"Where have you been all day, Hayden? I've been calling you over and over again?" There was a mixture of anger and worry in Elise Campbell's voice.

"I was driving around," Hayden answered. "It helps me think. What's wrong?"

"Everything is fine now." Elise sighed. "Only earlier it was . . . oh dear. Your father got upset. I forgot to hide the mail from him and he saw the hospital bill. He got so upset he started to feel pain in his chest."

"Did you take him to the hospital?" Hayden jumped up from her lying position and desperately reached for her shoes. She had to get over there.

"Well, I called the doctor," Elise said, "but he wasn't home. I paged him, but he never responded. How could they give us someone so irresponsible? I'm writing a complaint to the hospital and the HMO."

"Good, so will I. I don't know how we got him, Mama." Michael Kent's name quickly came to Hayden's mind again. "What happened next?"

"Well, I took him to the emergency room and he's alright now. We still couldn't locate Tom's doctor so a resident looked him over. I'm not happy with this at all."

"I know," Hayden said in a calm voice. She was upset, but needed to calm her mother down. Daddy always got upset when Elise was unhappy. "I know you're concerned, but don't let Daddy know."

"There is one bit of good news," Elise said. "Alan called out of the blue yesterday. He's decided to break down and be human."

"He's giving you the six weeks?" Hayden asked.

"Yes, and paid at that."

Hayden sighed, grateful that Cannon had kept his word. "Did he seem upset about it?"

"No, he actually sounded apologetic." Elise emitted a half-humored laugh. "He went on and on about loyalty and favors and all that."

"That's great, Mama," Hayden said. "I'm on my way over."

She hung up the phone and sat still on the edge of her bed for a moment. Disaster had been averted today, but what about tomorrow? At least Mother was getting her leave. This was a step in the right direction, Hayden knew that, but it didn't seem to make her feel better. What good was her mother's six week leave, if the bills kept piling on? She still couldn't pay them. What if they couldn't find the doctor again? Hayden would definitely call the hospital and let them know what she thought of that fiasco, but would it solve the problem? To the HMO, her father was a social security number. Nothing more.

"Daddy could have died today." She whispered the words to herself as she sat in the darkness of her small bedroom.

She clicked on the night light. There, staring at her with love and smiles, was a picture of her parents. It was taken last summer at Chicago's annual Taste of Chicago event, where people sample food of all kinds at several dozen booths. Seeing the barbecued ribs on a small paper plate in one of her father's hands and the slice of cheesecake in the other, took on a whole new meaning now and it almost brought tears to Hayden's eyes.

She loved them both so much. Despite their faults, as everybody had them, they had done everything, sacrificed all that was necessary and then some for her and Michael while he'd been alive.

With a beleaguered moan, Hayden reached into her purse and pulled out a little gray card. She knew what it was she had to do.

"Hello?" The voice came calmly over the phone.

"Cannon, it's Hayden Campbell." She cleared her throat, feeling the tingling of butterflies in her stomach.

"Yes, Hayden?"

"If the offer still stands," she said, "I accept."

"Very well," he said without emotion. "We need to get together and talk about the terms."

"Yes, we should meet sometime tomorrow." She felt he could have at least said *good* or *thanks*. "When is your interview with Tony Brown?"

"That's early afternoon. You can come to my office when you're through with work. Can you make it by six?"

"Yes. I'll see you at six." As she hung up the phone, Hayden wondered if she knew what she was getting herself into but she had no time to think about that now. Now, she had to see her daddy.

* * *

Monday, Hayden tried her best to block out the call she'd made to Cannon the previous afternoon. She didn't want to think of what she had done, but she couldn't help it. She still had not said a word to her parents or Donna. The truth was that she was embarrassed and that alone kept her mouth shut. In her heart, she believed marriage was for love and love only, despite what Cannon said. How could she face people in a lie? Did she have a choice? She was doing this for her father and mother. Family was everything and, after all, they had done for her, she owed them this. She was all they had now.

Hayden continued to remind herself of that as she stepped onto the sixth floor of the State Building. Noticing a couple of stares from a few of the late-leavers she began to realize that she would soon become a recognizable face in the city of Chicago and the state of Illinois. At least for a while. She ignored the tinge of excitement that she felt at the thought of that, considering it self-centered.

Outside Cannon's office, she was immediately met by Maryann's hostile glare as she was gathering her things to leave.

"Good evening, Maryann." Hayden wanted to be civil. She had learned to do so under the worst of circumstances being a public relations executive, only it was a waste of time with this woman. It was obvious Maryann had made up her mind about Hayden.

"Hayden." Maryann gave a curt nod. "Cannon is expecting you. I advise you to beware. He's not in a good mood."

"What happened?"

"Didn't you read today's paper?" Maryann asked.

"I didn't get to it." Hayden had wanted to. She usually read Donna's copy during lunch or at the end of the afternoon, but she'd been swamped with Coverling problems all day.

"How do you suggest to help Cannon with his publicity if you don't even know about it?" Maryann spat the words out contemptuously.

"I'm not solely at the service of Cannon," Hayden replied sharply. "I have a career. That that comes first."

Maryann gave her a seething look as she explained. "In today's tidbit, Sampson reported that he has sources to confirm that the reason why city employee health benefits haven't been reformed is because Cannon's spending the health budget on personal items and activities."

"He gave no proof?" Hayden asked.

"Of course not, why even ask? Cannon is fuming. John is in there now trying to calm him." She headed for the elevator. "Be careful and try to do your job."

Ignoring Maryann's last comments, Hayden entered the office where she saw a tall thin man, ginger brown in complexion, leaning against the window. His expression was one of deep, knowing concern, as if he was tormented by something. Cannon was sitting a few feet away at his desk, frustration and anger pervading every muscle and expression on his face.

"Hello," the man said as he walked toward her. Smiling friendlily he looked about the same age as Cannon. "You must be Hayden Campbell."

"Yes, I am." With a smile, she shook his hand firmly. Despite meeting the stranger, she found herself strongly distracted by the look of fatigue that settled in pockets under Cannon's eyes.

"Cannon was telling me about you. I'm John Dannell." He wiped his forehead and whistled. "He could have used you today."

"I heard." Hayden laid her purse on Cannon's desk and sat down. She gave him a compassionate smile, but he barely responded. She felt sorry for him even though she didn't know if she should. Was all of this a big lie or was he?

"Cannon, you have to stay calm," she told him. "Did Sampson give a source?"

"No, he refuses to," John interjected. "It's a waste of time to ask. A reporter never reveals his source."

"You're right there," Hayden agreed. "We've got to find

out some other way. Who are your enemies, Cannon? What about the guy you beat for this position?''

"That wasn't an election, Hayden," Cannon muttered hastily. Things were getting worse. Now they were attacking his job performance, something he'd thought was below even Sampson. "The mayor appointed me."

"I know." Hayden had to fight back a sudden urge to touch his shoulder. He seemed genuinely distraught. "But this is one of the most sought-after jobs in the city. There must have been someone else considered."

"Robert Marks is a distinguished surgeon at Cook County Hospital. His name was going around strong for a long time before I was mentioned." Cannon sensed a hint of affection in her eyes and felt it affect him deeply within. She was kind and soft under that courageous, stubborn exterior. He could tell that from the first time he saw her.

"You should have turned it down, Cannon," John said as he buttoned up his suit jacket. "You should have stayed with the practice. You made four times the money and you could have saved yourself all this craziness."

"Don't start with me." Cannon forced a smile and explained to Hayden. "John and I had a successful practice in Northbrook for eight years before I took this job. He's never forgiven me."

"You'd like him back?" she asked with an inquiring smile.

"Yes and the door is always open." John picked up his briefcase and winked at Cannon. "I've got to get home. Jesse's cooking my favorite dinner and I've been late three days in a row. It was nice meeting you, Hayden."

"Same here." She gave him a quick wave as he left, then turned to Cannon who was still very upset. "If you would rather go over this another day I would understand."

"No. I need this now more than ever." He leaned back in his chair with a tired sigh. "I'll go first."

"Sounds fair," she said, the stubborn girl inside standing alert, "but I reserve the right to interrupt."

"Fair." He sent her a smile that made her soft, bare cheeks flush. It gave him incredible confidence to see this. A great deal of pleasure as well. ''You will quit your job and completely devote your time . . .''

''Whoa!'' She held up her hand to prevent him from going any farther. ''Quit my job? Are you crazy?''

''No.'' He responded, looking at her as if she was the crazy one. ''You'll have plenty of money to pay . . .''

''This isn't about money, Cannon,'' she said, shaking her head. ''I have a career I'm committed to. And if I remember correctly, part of the deal was that I could acquire business contacts from you. How would that work if I wasn't employed?''

A suggestion of annoyance hovered in his eyes as he stared her down for a while, but compliance settled in as he realized there was no winning this fight. He was willing to compromise. After all, he was getting what he really wanted.

''Alright, you work,'' he said, ''but you will move into my condo.''

''No way.'' She shook her head as she realized this night would be a long one.

They were in his office for hours that night going back and forth. Hayden realized *stubborn* would be stitched on Cannon Factor's gravestone, but she stood her ground. An agreement was made for her to move into the lakefront condo after they were married. Hayden was extremely uncomfortable about it, even after he assured her the extra bedroom was well down the hallway from his. She found some comfort in the fact that, with such busy schedules, they would hardly see each other except for campaign work. He understood that she would spend many nights at her parents' house, especially while her father was still in his most critical state.

She would accompany him to all of his usual social events, such as charities and fund-raisers as well as campaign events after he declared his bid for the Congress. She agreed to come to every event as long as it didn't conflict with her career at R&D.

She made him promise not to lie or ask her to lie about their relationship to the public. If anyone questioned them, on the record, for print, radio, or TV, they would simply refer to it as personal. She refused to lie to the public and be quoted as saying she loved him. He agreed, and they both agreed the only people who would know would be the two of them and their lawyers if she chose to bring one in.

They would explain to family and friends that they met earlier last week and fell head over heels in love. Hayden was skeptical over the success of this because she had never been that impulsive of a person and wasn't sure those who knew her would believe this. She went over this with Cannon several times. She had never lied to her parents and was very uncomfortable with it, but Cannon worked to convince her it was for the greater good and after everything was over, she could tell them the truth if she chose to. It was a no-win situation in that sense. Either way, she would disappoint them, even if what she did could keep their family together.

They would demand that no one close to them talk to the press. Cannon would have Maryann draft a dry release on the marriage to be sent to anyone who inquired. He promised to call Dr. Kent the next day and Hayden's father would begin seeing him before the end of the week. Hayden felt some relief at the thought of no more medical bills to upset him, but knew that this would not be easy. At least she wouldn't have to lie about that. Dr. Kent was a friend of Cannon's and now that they would be family, there should be no harm in letting family do favors. Tom Campbell was a stubborn, proud man, but Hayden was prepared to fight for this. His care was what she was doing this for and she knew she'd have Elise on her side.

Both agreed to end any current relationships they had. Hayden was embarrassed to tell him she wasn't seeing anyone and decided Alec was not worth mentioning since it was clearly over. She gave Cannon a hard time on this topic. Even though they weren't going to be intimate, she refused to be humiliated in public. He promised to do his part and reminded her the whole purpose of this was, for him at least, to dispel any bad images people had of him so he would be a fool to see another woman while they were married. He mentioned he hadn't been seeing anyone seriously since he broke off with Joanne Pearl, a model he dated a month ago.

Wanting to get this started and over with as soon as possible, they decided to invite their families to Hayden's apartment Wednesday night to tell them. Cannon agreed to come over earlier to prepare with her. Their evening ended at midnight.

As she shook his hand before leaving, Hayden tried her best to see past the guilt she felt. Arriving home that night, she thought long and hard about what she was doing. It was wrong. Her conscience wouldn't allow her to ignore that, but there was more to it. Tom Campbell had always told her not everything was black and white. He'd said there was a gray area sometimes. This agreement was her gray area, Hayden believed. It was difficult to swallow, but she would have to make it workable and beneficial. It was now the end of March and the election would be in November. They would divorce in March of next year, citing their demanding careers as the reason. Time can go by fast, she thought. She hoped.

This was marriage! Even as she slipped into sleep, Hayden couldn't believe it. She had always imagined herself falling head over heels in love and getting married once and forever, but now she already knew when her first marriage would end.

Chapter Four

"I think I have it." Cannon rubbed at his goatee as he paced the living room of Hayden's apartment. "You've lived in Evanston all your life. Your father's name is Tom, he used to be a high school math teacher. Your mother's name is Elise, she is a bookkeeper at AG Enterprises. Your brother, Michael, passed away when you were seventeen and he was sixteen. It was a car accident while visiting friends in Detroit?"

"Yes." Hayden tried to keep the painful memory from showing on her face. It seemed so long ago when the police officer arrived at their door that warm night in August.

Cannon had noticed the painful flicker in her tender eyes when she spoke of her younger brother. His first inclination had been to reach for her, hold her and comfort her, but he barely knew her and wasn't certain she thought enough of him to want his comfort.

As a Sade CD played in the background, Hayden listened to Cannon and felt he was doing a pretty good job of remembering the basic facts of her life. Their families were expected at her place in half an hour and they wanted to give the impression

that, even in the small time they'd known each other, they had
learned a great deal about the other.

"You studied speech communications at Northwestern University?" he continued. "Then you worked as an assistant to
a journalism professor at Northwestern for a year before moving
on to R&D."

"Very good." Her smile widened in approval. She was doing
her best to conceal her preoccupation with his powerful well-
muscled body as he moved across the room. Having come
straight from his office, he looked devastatingly handsome in
a business suit. His jacket off, the crisp, cottony white button-
down shirt could not conceal the masculinity beneath.

"Don't I need to know more?" He felt a little nervous, but
never weakened his posture. That little voice in his head told
him Hayden's pleasant, but uncertain smile meant he could
be making a huge mistake. He kept reminding himself that
sometimes, if rarely, the ends justifies the means. Sometimes.
"I mean about your personality."

"You know enough for today." She felt a certain uneasiness,
as if she was giving up something too precious by telling him
about who she was inside. In her opinion, this was information
that should be earned in a caring, legitimate relationship.

"What if your mom asks me what it is about you I love the
most?" He sat his considerable figure in her black ottoman
chair. His eyes concentrated on her intently. In reality he wanted
to know the real Hayden Campbell for more reasons than to
convince people of why he wanted to marry her. He found her
a little mysterious and fascinating in her protection of herself
and her family. He wasn't familiar with that level of commitment in the women who had been in his life up until now.

Hayden felt terribly uncomfortable at his gaze. It seemed as
if he was trying to see through her. She was already angry with
herself for getting up extra early that morning to clean the
apartment for a second time. She tried to convince herself it
was for her mother and his, but she knew it was for Cannon.
She couldn't afford a luxurious condo like his, nor all the
expensive furniture and art, but she had a nice place and nice

things. Something inside of her wanted Cannon, more than anyone else, to know that. Selfish pride perhaps, she thought. There was a part of her that didn't want him to think he was doing any kind of favor for her personally. That she had all she needed for herself, which was the reason she refused a financial settlement after this marriage would end. Possibly, quite possibly there was a part of her that wanted to impress him. That was a very small part though, Hayden assured herself of that.

"I don't think she'll ask." She quickly stood up from the sofa, walking to the dining room. Neatly arranging the snacks she had picked up on her way home from work, she hoped he would not follow her. Every moment she saw him, she became more and more aware of his attraction, and it disturbed her that, despite all that should be her priority, his appearance was what she concerned herself with the most in his presence.

"What do you mean?" Cannon asked, as he followed her. He passed her a confused stare as he leaned in the doorway, his strong hands stuffed in the pockets of his streamlined ebony slacks. "She's your mother."

"Well, thank you for that information. I was wondering why she'd been hanging around me all my life." Hayden could see she surprised him with the sharpness of her tone. Take that Mr. Always So Calm, Cool, and Collected. "Listen, my mother is preoccupied with Daddy now. She won't get into all that."

"But she's your mother," he persisted, feeling a spark of excitement at her smart comment. Hayden Campbell could act very reserved when she wanted to, but he could see the fire inside of her every once in a while and he liked that. He liked it a lot. "Why wouldn't a mother be interested in her only daughter's wedding?"

"Cannon." She looked at him, his closeness effecting her in an odd way. She didn't like the direction of this conversation. "I don't want to discuss my mother. I just know she won't be overly inquisitive."

"Well if she does ask, I'll tell her it was your patience that turned me on like crazy." He gave her a sarcastic smile, knowing he was telling a bit of the truth. Everything about her turned him on, only he had to ignore that.

"I don't need your sarcasm, Cannon. I'm very uncomfortable with this." As she passed by him, the attractive scent of his cologne touched her senses and traveled sweetly to her head for a moment. "It's not every day I spend lying to my family."

"Would you get over this already?" His voice mocked a whining child.

"I'm sorry." She tilted a stubborn chin up as she turned to him. "Unlike you, I have what I like to refer to as a set of morals and there's a thing called guilt that sets in when I violate them."

"Okay, enough of that." He said indifferently in a tone meant to annoy her. He playfully smiled in response to her irritated expression. He was beginning to enjoy the wrinkle her little nose did when she was annoyed. "Getting back to the point, your best friend is Donna who works with you at R&D. You have no aunts or uncles, therefore no cousins. Your only grandparent is your mother's father, Perry, who lives in Memphis, Tennessee."

"You're right."

"Now your turn." He followed her actions by sitting across from her on the sofa. He could see he was irritating her, but instead of taking it personally, he chose to enjoy himself and tease her.

"Alright." She tried to concentrate on everything he had told her, hoping he couldn't tell how uncomfortable his closeness made her. "You grew up in Madison, Wisconsin. Your father, Craig, was an obstetrician who died of colon cancer four years ago. Your mother, Candace, is a retired nurse living in the Chicago area in Glencoe. Your sister, Mavis, is thirty years old, a sales rep for Lippert Products International and lives with your mother. Her son, Tyler, is four and a half."

"You should know that Tyler and I are very close, so he'll probably be at the condo often." Cannon smiled proudly, showing his great affection for the boy.

"What about his father? You haven't mentioned him." Hayden didn't mind the thought of having a kid around. She always enjoyed them, but most of her friends were still single and being an only child, she had no nieces or nephews.

"He isn't a part of our lives." An angry frown tightened his jaw muscles. "Mavis is . . . she's hard to explain. She used to be a little wild and made some bad choices in, shall I say, companionship earlier in her life. The guy was a loser and he skipped town as soon as she told him she was pregnant."

"Oh, that's too bad." Hayden could see Cannon's anger was genuine. Whatever questions there were about this man, his concern for those he loved wasn't one of them. "Maybe if he wasn't going to be a responsible father, it's better off he not be there. Don't you think?"

He looked at her in silence for a short time. His eyes had a burning, faraway look in them that made her want to know what this complicated man was made of.

"Yes, I suppose," he said finally. "It would be nice though if the idiot got a job so he could send some child support. All Tyler has now for his father is me."

Even though his feelings for Tyler had nothing to do with what was going on tonight, Hayden wanted to hear more. She liked this side of Cannon Factor, but she realized it was inappropriate. Theirs was a business arrangement. Cannon said himself it could get messy if it got personal. She agreed and planned to keep this situation as far from personal as possible.

"You have family spread across the country," she went on to say. "But you aren't particularly close to any of your cousins. Your family moved to Glencoe when you were seventeen. You attended Morehouse College like your father. What else?"

"I went to med school at Columbia University and performed my residency at Northwestern Memorial, going on to specialize in pediatrics. I opened a private practice with John Dannell, left that to become commissioner and you know everything since."

"Do I?" she asked. "What about the women, Cannon?"

"What women?"

"Set aside the current rumors." Hayden became uncomfortable as she sensed Cannon's uneasiness at the turn the conversation had taken. "What's this playboy past about?"

"Ninety percent were rumors." Cannon sighed, wondering if she was asking because she didn't want to be tripped up by someone mentioning one of his ex's or because she cared. "When I was younger, I liked the company of women. I was high profile. A lot of the women I dated were high profile. I was a little immature and curious. It's really not a big deal."

"Some people seem to think so." Hayden was disturbed by the nonchalantness of his tone. "Morality is important to . . ."

"I'm not an immoral person." He caught himself before letting his temper reach him. "I was a little wild, but it was my twenties. I gave that lifestyle up."

Hayden wanted to believe him, but she wondered if it was true or just convenient. How many ambitious politicians decided to clean up their lifestyle for the sole purpose of looking good to the public so they could get elected, only to return to that lifestyle once safely in office where their behavior was kept secret? Hayden didn't want to think about that right now. She was too nervous already, so she decided to return to safer topics. "So you like children?"

"Yes. I want to have some one day. Don't worry," he said with a quick laugh, noticing her sudden discomfort. "I know that's not part of our arrangement."

"Don't joke about this, Cannon." Suddenly it felt too warm in the room and she headed for the window to open it. "I'm doing this because I have to. I still don't approve of it and I certainly don't think its something to joke about."

Hayden jumped at the sound of the doorbell ringing. It seemed louder and more abrupt than usual. She felt butterflies in her stomach realizing it was all about to start. Would it work?

"It's them." She nervously straightened out the peach and yellow spring dress she had changed into and ran to the mirror to make sure she looked in place. She took a moment to survey her appearance, which she usually approved of. Her hair was neatly combed and pulled loosely into a long ponytail to keep it from her face. She took it easy with the makeup, choosing only a light lipstick and mascara. She never needed to wear much makeup, although sometimes she liked to dress up to look more sophisticated for an evening out.

"Are you going to get the door or enter a beauty pageant?" The tone of Cannon's voice slightly hinted at his increasingly nervous state as he quickly stood up. He was letting her uncertainty get to him and that was the last thing he needed to do.

"Oh, shut up." Hayden rushed by him quickly, rolling her eyes.

As soon as she opened the door, a small figure dashed past her and ran into the apartment.

"Hey, little guy." Cannon held out his arms to gather up the tiny person dressed in Chicago White Sox gear screaming in joy as he kissed Cannon on the cheek. Cannon's eyes lit up and his smile reached from ear to ear.

"I'm so sorry he ran right by you. He hasn't seen his uncle Cannon in over a week." The voice came as in walked a beautiful woman who looked to be in her late sixties with cocoa brown skin that barely showed a wrinkle. In a silk, sapphire blue pantsuit she carried herself with a distinguished grace.

"You must be Mrs. Factor." Hayden, held out her hand to shake, but the woman ignored it, and pulled her in for a warm hug.

"I think we're a little too late for handshakes. Call me Candace." She gave Hayden a gentle and welcoming smile. "Let me look at the woman my son tells me has his head spinning all day long."

As Candace stepped back to take in a full look at Hayden, a younger woman entered the apartment from behind her. Mavis Factor had a pretty face despite the unfriendly frown it formed. She looked older than her thirty years and was painfully thin.

"You are as beautiful as Cannon said." Candace smiled approvingly. "He said you swept him off his feet and I can see how."

"Alright, Mom, we get the point." Mavis walked slowly

into the apartment, a judgmental sneer on her face as she observed the decorations. "You're excited to meet her."

"Hayden." Cannon walked over to the women with the young boy contentedly in his arms. "This is my always polite sister, Mavis, and my mother, Candace."

"It's nice to meet both of you." Hayden gave a friendly smile to both women. Shaking Mavis's hand, she barely saw a smile form on her tight lips. Despite that, Hayden shook her hand vigorously before turning her attention to the young child in Cannon's arms. "And this adorable gentleman must be Tyler."

Happiness at being recognized lit up the boy's tiny face. "Yes, I am. Who are you?"

"I'm Hayden." She found him adorable with a precious smile that was infectious. "Your uncle Cannon told me you're a very good boy."

"Most of the time," he responded, his huge brown eyes wide open. "But sometimes he says I'm a smarty pants, too."

As laughter circled the room, Hayden noticed Cannon laughing harder than anyone. She watched him place Tyler on the floor and saw there was genuine endearment in his eyes. Tyler was where he could be touched. Tyler was where he was vulnerable. She appreciated that his tender look lingered on the boy for a moment before returning to the women.

"I hope you aren't starting without me."

Everyone turned to see Elise Campbell standing in the doorway. To Hayden's eyes her mother looked tired as usual. The past month and a half had been terribly hard on her.

"No, Mama, everyone just got here." Hayden kissed her mother tenderly on the cheek. "Is Daddy alright?"

"Yes, the nurse is with him," Elise said.

In an attempt to make up for the last unfortunate situation when her father's doctor could not be located, the hospital offered one week of free at-home nursing care. Hayden was at least happy it gave her mother some rest and the opportunity to get out of the house for a few moments at a time.

"Mama," Hayden said. "This is Cannon Factor."

''Hello, Mrs. Campbell.'' Cannon held out his hand to the kind, but cautious woman. He could see Hayden in her large eyes and the small, refined shape of her nose.

''I know you,'' Elise said as she shook his hand.

''Yes, Mama. I told you he's Cook County Health Commissioner.'' Hayden turned to Cannon. ''Mama's from the suburbs. She never watches the news and she only reads the *Evanston Review*.''

''No,'' Elise said. ''You dated Jessica Carey's daughter. What was her name?''

Cannon cleared his throat as he noticed Hayden's doubtful eyes set on him. ''I believe it was Jennifer.''

''Yes.'' Elise nodded. ''You dated Hedda Turner's daughter too, didn't you? She's mentioned your name. Yes, you dated her oldest, Farrah. Hedda says you broke her little girl's heart.''

Cannon felt a bead of sweat hit his brows as silence enveloped the room. ''Yes, I remember Farrah. That was a long time . . .''

'I'm sorry,'' Elise said, as she seemed to notice the tension in the air. ''I just speak without thinking. I've just been wondering why the name sounded so familiar since Hayden told me the other day. It just hit me, but please ignore me. I'm sure it's all in the past.''

Hayden hadn't taken her eyes off Cannon as her mother recalled two of his ex's. God, she thought. If her mother knew, then who else knew about him? So, Cannon had left a trail of broken hearts. So what? Hayden was certain no one would ever be able to say *''That's Cannon Factor. He broke Hayden Campbell's little heart.''* He'd never get the chance.

Hayden introduced everyone else and led them all to the dining room. Cannon had to chase Tyler around a couple of times before seating him. They spent over an hour introducing themselves a little further and engaging in small talk. She wasn't sure about Mavis, but Hayden knew she would like Candace. She was a vibrant, colorful woman who seemed to take enough pride in how she raised her son not to question his decisions.

''I hate to sound rude.'' Elise interrupted their conversations.

"I can't stay very long. The nurse is off at nine. What is this important news you both have to tell us?"

"Yeah, that's what we're all here for isn't it?" Mavis's tone was purposefully annoyed. "Some big news."

"Mavis, please be patient." Candace scolded her slightly. "Cannon said it was important, I'm sure its worth waiting for."

"I know it's a little late to be out on a week night, but we do have something important to tell you." Cannon winked at Tyler who had faded in and out of conversations throughout the evening. "We just thought you'd like to get to know each other better first."

"Well, if you're both as serious about dating as you say," Candace said, "we'll probably get to know each other very well."

Hayden cleared her throat. "Well we hope you like each other, because Cannon and I are getting married." There, it was out. There was no turning back. It was all beginning.

Intense astonishment filled the room as mouths dropped and eyes widened. Hayden turned to Cannon who was sitting beside her. The fear and uncertainty she felt must have shown on her face, because Cannon gave her a reassuring wink and firmly grasped her hand, which had suddenly turned cold. She was surprised at the strange sudden comfort the gesture gave her.

"Yuck, that's disgusting." Tyler gave an upturned nose as his squeaky voice broke the silence.

"It's not disgusting," Cannon said as he reached over and playfully rubbed the boy's head. "It's great news."

"It's unexpected news," Candace finally said, a look of incoherence on her face. "When did this come about Cannon?"

"That's what I'd like to know." Elise spoke quietly and slowly, arms tightly across her chest. Her eyes were intently on her daughter.

"Well, we pretty much decided it Sunday." Hayden felt confident in at least knowing that was the truth, but she found it difficult to look anyone in the eye.

"What Hayden is trying to say is, Sunday she agreed to be my wife and made me the happiest and the luckiest man alive."

Cannon spoke with confidence, trying his best to cover up the restlessness he felt.

Seeing him now, cool under pressure, Hayden was reminded of how attractive his control was.

"This is such a joke," Mavis said, with a spiteful laugh. "You two don't even know each other."

"That isn't entirely true," Cannon responded harshly. "We know that we love each other."

Hayden felt an unusual awareness at his mention of his last words. She assumed it was guilt because of the lie, but knew it could have been something more.

"Well I'm happy, I think." Candace stood up, still with a confused expression and walked across the table to hug her son. "I've always wanted you to find someone to settle down with."

"Well here she is, Mother." Cannon kissed his mother and turned to Hayden, who stood up.

"I really don't know what to say." Candace turned to Hayden. "I guess I should say welcome to the family."

Candace held out her arms to receive Hayden and hugged her tightly. Hayden was a little perplexed at the feeling of happiness that came over her. It was a satisfaction that she would expect to come to her if she had wanted this; really wanted it. She convinced herself it was only relief that their plan seemed to be working on the person she had once felt would be the hardest to convince.

"Thank you, Candace." As she stepped away from the older woman, Hayden turned to her own mother who was still seated at the table with bewilderment in her eyes.

"Mama, I know this is a surprise." She sat down next to her, feeling a sudden sense of loss in the knowledge that this was not real. She still dreamed of the day she would tell her mother she was getting married and wondered what the reaction would be. She had dreamt of a sudden change in their relationship to a closer, more caring one where they would share on a level they never had before. She dreamt it that way, but would it ever be? Hayden doubted it. "I don't know the best way to tell Daddy. I don't want to excite him too much."

"Why don't you let me tell him, dear." Elise took her daughter's hand and gave it a motherly rub. "Do you really know what you're doing?"

"Yes, Mama, I do." She wanted desperately to tell her she was doing this for her and Daddy, but they would never allow it. They would never understand. "I hope I have your support."

"Of course you do, dear." Elise nervously smiled and hugged her daughter. Her uncertainty was strongly evident. "I'll tell your father. I'm sure he'll be happy albeit surprised. By the time the wedding comes, he'll be healthy enough to dance the night away."

"That's the other piece of news," Hayden said, biting her lip as her mother's look said she wasn't sure she could take another surprise. "Cannon and I want to get married in April."

"April!" Candace yelled. "It's March thirtieth. This will never work. It takes at least eight months to plan a proper society wedding."

"That won't be necessary mother," Cannon said. "We're deeply in love and can't wait. We want to be married in three weeks."

Hayden was surprised at the ease with which he was handling all this. She, herself, felt as if she would explode.

"That isn't enough time for your father, Hayden," Elise said.

"I'm not sure about that, Elise," Cannon responded. "He won't be able to dance the night away, but I think it will be perfectly fine for him to attend."

"What about a dining hall and catering?" Candace stood up and began pacing the room, rubbing her temples in frustration.

"No, we don't want any of that." Hayden felt guilty enough. She couldn't bear it if this lie was made into a great celebration, costing tons of money and involving hundreds of people. "We just want an inexpensive, intimate ceremony with our immediate families and friends."

"We can all have a small dinner afterward," Cannon added,

throwing Hayden a grateful smile for temporarily calming his mother down.

"I get it." Mavis finally spoke, but kept her constant frown. "He knocked you up didn't he? He finally got one pregnant."

"Mavis, I've had enough of . . ." Cannon's voice rose as he faced his sister in anger. He never understood her desire to hurt him, but dealt with it. He would not allow her to insult Hayden. Ever.

"Cannon, please." Hayden took a gentle hold of his arm, catching him before he said something that could expose the both of them. She turned to Mavis, whose entire demeanor was filled with satisfaction at the explosion she just evoked from her brother. "Mavis, you couldn't be farther from the truth. Cannon and I just want to be married and neither of us wants a big hoopla. We're both very busy."

"Do you even know anything about him, Hayden?" Mavis stood up from her chair, straightening her thin shoulders. "Do you know how he is with women? Have you told her Cannon, about all your girlfriends?"

"Mavis, stop it!" Candace glared at her daughter. "Don't talk that way in front of the baby."

Everyone's eyes turned to Tyler who was completely ignoring them all. He had been long bored of their conversation when he found out his carrot sticks could be warriors fighting in a battle.

"Mavis, you know that isn't true." Cannon's voice was calm, but his eyes were sharp and assessing. "Do you always have to do this? Do you always have to cause a problem?"

"For you?" She gave her brother an evil grin. "It's not that I have to. I enjoy it, it highlights my day."

"Hayden, you must excuse Mavis." Candace rolled her eyes at her daughter. "She hates politics, government, and basically everything else her brother is involved in."

"Everything you do is bourgeois and fake." Mavis placed her hands firmly on her skinny hips. "You try to put up such a front, but the papers are showing . . ."

"I told you those rumors aren't true!" Cannon slammed a

strong fist on the table. "For Pete's sake. You were in one of them, remember?"

A cynical inner voice told Hayden it was possible that Mavis was the one leaking those lies to the press. That is, if in fact they were lies. The woman was obviously jealous and hateful of her older brother and appeared to hold a great deal of anger toward his success.

"Please!" Mavis continued her disruption. "You want everyone to think you're perfect, but you're not." She turned to Hayden. "You better be careful, Hayden."

"Mavis, please. Not in front of Tyler." Candace startled the young woman by firmly grabbing hold of her arm, like a mother trying to get control of an unruly child. "Must you do this every time?"

"Listen, Mom, I didn't even want to be here." Mavis spoke between clenched teeth. 'You begged me to come."

"Excuse me." Elise Campbell's timid voice entered the heated conversation. "I really must get going. It's after eight thirty."

"I'll walk you to the door, Mama." As she placed her hand gently on her mother's back, Hayden gave Cannon a stare that let him know he needed to handle this. It was definitely not going as she expected. Mavis was upsetting the plan and upsetting everyone.

"I'm sorry, Mama," she said as they reached the door. "I didn't know she was like that. Cannon said she was difficult, but I assumed she could behave like an adult."

"It's alright, dear." Elise held her purse to her chest and smiled. "I just don't understand why you haven't mentioned this love affair to me before. When I asked you about the photograph in the paper, you said it was just a business dinner."

"I know. I just didn't want to bring the relationship into the picture yet," she lied. "With Daddy just home and everything, I thought it was best. It was just . . . well, I guess we couldn't wait any longer."

"It's just so surprising to have your daughter call about

something important to tell you and it's that she's getting married to a man she met less than two weeks ago.''

"I know, Mama.'' Hayden couldn't stand the lies, so she decided to change the subject. "There's some more good news.''

Elise took a quick intake of breath. "You are pregnant aren't you?''

"No.'' Hayden smiled. "Although not being married yet, I'm surprised you would think that was good news. Do you remember that doctor we wanted for Daddy? Dr. Michael Kent.''

"Of course, I do. I'll bet you he would respond to a page.'' Elise frowned in her continued disgust at the past Sunday's events.

"Well he's a longtime family friend of Cannon's and he's agreed to start caring for Daddy this week.''

Excitement leaped into Elise's gentle face for a moment, only to be replaced quickly with disappointment. "That would be ideal, but he's far too expensive and the insurance won't cover it. We're already backed up in bills.''

"That's alright, Mama. It's a favor. He's going to do it free of charge. He went to school with Cannon's father and they were very close friends. Cannon's father saved his wife's life.''

Elise's lowered her eyes in uncertain suspicion. "I don't know about this. That's an awful lot to give for just a favor. Cardiac care is extremely expensive.''

"It is a great deal, but that doesn't matter anymore. We're all going to be family now so it's alright. Think of it as Dr. Kent's wedding gift to Cannon. What's important is that Dad will be receiving the best care available.''

After a moment of consideration, Elise's face lit up with a delighted smile that reached from ear to ear. "Tom will be so happy to hear about this.''

"Do you think so?'' Hayden asked. "You know how stubborn and proud he is. I'm counting on you to convince him to go along.''

"Convincing will not be necessary,'' Elise said with confidence. "I rarely put my foot down with Tom our entire marriage, but I'm going to now. Don't worry. He'll go along."

Seeing the excitement and determination on her mother's face, Hayden wondered if she was happier to hear about the doctor than about her own daughter getting married. She was afraid to ask and upset at herself for wanting to. She was making too much of this. It was a business arrangement and to connect it with her own personal problems was a waste of time.

After a peck on the cheek, the women said their goodbyes and with a deep breath Hayden turned and headed for the dining room. It was almost over, at least for tonight. In reality, she knew it was only beginning.

Apparently Cannon had done his best to settle everyone in the dining room, because when she returned they were sitting peacefully with smiles on their faces. As expected, Mavis wasn't smiling, but Hayden was at least happy she wasn't ranting and raving.

"How is everything in here?" Hayden gave a cautious smile in Cannon's direction, noting that his gentle eyes had calmed. She found confidence in that.

"Okeydoke," Tyler said, with a smile that showed several missing teeth.

"We've decided," Candace said, in a much calmer voice than before. "You can get married at my home in Glencoe. We have a very large backyard and I'm sure we can plan something respectful in three weeks. Everything will be fine."

Hayden wondered what had happened in the short period of time since she'd left the room and returned. What seemed about to become a disaster had turned into peaceful compliance. Cannon was a miracle worker.

As the evening continued, it became apparent to Hayden that Candace had been waiting for one of her children to marry for some time. Already she had a caterer and a list of relatives and longtime family friends in mind. After an hour or so, Hayden began feeling a little overwhelmed by it all and fortunately for her, Cannon noticed and encouraged his family to leave.

After promising to meet Candace for lunch the next day to go over plans for the wedding, Hayden waved a final goodbye and closed the door behind them. Cannon had already fallen exhausted, on the sofa. As she sat across from the him, staring at him, Hayden had to fight the attraction she felt from within. He was by far the most handsome man she had ever been this close to, but she knew this was business and only business. What she didn't know was if the rumors being spread about him and women were true or not. That alone was enough reason for her to remain cautious. Yes, the recent rumors were easily explained, but he never denied his past. Was he still living his past?

The physical was inconsequential, or so Hayden believed. Either on her part or his. He was probably attracted to her as he was to any fair-looking woman, but Hayden knew he cared nothing for her. She was useful to him now and that's all this was about.

"That little Tyler has got to be the cutest kid I have ever seen," she said in an attempt to break the silence and the tension that lingered because of it. They were alone again, without the noise of people or music. It wasn't fear that occurred to her, but an unusual sense of comfort. She didn't know him well enough to feel this comfortable. Did she?

"Yes, he is something." Cannon lifted his head from its resting position with a smile on his face. "He's the best kid in the world."

"He worships you completely." Hayden leaned in closer in an almost automatic response to acquiring his attention. "That must be some feeling. Every time I looked at him he was staring at you. Did you notice how he tried to sit like you and eat like you at the table?"

"Yeah." Cannon smiled again, not only at the mention of the boy he loved so much, but in response to the warmth and enchantment on Hayden's face. He found her so attractive and her closeness worried him a bit. He didn't want to mess this up by getting personally involved. "I'm the only father he knows. Sometimes I feel like I'm the only parent he has."

Hayden hugged a pillow to her chest, ignoring how much she enjoyed simply talking to him. "Cannon, what about Mavis?"

"I'm sorry about that." The happiness left his face, replaced with a disappointed frown. "I can't explain why she acts like that. She hates me and I don't know why. I've done everything I could to help her, be kind to her."

"Don't worry about tonight." She waved a dismissing hand. "What I'm wondering is, do you think she has something to do with the rumors?"

Hayden felt her pulse race as he looked at her with stark and vivid anger glittering in his eyes. It was so sudden, but there was no mistaking that implicating Mavis wasn't a good idea.

"How dare you bring her into this!" He leaped from the sofa with a force that made Hayden fall back against the pillows. He couldn't believe what he was hearing. The thought had never occurred to him and made him boiling hot to even think it.

"I'm not accusing her of anything." She stammered for the words to support herself. "I just saw how she reacts to you. You just said yourself she hates you."

"That's a personal thing, Hayden." Trying to calm himself, Cannon returned to rubbing his goatee. Could she? Would she? "She would never do anything like that. Not for the public to see."

"She didn't care about the public when you were at that Chicago Bulls game, remember." She was off the sofa now, following him to the large Victorian window that overlooked downtown Evanston. She was upset with him for turning his back to her. She was hurt more than she knew she should be. "I'm not saying she did it, but think about it. Your mother said she hates everything you're involved in. Mavis herself stood here tonight and said she thinks everything you do is fake."

After a short silence, Cannon finally turned around to face

her. The confusion and anger he felt was evident in his eyes and Hayden felt awful for putting it there.

"She wouldn't try to ruin me." He spoke the words almost in a question, as if he wanted her to reassure him that it wasn't possible. "She wouldn't do that."

"I don't know, Cannon." She felt an urge to reach out and touch his broad shoulder, but kept her hands to her sides. She couldn't understand why her concern for his feelings were so strong. She didn't know him and had made the decision, when she agreed to the arrangement. to keep her feelings out of this. Despite that, Hayden knew all she wanted now was to console this engaging man who stood before her. "I can tell you love her despite how she treats you and anyone with a pulse can tell you love her son, but you should think about it."

Cannon was looking at Hayden, but she knew he wasn't seeing her. He was looking right through her, thinking about his sister. Had he been purposefully blind to the possibility? Why would Mavis do this? Did she hate him this much? The questions came like a storm, and Cannon felt a sudden desperation for fresh air.

"I have to go. It's getting late." He wanted to be angry at Hayden for saying what she had, for bringing it up, but he couldn't. She wasn't to blame for being so observant. It was only the possibility that angered him. The fact that it was a possibility was a shame, but not a surprise and that was worst of all.

Hayden watched him as he slowly walked to the sofa and gathered his suit jacket and briefcase. He had just shut off to her presence, making her feel as if she wasn't even there. She didn't want to admit it, but she felt a hurtful flash by this as well as by his abrupt decision to leave.

"Cannon, I didn't mean to upset you or turn you against your sister." She tried to avoid looking into those compelling eyes as she opened the door for him. She was tired, her defenses weakening. She didn't want to say or feel something she'd regret.

"You didn't, Hayden." He paused to sigh. "I've got to think

about it, but I'm sure it's not her. It can't be. Good night. I'll call you tomorrow.''

"Good night, Cannon.''

As she closed the door behind him, Hayden was surprised to feel her entire body unclench at once. Had she been that tense all evening? It was understandable. Tonight she had lied to her mother, which was only the beginning of a web of lies that would last almost a year. Tonight she had also come to realize it would be harder than she thought to fight her attraction to Cannon. Her preoccupation with his appearance and his emotions told her that. She kept telling herself this was a business deal and assuring herself that Cannon's questionable past history with women was enough of a warning sign to keep her from feeling anything for him. She could do it and she would; for Mama and Daddy. A year would go by like nothing. They always did anyway.

Chapter Five

Hayden hadn't gotten any sleep last night. She was anxious about how her father would take the news of her impending nuptials, guilty about lying, upset that Cannon was now suspecting his sister because of her, and nervous over her upcoming lunch with Candace. She didn't even notice how her troubled spirits seemed to momentarily quiet at the sound of Cannon's voice when he called her at work the next morning.

"I want to apologize for leaving like I did last night." He spoke with an odd but gentle voice. "You gave me something to think about."

"I know." Hayden sensed a certain doubt in his voice that only made her want to understand him. Why, she wondered. Was it guilt over how the night ended? What else could it be? "I shouldn't have thrown it at you like that."

"I still can't believe Mavis would do something like that."

"She may not have," she said. "Like I asked before, what about Robert Marks? You said he was expecting your job before you got it."

"I don't know." Cannon's tone was cautious. "I've met him quite a few times and he seemed, to put it frankly, a little too spineless for something like this. My friend John is trying to find out some information on him. He suspects him as well. I'm going to let John handle it. I want to stay as far away as I can. If I got close, the press would be all over me. I wish there was a way I could find out more without letting on what I'm trying to do. It'd make me look scared and guilty, and I don't want that.''

''I'll think of something,'' Hayden said.

''Hayden, you don't have to worry yourself about this. I've got John and Warren—''

''I know,'' she interrupted, ''but if I think of something I'll tell you.'' She felt that possibly finding out who was at the bottom of these rumors would answer a lot of questions. For Cannon and for herself.

''Could you do me a favor?'' he asked in a soft and soothing tone.

''Yes.'' Her response came so quickly and with such surety, it frightened Hayden.

''Don't mention what you suspect about Mavis to my mother.''

''Of course not, Cannon. I wouldn't think of it.'' Hayden knew she wanted his trust even though she wasn't sure she could trust him. It was odd to her that she should feel this way. This man meant nothing to her. ''I like your mother and I hope we can get along.''

''Mom is great.'' There was a lighter tone in his voice now. ''She likes you a lot. She called me last night after I got home to tell me so. I hope you're prepared for her. She's very excited about this wedding and, if you let her, she'll overwhelm you with it.''

''I'm sure we'll be fine. After all, if we're going to be married, I need to get used to your family being around.''

Hayden's head flew up at the sound of a loud gasp in her office. Donna was standing in her doorway with her bottom lip to the floor, her eyes sparkling with astonishment. Hayden knew this would not be easy.

"I appreciate it, Hayden," Cannon said. "I appreciate every-thing."

"I'll talk to you later, Cannon." Preoccupied with Donna's entrance, Hayden forgot to address his last words before saying goodbye and hanging up.

Cannon felt an odd sense of disappointment at her lack of response as he hung up the phone. He knew it was stupid for him to want her approval. It meant nothing to his success. As long as she performed well as a PR professional and played the part of supporting spouse, he should be happy. But he wasn't, and Cannon was angry with himself for that.

Why should he care if Hayden Campbell thought he was a womanizer? If she stuck to their agreement, come March of next year her opinion of him would mean nothing. He would have what he really wanted. No longer the privileged son of a father who never felt he lived up to the standards set before him. He would be his own man. Make a name for himself. Nothing could stand in his way.

That was why he had to erase ideas of any relationship other than business with Hayden. That was also why he didn't want to make a big deal about the rumors. The more fuss, the more publicity and hence more obstacles to his goal. No, Cannon was only willing to make his dream of being a United States senator preoccupy his mind and as Maryann's voice came over the intercom to tell him John was on the phone, he vowed to himself to do so.

"Hey, buddy." Cannon pressed the speaker phone button and leaned backward in his chair. "How's it going?"

"I guess you haven't heard." John's voice came across solemn over the phone.

"What is it?" Cannon leaned forward, pulling the receiver to his ear. He felt chills run through him as John's voice sounded like a bad premonition.

"*Represent Chicago,*" John said. "You haven't seen today's paper. You might want to brace yourself."

After a long, hard swallow, with his heart falling to his stomach, Cannon said, "John, I'll call you back."

"I'm here anytime," the voice said before hanging up.

Almost in slow motion, Cannon pressed the intercom. "Maryann. Bring in today's paper."

"Cannon," she responded with reluctance in her tone. "I don't—"

"Just bring it in," he interrupted and clicked off.

Another day, another obstacle. Cannon ordered himself to be a man and not let it get to him. Only now it was different. He had always been concerned about himself, as well as his family, but now the cards on the table had changed. Now there was Hayden he had to be concerned with. Her personal and professional reputation could be harmed and that mattered to him. It mattered to him more than he expected.

He braced himself as the look on Maryann's face, as she entered the office with paper in hand, let him know the news was bad. Very bad.

"It's true!" Donna stomped angrily into the office. "It is true!"

"What are you talking about?" Hayden played dumb as she tried to buy herself some time to come up with an explanation that could fool her friend.

"I was just talking to Janice Sheldon." Donna spoke with utter disbelief. "She said Russell Falk came into the office and told everyone Cannon Factor was marrying you."

"How did he know?" Hayden asked.

She knew Janice Sheldon was planning secretary for the Chicago Chapter of the National Association for the Advancement of Colored People. Hayden and Donna were lifelong members and volunteered for the NAACP regularly. Russell Falk was chapter president.

"Russell knows everyone who is anyone in Chicago," Donna said. "What's going on?"

Hayden figured Candace Factor must have gotten on the

phone after leaving her apartment last night and told anyone she could find awake. This was not at all what Hayden wanted. She needed time to deal with this herself before forcing others to deal with it.

"I asked you a question." Donna's usual smile was nowhere to be found. "There is no way in heaven, hell, earth, or anywhere else you got engaged and I don't know about it."

"I don't know what to tell you Donna." Hayden was truly at a loss for words. Could she lie to her best friend convincingly? The best friend, who she swore sometimes, could read her mind? "It's all happened so fast."

"How could you?" Donna's face held a look of deep betrayal and confusion. "How could you not tell me? How could you get engaged to someone you met last week? That sounds like something I would do, not you. You're way too responsible."

"Well, contrary to what everyone thinks, you've been a good influence on me." Hayden's smile gave away her nervous state.

Donna eyed her suspiciously, not uttering a word as she slowly sat down in the chair across from Hayden. Her intense gaze caused Hayden to shift restlessly in her seat.

"What's going on?" The deep and slow paced tone of her voice left no room for misinterpretation. She knew something wasn't right.

Hayden hesitated, wanting desperately to hold onto the disguise, but decided against it. She had to tell someone the truth and she knew she could trust Donna with a secret.

"I'm going to tell you something in extreme confidence," Hayden whispered although she knew no one else could hear. "I'm serious, Donna, you can't tell anyone."

"You know you can trust me." She scooted closer to the desk, seeming to savor the idea of hearing the secret.

Donna's expressions morphed from confused to surprised to uncertain and finally amused as Hayden told her everything. She began with the visit to Cannon's office and ended with her impending lunch with Candace. Donna took a moment to take it all in, leaning back in the chair.

"I can't believe you're going to do this." She appeared

thoroughly impressed. "It sounds like a movie. Out of love and desperation to save her family, our heroine sacrifices herself to a man of ill repute."

"It's not a movie," Hayden corrected her. "It's a business deal. I'm not sacrificing myself to anyone. My life won't change that much."

"Hello," Donna said loudly as she raised her arms in the air. "Excuse me. We are talking about marriage here."

"I know," Hayden said. "But it's not a big deal. Only a small inconvenience for the greater good."

Donna's eyebrows rose mischievously. "You gonna have sex with him?"

"Are you insane?" Hayden asked in a amazement. "I told you it's strictly business."

"You mean to tell me," Donna said with a mocking tone, "you're going to live in this condo, which I'm sure is gorgeous, for almost a year with a man who is definitely drop dead gorgeous and . . ."

"Enough," she insisted with irritation. "He's not my type. You know that."

"What was it you said?" Donna asked with a playful grin. "Only a small inconvenience for the greater good. You do have a charitable nature. Giving of yourself—"

"You stop right there." Hayden put her hand up. She seriously wanted to change the direction of this conversation, but couldn't resist a smile at Donna's teasing. "Now this is serious."

"I'll agree with you there where the rumors are concerned," Donna said. "His behavior could hurt your career. No one wants their public relations counsel wrapped in scandal."

"I'm willing to risk that for my family." Hayden crossed her fingers together on top of the desk. "Besides, if I can find out who is starting the rumors, maybe I can stop them."

"You said you suspect his sister as well as the doctor who lost the job to him. You must think these rumors are lies then."

"Well I know the ones involving me were lies," Hayden

said. "I suspect someone is leaking these rumors to the press, but that doesn't mean they aren't based on some truth, considering his past."

"This is wild," Donna said. "You're really going to do this aren't you?"

"I don't want to." Hayden sighed discontently. "But I have to. I have to for my family."

"You've got to be careful around him," Donna warned.

"I know about his playboy past and all that," Hayden said, glad she hadn't told Donna of the emerging feelings she was developing for Cannon. "I'm not going to fall for any tricks."

"I'm not talking about that, although I'll bet you a thousand bucks you will." Donna placed her daily copy of *Represent Chicago* on the desk and said directly, "Check out page six."

A mixture of dread and disappointment crept through Hayden as she slowly turned the pages of the magazine. What was it now?

IS CITY GOVERNMENT MAKING PACTS WITH CHICAGO GANGSTERS ?
Lee Sampson

This reporter is very concerned about a package I received yesterday. In it, only this picture (center bottom) of Cook County Health Commissioner Cannon Factor, shaking hands with reputed Larch gang member Jackson Wells.

No note was added, but the picture was obviously taken in a medical facility setting. When questioned, Factor's assistant, Maryann Holly, said he was unavailable for comment.

This is the same Jackson Wells, currently in jail awaiting trial for the murder of a South Side Chicago woman who forbade her son to join the Larch's gang. Because of his violent past, bail has been denied.

Folks, we need some answers from Factor. Now.

Anger and concern conflicted within Hayden as she stared at the small picture of Cannon and Jackson Wells, shaking hands. Rumors were one thing, but pictures were another.

"That's serious stuff," Donna said. "You better talk to him about it."

"I will. I'm calling him now." In her confused state, Hayden was alarmed as she reached for her phone and the intercom switched on.

"Ms. Campbell," Marcy said with a hoarse voice. "There is a Joanne Pearl on line two for you."

Hayden didn't recognize the name, but assumed nothing in her current confused state.

"Hello, this is Hayden Campbell." She spoke cautiously through the receiver.

"This is Joanne Pearl." The voice on the other end was cool and harsh. "I'm calling to warn you about Cannon Factor."

At the mention of Cannon, Hayden immediately made the connection. Joanne Pearl was the woman Cannon last dated seriously. He told Hayden he'd broken things off with Joanne a little over a month ago.

"What can I help you with, Ms. Pearl?" Hayden made certain her tone was assessing. She wasn't about to take abuse from ex-girlfriends. That wasn't part of the deal.

"Nothing, but I can help you," she answered. "Cannon Factor is a lying, cheating bum. He's never been the marrying type, but I heard the news of your impending nuptials this morning."

"Where did you hear about it?" Hayden couldn't believe how fast the grapevine flowed.

"Don't worry about that, Ms. Campbell. You would be better to worry about Cannon Factor. He's a spoiled, self-centered playboy who gets what he wants by using his daddy's name and money. Before you it was me. Before me it was Cindy Last. Before Cindy, it was Karen Hart. Before that, I can't remember, but there were several before her. Cannon is a liar, a seducer, and a user. Only he's reached the end of that generous thread his daddy spun for him and you would be wise to get out while you can. He's no good and he's going down.''

Hayden's ears rang as the woman on the other end slammed the phone down hard.

"Who was that?" Donna asked as she noticed Hayden's startled expression.

"That was Joanne Pearl." She slowly let the receiver down. "She wanted to warn me about Cannon and his dirty deeds. He broke up with her a month ago."

"You're going to have to deal with a lot of jealous women," Donna said. "You've taken a prime rib off the meat market."

Hayden reflected for a moment on the conversation before saying, "She sounded more than jealous. She said Cannon's going down as if she knew it for a fact. She was angry."

Donna's eyebrows rose in curiosity. "When did you say he dumped her?"

"A month or so ago."

"I got suspect number three for you," Donna said triumphantly.

"How do you figure?" Hayden acknowledged her friend's victorious smile.

"Not much has been said about Cannon's personal life for a while. These rumors about his . . . private life began resurfacing about a month ago." She pointed to the paper. "She's obviously bitter to be calling you and saying awful things about Cannon, true or not."

"She has a great motive," Hayden added. "He dumped her and she wants to get back at him. She said he's going down, like she had a plan."

"There you go." Donna snapped her fingers. "Joanne Pearl is your rumor mill. More likely than his own sister, don't you think?"

"I'll look into it," Hayden said with a nod, "but I still want to check out Robert Marks. Cannon said he was expecting the position of Health Commissioner before Cannon got it. I'm thinking he may be jealous, not only because Cannon got the position, but also because he's done such a good job."

"How are you going to check him out?"

"I don't know." Hayden hadn't gotten that far. "I guess I'll start at the library. If he was in line for this job, he must be a very good doctor. If he is, then there might be some information on him."

"Ms. Campbell," Marcy's voice came again over the intercom. "There's a Candace Factor in the lobby. She says you have a lunch date."

Hayden was surprised to look at her watch and see it was already noon. She'd underestimated the time it would take to explain the past two week's events to Donna.

"You better put your love face on, sister." Donna stood up and placed her hand on her hip. "You can't fool me because I'm your best friend, but she's his mama. They can sniff out fakes better than anyone."

"I'm sure I can handle it," Hayden said in between laughs. She was grateful for Donna's jokes. She wouldn't be able to laugh at any of this if it weren't for her. She felt certain she would be needing her friend's sense of humor a great deal over the next year.

Candace insisted they eat at the famous Pump Room restaurant. She and her late husband ate there every time they traveled into the city.

"You know," Candace said, looking around after they were seated. "This place isn't as glamorous as it used to be. Or maybe I'm not as easy to impress as I was when I was younger."

"I don't see you as ever being easy to impress." Hayden spoke softly as she laid the napkin across her lap.

"I was when we first moved to Chicago. Madison is a nice town, but nothing compared to this place." She leaned back with a smile, seeming to remember very special, happy times. "The opera, the museums, the restaurants. You know, if it weren't for Cannon and Mavis being so young, Craig and I would have lived in Chicago. Right here in the middle of everything. But Craig wanted the kids to be brought up in the quieter suburbs.''

''There's a point to that.'' Hayden took a moment to thank the waiter for bringing menus and bread. She told herself a million times to stay calm, but the butterflies in her stomach wouldn't go away. ''I love this city, but I'm very happy I was brought up in Evanston.''

''Lived in Evanston all your life have you?'' Candace asked.

''Yes.'' As she browsed the menu, Hayden was aware of how staid the conversation was. She was expecting twenty-thousand questions, all very personal, but that wasn't so. Not yet at least.

''I hope you don't mind that I called a few friends upon hearing the news last night.'' Her decision quickly made, Candace folded the menu and placed it on the table.

''A few?'' Hayden raised disbelieving brows.

''Alright,'' Candace complied with a guilty smile. ''Around thirty.'' She reached into her purse, pulling out a sheet of paper. ''I've typed up a list of forty-five people that simply must attend. I'm going to make some more calls today.''

Hayden took a deep breath, realizing there was absolutely no way Candace would allow this wedding to be low profile. Going along as well as she could, she attempted to draw a line as to the number of attendees, but Candace simply ignored her. The older woman was excited and on a roll.

Hayden felt a little tension at Candace's suggestion of her own pastor performing the ceremony in her Glencoe church. Knowing the marriage was a lie, Hayden wanted to keep it as unreligous as possible. A justice of the peace was more what she had in mind. As the thought returned to her, despite her repeated desires to ignore it, the idea of such a sacred and spiritual ceremony, inside a holy place gave her chills. It was a lie! In her mind, Hayden saw a strike of lightning come down from the sky.

''Hayden?'' Candace bent her head slightly to the right as her brows centered with inquisitiveness. ''What's wrong? You look like you just got the chills?''

"I'm sorry." Hayden snapped out of her trance. "I guess . . . I . . ."

"I know, dear." With an understanding nod, Candace reached across the table and placed a tender hand on Hayden's own. "You're nervous. I was, too, when I got married, but don't worry. Everything will be fine."

"Thank you, Candace." Hayden smiled appreciatively. She wanted to believe everything would be fine, for reasons other than Candace knew of.

"I don't know how well you know my son." Candace reached for her glass of wine. "I trust him dearly and I value his opinion. He was a bit of a wild thing in his younger years, but he's really turned out to be a gem of a man."

Hayden wondered if Candace knew about the article in this morning's paper. She saw the sincere pride and love the woman had and it almost made her angry. She wasn't sure who at or what for, but she was. She wanted to believe it was at the paper or whoever was spreading the rumor, but she couldn't get the conversation with Joanne Pearl or that picture she'd seen this morning out of her mind. That had been Cannon with the gangster. The thought peaked Hayden's curiosity and urged her to ask about the man she was marrying.

"Candace," she asked, intending to sound like a young woman in love who couldn't hear enough about her man. "Tell me more about Cannon. I have my impression of him, which is obvious, but what about you?"

A peaceful smile came across Candace's face while she spoke. "Ever since he was a little boy, he wanted to save the world. He still does."

"What's wrong, Candace?" Hayden asked as she suddenly saw a vast change of expression on the older woman's face.

"I hope you're strong," she said with a concerned tone of voice. "Cannon has some issues, inner demons if you will, where his needs are concerned. Most of them originate with his father. Their relationship was rocky at best. I just need you to know that Cannon has dreams and he's intense about achieving them. He needs a partner to stick by him through thick and thin.''

"I know.'' Hayden sighed inside, dreading the day Candace would find out this was all a lie.

"You won't have an easy time,'' Candace said. "You read the papers.''

"Yes, I do.'' Hayden lowered her head for a moment, wondering what a woman in love would say. "I believe only what Cannon tells me.''

Hayden knew that was a lie, if she had ever told one. As she saw the look of confidence her words evoked from Candace, she wanted to disappear under the table. This woman deserved a loving and supportive wife to hand her son over to. Although she wanted to believe what Cannon told her, Hayden didn't. She wasn't sure if she ever could.

Before parting from lunch, Hayden agreed to bring her mother to Candace's Glencoe home Saturday morning to make catering and decoration choices. She was reluctant, wondering how close the two women would get. What would happen when it was all over? Hearts would be broken, Hayden knew that for sure. She could only hope everyone would understand.

Trying not to concentrate on her problems, Hayden hopped a cab to the Harold Washington Public Library, named after the city's first black mayor. She had already informed Marcy she would be late because of the lunch. She had made the decision earlier to find out more about Cannon herself. She knew what she was getting herself into this for, but wasn't so sure what exactly it was she was getting herself into.

She had no idea where to start, but maybe knowing a little more about Dr. Robert Marks, whom she suspected of leaking these stories to the press, would lead her to some answers.

Sitting at a table of approximately twenty computers, each with its own printer, Hayden typed in the name: Marks, Robert +Dr. The search printout gave three related articles, all available on microfiche. Two of them were in *Represent Chicago* and the third could be found in the *Chicago Tribune*. Hayden checked them all out and searched for a microfiche machine.

The first article was written by reporter Lee Sampson and covered several awards Marks had won a few years ago. Hayden found nothing of use and turned her focus to the second article.

DR. ROBERT MARKS DONATES $5,000 TO
THE UNITED NEGRO COLLEGE FUND

It wasn't the title of the story, but the name that caught Hayden's eye. Lee Sampson had written a half page about how gracious and generous Marks had been to the community, never forgetting to give back. Hayden's curiosity peaked, although she suspected Sampson would know Marks, being the health beat reporter.

The *Tribune* article was short, only four sentences. Reporter Andy Magers commented on Dr. Robert Marks receiving the Black American Medical Association's award for outstanding leadership. The words were of no interest to Hayden as she concentrated on the picture to the left of the column. It was small, but very clear. Marks held the award proudly in one hand while shaking hands with Lee Sampson with the other.

Hayden placed a dime in the coin slot and pressed the COPY PAGE button.

"That's not a big deal," Cannon said as he leaned across his desk. "Everyone in medicine is familiar with Lee Sampson. He's a medical reporter."

His quick dismissal of Hayden's news angered her. She had come directly to his office from the library. Excited, she showed him the picture, but her excitement was quickly deflated by his rejection of it.

"That's true," she responded persistently, but with a quiet voice as she knew Maryann was just outside the door and was probably leaning against it to listen. "But this picture makes them look pretty close," she responded persistently.

"Pictures are deceiving. That picture of us at the Metropolitan Club showed you that." Cannon couldn't help but be impressed by her determination although he wasn't sure he was happy she seemed to be developing an extreme interest in Dr. Marks. Underneath this beautiful and feminine woman was tenacity. He had suspected it the first moment he saw her and was glad he was right. He hoped she would bring that tenacity to his campaign.

When she walked into his office, he immediately felt that uncontrollable surge of energy. He was beginning to look forward to any opportunity to see her. It perplexed him that he had been disappointed when she began discussing the rumors. He wasn't sure why. After all, he had hired her to help him combat these rumors. What he would like was for her to just stop by to talk, to get to know one another, but he knew Hayden Campbell wasn't the least bit interested in him for anything other than what he could do for her parents.

"Don't you care about who is starting these rumors?" she asked in frustration. "You're saying these are lies and . . ."

"They are lies!" Cannon checked his tone. It angered him that she didn't believe him and he could tell she didn't. It hurt as well, but he tried to ignore that. He didn't want it to matter so much, but it was difficult not to. "Hayden, I'm aware that I hired you to help my PR, but I don't need you playing private investigator."

"Let me correct you," she answered stubbornly. "You didn't hire me. We have a partnership. You aren't my boss."

"Fine, I understand." He spoke in a conciliatory tone.

Cannon thought it peculiar that he found so much pleasure with her company. He had imagined time with her would remind him of the lie he was perpetrating, distracting him from his true goal. Instead, in addition to finding her beautiful and distractingly sexy, he also found her enchanting in an odd way. She was stubborn and strong-minded, but loyal and committed. If his life was in a different position with different needs, he knew he would want to get closer to Hayden Campbell.

Not in the mood to argue with this stubborn man, Hayden decided to let the topic go for now, but wouldn't give up. The possibility had peaked her interest and she wasn't willing to just throw it aside. She still suspected Robert Marks and wanted to know if her suspicions were true. But for now there were a couple of other things that concerned her.

"Your mother was in a great mood at lunch." She tried to sound cheerful, to break the tension she felt in the room. It was a tension she hadn't felt before in his presence. It was stronger, more personal than the general awkwardness of being close to someone you don't really know. "I guess she didn't see today's paper."

"She did," Cannon answered, "but I reassured her I would handle it. She's so caught up in the wedding, she hardly wanted to talk about it herself. It's alright now."

"How can you say that?" Hayden was deeply disturbed by his careless tone. "Your credibility is at stake. You need to draft a release and plan a news conference. You have to come up with something to say."

"Have to?" he asked accusingly. "Do you believe that article?"

"Well the article didn't really say anything, only insinuated, but . . ."

"Apparently that's all it has to do to get people like you to believe."

Offended by the angry tone of his voice, Hayden gave him a sharp glare. "I'm not interested in an argument with you, Cannon. Whether it's the truth or not, you should have responded immediately."

"I would have if I'd known." He knew she was right, but the thought of the article made his blood boil. When he'd read it this morning, he had to do everything to keep from breaking anything in sight. He knew he should have called Hayden, but at the time, all he wanted to do was be alone.

"Cannon," she said, "the article says Sampson contacted you and Maryann said you weren't available."

"I know." He sighed. "We've been yelling at each other about that all morning. Maryann took it upon herself to do that. She knew I'd be upset and make a stupid mistake that would come back to haunt me, so she told Sampson I was unavailable.''

"That's crazy!'' Hayden felt professional frustration at the back of her throat. "This man is a gang member, drug dealer, and a possible murderer. She should know that you needed to say something immediately.''

"I don't know what she was thinking.'' His voice held a tone of disappointment, but laced with sympathy. "She was trying to protect me, she says. Everyone's under a lot of pressure around here.''

A quick thought hit Hayden as she considered the possibility that maybe Maryann didn't want Cannon to respond. Maybe she wanted the article and picture printed, leaving speculation and suspicion rampant.

"Cannon,'' she asked, trying to hide her suspicion, remembering how he reacted the last time she hinted at someone close to him being behind the rumors, "what kind of relationship do you have with Maryann?''

"What do you mean?'' he asked. "She's my assistant.''

"I know, but are you close? Are you friends? Can you trust her?''

It only took a second for Cannon to piece together Hayden's inference and the idea angered him even more. "I don't know what you're trying to ask, but Maryann is a very loyal employee.''

"That doesn't mean you're friends.'' She had noticed Maryann's loyalty to Cannon herself, but wondered now if it was a front.

"It's a long story.'' The last thing Cannon wanted was for Hayden to hear another story about his rumored insensitivity toward women.

"Tell me.'' Just as I suspected, Hayden thought.

"Maryann was my secretary for six years at the practice I shared with John in Northbrook and she followed me here. She's been right with me through everything. She's saved my butt so many times.'' He paused for a moment. "About a month ago, after she learned I had broken up with Joanne, she . . .''

"What, Cannon? Go ahead." Hayden found herself somewhat touched by his apparent reluctance. His eyes showed a tender guilt that was mixed with regret. She could tell that whatever it was he was about to tell her, it was a painful experience.

"Maybe I did something wrong." He shook his head regretfully, not relishing a visit to this memory in any way. "I was upset about another failed relationship so I spilled my guts to Maryann. I should have never allowed her into my personal life like that, but I thought after eight years, we had developed a friendship at some level. Well, I was wrong. Maryann took it the wrong way. She had this crazy idea I was telling her everything, because I had awakened to some love I had for her."

"Was she completely mistaken?" Hayden asked, surprised at the strong interest she had in his answer to her question.

"Yes," he said convincingly. "I care about Maryann, but not in that way. Even if I had, I would never ever get involved with someone who worked for me." The composure in his voice at the last sentence showed his confidence in his words.

"Did she tell you she loved you?" Hayden couldn't help but wonder if that last comment was directed at her in some way.

"It never got to that. I stopped her before she could go on, but it was apparent she was close to saying that. She looked so stunned and hurt. After a silence that seemed to last a year, she looked at me with a vacant stare and said it was all a misunderstanding and everything was okay, but I had never seen her so upset. Things haven't been quite the same between us since."

"Okay, Cannon." Hayden could see it was difficult for him to continue. She had definitely added Maryann Holly, a woman scorned, to her growing list of suspects, but didn't want to push the issue with Cannon. She could tell from his tortured gaze, that the guilt he felt about the incident would never allow him to suspect Maryann of anything. "I have to get back to work, but I'll see you Saturday at your mother's house."

"Hayden?" There was a pleading tone in his voice as a part of him didn't want her to go for what he knew were all the wrong reasons. At least for now.

"Yes?" She felt a bolt of electricity shoot through her as he called out her name. The way he said it, as if he needed her.

"Don't you even want to know?" he asked.

"Know what?"

"The truth about the picture in the paper this morning?" He was angry at himself for caring so much, but he knew there was no fighting it.

"Cannon I . . . ," Hayden began, not sure she wanted to know.

"I want you to know," he said quickly. "The picture is over four years old. I treated his five-year-old daughter for measles. I don't know why, but he had a friend of his take pictures when he came to pick her up. He bought balloons and everything. I didn't know who he was then, but it didn't matter. I would never turn someone seeking medical attention away."

"Do you think he sent those pictures to Sampson?" She felt a surge of relief run through her at Cannon's explanation.

"I don't know. He mailed us double copies at the office a few weeks later with a thank you note. By then I had found out who he was. I gave them to Maryann and told her to do whatever she wanted with them."

"That's not important now," she lied. It was very important that Maryann was the last person to handle those pictures. "What's important is that you draft a release explaining the picture and refuting any acquaintance with him and send it to absolutely everyone. If you need to, you have records to prove you treated the little girl."

"I can't show those records without Jackson's approval," Cannon said.

"Fine, a release will have to do. Where are you on that?"

"I've taken care of that." He reached for a copy of a release he had drafted. "Maryann is typing it up now and faxing it to the news wires and local papers."

''This is good.'' Hayden gave the release a quick look over. ''This looks sufficient.''

As she stood up to leave, Hayden looked again into Cannon's eyes. She wanted to believe in him. She wanted to for more reasons than it would simply make her job easier to believe him, but it wasn't that easy. Nothing about their *arrangement* was.

''Thank you for explaining the situation to me,'' was all she felt safe to say.

Cannon simply nodded with a half-smile. He was tired. This was turning out to be a very bad day, but the sight of her gave him strength. It gave him an odd sense of strength despite the fact that she didn't believe in him. He could sense that, but still he hated to see her go.

''Call me,'' she said as she exited the office, ''if you get a question you can't answer. Remember, they'll try to trip you up. Always pause before you answer. Give yourself time to think first. It's very important.''

''Will do.'' His smile was wider now, grateful for the tip. Grateful for an excuse to call her and talk to her again even if it was over something that was giving him an ulcer.

After leaving Cannon's office, Hayden couldn't understand exactly what it was she was feeling. She was disturbed at the compassion she felt for Cannon and concerned at how much she wanted to believe him. His explanation of the picture seemed believable, but so had his explanations in the past. She wondered if she would have been so quick to accept another less accept-able explanation. Against her better judgement, she believed she would have.

''Violet and ivory will do perfect.'' Candace wrote those colors on the wedding planning sheet. ''Those will be the wedding colors, agreed?''

Without a word Hayden and her mother nodded in compli-ance. Candace had completely taken over. The plan was for all of them to get together Saturday morning at her home and decide on everything for the wedding and the reception, but in actuality Candace was deciding everything herself. Hayden and Elise seemed only present so they could be briefed and updated.

Hayden wasn't really there anyway. Her father had a difficult time accepting the idea of the marriage and was reacting stubbornly to the idea of seeing Dr. Kent for *free*. He explained to Hayden when she arrived at the house early Saturday, that he'd felt betrayed. They had always had a close relationship and he was usually the first person she told anything to.

Tom warned his daughter of making a hasty decision and it hurt her terribly to lie to him, saying she loved Cannon. He reminded her she was young and had time; that he wanted to meet the man first. Hayden left the house that morning feeling ripped apart with guilt. If only there was some way she could tell him she was doing this for him, for the family, but she knew it wouldn't have mattered. A man with as much pride as Tom Campbell would forbid her to go along with such a lie, no matter what the consequences to his health.

As she sat in the dining room of Candace's lavish home, she wondered what she could do to make her father more comfortable with this.

"Last night I received a couple of calls," Candace said. "Now my list is sixty, but I promise to keep it there. I need your names and addresses today. We have to get the invitations out by Monday and follow up with phone calls next Sunday."

"We have a small family and circle of friends," Elise said. "I've thought of fifteen who could make it on such short notice, but . . ."

"Fifteen is fine," Candace said, apparently ready to move on to the next topic.

"There may be more," Elise added.

"We can have several more at the reception." Candace pointed to her backyard. "As you can see, the yard is immense. Even with the band and food set up—"

"We want to keep everything small," Hayden interrupted. Mention of a band and all was making her a little apprehensive. She hoped it wouldn't arouse suspicion, but she wished she and Cannon could just quickly visit a justice of the peace and get it over with. "The wedding and the reception."

"Darling," Candace said, looking at Hayden with a politely serious expression, "my idea of a proper wedding is approximately four-hundred guests. This is as small as it's going to get."

"Fine, but no more." Hayden didn't want to argue. She could see the frustration on Candace's face. She was proud to pieces over her son and wanted his wedding to be perfect. Hayden almost felt sorry for her, but was sure she would have the opportunity to plan a proper wedding when Cannon was married for real. If he ever choose to settle down with one woman.

"You have my word," the older woman complied. "No more."

"Yeah, right," Mavis said as she entered the room from the kitchen. "There will probably be two, three hundred people here."

"Listen, Mavis"—Candace turned her head sharply toward her daughter—"if you aren't going to help us plan, then leave us alone."

"Where is that darling little boy of yours?" Elise asked with a smile.

"He's out back with Cannon." Mavis tone showed a certain disdain as she said her brother's name. "I told him he needs to take a bath before his piano class, but he won't listen."

"I'll try to go get him," Hayden said, getting up from the table. She was happy for an excuse to leave all this planning.

As she walked onto the back porch, she smiled at the sight of Cannon pushing Tyler on the swing set. She felt there was nothing that could lift your spirits more than the sound of a child's laughter, and at the sound of it, she felt the apprehension from earlier go away.

She couldn't help but be attracted to Cannon. She accepted that as a given under any circumstances. The man was fine. He looked handsome and rugged in a cotton brick red polo shirt and black denim jeans. His sturdy stance emphasized the force of his thighs and the slimness of his hips. She wondered how she was going to ignore this tough, lean body for a year. After all, she was only human. Part of her wished the rumors were true. At least then his character would repel her enough to make his appearance insignificant.

"Hey, little guy." She smiled at Tyler as she approached them. She knew she would get attached to the child quickly. He was terribly sweet and more than adorable. "Your mama says you're supposed to take a bath."

"I don't want to." He turned up his nose and shook his head. "Push me, Uncle Cannon."

"No, I think that's enough." Cannon held the chains of the swing tight and passed the boy an uncompromising stare. "Go take your bath. Now."

His emphasis on the last word was apparently enough for Tyler, who quickly leaped off the swing and hopped toward the house.

"Are they driving you crazy?" He slipped Hayden a charming smile that made her blush. He got that reaction from most women, but he loved getting it from her. It made sheer warmth flow through him.

"A little," she answered, lowering her head from his gaze. "I need a break."

"I needed one a long time ago. I hate to leave you in there, but I just can't get into the flower and napkin color stuff."

"It's alright." She leaned against one of the iron bars that held the swing set together. She regretted how conscious she was of her appearance in his presence. She looked casual in a pair of khaki brown leggings and a long button-down peach silk shirt. The colors complimented her dark skin. Her abundant hair in a ponytail tumbled carelessly past her neck. She looked nice and she knew that. She hadn't done a very good job convincing herself it was all to impress only Candace.

"Cannon," she asked, "I was wondering if you could come to my parents' house tonight for dinner?"

"Well, Hayden." He gave a wry smile. "Is that a personal invitation?"

"No," she said quickly, suddenly becoming uncomfortable at the suggestion. "This is all business and you know that. My father is a little upset about all this and I think it would calm him if he met you. He's old-fashioned. He needs to feel you seek his approval."

"That sounds like a good idea." He had never noticed before, but her eyelashes were a mile long, shadowing her large, piercing black eyes. He wished he hadn't noticed because now he couldn't turn away. "This is all for him after all."

"Yes it is." She wondered why she wasn't reassured that Cannon knew this? She told herself to stop thinking so much. None of this meant anything to Cannon, it shouldn't mean anything to her.

"We need to do a better job of this." He walked closer to her, making her terribly nervous. He knew what he was about to do would throw her, so fast and without warning was the best way to go about it. "Now that everyone on the North Shore knows about us, thanks to Mom, we need to back this up."

"Back it up?" she asked confused, as she saw him reach into his back pocket.

She gasped and almost fell backward as he pulled out a small black velvet box. He opened it to show a sparkling diamond engagement ring with more karats than Hayden had ever seen.

"Cannon!" She slapped her hand against her chest, feeling her pounding heart. "Is that real?"

"Yes." He laughed, amused at her response. He enjoyed the light he saw in her eyes. *Like it was real.* "I've been called a lot of things, but never cheap."

"But Cannon, you can't . . . it's too big. It's inappropriate." She felt herself breathing rapidly as he took hold of her left hand. His hands were big and warm to the touch.

"Hayden, to the rest of the world we are two people in love and about to get married. I'm not the richest man on earth, but people expect a certain standard from me. Therefore, this ring is very appropriate."

She was too startled to offer an objection as he placed the

ring on her finger. She recognized many of the emotions that battled within her such as fear, surprise, and confusion. She also recognized joy, but tried to ignore it was there. It shouldn't be.

"Looks perfect." He gave an accomplished smile, looking at her soft hand. "You have flawless skin."

"Thank you." She quickly pulled her hand away and lowered her head to hide her blush. She couldn't believe how she was behaving. This wasn't real.

Without warning, his large hand took her face and held it gently. As he cupped her chin, lifting her face to his, she felt a shiver of heat ripple through her. She knew what was coming next. She knew she had to prevent it.

Hayden opened her mouth slightly to protest, but before a word could come out, his lips were on hers. His kiss was slow and thoughtful, sending a warm surge through her. She wasn't only surprised at the kiss, but shocked at her own eager response to the touch of his lips. As his arms slid around her young shapely body, he encircled her with one strong hand on the small of her back pulling her closer. Her senses reeled as if short-circuited as she curled into the curve of his powerful body.

Cannon knew he'd wanted to kiss her from the moment he saw her. It was better than he imagined as the touch of her tender, soft lips set him on fire. He had convinced himself he needed to do this to reach his goal, but that myth was shattered the second he held her body to his. He wanted this with every fibre of his being and as his lips pressed against her, he only wanted it more.

Hayden felt her body begin to melt as she gave herself freely to the passion of his tongue. As he used it to tease her mouth she felt the pit of her stomach fall into a wild swirl, hearing a soft and quiet moan leap from within her. Was this real, she asked herself.

Then, as fast as it began, his lips parted from hers. Hayden felt herself gasp for air as her large eyes opened to see his handsome face lift from hers. Confusion overwhelmed her as he relinquished his hold. She hadn't known when, but sometime during the kiss she had lifted her hands and placed them on his broad chest. As she lowered them, she gazed into his eyes, pleading for an explanation.

"This is definitely one part of keeping up appearances I will enjoy." He spoke with slightly heavy breath, a mischievous smile appearing on his face. "They were staring. We had to do something."

Hayden, still speechless, turned her head in the direction Cannon nodded. Candace and Elise were standing on the back porch both smiling with affection and pride. Hayden was jolted back to reality.

"Next time," Hayden said, eyeing him harshly, "give me some warning." With that she quickly walked into the house, stopping momentarily to paste a happy smile for both mothers as they observed the ring.

As he watched her walk away, Cannon felt a tiny tug at his heart. Had he hurt her or merely annoyed her? It took all the strength he had to pull away from her, but he had to. He hadn't expected to feel the way he had when their lips touched. Getting involved with Hayden would be impossible. He had to fight the feelings arising within him and vowed to never kiss her again. Not for any reason, including appearances.

Hayden sat emotionally exhausted on the living room sofa. Still dazed by the kiss, she was fuming at Cannon for surprising her that way. She was angrier with herself for allowing it to affect her so strongly. Despite its brevity, she knew it was without a doubt the most breathtaking kiss she had ever experienced. She knew the last thing she needed was to develop romantic feelings for Cannon, but began to wonder if she already had. Why else would it upset her so much to realize the kiss had been nothing more than appearances to him?

Her somber mood quickly turned as Tyler ran, stark naked and screaming at the top of his lungs into the living room. Hayden jumped backward on the sofa as he rushed past her and hid his tiny body behind the end table.

"Boy, where are you?" Mavis entered the room with her

sleeves rolled up and a wet rag in her hand. "You better come get in this tub."

Hayden gave Tyler a chance to answer, but he remained silent. Without saying a word herself she pointed out where he was hiding. Only it was her engagement ring that stole Mavis' attention, not her son.

"When did you get that?" Mavis pointed at the ring.

"Just now." Hayden quickly pulled her hand from sight behind her back.

"So you're really going to go through with it, huh?" She placed a wet hand on her hip.

"Hey, what about me?" Tyler popped his little head out from the side of the sofa.

"You!" Mavis pointed a scolding finger at him. "You better get upstairs and sit in that tub or you won't be able to sit anywhere for a week."

His innocent eyes widened at the threat and he quickly ran out of the room. Hayden smiled at the sight of his little bare bottom, then turned with a serious look to his mother.

"Mavis, what is it?" she asked. "Why do you hate Cannon so much?"

"I don't hate him." Mavis eyed Hayden contemptuously, as if she didn't care to be questioned. "It's none of your business anyway."

"Fine," she replied sharply. "Then Cannon and I are none of your business."

"Trust me, I don't care." Mavis began walking out of the room, then turned to Hayden again. "I just thought you would care."

"What do you mean by that?" Hayden was sure she'd regret asking, but her curiosity go the best of her as she knew the answer could be a clue to Mavis involvement in spreading the rumors.

"You're familiar with that wedding vow that says you shall forsake all others?" She didn't wait for Hayden's response. "Well Cannon is going to have a problem with that. This morning, before you and your mother came over, he made a little call while we were eating breakfast. It was to his old girlfriend Tiffany Shields and oh boy was he happy to talk to her. I heard him telling her he would visit her in Los Angeles this summer. He didn't mention a word about you. Kind of weird seeing as how you're getting married in a two weeks."

"I'm good friends with many of my ex-boyfriends," Hayden said, trying to hide the anger that swelled inside of her at the news. They had an agreement and he was already breaking it before it started!

"Aren't we all?" Mavis's small mouth formed a sly smile. "Cannon's just a little friendlier than most. I think it's to your benefit to get used to it."

After Mavis left the room, Hayden fumed in anger. Unfortunately for him, Cannon walked into the living room just in time to receive her wrath.

"How dare you?" She shot up from the sofa, not even trying to get in handle on the tone of her voice.

"What?" He gave a half amused, half confused stare. "You still upset about that kiss?"

"Forget the kiss," she said, knowing very well that she couldn't forget it herself. "What's this about Tiffany Shields?"

"Tiffany? Oh yeah, good ole Tiffany." He leaned against the wall, crossing his thick, dark arms across his chest. "How did you . . ."

"Never mind that." She took a short breath, trying to control her temper. "We made an agreement to keep away from other men and women during this arrangement."

"Yeah, but Tiffany doesn't . . ."

"That would include making summer visits to see them. Just because she's in LA doesn't mean she doesn't count." She found some satisfaction in his annoyed expression at her interruption. "And what about Joanne Pearl?"

"I told you I haven't seen her in over a month." Cannon wasn't used to being yelled at this way and wasn't sure how to respond. He didn't want to fuel the flames of her obvious anger.

"Why is she calling me at my job to warn me about you?"

WE INVITE YOU TO JOIN THE ONLY BOOK
CLUB THAT DELIVERS HEARTFELT ROMANCE
FEATURING AFRICAN AMERICAN HEROES AND
HEROINES IN STORIES THAT ARE RICH IN
PASSION AND CULTURAL SPICE...

And Your First 4 Books Are FREE!

Arabesque is the newest contemporary romance line offered by
Pinnacle Books. Arabesque has been so successful that our
readers have asked us about direct home delivery. We
responded to your requests. You can start receiving four
bestselling Arabesque novels a month delivered right to your
door. Subscribe now and you'll get:

◇ 4 FREE Arabesque romances as our introductory gift—a value
  of almost $20! (pay only $1 to help cover postage &
  handling)
◇ 4 BRAND-NEW Arabesque romances
  delivered to your doorstep each month
  thereafter (usually arriving before
  they're available in bookstores!)
◇ 20% off each title—a savings of
  almost $4.00 each month
◇ Just $1.50 for shipping and handling
◇ A FREE monthly newsletter,
  Zebra/Pinnacle Romance News that
  features author profiles, book previews
  and more
◇ No risks or obligations...in other words, you can cancel
  whenever you wish with no questions asked

So subscribe to Arabesque today and see why these books are
winning awards and readers' hearts.

After you've enjoyed our FREE gift of 4 Arabesques, you'll begin
to receive monthly shipments of the newest Arabesque titles.
Each shipment will be yours to examine for 10 days. If you
decide to keep the books, you'll pay the preferred subscriber's
price of just $4.00 per title. That's $16 for all 4 books with a
nominal charge of $1.50 for shipping and handling. And if you
want us to stop sending books, just say the word...it's that simple.

*See why reviewers are raving about ARABESQUE
and order your FREE books today!*

Hayden asked. "She reminded me of some of your past dalliances in romance. She forgot to mention Tiffany, but Mavis helped me with that one. I'd also like to know how Joanne knew the day after we told our families about our marriage?"

"I don't know," he said, throwing his hands up in the air. "How does everyone in Chicago know? When did she call you and what did she say?"

"She warned me about your moral character." Hayden placed her hands on her hips, her tone faintly mocking. "She practically threatened you."

"Who threatened him?"

Candace Factor stood in the doorway to the living room with Elise right behind her. "What are you talking about Hayden?"

"Nothing, Mother." Cannon gave Hayden a curt look, ending the conversation. "Just a bitter ex, upset about the engagement."

"Oh, alright." Candace's concerned expression calmed, but didn't completely disappear. "Well Elise says she must get back to her husband. We're all welcomed to her home for dinner tomorrow evening. I'm looking forward to meeting Tom."

"Well actually," Cannon said. "Hayden invited me over for dinner tonight. Maybe we—"

"No, Cannon." She interrupted him purposefully, still angry. "I forgot I'm busy tonight. Let's make it tomorrow."

"That's fine," he said after a short pause and walked out of the room. If she wanted to be that way, fine. He didn't have to explain himself. So what if she didn't trust him. So what.

Too involved in her wedding plans, Candace ignored her son's abrupt exit. "Now you have your maid of honor. Donna was her name, right?"

"Yes, Donna Nouri," Elise answered, for Hayden who was no longer paying attention either women. "She's Hayden's best friend."

"That's taken care of." Candace smiled. "Of course John Dannell will be best man. Then little Tyler. I've already booked the caterer and we can decide tomorrow night what to serve. We'll see you tomorrow evening."

Later that night, alone in her bed, Hayden was overwhelmed by an influx of emotions. She was angry at Cannon for arranging the summer rendezvous with his ex-girlfriend. She kept telling herself her anger was concern over appearances, but she couldn't help but feel a sense of personal betrayal and for that, she was angry with herself. Cannon had absolutely no problem keeping everything on a business level, so why couldn't she? The kiss they shared earlier that day was, for him, merely for the sake of their on-looking mothers. For her, it was much more and she knew she had to do something about it, or this would be the longest year of her life.

Chapter Six

The next two weeks were chaotic for Hayden. Thankful for Candace's obsession with the wedding, she didn't have to bother with it too much, with the exception of a couple of wedding gown fittings. She had picked the ready-made dress out of a Michigan Avenue boutique. It was simple and understated, but Hayden felt that appropriate considering the situation. She knew when she would be married for real, her dress would be spectacular.

She felt guilty for taking a week off work after the wedding even though she would work at home as much as she could. Everyone assumed it was for a passionate honeymoon and that was the idea, but Hayden knew Roger was concerned about her attention to the Coverling account. To ease her guilt about the wedding, she demanded that no one buy gifts for them, but make a donation to the NAACP or The United Negro College Fund in their name.

She spent a lot of her time reassuring Roger that she would not desert R&D now that she was marrying a wealthy man. Although she reaffirmed her commitment to the Coverling account, she did request an assistant in addition to Marcy. She told Roger nothing about Cannon's bid for the Senate seat, but knew she might be spending a lot of time with him when he campaigned.

A burden was lifted off of Hayden's shoulders as Cannon's relationship with her father got off to a great start. Reluctant at first, Tom was distant and unresponsive the evening Cannon and Candace came to the house for dinner, but Cannon was smart and determined to gain Tom's approval. He persisted with the topic Tom could not resist, sports. By the time they all sat down to dinner, both men were talking as if they'd known each other forever.

Mavis had declined the invitation to dinner and Hayden was thankful for that. Candace brought Tyler along and by the end of the evening, he had a permanent seat on Tom's lap. Things were going so well that Tom almost gave everyone a scare because he got excited over Cannon's invitation to attend a Chicago Bulls playoff game at the United Center. Hayden knew she would never feel completely comfortable about what she was doing, but at least she felt better after that evening.

The only thing in the papers about Cannon was positive. Maryann had sent a brief press release to all local papers and radio and TV stations. There was a full-page spread on the upcoming wedding in *Represent Chicago*. There were also short articles on the event in the *Chicago Tribune* and *Chicago Sun Times,* the city's major daily newspapers. There hadn't been enough time before the actual event to put the news in the local society specials, which were published only once a month. Maryann promised them all pictures for follow-up articles. The themes were all the same. Beautiful and successful PR exec tames playboy health commissioner. Inevitably, the late Dr. Craig Factor's name was mentioned in every article.

When called by reporters, Hayden never said she was in love, only telling them she was looking forward to her wedding day and was very happy. She felt she might as well have said she loved Cannon. It was no greater lie than what she did say. She wasn't looking forward to marrying for convenience, nor was she happy about lying to her family and friends.

She had Marcy screen her calls as more than half of them were from people, most she had never heard of, calling to congratulate her and ask if they could attend. The papers had not only given Hayden's name but also mentioned she was an account executive at R&D Public Relations. Her boss, Damon, appreciated the free publicity.

Two days before the wedding, John Dannell and his wife Jesse invited the two of them to dinner. The couple had just returned from a week-long vacation in Europe and were dying to show their pictures. Hayden obliged, knowing that John was Cannon's best friend and she would be seeing a lot of him.

Jesse Dannell's constant talking about the trip would have normally annoyed Hayden, but that night she was grateful for it. There was practically no opportunity for John to ask Cannon or Hayden personal questions about their relationship. She wondered if it was because she and Cannon were convincing enough, or did John and Jesse feel so uncomfortable about their hasty union that they didn't want to talk about it.

She also wondered how much about their arrangement Cannon had told John. As she watched the two men throughout the evening, she could tell they were very close. They laughed and joked all night, making fun of each other in that peculiar way men do; insulting one another.

Hayden felt the thickening tension that existed between her and Cannon despite the fact that they were more than polite to each other. She had felt it picking up steam since he appeared on her doorstep that evening. Every time she saw him, all she could think of was the kiss and how it had made her feel. It held the climactic combination of something sweet and familiar, but at the same time excitingly new and dangerous. It was as if nothing had been the same since. She knew it was unnecessary for her to be so conscious of him since the evening was like nothing more than a few friends getting together, but she couldn't help it. In Cannon's presence, *the Kiss,* was emblazoned on her mind.

Hayden noticed that John and Jesse weren't a very intimate couple, at least not in front of others and she was grateful they

didn't encourage it from her and Cannon. Cannon encouraged
her several times to hold hands, but Hayden was very reluctant,
not welcoming the uneasy awareness the thought of his touch
brought her. When she finally gave in, the safe feeling that
began to set in with his strong hands gripping hers bothered
her even more. She didn't really know whether or not it was
a good sign that she was getting used to being near him or the
whole idea of their fake marriage.

"You're very lucky, you know." Jesse Dannell handed Hayden a glass of wine and sat beside her on the plush, hunter
green sofa.

Hayden had anticipated this. John asked to have a moment
alone with Cannon to discuss a serious issue, leaving the two
women together the living room of the large north suburban
home. Hayden had done everything she could to keep the topic
off of herself and Cannon. She asked about the decorations,
Jesse's career, upbringing, and more, but Jesse wasn't the least
bit interested in discussing those topics.

"That is," she continued, apparently not expecting a response. "You're lucky because Cannon is such a catch. Don't
you agree? Of course, you do. After all you're marrying him.
When John told me I was flabbergasted. I mean Cannon, settling down? That is the news of the decade. Not that he never
wanted to, he just couldn't find the right woman. He's dated
so many . . ."

Hayden simply stared as the fair-skinned woman went on
and on. She stopped only occasional to flip her naturally curly
brown hair back or lean her small figure forward or backward
on the sofa. Hayden was fine as soon as she realized nothing
was expected of her. Jesse liked to do all the talking and simple
nods and head shakes with an occassional understanding smile
would suffice.

As long as it lasted, Hayden did learn a few things about
Cannon she hadn't known. Through stories of their times
together, she learned that Cannon liked to joke around and have
a good time. He had always loved to help others, volunteering
his medical services to the poor as a young doctor, devoting

his life to pediatrics before turning to public service. The man Hayden was hearing about was one she could easily respect. Could it be the same man she had so many moral questions about?

"Is she talking your ear off?" John asked, as he and Cannon reappeared from the study.

"No," Hayden lied with a hopefully convincing smile. "Not at all."

Turning to Cannon, she noticed a peculiar look on his face. His mouth was tight and grim, his eyes seeming bothered, making her wonder what he and John had discussed.

"It's getting late," Cannon said, sounding as tired as he felt. "We need to get going, if that's all right with you Hayden."

"Yes," she answered, rising from the sofa. "Tomorrow morning will be the last time I can get a lot of work done for a while. I'd like an early start."

"Are you and Cannon finished?" Jesse asked.

"Yes, dear." John attempted a smile, but it was halfhearted and unconvincing.

Hayden watched as Cannon quickly said his goodbyes. She followed with her own and almost had to run to catch up with him at his BMW. As he opened the door for her, his silence began gnawing at her nerves. Her curiosity had always gotten the best of her. Sometimes she regretted its strength, but it was useless to challenge it tonight.

"Cannon," she asked, not turning to look at him, but keeping her eyes straight ahead, "what's bothering you? You were having such a good time this evening. Then you and John had your discussion. Is there something I can do?"

"No, Hayden," he said flatly. Her concern touched him as it appeared genuine, but he wouldn't bother her with John's problems. "This isn't a PR problem."

"Then, what is it?" Hayden asked. Maybe it was none of her business, but she wanted to know why he seemed so unhappy all of the sudden. "I know our relationship is strictly a professional one, but we're going to be spending a lot of time together this next year. We might try and be friends."

"Friends?" he asked, with a cold laugh. The irony in her statement stuck at his throat. "You seem to think I'm a moral louse. You sure you want to be friends?"

"I never said that." Hayden felt crushed by his words. More so than she expected anything he would say to her could. "Never mind."

Realizing what he had just done, Cannon wanted to kick himself in the head. Instead, he pulled over, put the car in park, and turned to her. The hurt he saw in her eyes stung him. The last thing he wanted to do was hurt this woman who was doing everything she could, everything she didn't want to, just to keep her family together.

"Hayden," he said with earnest eyes. "I'm sorry. I'm very sorry."

"Don't bother," she answered, uncomfortable with the surge of affection she felt knowing his eyes were on her, touching her.

"No." He shook his head, removed his seat belt and turned his entire body to her. Her eyes mesmerized him. "You extended me courtesy and I insulted you. I'll tell you what's wrong with me."

"Don't do so on my account." Hayden knew her pride was talking now.

"I want us to be friends." That now familiar voice from within that told him he wanted to be more than friends. "So I'm telling you for me. It's John."

"Did you tell him about us?" she asked.

"No. I've decided against that. It'll be hard because he's my best friend, but the less people know, the better. Besides, John has problems of his own, which is what we were discussing."

"He didn't seem too happy when you both returned."

"The practice isn't doing so good. Financially, we both expected some windfalls after I left, but its been over two years. Some of my clients stayed with John, but most didn't. He's been unsuccessful finding another partner willing to take on the financial burden. I feel awful."

"Why should you feel awful?" Hayden asked. "You can't be responsible for his practice and do your job at the same time."

"I know." Cannon nodded in agreement, turning his head. Looking out the front windshield, the sky was full of stars. He hadn't remembered seeing a starry night in the longest time. "It's just that we built the practice together. We were going to stay together till the end. Then I left."

"You moved onto another stage in your life." Hayden, unknowingly placed her hand on his shoulders. Shoulders, she began to understand, that carried a lot of weight. "John understands that, doesn't he?"

"It's not John," Cannon said, feeling a comforting warmth from her touch. Everything about her touch was soft. It made him think of silk and cream. "John and I are as thick as blood. It's me. I just feel so guilty."

"Your mother was right." Hayden smiled as he turned to her with a confused look in his eyes. The urge to console him was becoming a desire and that frightened her. "She said you want to save the world. You always have. Well you can't. All you can do is your part and you've done so much already. Don't tear yourself up about it. All that will do is take from you what you need to keep doing what you can."

As he looked longingly into her eyes, Cannon knew what he felt for her was more than an attraction. She was what he'd been looking for, but hadn't found in all of those failed relationships. She was a sexy, beautiful, intelligent, and strong black woman with a heart full of kindness and a determined loyalty as strong as the sun was bright. He wondered what he was to do now.

Hayden felt the connection that was created by the silence as they both gazed into each other's eyes. Inside, she yelled at herself to turn away, even begged, but to no avail. His eyes held hers like she was in a trance. The kiss they had shared quickly returned to her thoughts and as she realized that was what she wanted, Hayden became scared to death. This couldn't be happening. She barely knew him, didn't know if she really wanted to. Two days from today, she would be marrying this man. It was all a mess and facing that fact gave Hayden the strength to tear her eyes, her face away from his.

"It's getting late," she said in a voice she barely recognized. "We should get going."

Cannon knew in his heart he wasn't ready to let this end. It could be the stars, the night air, or simply her arresting face, glistening skin, and rich eyes. Whatever the case, more than water or air, he wanted to taste her lips.

Gently, he took her face in his hands and leaned across the seat. Hayden felt her heart hammering away as she saw his face come down on hers. The undeniable magnetism that was building between them could only lead to this, Hayden knew that. She knew it, and the demanding way with which he took her lips, told he he knew it, too.

His lips pressed against hers and covered her mouth with force, sending an aching sensation throughout her body. Her arms instinctively went to him and, to her surprise, grabbed his arms and pulled him to her. Her body stirred at the feel of his tongue entering her mouth. The pleasure made her intensely weak with desire.

No, no she begged herself. She couldn't take it, but she couldn't back away from him. She could only drink it in. The passion, the desire, the feeling of insane hunger as his mouth devoured hers.

The honking of a passing car's horn shot them both back to reality. Cannon jumped so high, his head almost hit the ceiling of his car. Hayden pushed away so hard her back hit the car door. The pain made her wince and moan out loud.

"Are you alright?" Cannon's first instinct was to reach out to her, but he couldn't trust himself to touch her anymore. It was as if he lost control of himself this close to her.

"I'm fine," she lied, turning her back to him. What had just happened? Was she crazy? Her mind told her that she was, but her body told her something entirely different.

"Hayden." He spoke with caution, not just because of her obvious rebuttal of him, but also because he wasn't certain what to say. He was feeling everything right now. No woman had ever done this to him.

"Don't say anything, please." She couldn't look at him as she held her hand up to stop him. Back in the real world, it suddenly hit her what she had just done. She wanted to take back time, certain she could have stopped it if given a second chance. Certain.

"I have to say something." His voice was still a little choked. They weren't in an embrace, but he could still feel her. He could still feel the effect she had on his manhood.

"Cannon," she said, each word coming out of her mouth a labor of pain. Couldn't the last five minutes just go away? "No one has to say anything. We're both human. We got caught up in an emotional moment. Alone, the night sky. These things happen."

He wanted to tell her this wasn't a *thing*. This wasn't the night. What he felt was genuine, but he couldn't. To say that would be a colossal mistake.

"It was my mistake." Her eyes stared straight ahead. She couldn't bear this much longer. She wanted to, needed to get away. The issue before had been trusting him. Now, she couldn't even trust herself. "It was my mistake."

"Don't blame yourself." He wanted to smack himself for hurting her. She was terribly upset, it was obvious and it was his fault. He wanted her to believe he was different than he used to be, no longer a playboy. Only now he had destroyed that by forcing himself on her.

"I opened the door up to this," Hayden said. "I thought we should be friends, but that isn't going to work. We need to keep this professional. No more personal stories. No more getting into each other's personal lives or pasts."

After taking a moment to gather his thoughts, his feelings, Cannon started the car. It burned him inside to know she was thinking he was a man only interested in one thing. Despite how much it hurt him, he thought maybe it was for the best. He couldn't allow this to get so complicated. He had to keep his eyes on one goal, focusing his emotions on that. There was no time for a woman to cloud his thoughts or his heart. Not even one as beautiful as Hayden Campbell.

They drove in silence the rest of the night, Hayden doing her best to think of anything other than the intimate moment they had just shared. It was impossible as she realized this arrangement would be ten times harder than she originally thought. The blacks and whites of the situation were melting into gray, a fierce gray that she feared she had no control over. She could no longer ignore it. She was headed for trouble.

The day of the wedding finally came and Hayden wasn't at all prepared for how nervous she'd be. She kept trying to tell herself it wasn't real, but her heart was aflutter from the night before, on into the next day. She couldn't get the kiss out of her mind, out of her heart, no matter how hard she tried. Everyone around her, including Donna who knew it was all fake, seemed so excited for her. Everyone, including Tom Campbell.

While waiting in Candace's kitchen, Hayden squeezed her father's hand tight. She knew she wasn't so nervous about lying. Somehow she had found a way to deal with that. Having her father standing next to her, looking the best he had since before the attack was how she dealt with it. Whenever she felt guilt at what she was doing begin to overwhelm her, and fear at what she was feeling for Cannon, she thought of her father. She thought of how everyone's attitude seemed to be a little bit more optimistic the past couple of weeks.

No, the lie wasn't what made a million butterflies in her stomach stir. Today was her wedding day! She was the picture of beauty and grace in her dress with her loving father ready to walk her down the aisle. Everyone's eyes were on her. She knew it wasn't for real—for love—so why did she feel something magical? Who knew? Hayden had made the decision to second guess all her feelings from now on, especially after her last kiss with Cannon.

"Now, baby," Tom said, looking tenderly into his little girl's eyes, "if this boy doesn't treat you right, you come right home to me and your mama."

"We aren't even married yet, Daddy." Hayden was touched to her heart by his words, although they weren't necessary. Not this time around. She knew her father would always be there for her. "Give him a chance."

"I'm just saying,"—he shrugged, turning his head to face the sliding glass doors—"if he ever cheats on you or raises his hand to you, you don't have to stay. Don't ever feel trapped like these women do today. I don't care how old you are, I don't care if you have twelve kids. You pack their things and bring every single one of their nappy little heads home to me and your mama."

"Oh, Daddy." Hayden laughed out loud, feeling herself about to cry. He was returning his old self again. "I wish I could marry you."

"Well." He passed her a quick wink. "That's what all the ladies say. But I'll tell you like I told them. My heart was stolen thirty years ago and that little thief still has it."

Hayden saw the love in his eyes as he referred to her mother and it melted her heart. One day a man would look like that when he mentioned her. She knew it. She had to believe it.

Their cue was when Tyler, adorable in his tiny tuxedo, reached the pastor and took his seat next to Candace. When he did, Hayden felt her heart leap.

"You ready, princess?" Tom asked.

"As much as I'll ever be." She made sure her vail was in place and took a deep breath.

"You know," he said in a whisper, "you're still my baby and always will be."

"I know, Daddy." Hayden wiped away a tear as she kissed her father on the cheek. Her heart wanted to tell him that because of this, he would be around a long time for her to be his baby.

"Let's go," he said as he led her onto the back porch and down the aisle.

The wedding itself was quick as Hayden and Cannon had

instructed the pastor they wanted a brief ceremony. Hayden was nervous throughout, especially when it was time for the kiss. Thoughts of their last kiss swept through her, but she knew there was no avoiding it in front of all these people. It was brief, as she expected, but still she felt the sparks in the pit of her stomach and it frightened her. She wondered how she was going to keep this a business arrangement if every time he kissed her she felt her mouth on fire. To make it worse, every time she saw him, all she could think of was how handsome he looked.

The reception was like most, a fun celebration. Hayden enjoyed meeting members of Cannon's family and close friends even though she knew most of them thought she was pregnant. She found many of them to be well-connected in whatever city they were from. There were at least twice as many people as Candace had promised, but Hayden didn't care and Candace seemed happy.

Sometimes overwhelmed with well-wishers' questions, Hayden was filled with relief whenever Cannon was at her side. He rescued her several times throughout the evening and shouldered the responsibility of answering the difficult questions. She was glad she and Cannon were getting along tonight despite the ever-growing tension between them since the last kiss. She enjoyed watching him interact with Tyler and several other children who attended. She could see he had a connection with kids that made them swarm to him and delight in his attention.

As the guests demanded they do so over and over again, Hayden and Cannon shared brief kisses to appease them. Each time, she felt a heady sensation and knew that wasn't a good sign, but she was having fun. She would worry about that later.

She let all the champagne she was drinking be her excuse for her physical distraction while dancing with him. The entire time her mind was obsessed with wondering if Cannon felt the same. She was bothered by his seeming indifference. He was obviously having a good time, smiling at everyone, speaking to her throughout as if they were the best of friends. As if what was going on between the two of them was nothing.

Cannon put on the best face he could all evening. He wanted to appear happy to please the onlookers and unattached to please Hayden. After the kiss the other night, he was certain there had been a connection, but she had turned away. She had made her feelings clear with that one motion, and even went so far as to dismiss the kiss as nothing more than an emotional release. She didn't even want to be friends, let alone more. He knew she wouldn't like it if he showed his true feelings, but the truth was, he'd never been as happy as he was tonight. In his opinion, Hayden was the most beautiful woman in the world, looking like an angel in white. Cannon knew he was falling for her, hard and fast. It didn't matter that he didn't want to, but he had always feared love was like that. Ready or not, here it comes, and it was coming.

"Did you see that?" Donna stepped into Hayden's sight off from the dance area. She looked beautiful in the violet dress she wore. Jokingly refusing to be in the wedding if Candace forced her to wear an ugly bridesmaid's dress, Hayden let her chose her own. She decided on a Valentino, similar to one she'd seen actress Angela Basset wear to a movie awards show.

"See what?" Hayden asked. Taking a break from everything, she attempted to hide behind the band's sound equipment, but was happy Donna had found her.

"That gorgeous guy I was dancing with." Donna stole an olive off of Hayden's tiny food plate. "I think he's the mayor's aid or someone in the mayor's office."

"I wasn't looking. I'm sorry."

Donna studied Hayden's face for a moment. "What is with you?"

"What do you mean?" she asked. "I couldn't see you. The dance area is packed."

"I'm not talking about that anymore. You've been goofy all evening." Donna placed her hands on the curves of her hips. "You act as if you're really married. You don't have to put on a show for me, hon. I know the truth, remember?"

"What show?" Hayden wasn't sure what she meant. Of

course she had been putting forth the appearance of a happy bride, but was she overdoing it? Can one overdo a happy bride?

"You've been acting like a giddy young girl who found her prince and can't see anything in the world except him." Donna rolled her eyes, mocking an impression of a young girl senselessly in love.

"I have not." Hayden stuck a carrot in her mouth.

"Maybe you haven't noticed, but I have. Is it a facade or for real?"

"Don't be silly." Hayden laughed nervously. "We want to convince everyone."

"Look at your eyes, baby." Donna leaned her face in closer to Hayden's, looking into her eyes. "They're almost bouncing. Maybe you're trying so hard to convince everyone else, you've convinced yourself."

"Donna, don't be ridiculous," Hayden said, waving a dismissing hand. "I'm just having a good time. I'm drinking champagne. It's a party."

"You're right. It's your wedding day!" A relaxed smile spread across her face. "Which reminds me. Tonight is your wedding night."

"Don't even go there." Hayden threw Donna a serious look, feeling the heat rise to her face.

"You're going to live in his condo aren't you?"

"Yes, I am." The move was still in progress and Hayden had only two months left on her lease, so decided against bothering to sublet. She had several of her favorite items and necessities moved into Cannon's condo over the past couple of days and planned to spend tomorrow unpacking.

"What have you two talked about . . . you know . . . tonight?" Anticipation on Donna's face gave her thoughts away.

"Would you stop?" Hayden really wanted her to quit this. After everything that had happened between her and Cannon, she was terribly uneasy about the topic and tried to avoid thinking about their first night alone under the same roof.

"The rumor is you have a room at the Ritz Carlton downtown."

"That's what Cannon told his mother and we know how fast her mouth moves. We've told everyone we're too busy with our careers right now to go on an extended honeymoon. He booked a suite, but it's just for appearances." Hayden was beginning to hate saying that word. "He wanted to go to the hotel, promising he'd sleep on the sofa. He felt it was the icing on the cake to make everything believable, but I was too uncomfortable."

The thought of being in a beautiful hotel suite on her wedding night with a man as attractive and well versed in the art of seduction as Cannon, was a bit much for her. It was especially so now that they were both aware of the strong physical reaction each evoked from the other. The few glasses of champagne didn't help either.

Of course she didn't tell him that, only saying it wasn't necessary. All they really needed to do was check in, which Cannon did early that morning. He also told the front desk not to disturb them. Cannon agreed to return to the hotel Sunday to pay the bill and check out. She offered to pay for half the room, noting his disapproval of her decision not to stay, but he refused her money.

"It's a shame," Donna said, shaking her head in disappointment. "It's your wedding and . . . well nothing. I bet you never dreamed . . ."

"Can we stop talking about it?" Hayden lowered her eyes to the ground. She was tired of not being able to hide her feelings and emotions.

"Fine," Donna said. "Just remember who this man is."

"Was," Hayden corrected. "That's the past."

"Do you really believe that?" Donna asked skeptically.

"I want to." Hayden raised her head, looking at her friend with vulnerably honest eyes. She really wanted to.

"Can you risk that?" Donna asked. Hayden didn't answer that question. Not because she didn't want to, but because she couldn't.

''There you are!''

From around the six-foot speakers came Cannon with a lazy smile on his handsome face, his tuxedo a little undone from dancing the night away.

''Sweetheart, John and Jesse want to take another picture with us.'' He reached out, took hold of her hand, and pulled her out in front of the band area. A compact disc of Boyz II Men was playing now that the band was taking a short break.

''Alright.'' Hayden's delayed response was unnecessary as Cannon had already assumed position for the picture. She noticed he'd called her sweetheart for the first time. She assumed he did so for Donna's sake and wondered if she should tell him Donna knew the truth.

''Can you take the picture?'' John Dannell offered the camera to Donna.

''Sure, no problem. Get over there. How does this work?'' Donna eyed the angles of the camera.

''It's all set,'' Jesse said in her high-pitched voice. ''Get us in your sights. Wait until you hear the beep and press the red button.''

''Okay.'' Donna situated the camera. ''Alright everyone, say cheese.''

After the picture was taken and everyone unlocked arms, Jesse turned to Hayden and said, ''Oh dear, you look pretty tired.''

''Yes, she does,'' John agreed. ''You better get her out of here, buddy.''

''I'm ready myself.'' Cannon again took Hayden's hand in his and felt her lean against his strong tall body. A feeling of tenderness swept through him at the touch. *If only.*

''Well, Hayden,'' John said as he took her free hand in his. ''You've done what I never thought possible—settled Cannon. Now, if you could only convince him to come back to our practice.''

''I'll see what I can do,'' Hayden said with a tired smile, unaware she was leaning against her husband. John had been nice to her since the moment they'd met and she hoped they could be friends, even after this was all over.

After John and Jesse thanked Donna for taking the picture, the three of them decided to try for another piece of cake, leaving Hayden and Cannon alone.

"Are you ready to go?" He looked down at her with a protective smile. Even after a long, exhausting summer night, she still looked radiant.

"Yes, I am," she responded, lifting away from him enough to look up at his arresting face. She tried not to acknowledge the warm comfort she saw in his soft eyes. He had the most gentle eyes she had ever seen. It was as if they said, *I understand.*

"Where are your parents?" he asked. "We'll have to say goodbye to them first."

"They left a half hour ago." Hayden was happy to see her father enjoying himself. The wedding was the first social event he'd attended since the surgery. To be safe, Elise decided to leave earlier than Dr. Kent recommended. "They wanted to give you a hug and wish us both well, but you were surrounded by a bunch of people and Daddy was tired. You can call them later if you'd like."

"Alright." Cannon looked around the yard. "Okay, sweetheart. A couple of kisses and hugs. Maybe a quick speech and we can hit the road. Let's start making the rounds."

As she took his hand and followed him to the crowd, Hayden realized he had said the word *home,* as if it had the same meaning for the both of them. Then another word echoed in her mind. He had called her sweetheart again. No one was within ear distance to put on the disguise for. She wanted to analyze the whys of it, but decided against that. He was probably tired, as she was, and hadn't even realized he said it. Yes, he was just tired.

The ride to Cannon's condo was a long one. Hayden thought she'd come to grips with what she was doing, but that had changed with their kiss the other night. It was settling in now. There was something about the long silent drive to her new home that brought on a whole new set of fears and doubts. With some satisfaction, she assumed Cannon's silence meant it was finally hitting him, too.

It irritated her that he was so polite, showing her around the place for a second time. She was grateful her bedroom and bathroom were far away from his. Despite that, in the silence of the night, she could still hear him rustle around in his room as she lay in her new bed trying to fall asleep.

It made her angry when the noise stopped and there was nothing but loud silence. How could he fall asleep so fast? Was this all so simple for him? Hayden tossed and turned, missing the familiarity of her old bed. After countless minutes of staring at the ceiling, she had had enough and decided to head to the kitchen for a late night snack.

Some wedding night, she thought to herself as she flicked on the night lamp next to the bed. Her eyes shut tight as the pain of the light hit them. The shade to filter the bulb's power was still packed in one of the boxes marked BEDROOM. She whispered a curse to herself as she realized her robe was in one of the suitcases underneath all those boxes. She was wearing the primrose yellow satin top and shorts she wore almost every night to bed. Since Alec had left for Atlanta, her more exotic nighties were gathering dust.

She hesitated for a moment, but decided to chance it. After all, Cannon had been quiet in his bedroom for a long time. She was sure the insensitive brute was sleeping.

Hayden tiptoed across the carpeted hallway past Cannon's closed bedroom door. Looking at the crack underneath the door, she felt more confident as she saw the light was off. Forget him anyway for sleeping like today was any other day.

As she turned the corner toward the kitchen, she noticed the light was on. She would have to have a say in that if he expected her to go half on the utility bill.

Just as she stepped into the kitchen, her heart leaped into her throat and she let out a gasp.

"Sorry," Cannon said as he swallowed a mouthful of vanilla ice cream. "I didn't mean to scare you."

"I thought you were sleep." Hayden stood, frozen in the doorway.

As he leaned casually against the countertop, she found herself extremely conscious of the fact that he wasn't wearing a top, but only satin pants. His dark brown shoulders, forever wide, were proportioned perfectly to his chiseled chest. The brown paisley pants fell on his body, laying softly on his skin and showing the thickness of his thighs.

Suddenly aware of her own attire, her usual yellow pajamas didn't feel so usual anymore. She realized now her top button was undone, revealing a generous amount of cleavage. Her shorts, which seemed perfectly innocent in the past, now felt too high up on her shapely thighs.

"I thought you were asleep." His eyes roved and lazily appraised her. It wasn't as if he needed a reminder of how sexy she was, but he got one. "I like that outfit."

"Thank you," she said nonchalantly, lifting her head as she brushed passed him to the refrigerator. "What about yours? Could only afford half?"

"Very nice," he said with a humorous smile. "Midnight comedy."

"Why couldn't you sleep?" She opened the cap of one of the cherry yogurt cups she had brought from her own apartment. Besides her own food, Cannon's refrigerator was bare, maintaining the stereotype of bachelor's refrigerators.

"I usually don't get to sleep until one in the morning anyway." He handed her a spoon from the dish rack, noticing she was reluctant to reach over him. "What about yourself?"

"I need more sleep than that, but I guess I'm unfamiliar with the place." She refused to look at his compelling chest, instead allowing her eyes to roam the kitchen and appreciate its fine black and white decor.

"I can understand that." He took another mouthful of ice cream. He could stand there and stare at her all night. "I like your ice cream."

Hayden smiled as she realized it was her vanilla ice cream he was eating straight from the pint-sized carton. ''Well, you're welcome.'' If he wasn't so attractive this wouldn't be so difficult.

''So what is with you and your mother?'' he asked, thinking of anything he could to keep her in the kitchen.

''What do you mean?'' Hayden quickly stole a moment while he turned his head to lower her shorts an inch or two. He could tell she hadn't expected to see him there.

''I've been to quite a few weddings in my time and usually the bride's mother is all over her. I barely saw you with her all night.'' He returned the ice cream to the freezer and carelessly threw the spoon in the sink. ''Are you two close?''

''Of course we are,'' Hayden said, her eyes widening in alarm she knew there were issues between her mother and herself, but usually no one noticed. It bothered her that he had.

''It just didn't seem like . . .''

''Is it necessary for you to analyze my family relationships?'' She firmly placed the yogurt cup on the counter. ''My mother was very preoccupied with her husband. This was his first outing since surgery, if you recall.''

''Fine,'' he said, raising his hands defensively. Hoping to spark a meaningful conversation, he realized he had struck a personal chord with her.

''It's not fine,'' Hayden continued. She hid her embarrassment at his insight under anger. ''I don't want you questioning my family relationships.''

''Well seeing as how we're supposed to be playing house for a while, I don't know how that can be avoided.'' Cannon mocked her by placing his hands on his hips and saw that his movement only angered her even more.

''If that's so, then what about your sister?'' She regretted the question as soon as she asked it, but it had been in anger not with intent to hurt. She watched with apprehension as the amused expression on Cannon's face immediately turned to anger.

"I don't want to discuss her with you." A serious calm came over his face as he stared at her intently.

"Fine," she said, turning her face from him. "Then I don't want to discuss my mother with you."

"You know, Hayden," he said, with a loose voice. "I know the other night was uncomfortable and I understand your desire for us not to be friends, but we're going to be living together and attending social functions together. We don't have to be buddies, but we do have to get along. It's really not a choice. This will never work if we don't."

"I know," she agreed apologetically. She couldn't tell him it was easier to be angry at him, than try and get along. At least when she was angry she wasn't so attracted to him.

"After all," he said with a slow seductive tone of voice, "this is our wedding night. We could at least not fight."

"Cannon, don't joke about that." Hayden quickly buttoned her top button with nervous hands. He was practically naked. Why should she feel ashamed? "It isn't funny."

"This situation isn't ideal for either of us." Cannon turned to walk out of the kitchen, tilting his head backward at her. "If we don't find a way to laugh at it, we're doomed."

As she stood alone in the large kitchen, Hayden had to agree with him. They would have to learn to get along and find a way to laugh at their situation. It would be brutal otherwise. Laughing wasn't the hard part. March was a long way away and if Cannon insisted on walking around the apartment without a shirt on, Hayden knew it wasn't her sense of humor she needed to worry about.

Chapter Seven

The day after she became Mrs. Cannon Factor was relatively eventless for Hayden. She spent most of it unpacking and decorating her room. Cannon told her she could change anything around the apartment she wanted to if it would make her more comfortable. She was correct earlier in thinking the place had been professionally done. It was, and Cannon wasn't particularly attached to anything except the universal symbol for medicine statue his father had left him. Hayden noticed an unfamiliar sense of personal importance as he mentioned his late father's statue.

She appreciated the gesture of welcome, but felt uncomfortable making his home hers. Neither did she want to get attached to anything new in this stage in her life. This was all only temporary and reminding herself of that was what would get her through. Instead, she bought everything of sentimental value into her room, which was generous in size.

She moved everything that didn't fit in her room into Cannon's large storage closet in the basement of the building. She also did a little grocery shopping to fill the barren refrigerator and cabinets. It surprised her how little she actually came in contact with Cannon. Although breakfast was a ritual for her, he never ate it. He woke up early, exercised in the building's gym, and went straight to his private office which was down the hall from both their bedrooms.

She heard him preparing lunch as she set up her laptop computer in the living room to get some work done and decided to wait until he finished to eat her lunch. By the time he'd washed his dishes and left it was two thirty in the afternoon, and she was famished. Realizing they couldn't continue to avoid each other at all cost, she asked him to talk over dinner and he agreed before returning to his office.

"I don't mind if you eat with me, Hayden," Cannon said as he twirled the spaghetti she'd prepared with his fork. "I think it would be nice."

"It's just a little awkward." Hayden felt a more than normal sense of pride as she watched him enjoying her meal. She meant it as a gesture of peace, hoping he understood she beared no hard feelings from the last night or that night in the car. She hadn't cooked for anyone other than herself since Alec. "We go from not even knowing each other a month ago to living together. We tried to prepare for this, but you really can't deal with a situation like this until you're in it. We have to discuss this."

"We already agreed on rent, bills, and all that." Cannon wasn't sure he wanted to have this conversation, although he knew it was necessary. He had sensed the tension all day. He could never tell her he felt uncomfortable around her because he was falling for her and didn't want to know that she felt uncomfortable around him because of what he suspected was her opinion of his reputation with women.

"What about our personal interaction?" she asked. "We need to make it more comfortable."

"I didn't know you were so uncomfortable." His expression showed an amused disappointment. "You know some people actually believe I'm a nice guy."

"It's not about your personality, Cannon. I'm just wondering, are we going to eat meals together or are we going to avoid each other? What if we both want to watch something on TV? What if I want to invite some of my girlfriends over or you want some of your buddies over to watch a game? Those sorts of things."

"We'll do like every other married couple," he replied casually. "We'll see what happens and go with what works best."

"Oh, that sounds good," she said sarcastically. "You should write a book about marriage. That will work out just fine."

"What is that supposed to mean?" He was confused at her disapproval. He was doing his best to make this a lighter situation for both their sakes, but it only seemed to aggravate her.

"We aren't like every other married couple," Hayden said, perturbed at his nonchalantness. "Newlyweds are clouded by love and passion. They live for compromise and want to spend every waking moment together."

"Sounds good to me." He collected some marinara sauce with a bread roll and ate it.

"Cannon, I'm serious." She wondered if he found pleasure in annoying her to such a degree or if she was overreacting.

"I've never lived with a woman in my life, Hayden." Cannon twisted restlessly in the black lacquer dining room chair. "I don't know what to do. You tell me what you want."

"Okay, I'll start." Hayden gently wiped her mouth with a napkin. "I'm used to working over dinner, so I'd like to continue that. If there's something we need to discuss, I think we should leave a note somewhere. Let's say the foyer ledge. That's pretty open and obvious. That way we'll know if we need to be home for dinner or come home early, if someone will be joining us . . . whatever."

"I work late at the office pretty often." Cannon noticed she was avoiding eye contact with him and couldn't ignore that it hurt his feelings.

"I do as well." As structure returned to the conversation, Hayden felt more comfortable. "If we plan to, we can leave a note or call each other at work. I can do likewise if I plan to stay at my parents' home for the night.''

"Sounds very civilized.''

"Now about the television,'' she said, ignoring his snippy comment. "I don't watch it too often and I have a small one in my room so unless I'd like to watch something on cable . . .''

"Are you planning on locking yourself in that room for a year?'' he asked, irritated by the coldness in her demeanor.

"No, of course not,'' she said defensively, remembering she had thought of the idea at once. "It's just that until we get used to being around each other, we need ground rules and space.''

"You can watch the big television as much as you want. Who knows, maybe if I behave, you'll let me come join you for the ten o'clock news.'' The sarcasm in his tone was evident. "I'll eat dinner in my office. I usually bring it home from work anyway. I'll stay out of your way.''

"Cannon, I don't want you to be upset with me,'' she pleaded, not knowing any other way to handle this.

"I'm not upset, Hayden,'' he said despite the frown on his face making it obvious he was. "It just seems like you're doing everything to avoid me. It's as if''—he hesitated—''as if you believe everything that's being said about me.'' He lowered his eyes to his plate. Hungry before, now he merely played at his food to create a distraction. He was embarrassed for acting like a baby; complaining. It was unlike himself to behave this way toward a woman, over a woman.

Hayden didn't know how to respond, so she chose to say nothing. Her disappointment grew as they ate in silence, wondering what she had said to upset him so much. She didn't want to believe the rumors on one hand, but couldn't totally dismiss them on the other. Aside from the rumors, she couldn't ignore Joanne Pearl's comments over the phone weeks ago, naming all the women before her. Then there were Mavis's comments. About her own brother at that. Then the waiter at the Metropolitan Club mentioning Cannon's previous visits. Even her mother knew of two women who had their hearts broken by the good doctor. She was frightened of getting close to him. What would happen? It couldn't be good, not after their entire relationship was founded on a lie. After Alec, the last thing she needed was another broken heart. She wasn't sure the one she'd just had was completely mended yet. No, she couldn't risk being the next Joanne Pearl.

As he quietly excused himself from the table, she wondered if this would work. They'd seemed able to get along at first, but she'd felt a level of tension growing between them ever since he kissed her that day outside his mother's home. It had grown tenfold after the kiss they shared in the car. She would have to remind herself that this was for her family and her own personal comfort was not a priority.

"So you two done it yet?" Donna asked Hayden the question as soon as both women sat down for lunch at Chicago's trendy Everest restaurant.

"I'm leaving right now if you continue with this line of questioning." Hayden gave her friend a stern stare. Thankful for a moment away from the condo, the last thing she wanted to talk about was Cannon and the tension that continued to exist between them.

"Okay, your honor!" Donna mockingly bowed her head to Hayden's insistent tone. "How has it been going, really?"

"Alright," she said, shrugging her shoulders. "It's just very weird living with someone you hardly know."

"Well it's only been four days." Donna placed her napkin on her lap and opened the menu. "I'm sure things will get busy when you both go back to work next week."

"Actually, Cannon's been back at work since yesterday," Hayden said.

"Better for you," Donna said. "You don't have to see him as much."

"I know," Hayden weakly agreed. "I'm sure you're right about next week."

"I haven't seen anything in the paper all week." Donna's smile was hopeful and encouraging.

"Fortunately." Hayden was at least grateful for that and for more reasons than her role as Cannon's public relations counselor. Now that she was Mrs. Cannon Factor, she couldn't help but take it personally. Even if she was in name only.

"This is a good long break from negativity before he makes his bid for senator public," Donna said. "When is that again?"

Hayden waited until they gave the waiter their orders before answering.

"We're planning it for Friday," she said. "We'll be attending a charity function Saturday night and he wants to use it to drum up some support."

"You mean money?"

"Yes, money."

"Isn't Cannon loaded?" Donna asked. "His dad was one of the leading doctors in the country. He made millions from books and speeches."

"I don't know Cannon's exact worth," Hayden said, "but he's definitely well off."

"And so are you, now that you're his wife." A quick smile curved Donna's mouth.

"I want nothing to do with Cannon's money," Hayden stated emphatically.

Although she willingly signed a prenuptial agreement, she had been offended when Warren offered to write up an agreement including a generous divorce settlement. She refused it immediately. She also refused a standing bank account Cannon offered to set up for her during the marriage. The only concession she made was to pay less than half of the mortgage on his condo. Amazed that half would still be three hundred dollars more than she paid in rent at her old apartment, she agreed to pay only what she had been paying for herself after her current lease was up. At first, Cannon refused any money, but she insisted and he reluctantly agreed.

"Well," Donna said with a shrug. "You were never too smart."

"Thank you." Hayden laughed, glad to have something to laugh at.

"Are you excited about this fund-raiser?"

"I don't know if excited is the word. It's a fund-raiser for educating inner city families on sickle cell anemia." Hayden had to admit she was anxious about dressing up and attending a party with the who's who in Chicago society. She was also nervous because it would be her and Cannon's first time in public since the wedding. "It's one of several organizations Cannon belongs to."

"It sounds intriguing," Donna said as the waiter brought their appetizers. "First thing Sunday morning, I want you to tell me all about it."

Hayden heard Cannon call her name from the living room for the third time in the past ten minutes.

"I'm coming," she shouted to him from her bathroom. Putting on the final touches for the evening's event, she wanted to look good. It wasn't often she got to dress up this much and she wanted to do it right.

"Hayden, it's already seven. We should have been there by . . ." Cannon stopped cold in the middle of his sentence at the sight of her coming around the corner.

His eyes raked boldly over her. He couldn't remember seeing any woman so beautifully elegant. His eyes moved from her shining, flowing hair and rested a moment on the arrestingly well-modeled and feminine features of her coffee brown face. The short spaghetti-strapped black pearl dress gave grace and calmness to the sensual suggestion offered by the young nubile curves it covered. The uptilt of her full breasts and the roundness of her hips were softly contained underneath the lanky dress. She looked so regal, yet touchable at the same time, making Cannon swear he could feel his heart flutter.

Hayden confidently basked in his approval. That confidence veered to faint shyness as his gaze, as soft as a caress, trailed her body. His eyes were riveted to her and Hayden couldn't deny the race of her pulse and the slight pull in the pit of her stomach in response to it.

"You are truly gorgeous," Cannon said slowly, never taking his eyes off her.

"Thank you," she responded, with an affectionate smile.

"You looked like an angel at the wedding and I thought you looked so together in that dress at the press conference yesterday, but"—he stammered a bit, his soft eyes wide with intrigue—"but tonight . . . tonight you look fantastic."

"You look okay yourself." Hayden gloried in the brief moment of joy she felt at the thought of him feeling this way about how she looked. It was deep within her, not wanting to be acknowledged, but she wanted his approval. She wanted him to find her attractive.

In return, she found him dynamic and powerful in his tailored tuxedo. There was an air of masculinity about him that fascinated her. Clean cut, yet rugged and sexy, his respectable arrogance showed as he held his tall, dark, and strong body so well.

"I guess we better get going." She wasn't sure, but she thought she saw a hint of embarrassment on his face as well. Moderate humility was becoming on him. Then again, what wasn't becoming on him?

"I guess so," he responded, holding his arm out to her.

As she took his arm, sliding her hand down it gently, she felt uneasy about the victorious knowledge that she had some effect on Cannon Factor. She knew this wasn't a good thing, but nevertheless . . .

One thing was definite and that was that Cannon Factor had an effect on everyone else. As they arrived at the Four Seasons Hotel, Hayden was thoroughly impressed as the evening's attendees stopped whatever they were doing to address him as well as congratulate them both on their marriage and his decision to run for senator.

"We're behind you, Cannon."

"Good luck to you, kid. We know you'll do good."

"Love and happiness for you both."

After John and Jesse arrived, the four of them took their

seats. They were placed at the same table as the lieutenant governor of Illinois and his wife as well as the owner of the *Chicago Tribune,* Chicago's top selling newspaper and his wife. Hayden understood now why it was so important to Cannon to announce his bid before tonight. Everyone in a power position in this politically powerful city was there that evening. She had attended awards and association dinners before, but they were mostly business affairs for her peers, at the relative same level she was at in their careers. Here, there were politicians and big spenders. *Power brokers* was Cannon's name for them. Hayden wondered for a moment what she was doing there before remembering she was the health commissioner's wife.

They chatted among themselves, with Jesse doing most of the talking. Cannon was a little preoccupied with John, who wasn't in the best of moods. Hayden was touched by Cannon's commitment to his friend. Likewise, the few times John spoke, it was in praise of Cannon.

The pleasant chat ceased as the executive director of the Fight Sickle Cell organization stepped to the microphone. She spoke eloquently for a long time about the disease that effects mostly African-American and Mediterranean cultures and how, although there is effective treatment, there is still no cure and more work must be done. She then proceeded to name various doctors in the Chicago community who have led in the fight against the disease. Hayden was intrigued at the last name mentioned.

As he stood up to acknowledge the applause, she recognized Dr. Robert Marks from his picture in the *Chicago Tribune.* She noticed he looked a little older and thinner now, but understood the picture was a couple of years old. As it always did, her curiosity got the best of her and she saw an opportunity.

After the ceremony session of the evening was over, Hayden tried to keep an eye on Marks with the intention of confronting him about the rumors. It was difficult as she was required to stay by Cannon's side while he introduced her to well-wishers and old friends. Hayden was pleased that everyone they met seemed very impressed with her, several mentioning that they knew there was one woman out there who could tame Cannon. Hayden felt a tinge of guilt creep in as she eyed Cannon adoringly and spoke of his many attractions, but her curiosity for what Dr. Marks would have to say stayed with her.

She finally got her opportunity to approach him as Cannon excused himself to the men's room. By that time she had lost sight of Marks, but went in search of him.

"Mrs. Factor! Mrs. Factor!"

Hayden heard the name several times before remembering it was hers. Turning around she came face to face with Lee Sampson. The short man looked awkward with his large camera wrapped around his small neck. His tuxedo wasn't new, neither was it tailored.

"I'm sorry, I didn't know . . ."

"It's okay," he said with a quick smile. "I'm sure the name will take some time to get used to."

"What can I do for you, Mr. Sampson?" she asked, placing a judgmental hand on her hip. She eyed him harshly, wanting him to know from the start she was not one to be pushed around. "Looking for more rumors to spread about my husband?"

"Rumors?" Sampson took a step back, appearing surprised by her suggestion. "I'll have you know I don't print a single thing without a reliable source."

"And who is this reliable source?" She knew he wouldn't tell her, but she held a level of resentment toward the little man and wanted to bother him. "If it exists."

"You're in public relations, Mrs. Factor. You should know enough about journalism to know I can't tell you that." He crossed his arms in a self-assuming manner. "But I can tell you it is a reliable source. Someone who knows Cannon."

Maryann Holly and Mavis Factor came to Hayden's mind, but she also considered that Sampson wouldn't tell her that if it was true. It would be too easy. He would try to set up a decoy to distract her.

"My husband admits to a playboy past as I'm sure some men have," Hayden said defiantly. "But he has matured and become a responsible man who does a very good job as health commissioner and will be even better as a United States senator.''

''Of course you think that, you're his wife,'' Sampson said. ''But I'm a reporter and I deal in facts. My source is very, and I stress the word *very*, reliable and on top of things. You ought to think about that.''

As he walked away from her, she cursed him inside because she was thinking about it. Despite what she said, she wasn't sure if it was true herself. She believed Cannon wanted to be Senator, but to serve your country in such a way was as much privilege as a burden and Hayden wasn't sure Cannon deserved that privilege. Determined to find out if her doubts were valid or not, she resumed her search for Marks and found him at the bar ordering a glass of wine. The smile on his face made it appear as if he was happy to see her.

''You and Cannon have been the talk of the town.'' He raised his glass to her after the bartender handed him his drink. ''Cheers to your marriage and good luck to him on his decision.''

''I thank you for both of us, Dr. Marks,'' she said, issuing a graceful tone. ''I wonder, though, if you mean that?''

''What are you saying?'' Hayden guessed Marks was a man of about fifty, but looked older.

''I'm sure you've been reading those awful lies in *Represent Chicago* about Cannon.'' She accepted a glass of wine offered her by a passing waiter.

''Yes, I have.'' He sighed, shaking his head sympathetically. ''It's awful that someone would try to do that.''

''I agree, but I'm wondering who that someone would be.'' She feigned a confused expression. ''My guess would be someone who lost something to Cannon and wanted to get back at him for it.''

He paused a second as it seemed he was putting together her meaning. An angered expression came to his face as he did. ''I don't like what you're insinuating, Mrs. Factor.''

''Insinuating?'' Hayden asked. ''It wasn't my intention to insinuate, doctor. I meant to be very clear. I know you're close to Lee Sampson and I believe you're his source or have some connection to these lies and I intend to find that out.''

''I hope you do find out who is at the bottom of this,'' he said, challenging her look with a direct one of his own. ''And when you do, Mrs. Factor, I'll be waiting for your apology. Good evening.''

As he swiftly turned and walked away, Hayden felt her nervous body let go in a sigh. She wasn't sure what to think of what had just happened. She wasn't well versed in the art of interrogation, but Marks hadn't blinked for a second. Despite that, she felt accomplished in at least having made contact with him.

''Well aren't you a pretty young thing?''

Hayden broke from her thoughts, turning to a woman who, despite the negative expression on her face, was very beautiful. Possibly in her mid-thirties, she looked striking in a strapless white beaded gown. Her hair was cut very short, only an inch or two from her head and slicked back, exposing a daintily featured, caramel-colored face with hazel eyes and ruby red lipstick.

''Excuse me?'' Hayden wasn't sure she heard the woman correctly.

''Cannon does have taste,'' she said with a wry smile. ''I should know.'' She held out a long arm, extending a jewelry adorned hand to Hayden. ''I'm Joanne Pearl.''

Hayden hesitated, but cautiously shook the woman's hand. She surveyed her, admiring the height and distinct beauty of the woman she also suspected as having part in the rumors.

''So you've become the wife.'' Joanne studied Hayden, a look of bitter amusement on her face. ''So many have tried, so many have failed.''

''You among them I presume?'' Hayden, still fueled by energy from her confrontation with Marks, decided to continue her personal investigation.

''Yes, I admit being Mrs. Doctor Cannon Factor was a dream of mine.'' Joanne's eyes looked into the air as she said the name, giving the illusion of some foreseen grandeur connected to the title. "It was a dream of mine as it was for so many other women, but that was before I woke up."

"Woke up?"

"Yes. Cannon is a liar and a cheat." Joanne leaned in closer, standing only a couple of feet from Hayden. "He'll tell you he cares and wants you to trust him, but it's all a game. I was warned, but I didn't listen. I was certain I was different. I was the one. Well I was for that time and so are you for this time. I hear you're not pregnant, so why he went so far as to *marry* you I don't know, but . . ."

"Excuse me, Ms. Pearl." Hayden spoke firmly as she took one step closer to the woman, forcing her head back. She hid the discomfort Joanne's words gave her. She made Cannon seem like such a horrible person. "Why he married me is none of your business. Say what you want about Cannon, but if you thought those things you've said about him were true, you wouldn't be so bitter about losing him."

"Bitter!" The woman suddenly became furious, her ample chest heaving. "How dare you!"

"How dare I?" Hayden persisted. "How dare you come to me and ridicule my husband? How dare you question his affection for me and our marriage?" She wanted to continue, but ceased as an embarrassed and surprised expression came over Joanne's face. Hayden turned to see what was causing it.

"Would you please excuse yourself, Joanne?" Cannon placed his strong hands firmly on Hayden's shoulders. "I would like to speak with my lovely wife."

"I'm sure you would." Joanne gave Hayden one last spiteful glance before slowly walking away.

Aware of the heat that emanated from his hands onto her bare soft shoulders, Hayden stepped away from Cannon and turned to face him. She eyed the man whom she had so many unanswered questions about.

"How did that get started?" He placed his hands awkwardly in his pockets as they begged to touch her again.

"You don't end relationships gracefully," she said, one eyebrow raised in accusation. "I hope our marriage ends with more civility than your relationship with her did."

"Is that so?" The smile on his face faded, replaced by a heavy frown. It affected him deeply when she spoke to him with such disdain in her voice, in her eyes. "Well, my relationship with Joanne ended a little hot and heavy because it always was hot and heavy. You obviously can't stand to be touched by me so I don't think we'll have that problem."

She permitted herself a withering stare before turning away from him. She didn't want him to see how much his words had affected her and was surprised herself to realize it wasn't so much anger she felt as it was hurt.

"What are the two of you up to?" John asked as he approached them, an empty martini glass in his hand. "You keeping him all to yourself, Hayden?"

"You can have him," Hayden said with contempt in her voice. Without even a glance in Cannon's direction, she placed her wine glass on the table and walked away.

"What's with her?" John leaned over the bar table and ordered another martini.

"She's tired." Cannon kept his eyes on Hayden until she disappeared around the corner. He wanted to go after her and apologize, but at the same time he didn't. Let her storm out. He wasn't going to attend to her tantrums.

"You two about to step out?" John asked as he paid for his drink. Cannon wasn't paying him attention, that was obvious. "Hey, Cannon."

With a slight jerk, Cannon turned to John. "What? What did you say?"

"Before you head out," John said, "I need your help with something."

"Anything, buddy." Cannon paid a hard slap to John's back. "Name it."

"There are a couple of people here I would love to get to know." John leaned over, whispering. "Their influential parents. If I can see their kids, well you know. They'll get the word out. Right now I'm nothing to them, but with you . . ."

"Say no more." Cannon took a deep breath. Anything to get his mind off Hayden. "Lead the way."

The rest of the evening was spent in relative silence between Hayden and Cannon. After she returned to the room, her hurt feelings allowed the words of Lee Sampson and Joanne Pearl to sink in. As she stole quick glances at Cannon, her doubts grew. She knew it was aided mostly by her anger toward him, but nonetheless they grew. The two barely spoke during the ride home. The only words exchanged were cordial, expected and somehow this only served to make Hayden even angrier. She knew she had to do something about how much she allowed him to affect her, but what? What could she do? It seemed to her that the situation was getting out of her control.

The next morning, Hayden awoke to the sound of birds chirping outside her window. As she had been for the entire week, she first thought she was in her old bed at her old apartment, but soon realized it was just a dream as she looked around. She wasn't at home. She was in her lie. The lie she would been in for the next year.

As she showered and dressed, Hayden resolved within herself to face Cannon that morning with politeness and friendliness. She still felt hurt by his comments from the night before, but wouldn't allow him the benefit of knowing he could hurt her feelings. She was disappointed at how an evening that started so well ended on such a sour note. She thought herself silly for entertaining the idea that she had some affect on Cannon. She would be stupid to even want that. The tension was thick enough between them just living together, despite Cannon's indifference. She didn't want to hold any grudges and make things worse. After all, this is where she was and would be for a long time.

As she passed his bedroom, the door was open and the black and forest green decorated room was empty. Hayden took a second look around, noticing the king-sized bed and the glazed-wood dressers. She eyed the door that led to the private bathroom before leaving and walked toward the kitchen.

She was surprised he wasn't there. Now interested, but not wanting to admit so to herself, she went to his study and found the door was locked. She then tried the dining room and, for the second time, the living room. No Cannon. The condo was big, but not so big two people could be there and not know where the other one was. Just before giving into calling out his name, Hayden saw the pink sheet of paper laying on the foyer ledge. She didn't notice how quickly she ran across the living room to pick it up.

> *Hayden—*
> *A situation has come up with John and I have to help him. I'm off to LA. I'll be staying at the Sheraton Grande. Be back Wednesday. Please help Mother plan the campaign party.*

Hayden knew she should be happy at the thought of not being forced to deal with Cannon for three days, but she wasn't. She was upset that he left without speaking to her and was mad at herself for remembering the idea of leaving notes was hers.

Her heart leaped as she jumped at the sound of the phone ringing, its call reverberating through the empty home like a canyon echo.

"Hello?"

"So, who did you meet?" Donna's always cheerful voice came over the receiver.

"Donna, I know I told you I'd dish with you," Hayden said. "Only right now isn't a good time."

"What's wrong, honey?"

"Nothing. I'm just not in a good mood right now." Hayden regretted saying that, knowing that as a result, Donna would never let her go.

"What happened?" Donna asked quickly with a concerned voice.

"Cannon," she started. "Oh, I don't even know why I'm upset."

"What did he do?"

"He didn't really do anything," Hayden said, sounding almost as confused as she felt. "He's not even here."

"Oh my . . ." Donna paused, then whispered into the phone. "Did he go home with another woman last night?"

"No!" Hayden yelled, upset by Donna's suggestion. Is that what she really thought of Cannon? Is that what most people thought of him? "I'm just a little ticked off that he left without talking to me. He went to Los Angeles to help John with something. You remember John Dannell, the best man?"

"Yeah, I remember him." Donna paused again. "So you believe him?"

"What do you mean, do I believe him? Why wouldn't I?"

"I don't know. I guess you trust him more than I would. So who did you meet last night?" Donna's last sentence took on a much lighter tone than before.

"No one really," Hayden lied. She didn't feel like getting into an involved phone conversation now. She was also hesitant to mention her run ins with Lee Sampson, Robert Marks, and especially Joanne Pearl.

Hayden feared she was losing what little strands of her objectivity she had left, wondering if everyone saw Cannon as Donna did? She wouldn't lie and say she wasn't attracted to Cannon, but had that attraction begun to cloud her better judgment? She realized then, that although her only objective in this marriage had been to help her father get well with her mother at his side, Hayden knew there was now more to it. She had to find out who was spreading these rumors about Cannon and if the rumors were founded in truth. She needed to start by first finding out who this man she married really was.

Although she had spent her off-week keeping herself up to date on client issues, Hayden found herself seriously backed up at work Monday morning. She was disappointed that certain tasks had not been attended to by her assistant, but had to admit some satisfaction came from realizing the company couldn't get along as well without her. Her career at R&D was important to her now more than ever. She felt it was one of the very few things in her life she had some control over.

Intending to drop by Cannon's office on her lunch break, she was too overwhelmed at work and couldn't. She tried to duck out of her office a little early, only to run head on into a congratulations party put together by her coworkers. Determined to follow through with her plans, she finally made it to the State Building at six.

Feeling a little embarrassed as she walked through the heath department's offices, Hayden wasn't sure how to respond to all the well-wishers still working. None of them knew her at all, but were excessively kind. She was the boss's wife.

"What are you doing here?" The words jumped quickly from Maryann's lips as she first set eyes on Hayden.

"Maryann, it's nice to see you as well." She extended the woman a cordial smile. Although invited, Maryann chose not to attend the wedding. She told Cannon she was ill, but Hayden knew that wasn't the reason. She knew Maryann still had feelings for Cannon. Feelings strong enough to evoke revenge for a broken heart.

"I only say it that way because Cannon isn't here." Maryann made no attempt to hide her dislike for her boss's wife.

"I know he isn't," Hayden said, as she passed by Maryann and headed for the office. "He called and asked me to retrieve something for him for when he returns home."

"Why would he ask you?" Maryann jumped up from her chair, following Hayden into the office.

"I'm his wife, remember?" Hayden noticed Maryann's quick reaction to her entering Cannon's office. Was she afraid of Hayden finding something that would point to her?

"I know, but I'm his assistant." Maryann kept a watchful eye on Hayden. "He would call me if he needed something from the office. He just called me this morning and didn't mention you at all."

"It has nothing to do with work." Hayden couldn't ignore

that she felt a little something, knowing that Cannon took the time to call Maryann and not her.

"What is it?" Maryann asked, stepping closer as Hayden sat in Cannon's chair. "I know where everything is. I can get it for . . ."

"Maryann, please." Hayden was intrigued by Maryann's excessive interest. All the more reason for her to begin her search here. "I don't need your help. Cannon has told me where everything is. You can return to your desk."

Maryann's expression showed her distaste for Hayden's curt dismissal of her, but after a short hesitation, she openly rolled her eyes and sauntered out of the office, closing the door behind her. Hayden wondered if it was Maryann's desk she should be investigating instead of Cannon's.

After some time, frustration edged Hayden's nerves as she wasn't finding anything of interest either way. Ten minutes had gone by and Hayden knew Maryann would be returning soon. Office supplies, speech drafts, every health insurance form in creation, but nothing of use to give her a better idea of who Cannon Factor really was. She didn't even know what she was looking for as she moved to the dresser behind the desk and only found health magazines and newspaper articles.

She took a moment to look over some bills and run through his Rolodex. She found the phone numbers of several women listed only by their first name, including Joanne. She saw Farrah and Jennifer, the two women her mother spoke of. She also saw Cindy, one of the women Joanne said had come before her. Hayden wondered why they were still in his Rolodex, if they were really in the past like Cannon had told her. She didn't know if she could believe a word he said, and that bothered her more than she could have anticipated.

Deciding she would find nothing else, Hayden realized Cannon didn't keep many personal items in his office. With the exception of a picture of Tyler and another of his mother, his desk was bare of mementos.

"Did you find it?"

Hayden almost screamed as she jumped and looked up. She

wondered how long Maryann had been standing there. Fortunately at the moment, Hayden was simply admiring Cannon's awards and degrees nailed neatly on the wall behind his desk.

"Yes," Hayden said. "Yes I did." She felt the older woman's vehement stare as she passed her casually, wishing her a pleasant evening.

That evening Hayden attempted to go through Cannon's belongings in his bedroom, but the ringing of the phone in his office down the hall scared her so much she decided against it. She felt too guilty to enter his bedroom. She was still curious to find out about Cannon, but couldn't justify going through his personal belongings. Besides, she was afraid to find even more personal mementos to past or present secret affairs.

The ringing of his private office phone, reminded her that the office door was locked. She expected as much but couldn't help but wonder why? Was he hiding something in there? How would she know? How could she find out?

Her doubts about Maryann grew as well. Her suspicious behavior at the office intrigued Hayden. Thinking about Maryann, along with Joanne Pearl, Mavis, and Hayden's first choice, Dr. Robert Marks, made her head spin. By the time she went to bed, Hayden had been thinking about these suspects so much that she didn't even realize how alone she felt in the big empty condo.

"Hello?" Hayden's tired voice came through hoarse over the phone, which rang so early in the morning it startled her out of a comfortable sleep.

"Hayden, are you awake?" Cannon's voice came through strong and clear.

"Cannon? Is this you?" She sat up in bed, wide awake at the sound of his voice.

"Yes it is," he said. "I woke you, didn't I?"

"Sort of, but my alarm is set to go off in twenty minutes."

"How are you?" he asked.

"I'm fine." She could sense a sort of apprehension in his tone. "Is something wrong?"

"No, everything's fine."

"Cannon, it's seven in the morning here," she said. "That means its five in Los Angeles."

"I know." His voice sounded hesitant and uncertain. "My body is still on Chicago time. I feel like I have to get up."

Hayden waited in silence for a moment before speaking again. "Why did you call, Cannon?"

"I don't know." He paused for a moment. "I guess . . . Well I wanted to tell you I'll be home tomorrow."

"Okay." Still a little tired, she wasn't sure if he was talking slowly or she was interpreting it slowly, but something seemed odd about the entire conversation. "I got your note. You said so on it."

"Have you and Mother made any plans for the party yet?"

"Not really." Hayden sensed he was stalling for time. Time for what? "I mean, not us. We talked on the phone yesterday. As you might have guessed, she's pretty much planned everything."

"That's Mom." There was a quick, thin laugh. "Well, I guess I better go."

"Is everything okay with John?" She asked, remembering what his purpose for going to Los Angeles was.

"I guess things will be alright." Cannon sighed. "He's done what he's had to do."

"Is it about the practice?" She had thought to call Jesse, but wasn't sure if she had any right.

"Not so much the practice as John's personal financial problems. I'm helping him sell some property and get a loan from some old friends out here. Everything should be fine now."

"That's good news." Hayden felt the urge to console Cannon return as it had several times before. It was coming too often. "Is there anything else, Cannon?"

"No." He cleared his throat. "I do have something I'd like to talk to you about when I get back."

"What's wrong?" Apprehension swept through her remembering how they had left things between them.

"Nothing's wrong. Actually I hope it's something good."

"Okay, then I'll see you Wednesday when I get home from work." She felt an uneasy warmth as she said the word home. Like a married woman talking to her husband.

"Alright," he said. "My flight gets in at three. Maybe I can make dinner for us?"

"That sounds good." Actually, deep down inside Hayden thought it sounded great, but she wasn't ready to admit that to herself. "Goodbye, Cannon."

"Bye-bye, Hayden."

Cannon's phone call placed Hayden in a good mood for the first time in a while. She was glad the tension from Saturday seemed to be gone and looked forward to seeing him tomorrow evening. She was sure his news was an apology for his inappropriate words about Joanne Pearl the other night. She would forgive him, apologize herself and, they would try to be friends. Everything would be fine.

"Mrs. Factor! Mrs. Factor!"

Before entering her office building, Hayden turned her head at the sound of her name. She had been married for only a week and a half so it was understandable that the name still wasn't familiar to her.

"I've been waiting for you." Lee Sampson glanced at his watch. "It's nine thirty. You're a little late for work."

"What do you want, Sampson?" Hayden firmly gripped her briefcase at her side, standing tall against him.

"First," he said, placing a pen behind his left ear. "I would like to thank you for the invitation to the commissioner's announcement party. I plan to attend."

"Don't take it personally, Sampson," Hayden said sarcastically. "All of the health beat, as well as the political, reporters were invited."

"Nevertheless." He turned to walk away, but halted, pretending to have forgotten something. "Oh, yeah. I thought you'd like to see this."

Hayden watched as he reached into his torn-up purple duffle bag and pulled out a sheet of paper and offering it to her. She hesitated, throwing him a cautious glance, before accepting it. She felt a rush from her gut to her head as she saw a paper copy of a picture of Cannon just releasing from an embrace with a very beautiful woman.

"That picture was faxed to me this morning." Sampson retrieved the photo from a shocked Hayden. "As you can see from the background, it's in front of the Sheraton Grande in Los Angeles. It was taken last night."

Hayden swallowed hard, trying to hide the anger boiling within her.

"My source is superb, Mrs. Factor. They told me Cannon would be in Los Angeles and I asked a friend at a local paper to help me out a bit and trail him for a couple of hours." He seemed to notice the hurt look on her face. "Despite what you think, I'm not trying to hurt you. I just think Factor is a foul brother and I also think you have a right to know as well as the public that pays his very generous salary with their taxes."

"Obviously you want everyone to know. No matter who it hurts, right?" She was surprised at the choking sound of her voice. She was more upset than she thought.

"Okay." Sampson held up his hands, expressing guilt. "Sometimes I go too far. I'll tell you what. I won't print this picture or write this story, but if this goes on, I won't have a choice. This man wants to represent this state in Congress. The voters have a right to know."

"Thank you," was all Hayden could say as she watched him walk away. She sensed her own hot anger and flowing rage, but there was more. As ice spread through her entire body, she was assailed by a sense of bitterness. It was a feeling she wasn't accustomed to. How could he betray her? How could he lie to her?

What was the purpose of his call that morning? She went over every word again and again as she sat in her office. It could be as innocent as it sounded. It could have been about good news. She couldn't be sure, but wondered if it was about guilt. Had he spent the night with that woman and called Hayden out of guilt because he had broken their agreement? Had the woman just left Cannon's room that night before he called or had he just gotten back to his room from hers? What if she had been lying right next to him while he was on the phone with her? Hayden wasn't sure, but the thought made her feel as if she would be sick. Was Cannon returning to his old self? Hayden didn't want to believe it. Despite their occasional disagreements she had come to like him as a person. She wanted to believe him, but was that practical? This was the same man who, despite his charm and kindness, orchestrated a lie as big as a marriage to get something he wanted. Power he wanted. Would cheating be beneath him? Especially, when the marriage wasn't even real. It wouldn't take such a playboy heart not to be committed to something that in itself was a lie.

She purposefully avoided everyone at the office, allowing her despair to deepen as the day went on. She even put her foot down with Donna, refusing to discuss what was bothering her. Hayden knew she was stupid to let a mental picture of Cannon with the woman invade her mind and distract her all day, but she felt powerless to stop it. She tried over and over again to tell herself she was upset because this was a bad public relations move and her concern was about the public's perception, but it was the feeling of personal humiliation that told her differently. Forget the public.

As she drove through rush hour traffic toward the condo, she was forced to acknowledge the emotion that had threatened her peace of mind all day. It had nothing to do with appearances. She was jealous that Cannon was with another woman and frightened by her awakening to these feelings. Although the physical attraction was inevitable, the vow Hayden had made to stay uninvolved emotionally was now shattered. Despite his past, despite the rumors, she had found a way to develop strong feelings for Cannon, worse of all, it hurt her that he didn't feel the same.

Remembering their morning conversation, she wondered what he had to say to her upon returning? Was he going to tell her about the woman? Was he going to lie? Hayden decided she wouldn't give him the chance. Unwilling to face him or another night in the empty condo, she decided to pack some clothes and stay with her parents. She didn't care who knew.

"You miss him, don't you?"

Hayden looked up from her laptop computer to see her father standing in the doorway dressed in those same pajamas she could swear he'd worn since she was in high school.

"Who?" She turned away from the desk in the corner of her bedroom. Her parents had barely changed the room since she moved out five years ago. Its familiarity was a great comfort to her hurt feelings.

"I can tell from the way you've been acting." Tom Campbell walked into the room and sat on the edge of the twin bed, facing his daughter. "You've been in a bad mood since you arrived. It's your first time apart."

"I suppose." Hayden felt emotion catch in her throat at her father's words. She would give anything to fall on his lap and sob about what a mess she's made of her life.

"I remember that," Tom said with a gentle smile. He looked past Hayden, out the window and into sweet memories.

Forgetting her work, Hayden turned her full attention to her father as he spoke. She loved sharing his memories with him.

"Your mother and I were married for only three months before her mom, Alva, died." He lowered his head in respect for a moment. "Your mother left for Tennessee immediately, but I had to stay behind. I'd just gotten a new job at the junior high and couldn't leave until the weekend."

"It was hard on you wasn't it?" Hayden joined her father on the bed. It had been a while since they had shared like this. She could tell he was feeling much better and it made her heavy heart rejoice.

"Terrible," he said. "I wanted to be there for her more than anything. I felt selfish, because I couldn't help but feel sorry for myself because I was so lonely.''

''I felt the same.''

They both turned to see Elise standing in the doorway, her eyes set tenderly on her husband.

''You think you felt guilty?'' She rolled down her sleeves, having just finished washing the dinner dishes. ''My mother, that I loved with all my heart, had died and I couldn't stop wanting to be with my husband.''

''Nothing in this world could compare to the relief I felt when I saw you again.'' He held out his hand to Elise.

Hayden felt her heart warm and tears swell in her throat as she watched her mother grasp her father's hand tightly. She could feel their love for each other as thick as a dense fog.

''One thing could,'' Elise said, ''and that was my relief when you held me in your arms. I knew then, everything was going to be alright even with Mama gone.''

Tears trickled from her eyes as Hayden witnessed the love and affection a real marriage held. It made her hurt all the more, stuck in a loveless marriage for the next year.

''Don't cry, princess,'' Tom said as he reached his other hand out to Hayden. ''He'll be back tomorrow.''

''And tonight you're here with us.'' Elise gave Hayden a wink. ''Maybe we can't compete with the love of a new husband, but we'll have to do.''

''I think you'll do,'' Hayden said through her tears, thinking only of how she could ever bring herself to tell her parents the truth after it was all over. She couldn't take the lie to her grave, it was killing her already. She would have to find a way.

She also knew she would have to find a way to handle what was going on between her and Cannon, no matter how much it upset her. It would take time, but whatever she came up with would be worth it. Her family hadn't felt this close since before the attack and anything was worth that.

Hayden vowed to find a way to fight her emerging emotions for Cannon. It would all be worth it in the end. One day she would get married for love and feel those same feelings expressed before her now. What she was going through at the moment was no big deal. She thought it fortunate she had pinpointed her feelings at their start and was sure she could end them just as quickly as she had discovered them.

Chapter Eight

The next day, Hayden felt no better. Again she did her best to avoid everyone at work and fortunately for her, Donna was busy planning a publicity tour for another of R&D's clients, leaving her too swamped with work to harass Hayden about her somber mood.

Heading down the street to pick up her lunch and bring it back to her desk, she saw Robert Marks at the newsstand. She was surprised to see him out of the blue that way, but wondered if it was a coincidence. Was he hanging around her office, purposefully trying to tease her, knowing that he had linked the news of Cannon's betrayal to Sampson? She had half a mind to approach him and chew him out, but her emotions were drained. So much for the master sleuth. Cannon had even succeeded in robbing her of her ever-present curiosity.

When Marcy came over the intercom to tell her Cannon was on the line, Hayden sharply ordered her to tell him she was busy. She knew she needed to speak with him, but wasn't ready yet. She didn't know what to say to make things better. She couldn't get past the hurt and anger she was feeling toward him. She was also worried about what it was he had to say to her.

Sensing the hostility, Marcy only gave a cautious smile as she delivered the message from Cannon to her desk. The note read:

Back home. See you for dinner. Can you get off early?
                                                    Cannon

Was that sweetness she sensed in the message? Little did he know what she knew. Get off early, he asked. Her vindictive side had a short spurt as she decided to return to her parents' home instead of the condo. To avoid having to speak with him, on her way out of the office Hayden had Marcy call Cannon at home and leave the message with him. He could have dinner alone.

In all of her childish planning, Hayden forgot she had already told her parents Cannon would be home Wednesday afternoon. She was reminded when she saw their surprise as she stepped into the house.

"What are you doing here?" Elise looked up from the sofa, her eyes wide with unexpectedness.

"I had to visit our copy supplier in Skokie." Hayden placed her purse on the coat rack as she smiled at her father. Tom gave her a quick wink before returning to the basketball game on the television. "I just thought I would stop by for a while."

"Isn't Cannon expecting you?" Elise asked.

"Uh . . . uhm, his flight is later than I thought." Hayden turned from her mother's unassuming stare. She hated saying lie on top of lie. She would have to go home to the condo that night, but wanted to buy as much time as she could to build up her confidence. As long as Cannon realized she wasn't about to run home from work to see him, then her message would have gotten across.

"Really?" Elise looked to her husband in confusion. "Tom, didn't Cannon call?"

"Yeah," Tom responded without turning his head from the game.

"What was he . . ." Elise sighed impatiently in the middle

of her sentence as she walked into the living room and turned the television off. "Dr. Kent said you can't watch this stuff."

"It's the playoffs, baby," Tom pleaded.

"All the more reason." Elise clicked the remote, turning the television back on, but to the nature channel. "You get too excited."

"Cannon called?" Hayden felt anxiety begin to set in. She would never be able to keep all the lies straight. "What did he say?"

"He said he thought you would be coming here," Tom said. "At first he asked if everything was okay. He seemed to think you were coming over because something was wrong with me. When I told him I was fine and we weren't expecting you, he said okay and hung up."

"Where would he be calling from?" Elise inquired. "The plane? Is he at O'Hare airport?"

"I'm not sure." Hayden wished her mother would stop asking so many questions, but why wouldn't they be concerned? After all, she was his wife, his newlywed wife at that. Shouldn't she know where he was?

"You should beep him on that pager thing he has," Elise said, walking toward the kitchen. "We already ate, but I'll fix you a plate."

"Thanks, Mama." Hayden's mood quickly improved at the thought of home-cooked food for the second night in a row. It had been a while. She herself, was nowhere near a chef and Cannon was even worse.

"Hand me that remote, baby girl." Tom pointed at the television remote control next to Hayden as she sat down on the living room sofa.

"What do you want to watch, daddy?" Hayden hid the object from her father's eager eye "I'll flip to it for you."

"Turn to the game real quick." He gave her a sneaky wink.

"No, Daddy." Hayden cruised the channels for something to watch. With the exception of a few shows, she rarely watched television and had no idea what was on.

"Come on, honey," he said, eyebrows folding downward in frustration. "While she's in the kitchen."

"When your heart gets better, I'll buy you a satellite dish and you can watch three basketball games a day."

"The playoffs are going to end soon." He lowered his shoulders in defeat.

"Fine, then next year." She set the television to WGN, Chicago's Superstation. "Perfect. A Cubs game. Nice and slow. This will be good for you." She smiled as he mumbled under his breath, leaning back in his favorite used and tattered Lazy-Boy chair.

"Hayden," Elise called from the kitchen. "Do you want peas or corn or both?"

"Both," she called back.

"How much?" Elise returned.

"What is this yelling?" Tom asked. "I can't enjoy my game."

"Oh, please." Hayden jokingly tapped him on the shoulder as she headed for the kitchen.

Her senses enlivened by the wonderful smells, Hayden took the plate her mother handed her and placed a healthy portion of everything she could find. With a prideful grin, Elise watched her daughter gather up the food until the doorbell rang.

"So much for the leftovers I was planning for tomorrow." She laughed as she left to answer the door.

Hayden smiled a playfully guilty smile at her mother as she watched her walk out of the kitchen. Something was changing between the two of them. She couldn't put her finger on it, but she didn't feel that missing feeling as strong as she used to. Not as strong, but it was still there and Hayden knew she needed to take advantage of the good vibe going between them and reveal her feelings.

As she placed her plate on the counter to raid the refrigerator for a soda, Hayden felt chills run down her spine. It wasn't the cold from the refrigerator that caused it, but Cannon's voice as he said her name.

She turned to face him, standing in the doorway to the kitchen and was amazed that her first emotion was contentment. Despite the anger and anxiety she'd been feeling because of him over the past couple of days, more than anything she was glad to see him again.

"Hello, Hayden." Cannon stared at her with tired and confused eyes.

"Hello." Her gaze focused on his long, lean form. He looked his usual ingenuously appealing self in black jeans and a gray button-down polo shirt. He stood tall and confident, exuding an unintentional sexual magnetism that gave her a strong enough discomfort to make her return to the refrigerator.

"Hayden," Cannon whispered as he walked toward her. He wanted to touch her, to tell her all he felt inside, but her hostility toward him was evident. "Don't you think we should hug or something? For your parents, at least?"

"No," Hayden said curtly, grabbing a cola and slamming the refrigerator door shut. She looked directly into the living room. "They can't see us."

"Alright." He continued to follow her as she took her plate and settled herself at the kitchen table. What was wrong with her? "Why are you here? I told you I was making dinner. I have something to tell you."

"I miss my parents." She refused to look at him, although the tenderness of his voice gave her a sense of urgency, wanting to touch him. With her appetite all of a sudden gone, she merely played with her plate.

"I understand." He paused for a moment, observing her with a half smile. She was the most beautiful women he'd ever seen. Her face held a look of glamour, yet maintained a tender sweetness. He could look at her forever. "It's nice to see you."

Like a knee-jerk reaction to his words, Hayden lifted her head, her eyes catching his. She was touched deep within by the gleam of eagerness in his eyes.

"That's what I wanted to speak to you about." He smiled nervously and took a seat across from her at the table. He felt the butterflies in his stomach flutter wildly. "I really don't know how to say this."

"What? What is it?" Her own eagerness and curiosity showed in her wide eyes.

"Something happened when I was in LA," he said, hoping he wasn't about to make a mistake. No, it couldn't be. This was right, he was sure of it.

So this was it, Hayden thought, leaning back in her chair. He was going to tell her about this woman, and in her parents' kitchen at that! He had followed his pants' zipper instead of his head and could no longer go along with the charade. Well, Hayden thought, she would have her say first.

"I think it's utterly shameful what you've done." She spoke in a strong whisper, firmly entwining her arms across her chest.

"What?" he asked with a dazed expression.

"That's right, Cannon." She eyed him assessingly. "What you're about to tell me, I already know and I felt like a fool at first for being surprised. I knew you lacked morals or standards of any kind, but I assumed you were a competent businessman that could keep a business agreement. That was my fault."

"What in the hell are you talking about?" Confusion turned to anger as a frown set into his features. Her insults were like stabs at his heart.

"What's the matter?" She gave him a cold, teasing glare. "Did my knowing ruin the story you planned?"

"Hayden . . ." he began in a harsh whisper.

"How could you, Cannon?" She cut him off, her anger from the previous two days rearing her on. "Not that I care who you sleep with, but how could you enter into this . . . this arrangement so strongly and go weak so soon? Is it that hard for you to control your needs?" She felt her throat fill with emotion and quickly turned her face from his view. She couldn't stand for him to notice her jealousy.

"Hayden, I suggest you calm down now and tell me what you're talking about." His voice was low and cool as he stared at her frankly, hiding his pained emotions. "Has Sampson written another lie about me?"

"No, he didn't." Hayden cleared her throat, mustering all the strength she could to maintain her composure. "He showed me the picture of you with that woman in Los Angeles in front of the Sheraton Grande. Out of pity for me, your betrayed wife, he promised not to run it. Do you have any idea how embarrassing an experience that was?''

After a short silence, Cannon sighed and shook his head, wondering how in the world Sampson followed him to LA. ''Hayden, was the woman wearing a candy apple red dress with short black hair?''

''Of course.''

Cannon smiled in amusement and said, ''He followed me to LA.''

''You think this is funny?'' Her anger boiling to the top, she wanted to slap him now. ''You make a fool out of me and it's funny?''

''No, Hayden, but it's a misunderstanding.'' He leaned across the small table. ''That was Tiffany Shields. You already know about her.''

''That was Tiffany?'' Hayden remembered the name as the woman Mavis told her Cannon spoke with on the phone the morning they were planning the wedding at Candace's Glencoe home. The day Cannon kissed her for the first time.

''Yes.'' He reached into his back pocket and pulled a picture out of his wallet. ''She gave me this picture before I left.''

Hayden didn't take the photograph but leaned over to look closely at it as Cannon held it out to her. There was no doubt Tiffany was the woman in the picture with Cannon before. She looked just as lovely in this picture standing with a handsome bearded man and a young boy.

''She's very pretty.'' Embarrassed beyond words, Hayden lowered her head to the table. She did her best to hold onto some pride.

''It's the glow,'' Cannon said, as he returned the picture to his wallet and placed it back in his pocket. ''She's three months pregnant. The man is her husband, Geoffrey, and her son is Jake. Tiffany and I had dinner after she stopped by my hotel.''

''Oh.'' Hayden felt even worse now, if that was possible. I'm . . . I'm sorry.''

"You really think I'm some kind of animal with uncontrollable urges, don't you?" His voice was stern, his expression serious.

"I said I was sorry." She attempted to make eye contact with him, but was only able to look at him briefly. Shame veered her eyes to the left. "I've just made a complete fool of myself. Please don't make it worse."

"That would take a lot," he said. "I don't think I could top the show you just performed here."

Hayden merely rolled her eyes, unable and unwilling to respond.

"What do I have to do, Hayden?" he asked desperately. "What do I have to do to make you believe I'm not that kind of guy?"

"I'm sorry, Cannon." She forced a friendly smile his way. "It's me. I'm tired and hungry."

"So am I, but you don't see me taking it out on anyone." Cannon made sure to keep his voice low. "And it isn't just now. You've always felt this way about me."

"What do I expect?" she asked defensively. "I see you in an embrace with her. I know about your past. You've admitted to it."

"That was long ago." His expression was a mask of stone, mimicking the hardness of his heart at the mistrust in her eyes. "How long does a person have to answer to his past? Or should I ask, how long do you use a person's past against them?"

"I'm not using it against you." She returned to playing with her food, fighting to keep her emotions out of this conversation. She didn't trust herself not to say something utterly foolish. "I'm not some holier than thou type of person."

"You could have fooled me."

"I'm sorry, Cannon," she said, hurt by the disappointed tone of his voice. "I jumped to the wrong conclusion."

"Yeah, whatever." Cannon waved a dismissing hand, standing up. He wanted to be grateful this unfortunate scene took place before he told Hayden what it was he had really wanted to tell her, but he wasn't. He was tired and not looking forward to work tomorrow. He didn't want to feel a thing, only get some food and some sleep. "It really doesn't matter now, does it?"

Hayden wasn't exactly sure what he meant by those words, but they hurt regardless. Things had gone from bad to worse and no matter how much she wanted to spread the blame, she couldn't help but feel it was all her fault.

Neither of them spoke barely a word to each other for the next couple of hours. Elise offered Cannon a plate, which he readily accepted and they all sat in the living room watching television and talking about this and that. Cannon put on the charm for her parents, but Hayden could tell he was upset and withdrawn and she felt awful for it.

On the ride home, he spoke briefly of the campaign party, finding out Hayden hadn't paid much attention to how it was coming along. He wanted her to care. Not only because it was her job according to their deal, but because it was so important to him. He was stupid to think she cared about his future. After all, she'd made it clear she wanted nothing to do with him. Cannon was angry at himself for letting it hurt him so much. He thought maybe Hayden had just done them both a favor.

As they finally reached the condo, Hayden was relieved. She could finally get away from Cannon and the guilt that his presence was making her feel. She wanted to lock herself in her bedroom forever. She wanted to be angry for having to lie to her parents. She wanted to be angry at Cannon, but knew she had no cause. She had jumped to conclusions and attacked him ruthlessly. So much for wanting to decrease the tension that existed between them.

As she walked through the foyer, she quietly said good night. Cannon didn't respond as he turned to the answering machine and listened to the message. As Hayden passed the dining room the sparkle of the chandelier caught her eye and she looked in. Candace's voice on the machine faded into the background as Hayden saw the dining room table.

It was as beautiful as anything she'd ever seen, covered with a white terry cloth sheet braided with speckles of soft pink, which draped the edges of the round table. Two china plates and saucers were placed neatly across from each other with silverware and white cloth napkins laid beside them. Next to the table, a bottle of wine stood, sweating in its holder, surrounded by water that was once ice. Two peach candles, melted to deformity, lay in the middle of the table, the flame long since blown out.

"I made filet mignon."

Hayden looked over her shoulder as Cannon stood in the doorway. He wasn't looking at her, but at the table with a grim expression on his face.

"What is . . . ?" She was speechless as she briefly lifted the bottle of wine, then lowered it as it seemed to weigh one hundred pounds.

"It was our dinner." He walked to the table and began gathering things together. He was too tired to protect his pride. "It was what I wanted to talk to you about."

Hayden suddenly remembered that before she'd made a fool of herself in her parent's kitchen, he had told her he wanted to tell her something. *Something that happened in Los Angeles.*

"What was it, Cannon?" She tried to correct her eyes as she stepped out of his way so he could place the silverware in the breakfront against the wall, but he wouldn't look at her.

"It's not important," he said, only wishing that were true.

"I want to know," she insisted, feeling herself pulled to him, wanting nothing more than to hear him speak to her, look at her.

"Alright." He stood still, tall and firm like a tree, staring at her boldly. He felt he had nothing to lose. At least nothing he hadn't already lost. "I planned a romantic dinner for us."

"Romantic?" Hayden asked, her eyes widening in wonder.

"Yes, Hayden." A look of disappointment centered in his eyes. "When I was in Los Angeles, I was in a constant state of restlessness and distraction. It didn't take me long to figure out why. I missed you. It hit me weird, I mean I knew I was attracted to you. You're just about the most beautiful woman I've ever met, but I didn't know I cared. At least not like I really did. I thought maybe I could try. Maybe I could try to make this, what we have, something real. Something more than what it was.''

Hayden stood stunned as Cannon turned his back to her and walked toward the kitchen. Something in her drove her to follow him. She wanted to hear more, but at the same time did not. Her head was spinning, her heart pumping wildly.

''I didn't know.'' She wanted words to express her emotions, but could find none.

''What difference would it make?'' His tone wasn't angry, but still harsh. ''All that's ever on your mind is how much of a moral louse I am.''

''Cannon, I . . .'' She felt her words catch in her throat as emotion threatened to overcome her. She would have never expected to react this way to news that he cared for her, wanted more with her.

''Don't worry, Hayden.'' He covered the two steaks with plastic wrap and placed them carelessly in the refrigerator. He was doing everything he could to control his own emotions. He was determined to hold onto what pride he had left. ''It was a stupid idea in the first place. I'm glad you stopped me. If this is going to work, we have to keep things strictly professional. If your believing I'm a player accomplishes that, then go right ahead.''

After watching him walk away, Hayden fell helplessly into a chair. As she stood alone in the kitchen, thoughts came as fast as lightening. What had just happened? she asked herself. Was it real? Had she been wrong all along? Not only was Cannon not with another woman, but he was missing her! He had planned this beautiful, romantic evening and she had ruined it all. She let her jealousy and insecurity get in the way of everything.

What was everything anyway, she wondered? It was more than physical attraction, that was agreed. Hayden had found out the hard way two days ago that she had feelings for Cannon and now he had admitted he had feelings for her. At least he did before she had blown up, accusing him of being weak and promiscuous.

As she tossed and turned in her bed that night, Hayden forced herself to believe it was for the best things hadn't worked out. Cannon was right. If this *marriage* was going to work for both of them, they had to keep it professional. If one good thing came from tonight, it was that she was certain her actions had turned off any feelings Cannon was beginning to have for her. Hayden saw it as an incentive for her to do the same with her emerging emotions. The closest they could ever be was friends, but Hayden wasn't sure that was even possible after tonight. Not only had she made a fool of herself, but she had seriously hurt his feelings. She was certain of that from the look on his face as he cleared away the table. Besides, she wasn't sure what kind of relationship they could have had that was based from its beginning on a lie.

The next morning Cannon had already left for work by the time Hayden came out of her bedroom to make breakfast. Disappointed, she was certain he was trying to avoid her. Reflecting back she felt even worse about what had happened last night and try as she would to forget it, she couldn't. The last thing she wanted was for him to feel he had to leave his own home to avoid her merely because she had made a stupid assumption.

Feeling terribly alone as she ate her cereal alone in the kitchen, Hayden was determined to fix things. Fix or at least repair them as best she could. A lot of damage had obviously been done not just last night, but from the onset as Cannon had indicated. Hayden knew she couldn't take her biting words back, but she would try to befriend him, being as supportive as possible from now on. She would try to trust him and at the same time try to control any personal feelings she had for him.

All in all, she thought he was a nice guy. He was extremely intelligent and caring. He was committed to his goal and willing to work hard for it. He was friendly and charming. Yes, she had questions about his moral character, but she wouldn't be personally involved with him so she determined not to make that an issue between them. As business partners they could come to civil terms and as friends they could actually enjoy each other's company. Even if that was a long shot, Hayden at least wanted the uncomfortable tension between them to go away.

She wasn't too encouraged for that to happen as she found a note on the foyer ledge on her way out the door.

Mother will take care of everything for the party. Maryann and Warren will be over at seven tonight to go over the speech. Remember, Maryann is not aware of our situation, so make sure your bedroom is locked. If you're going to need anything, put it in my room.

Hayden would not allow the cool, authoritarian tone of the note get to her. She was still committed to her goal of getting along with Cannon. She would go out of her way to help Candace plan the party and help Cannon prepare his speech. As an added gift, she would put forth an extra effort to be nice to Maryann, although she still suspected her of possibly leaking rumors to the press.

It was six fifteen when Cannon arrived home that evening. Hayden stopped preparing the dining room table, and stepped into the hallway to greet him.

"Hi." He responded to her kind greeting with a little surprise. Looking her over quickly, he observed the teal green jumper she wore. He was beginning to believe this woman could be a knockout wearing a potato sack. "Is that what you wore to work today?"

"No, of course not, silly." She returned to the dining room, knowing he was following her. "I left work a little early and changed for the evening."

"What is this?" He watched as she placed the silverware and napkins on the table.

"They'll be here at seven, right?" She made sure her tone was jovial, as if they had never argued. As if last night was forgotten. "I thought I'd whip up a little something. Do you think it's too much?"

"What did you make?" Her mood was contagious. He pleasantly smiled and followed his nose to the kitchen.

"Spaghetti." This time Hayden followed him. She briefly flushed at how athletic his physique was from behind. With his suit jacket off, the definitions of his firm muscles were visible underneath the white cotton Calvin Klein shirt. "It's not very glamorous, but if you hadn't noticed yet, it's the only thing I know how to make."

"You make it great." He quickly dipped his index finger in the low boiling saucepot over the oven. Tasting a bit, he savored the garlic taste.

"It's one of those hard to mess up meals." She shooed him aside in order to check the bread in the oven. Not wanting to feel uncomfortable, she did her best to ignore the strong desire within her for his praise and approval. "I can't take credit for the garlic bread. I picked it up on the way home."

"My mother called this afternoon." He placed his black leather briefcase on the kitchen table. "She said you called earlier today and spoke. She appreciated your help."

"I did nothing, really," she said nonchalantly. "I made some changes with catering and decorations, updated the RSVP list, and reconfirmed with the band."

"You didn't have to," Cannon said.

"I wanted to." She gave him a wide smile, amused by his confusion. "It's what we agreed. What would your mother think if I, as your newlywed wife, appeared too busy to help plan your campaign party? I'm actually pretty excited about it all."

"I'm just surprised," he said, wanting to say more, but decided against it. He could only stare at her with an electrifying interest glowing in his light eyes. For a moment, he pretended it was real. He was sitting in his kitchen talking to his beautiful wife. They were a family.

She pretended to be unaware of his gaze as she went about her business in the kitchen, but she knew he was there. He was leaning against the wall, watching her. After a short while, she flipped her head back casually and said, ''You have time to change, too, but you'd better hurry. They'll be here in a few.''

''I suppose so,'' he said, grabbing his briefcase and heading for his bedroom.

She wasn't completely facing him, but she thought she saw a very wide smile on his face. She hoped now that last night could be forgotten.

Being nice to Maryann was difficult, but Hayden managed to do it throughout the evening. By herself, Hayden went over Friday night's speech, written by Cannon while he was in Los Angeles. She was impressed by the clarity with which he stated his intentions and goals and the understanding way he expressed the needs of those he wanted to serve. Hayden felt almost unnecessary as she made very few edits. They made the decision that his campaign theme would be, *returning politics to the people,* portraying him not as a politician, but as a caring citizen with the opportunity and desire to improve life for everyone in the state of Illinois by taking their grievances to Washington. It went very well with a speech that came across as personal and informal instead of political and ambivalent. Hayden particularly liked his emphasis on children, with his reason being that they are the focus of everything in the present and the future of Illinois. She found his supporting points to be strong and substantiated, but not overly aggressive or intimidating. In her opinion, Cannon was fully qualified and perfectly capable of being the next senator for the state of Illinois.

Cannon seemed very flattered by Hayden's compliments as she reviewed her suggestions with the three of them. She felt a strong sense of pride as he, as well as Maryann and Warren, listened quietly and attentively as she clued them in on how to handle the press and scheduling.

Cannon showed respectful acknowledgment of Hayden's career as well as his own by planning most of the campaign visits in the evenings and on weekends. Hayden's suggestion was for an initial saturation of the news for the next two weeks, then a gradual slow down focusing more on fund-raising until two months before the election. Then the saturation would resume. The first plan of action was to acquire volunteers for the campaign. Warren suggested it would be no problem, especially since the college year was ending. There would be plenty of young, eager volunteers. Cannon was working very hard on the mayor's endorsement, which would not only bring in tons of campaign contributions, but would allocate some of the city's campaign volunteer resources.

They would visit every hospital in Chicago and its surrounding suburbs next week since health care was his strong point. Their focus would be the children's wards. From there, nursing homes and public housing districts. Hayden was sure Cannon's youth, vigor, and vision for the future would appeal to the university set, but since most college semesters were over, they would wait until late August to visit the schools across Illinois. They would start with Northwestern University, then the University of Chicago, DePaul, and Loyola. The next step would be to move outside Chicago to the University of Illinois, and Southern and Northern Illinois Universities.

"You've got to go to Springfield at least once a month," Maryann said, as she took notes in short hand.

Hayden had been studying Maryann's behavior closely all night. Although she showed no enthusiasm or excitement, Maryann was a constant participant in the planning. This led Hayden to wonder why would she want to ruin Cannon's reputation? Knowing that Cannon had spurned her right before the rumors started and that she was the last to have known possession of the incriminating picture of Cannon and Jackson Wells still made Hayden suspicious of her. That, coupled with the fact that she was one of the few people initially aware that

Cannon was in Los Angeles. As city officials are obligated to leave their whereabouts with their office, there were several people who could have found that information out, but Maryann could have been Lee Sampson's source.

"We'll do that before the end of June." Cannon, now changed into comfortable, baggy sweats, squeezed his eyes shut several times. It was late and he was getting tired. "I know several people downstate who will support me. That can be our first official fund-raiser, ASAP."

"Sounds good." Maryann wrote a reminder on her pad. "Plan Springfield fund-raiser."

"I don't know about you guys," Hayden said, unable to stifle a yawn. "But I'm really getting tired."

"You're right," Warren agreed, as he began gathering his things together. "It's almost one in the morning and I told Gladys I'd be home by midnight. We've gone over everything we need for tomorrow at least. I'm having lunch with the mayor in the afternoon. I'll let you know what he thinks."

"Sounds good." Cannon stood, holding out his hand to help Maryann off the sofa, but she refused. Hayden noticed the rejection, and wasn't sure what to make of it. It could be disdain, but also an effort on Maryann's part to avoid any embarrassing miscomfort. She knew Maryann still cared for Cannon and was possibly too unsure about what reaction his touch might evoke from her. Hayden knew from experience there was a certain feeling she got from Cannon's touch, even casually. That was why she purposefully avoided physical contact.

"I wouldn't mind," Cannon continued, too tired to notice Maryann's rejection, "if you were late for work tomorrow. I'm sure I will be."

"I'll be in at nine sharp," Maryann added, with a defiant smile. "I'm sure the phones will be as busy as they have been all week."

"Okay." Cannon led the two guests to the door. "At least you should leave early. I need you to be at the Hyatt before the press shows up."

"Of course." She spoke in her usual short tone as she nodded in Hayden's direction. "Good night."

"Good night, Maryann," Hayden said with a wide smile. She felt almost sorry for her. It's hard enough to have to face the man you love every day after he rejected you. It must be even worse to visit the home he shares with another woman, believing they were in love. Could anger over Cannon's rejection of her have caused her to start the rumors?

Hayden began clearing away the food as Cannon shared a few words with Warren. As she placed the silverware and dirty dishes in the dishwasher, she felt proud of the effort she had put forth in reversing some of the prior night's damage. Although tired, Cannon seemed to be in a great mood, focused on the campaign and eager to face the task ahead. Hayden still sensed tension between them, but it wasn't an unbearable kind. It was still strong, but she was certain it would go away as soon as they immersed themselves in the overwhelming obligations of the campaign.

"Why don't you go to sleep?" Cannon asked as he entered the kitchen. "I'll take care of all this."

"No, you've done enough." She smiled easily at him. "I'm just going to throw these dishes in the washer and put the food in the fridge."

"Then I'll help." He rolled up his sleeves, helping her place the food in tupperware cartons. "You have to get your sleep. You don't want to be in late for work tomorrow."

"I won't be at work at all tomorrow," Hayden said. Roger was understanding when she'd asked for the day off. She had worked extra hours as well as through lunch the day before and Roger always had confidence in her ability to more than make up for time off.

"You're taking the day off?" Cannon was confused by this sudden and cheerful commitment she seemed to have developed, but he wouldn't question it. He would only enjoy it.

"Yes," she answered, as she turned the dishwasher on. "I knew the evening would last long and I have a lot to prepare for tomorrow."

"You and Mother are doing a great job. What more needs to be done? Maybe I can help?"

"Everything is taken care of, thanks. I thought I'd spend the day connecting with my contacts at the newspapers and television stations. I want to make sure we get as much free publicity as possible." Because of her line of work, Hayden had made several associates in the media industry. They were mostly in the business arena, but had influence across the board.

"That would be great." Cannon kept his eyes straight ahead. He could see her, from his side view, bending over the dishwasher and he fought the arousal that wanted to grow. Don't mess this up, he ordered himself.

"I also have a hair appointment at two and I have to pick up my dress." She leaned against the sink, watching with amusement as Cannon strained to find room in the refrigerator for the food. She knew he wasn't accustomed to seeing so much food in there.

"I know you'll look incredible," he said, turning to face her, his eyes catching hers. If she wasn't so beautiful it wouldn't be so hard to be this close to her and not touch her lustrous hair, her soft cheeks, or her full lips.

"Thank you." Hayden turned away, disturbed by his gaze. His tender eyes, as tired as they were, looked incredibly seductive under the dim light of the kitchen.

"You've really gone out of your way today." He took a step closer to her, his voice gentle and warm. He couldn't fight it, although he heard the distant voice that reminded him she wanted nothing to do with him on a personal level. She was gorgeous and the pull was stronger than that distant voice.

"Not really." Hayden removed her apron and placed it on the hook against the wall. Something told her to run, but somewhere else a voice said to stay. Which would she listen to? "This was our agreement, Cannon. You help my father get the best care possible at no cost and I help you run for senator."

"Yes." Cannon's voice went flat as his mouth spread into a thin-lipped smile. He was angry at himself for expecting there to be more to it than that. Even after last night, he hadn't learned his lesson. "Good night, Hayden."

"Good night," she said back, noting the distinct hardening of his expression and the long exhausted sigh he heaved before leaving the room.

She wondered if she'd said something wrong. It was not overt, but it was obvious to her that his mood had suddenly changed. She had thought he'd be happy to hear she was interested in doing her part. He had, without a doubt, done his.

Not wanting to ruin the feeling of success she felt after a good night, Hayden decided to attribute Cannon's reaction to fatigue and sleepiness. She knew if she became negative and focused on her personal feelings, things would never work. She had to stick to the business at hand and make this arrangement as pleasant as possible for everyone. Blowing every expression and look Cannon made out of proportion wouldn't help things.

"You're a genius, Carla," Hayden said, looking at her new hair style in the mirror. She had thought an up-do would be more elegant, but Carla assured her, a flowing wave, parted in the middle would look perfect and she had been right.

"Girl, you say that every time." Carla Houston stood back, admiring the work she had done. Founder and owner of Carla's Place on Howard Street, where Evanston met Chicago, Carla had been doing Hayden's hair since Hayden was fifteen years old.

"It's true," Hayden said, swiveling her chair around in order to observe the back. "You deserve compliments every time."

"Forget the compliments." Carla held up the small mirror for Hayden to get a better contrasting view. "If you keep letting your hair grow, I'm going to start charging you more money. Especially now that you're a future senator's wife."

"Anything you want." Hayden stood up, giving the fifty-year-old woman a quick hug. "No price is too high for this magic."

Hayden knew she appeared vain as she twisted and turned

her head, her hair flowing back and forth as light as a feather against her soft delicate neck. She stopped with a flush, realizing her first thought was how impressed Cannon would be when he saw her. She had to remind herself to put an end to those kinds of thoughts.

"So what's next on the list?" Carla stepped behind the front desk, running Hayden's credit card through the machine. "You know, I can give you a manicure real quick."

"No time," Hayden said. "My nails are in good shape. Thanks anyway. I'm on my way to pick up my dress."

"You'll look like Cinderella." Carla sat back in her torn-up old chair. The shop had been newly decorated two years ago with an LA chic design, but Carla held onto the chair, saying it was the first thing she brought into the store and would be the last thing she brought out.

"Well, I am a little excited." Hayden could feel the butter-flies in her stomach.

"Why does every woman say that when I enter the room?"

Slipping her purse over her shoulder, Hayden turned to face the voice.

Alec Gavin was a handsome young man. As he stood in the doorway to the salon, Hayden was reminded of why she'd been so attracted to him. He had an athletic, college boy look, his tawny brown skin blended perfectly with the neutral-colored clothes he always wore. His appealing face was friendly and confident.

"Alec?" Hayden almost whispered his name in surprise at the sight of him.

"Hello, Hayden." His mouth softened as he rapidly glanced her up and down.

"What are you doing here?" She walked toward him, want-ing to hug him, but not knowing if she should. She searched inside herself for feelings she expected to resurface, but couldn't find them. At least they weren't as strong as they used to be.

"I'm in town for a wedding." He took hold of both her hands and held them in his own. "You remember my cousin, Clive?"

"I remember him." She felt a slight sense of satisfaction as she detected the attraction in his eyes at the sight of her. He must miss her some. He must regret, at least some of the time, never asking her to come with him.

"He's getting married tomorrow. I went by your office down-town and Marcy said you had a hair appointment around two today." He looked around the salon. "I remember picking you up from this place a lot, so I tried it. I guess I'm lucky."

"Lucky," Carla mumbled from behind the front desk. "Lucky, but a little too late."

"Now, Carla." Hayden swung around, winking at the woman whose arms were crossed defiantly. As most people do, Hayden had told her hairdresser the details of her relation-ship with Alec, including the pain his leaving caused her.

"It's alright," Alec said with a laugh. "I heard the news. My sister Bobbi called me in Atlanta last week." He swallowed hard before saying, "Congratulations."

"Thank you." Hayden lowered her head, hoping he wouldn't read the shame on her face at her lie. Alec wasn't a very sensitive man and was never too good at reading her feelings, but she didn't want to take any chances.

"It's so great seeing you again," he said, shaking his head as if not believing she was there. "I've been thinking about you a lot, Hayden."

She wasn't sure how to respond to those words. A couple of months ago she would have jumped into his arms, forgetting and forgiving all that was done in the past, but now things were different. She couldn't ignore the tiny tug at her heart at the sight of him, but those feelings that had kept her up crying all those nights were gone.

Noticing Carla's annoyed expression at his presence, Alec suggested they get some coffee and talk.

"I don't drink coffee, remember?" She waved goodbye to Carla and led Alec out onto the sidewalk.

"Just a figure of speech." He shoved nervous hands into his khaki pants.

"I really can't, Alec." She faced him with more confidence

than she had figured she would be able to, seeing him again
for the first time, and so soon after. "I've got to pick up my
gown and get home."

"I guess you have some big plans," he said. "Your husband
running for the U.S. Senate has everyone buzzing."

"Yes, I suppose it does." She walked alongside him down
the sidewalk. She was surprised at how little his staring at her
seemed to affect her. Hayden never thought herself a vengeful
person, but it felt good to think Alec was under the impression
that she had fallen in love with such a successful and dynamic
man so soon after he had practically thrown her away.

"Suppose so?" Alec laughed. "African-American senators
aren't around every corner. I hate him for getting you, but I'm
pretty excited about it myself."

"Hate him?" So he was jealous, she thought to herself with
a smile. She had wondered often in the last few months, if he
had realized what he gave up. Hayden knew she wasn't perfect,
but she had a great deal of love to give and she didn't like the
thought of it being rejected. "Don't be silly. I'm sure you have
beautiful sisters falling all over you in Atlanta."

"Forget that, kid," he said. "I'm still trying to unpack."

"I'm sure any day now those southern belles will start lining
up for you." She gave a friendly smile, proud of her civility.

"Yeah," he moaned, his eyes to the ground. After a quick
sigh, he turned to her again. "Hey, I heard about your dad.
I've been meaning to call. I'm really sorry."

"Thank you. He's doing great now. You should stop by to
visit."

"I'd love to. I'm only in until Tuesday. I wonder when . . ."

"Why don't you come tonight?" Stopping at her car, Hayden
realized she might have taken her civility one step too far.

"You think I could?" His face lit up with the eager excitement of a child. "I thought only important people were
invited."

"Oh, please," she said, waving a dismissing hand. "There's
going to be some press city people, but it's just a party."

Alec nervously tugged at his collar. "Do you think . . . he . . . Dr. Factor would mind? I mean . . ."

"Don't worry about him." Hayden remembered she had never told Cannon about Alec. "Mama and Daddy will be happy to see you."

"I wonder," he said with doubt. "I saw Donna when I was at R&D and she wasn't too happy to see me. Actually I was a little nervous about coming back until I heard you got married."

"Why is that?" she asked, knowing full well the reason why, but the proud side of her wanted to appear unfazed by his virtual desertion.

"I don't know," Alec said, his voice holding a fragile tone. "I wasn't sure how you felt about me. Then I heard you got married and when I got over my jealousy, I knew at least you were over the breakup."

"Yeah, I am," she said honestly. She wanted to tell him not to overestimate himself, but being bitchy wouldn't make her look good.

"I guess you fell head over heels in love with this guy."

"Everything did happen quickly." She thought that was at least the truth.

"I guess he's the kind all the ladies are crazy about." Alec's eyes fluttered nervously.

"Pretty much." What did he want, she asked herself? Did he want her to express her undying love for Cannon? She had told enough lies this week.

"Well, I can see you're getting a little restless." He took a couple steps backward. "You're very busy. I'll see you tonight."

"I'll leave your name at the door," she said. "It's the Hyatt Regency Gold Coast Room at seven."

"I'll be there." He waved again before turning to walk down the street back the way they had come.

In her car, Hayden sat in silence as she tried to examine her feelings closely. This was the first time she had seen Alec since the breakup. Expecting a whirlwind of emotions, she was surprised at only a small tinge of affection and remaining anger.

She didn't doubt that she had loved him, she knew she had. She wondered how her feelings could disappear so quickly. She always believed that something good came from even the worst of events and rationalized getting over Alec was one good affect from her father's heart attack. Realizing what was really important, breaking up with a boyfriend wasn't such a big deal.

She was certain Alec's appearance at the party wouldn't be a big deal either.

Or so Hayden thought, until she saw the look on Cannon's face when he saw Alec enter the room that evening.

"What is he doing here?" Cannon asked, not taking an eye off Alec. He couldn't hide his jealousy as the young man sauntered into the ballroom.

"How do you know Alec?" Hayden was unprepared for his reaction. She had planned to introduce Alec as merely an old friend, but seeing the angered expression on Cannon's face, she knew she would need to come up with something more.

"He's your ex-boyfriend, isn't he?" He turned to her, his eyes sharp as tacks.

"Yes," she answered, "but how did you know?"

"I saw a picture of the two of you in your parents' living room and asked your father who he was."

"It wasn't too long ago, I guess." Hayden wasn't sure why she felt guilty all of the sudden. The past was the past, wasn't it?

"You haven't answered my question." He eyed her intently, his handsome features hardened.

"He's in town for a cousin's wedding. I thought he would enjoy being here, meeting people." Not one word she said softened his expression.

"I wish you had told me it was that kind of party," he said in a cold tone. "I would have invited my ex-girlfriends."

"I'm glad you didn't. We would have needed a bigger room." She titled her chin up, smiling victoriously at his angry glare.

"Now now, Hayden," he spoke between gritted teeth, forcing a smile. "Let's be the supportive wife."

"Yes, and let's be the adoring husband." She responded with a saccharine smile of her own. "The cameras are rolling."

Hayden tried to hide how upset she was at Cannon's comments. She had been playing the supportive wife role quite well that evening. Gentle, serenely wise, and beautiful, she greeted everyone as they entered the room. She was even polite to Lee Sampson, making a point to correct him as to the identity of Tiffany Shields and Cannon's relationship with her.

She was surprised at herself as she sang Cannon's praises to anyone who asked. She felt so confident in every word she was saying. The surprise for her wasn't because she was doing such a good job as a seasoned public relations professional, but that she believed in what Cannon stood for politically and wanted others to know.

She watched with some pride as everyone attending was impressed with his confidence and vigor. He was the perfect candidate after all; young, handsome, intelligent, and wealthy. The press fell in love with him as he portrayed dignity and power in discussing his views, and appeared soft and approachable as he played with Tyler.

Hayden's parents enjoyed themselves for a couple of hours before returning home. She could see at least Donna would enjoy this next year. She was hobnobbing to her heart's delight, particularly with the male attendees.

"Do you ever get tired?" John Dannell offered Hayden a glass of champagne, which she refused.

"I was tired a couple of hours ago." She took a seat next to him at one of the tables. "I'm half asleep now."

"You look great." He sighed. "Boy, Cannon has always been a lucky one."

"Are you alright, John?" Hayden placed a comforting hand on his. She had noticed his somber mood as well as his many trips to the bar all evening.

"Yes, I'm fine." He gave a half smile.

"Jesse looks real tired," Hayden said. "Maybe you should

both hop a cab home. Everyone's pretty much gone anyway.''
She was aware of his financial problems, but knew now was
not the time to bring them up.

"I think we will head home," John said, stretching as he
stood up. "Do me a favor?"

"Anything." Resting her chin on fisted hands, she gave a
bemused smile. She liked John. He was a kind person, although
he always seemed bothered. He had been friendly to her from
the start.

"Tell Cannon, whenever he gets sick of kissing babies, he
always has a job examining them."

"I'll be sure to pass that along." She returned his wink and
watched as he walked away. She hoped things would be all
right for John and Jesse.

As John faded out of the picture, Alec faded in, taking a
seat across from Hayden.

"Who is that Maryann lady?" Without asking, he took a
sip from the champagne glass Hayden had just refused.

"Maryann Holly is Cannon's assistant." She ran her tired
fingers through her thick mane. She had spent most of the night
avoiding Alec because merely saying hello seemed to upset
Cannon. He seemed especially perturbed when she reacquainted
Alec with her parents.

"I just met her on her way out." He shook his head feigning
caution. "She's not the nicest lady I've ever met."

"Trust me, it isn't you. She's that way with everyone."
Hayden had noticed Maryann's mood as well, arousing her
suspicion. She had also noticed Mavis Factor's mood before
she left with her son earlier in the evening. Neither of the
women seemed happy at Cannon's successful evening. Hayden
had purposefully extended an invitation to Dr. Robert Marks
so as to study his behavior, but he hadn't shown up. That in
itself she saw as a sign.

"I didn't think so." Alec spoke with a tired voice and tired
eyes. "You were great tonight."

"What do you mean?" Alarmed by his words, she wondered

if he knew she had been acting. Then she wondered if in fact she had been acting.

"Nothing, except you were great." He laughed heartily. "I wonder if I should have stayed in Chicago."

"Don't think that way." She wondered if he could possibly believe he should have at least asked her to come along? "What's done is done."

"Your husband wasn't too happy to meet me when you introduced us."

"Just ignore him," Hayden said, feeling sorry for not having done a better job of covering up Cannon's rudeness toward Alec. "He's just anxious about the evening."

"I would be as . . ." Alec stopped in midsentence as he looked past Hayden before quickly lowering his head.

"Hayden, it's time we get going." Cannon placed a possessive hand on his wife's shoulder, but kept his eyes on the younger man. He wasn't usually a jealous man and never so over a woman who wasn't even really his. Despite that, he couldn't help but envy the man he saw before him. This man had enjoyed the pleasure of holding Hayden in his arms, possibly even making love to her. It was a pleasure Cannon wanted, but knew he would never have.

"Alright, Cannon." Hayden felt an unusual sense of comfort at his touch, reminding her of how tired she was.

Watching Alec's face, Hayden could tell he was obviously intimidated by Cannon. She had noticed Cannon had that affect on most men in social settings. She assumed the powerful stature and confident pose that drew women to him also compelled men to defer to him.

"I gave you my number, Alec," she said standing up. "Please call me so we can get together before you leave. I want us to be friends."

"I'll call you tomorrow." Alec reached over, giving Hayden an unassuming kiss on her cheek.

"Good night, Alec." Cannon spoke in a cold impatient tone to match his constant stare before leading Hayden away by the arm.

"Can you tell me why that was necessary?" She slid her arm from his grip, giving well-wishers a smile as they passed.

"Sure," he responded, walking briskly. "As soon as you tell me why it's necessary you flirt with him in front of everyone."

"Don't even go there, okay?" She pressed her lips together to keep from saying any more as they rode the escalator up to the hotel's lobby. "There's no one around. The possessive husband role is a waste of your time."

"Did he have to stay the entire night?" He stubbornly stuck out his chiseled chin.

"He was excited about meeting some interesting people." She crossed her arms, not knowing why she had to explain anything to him. She'd made a direct point not to appear too friendly with Alec.

"Anybody important left hours ago," he said.

"You're right, Cannon." She threw her hands up in defeat. "He was just there for me. I still love him and . . ." Seeing the threatening anger in his eyes and the tight set of his jaws, Hayden ceased her joking and they walked through the hotel lobby in silence until a bellboy stopped them.

"Dr. Factor, I've been waiting for you since your limo showed." A young man, out of breath from running, approached them. He looked awkward in a hotel uniform that was at least two sizes too big.

"What is it?" Still angry, Cannon was curt with the young man.

"This message was left for you at the desk," he said quickly in response to Cannon's tone.

"What is this?" Cannon snatched the envelop from the boy's gloved hand and opened it as Hayden looked on.

"Someone left it for you, sir." The boy spoke quickly as his nervous eyes darted in every direction. "I'm not exactly sure when. It could have been any time within the last half hour. I didn't get a look at them, but they left it at the desk."

Hayden watched Cannon as he opened the letter inside the envelope. Her curiosity grew as she watched his jaw clench and his eyes narrow in anger.

"What is it, Cannon?" She reached for the paper, but he held it away.

"Who left this?" He yelled loudly as he faced the bellboy. "Who was it?"

"Like I said," he responded, his eyes shifting in fear. "I didn't see. I haven't been at the desk hardly the past half hour. I was hooking a guest's bags to the trolley when I noticed it there."

"You must have seen someone!" Cannon yelled. "Think!"

"Show me, Cannon." Hayden reached again for the paper, crumpled now as Cannon gripped it in his clenched fist.

"I'm s-sorry s-sir," the boy stuttered nervously. "There were a-a million p-people passing through here. There's about f-four separate p-private parties letting out."

"Who else was on duty?" Cannon looked toward the empty front desk.

"Vicky is supposed to help me, but she called in sick." His eyes turned to Hayden, begging for help.

"Thank you, young man." She spoke in as soothing a voice she could manage. "You can go now."

"Thank you." In less than a half second, the young man was gone.

"Stop grabbing," Cannon said in irritation at her continuous reaching and handed her the letter.

FACTOR—
NOT A GOOD IDEA. DROP OUT OF THE ELEC-
TION OR IT COULD BE DANGEROUS.

Hayden read the note, made up of individual unusually shaped letters cut from magazine clips. She gasped aloud in amazement at the last word.

"Give me the letter," Cannon ordered, holding out his strong hand.

"What are you going to do," she asked, reading the note one last time before returning it to him.

"Nothing." He turned and resumed walking toward the limo.

"What do you mean nothing?" She followed quickly behind. It annoyed her how she almost had to jog to keep up with his calm stride.

"Nothing is one word, Hayden." He slid into the limo's back seat. "Which part of it didn't you understand?"

"Cut the sarcasm, Cannon. This is serious." She slid in next to him and waited for the driver to close the door. "This person is threatening your safety."

"These things are usually pranks," he said with a shrug. "I'm sure everyone who runs for a high-profile office receives these."

"Well, we'll let the police decide how much of a joke it is," she said. "Let's tell the driver to take us to the station now."

"No! No police, Hayden. I can handle this." He slammed his fist on the leather seat, doing everything he could to keep from exploding in anger.

"What are you talking about?" She was astounded by his behavior, never having seen this level of anger from him before. "You could be in danger."

Thoughts of all the possible suspects ran through her mind. Mavis and Maryann had left before them, so it could have been either of them. Robert Marks had been invited, so he could have dropped it off. The event was covered in most of the papers, so Joanne Pearl could have dropped it off as well. Or any one of them could have paid a street kid five dollars to bring it in.

"Hayden, you don't understand." He gave a deep sigh, lying back in the plush seats of the limousine. He felt his surroundings closing in on him.

"Make me understand." She experienced an involuntary need to hold him, to try and make him calmer and feel better as she noticed the anguish on his face.

"I've come so far. I can't let anything stop me." He raised his head to look at her, an unexpected calm resting his soul as he gazed into her eyes. "You can't tell anyone about this. Not your mother, Donna, or anyone. This is too important to me."

"Cannon, threats to your person shouldn't be kept a secret." As if it was a natural occurrence, she slid closer to him on the seat. "Maybe this isn't worth it."

"That's what I'm talking about." His brow lowered in frustration as he reached for the mini-bar across from him. "That's what everyone will say. You, Mama, John, Warren. Everyone."

"Cannon." She reached out, grabbing hold of his hand before he could grab the bottle of scotch. "This is not the time to drink alcohol."

Cannon grasped her cautioning hand in his, turning his face to hers. His voice was deep and slow, his eyes holding hers. "You're a smart woman, Hayden. I'm lucky to have you for a business partner. I'm lucky to have you for a wife."

The gentle flame that lit his eyes drew her like a magnet to him as he gathered her in his arms. She closed her eyes as his full lips captured hers. A swell of fire slid through her body like an arrow and her heart rose from its usual place as his hard searching lips possessed her like a spirit.

As he moved his lips over hers, devouring their softness, she let out a hungry moan. She realized, through all the sensation, this was what she had been waiting for since that night they kissed in the car. She had been waiting to be kissed again and return to this madness. She had been waiting to feel like she was floating on air again, and her wants were satisfied and then some as the passion now surpassed that of the previous kiss tenfold.

"Hayden," came from his lips in a deep breath as he left her mouth. His lips seared a hot, devilish path down her neck and shoulders. His mind left him and his body exploded at the touch of her. The touch of her petal soft skin against his lips made him forget any and every problem he'd ever had. He felt the sensuality and sweetness of forever and could only want for more.

The delicious intimacy of his moist tongue as it briefly trailed her neck, sent a shiver through Hayden's body. She heard herself call out his name in a moan, almost ready to lose control. He responded to her call by capturing her mouth again with his, this time penetrating her lips and entering her mouth with his hot tongue. She returned his kiss with reckless abandon as she gave in to a burning desire and aching need she had never experienced before.

As she lifted her shaky arms to wrap around his neck, his hungry hands slid up from her waist to cup her full breasts. She felt her body melt as his fingers found the outline of her nipples that had hardened beneath the thin dress she wore. Just at the point of losing all of her senses, Hayden felt his hands release from her supple breasts and his mouth reluctantly part from hers.

"I can't, Hayden." The words came as a whisper under his fast deep breathing. He allowed her to release her arms from his neck. He knew he had to stop this before he lost all control. He wouldn't do this to Hayden nor to himself.

"Why not?" Forgetting her pride, Hayden only wanted to resume the intense ecstasy and passion that had just threatened to consume her.

"Because I want you." He slid away from her, unable to trust himself so close. "I want you more than I've ever wanted any woman in my life."

"I don't understand." She licked her lips, savoring the feel of the touch they'd just experienced.

"I care about you, Hayden, and I want a real relationship with you, but I can't." Passion as strong as a tornado was still in his eyes and his heart as he spoke.

"What's stopping you?" Hayden didn't try to hide the confusion she felt at her emotions and his reaction.

"You don't trust me, Hayden," he said, feeling the hurt he heard in his own voice. "You still question my moral character and that hurts. It's what I am."

"Oh, Cannon." She spoke in a pleading tone, hurt that he hadn't gotten over the other night's misunderstanding. "That was my fault. I jumped to conclusions. I was only trying to combat the feelings I was beginning to have for you."

"Maybe so," he said, "but how do you explain rummaging through my office at the State Building?"

She had no response for his words as she remembered her

search through Cannon's office for clues about him. She was too embarrassed to ask how he knew.

"Maryann called me and told me about it," he said in a somber tone. "I hadn't called you and asked you to search for anything. I can only assume you were conducting some kind of investigation."

Shame overwhelmed her as she lowered her head to avoid the disappointment in his eyes. "Cannon, please stop. I'm so ashamed already."

"Don't be." His tone wasn't sympathetic or angry, but unemotional. "I know you've had so much thrown at you. I think you've handled it as well as can be expected and I know you'll figure everything out in enough time."

"I'm sorry." She wasn't sure what to say and could only apologize. She wanted so badly to throw herself at him and convince him to forget everything that had been done in the past, but deep down inside she knew he was right.

As he looked into her eyes, Cannon was filled with a hope that superseded any apprehension he'd felt before. He could see that she cared something for him from the tenderness in her large, beautiful eyes. Maybe there was hope for them.

As they rode home in silence, bidding only a civil good night before they parted to go to their separate bedrooms, Hayden thought about what Cannon had said. She would come to figure out everything in enough time. She had figured out one thing at least and that was that she was falling for him. She didn't want to fight it, although she knew it might be best if she did. After experiencing the desire and affection of his kiss, Hayden knew she wanted to be with him.

It was true, she didn't completely trust him and that was not good. She would have to find out who was behind the rumors and the threatening letters and present that person to Cannon. Then everything would be settled and he would know she was ready for a relationship with him.

As she fell asleep that night, hoping to dream of the kiss they had shared, Hayden laughed to herself at one thought. She was falling in love with the man who was already her husband.

Chapter Nine

Hayden was very busy over the next few days, but not enough to keep her mind off her feelings for Cannon. Although she spent most of Saturday planning the campaign, when she was alone, her mind would wander and reflect on the intimate moment they had shared. Reliving the ecstasy of being held against this strong body, she felt a pull of desire in her lower belly. What she recalled most, despite all the passion and heat racing through her veins, was that she had felt very safe and comfortable the entire time. It was as if she knew that in his arms was where she belonged.

With a chill she remembered how he had pushed away from her as quickly as he had pulled her to him. She had felt as if a part of her body had been detached from her. It took a power from within her she didn't know she had to keep from begging him to take hold of her again.

She knew he was right to pull away. She tried hard to put herself in his position to keep from being angry at him. After thinking it through, she felt a little flattered by his action. If Cannon had continued his seduction, which she was obviously not about to thwart, it would have meant his interest was purely sexual. It would have confirmed all the misgivings she'd had about him. Only he admitted he cared about her enough that her opinion of him, on a level of respect, was important to him. Maybe she had been wrong about him all along. She hoped it was so.

As the next few days passed, Cannon was the perfect gentleman. He seemed to go out of his way to say hello and talk to her as they passed each other in the condo. It was difficult, but Hayden controlled her awakening emotions and returned the friendliness. He was charming and humorous, and every time Hayden heard his footsteps come her way, her heart gave a little jump.

"You've been so quiet. Did I say something wrong?" Alec's brows centered as he eyed her from across the table at Rosebud's Italian restaurant.

"I'm sorry Alec, I've been so rude." Hayden smiled apologetically. She couldn't help but feel a little guilty after agreeing to see Alec for lunch now that her relationship with Cannon was changing. Yet it had been her idea they get together before he returned to Atlanta.

"No, you haven't been rude," Alec said. "You look like you have a lot on your mind. I'm surprised you had time for lunch with me."

"You know I can't resist Italian." She looked around the popular downtown restaurant she and Alec had eaten at so many times in the past. The food was delicious and the portions so big, she usually had two days' worth of leftovers if she wanted.

"I remember." He laughed, lowering his head. When he lifted it again, there was a softer expression on his face, void of humor. "I remember a lot. I remember you telling me you loved me here one night."

"Alec that was a long time ago," she responded awkwardly, not knowing how to handle discussion of their past. It seemed like a long time ago. "That was before you left and before Cannon."

"I know," he said, "but has it all gone away?"

She searched within herself. Yes, she had loved him, but he had left her. Then her father became sick and now . . . well, now Cannon had kissed her with more passion than she had ever felt before, including with Alec. He had enlightened her with his care and concern for those less fortunate and given her hope that he could do something to change things. Still, Hayden believed there was something inside of her for Alec. Something, but she wasn't sure what.

"I'll always care for you." She placed her hand tenderly over his across the table. "I thought I would want to hurt you because you'd hurt me, but I don't. I guess it is gone."

"I should have been honest with you," he said, shaking his head with regret. "I should have asked you to come to Atlanta with me."

That was it. Hayden felt a light blink inside her head at his last words. She smiled inside as she realized that was what she had been waiting for. That was the something. The tinge of emotion, that smudge of anger, that something was now gone. All she had wanted from Alec was for him to admit he'd made a mistake. He should have at least asked her to join him in Atlanta. Maybe she would have refused, maybe she would have gone but either way, he should have asked. The eight months they shared were worth at least that.

"Should have, could have, would have," Hayden said. "We would never get anywhere if we depended on hindsight. What's done is done. We learn from it and move on."

"Apparently you have." Alec gave a brighter smile than before. He took hold of the hand she had laid on his, concentrating on the generously adorned gold wedding band. "I hope Cannon Factor is smarter than me. I hope he knows what he has in you."

"I believe he does," she said with a blush as he kissed her delicate hand. She was over Alec Gavin. Now if, she could find a way to trust Cannon completely and prove to him that she trusted him. Then, who knew what her future held?

The camera flash in the dimly lit restaurant almost blinded Hayden. Regaining her sight, she was only able to see a restaurant full of people staring at her wondering who she was that someone would want to take her picture.

"What was that?" Alec blinked repeatedly and shook his head.

"It was probably Lee Sampson with *Represent Chicago*," Hayden responded angrily. "He has it in for Cannon and looks for every opportunity to print something negative about him."

"I guess a picture of his wife having a lunch with another man doesn't help." Alec threw his napkin onto the table, leaning back in his chair.

"Don't be upset, Alec." Hayden was doing her best to keep her cool. "We haven't done anything wrong so he can't say we have."

Hayden hoped the lack of confidence she felt in her own words didn't show.

Returning to her office, Hayden went over in her mind what Lee Sampson would say about her lunch with Alec. She should have known better than to have lunch with Alec right now. Especially in such a popular downtown restaurant. Their objective was to saturate the media with positive news about Cannon and his plans for Illinois. She knew there was someone out there who wanted to combat that and Hayden felt a sense of dread come over as she realized she had to tell Cannon she had helped whoever that was.

"Hayden, where have you been?" Cannon asked over the phone.

"I was at lunch." She sat up in her seat noticing three phone message sheets next to her phone, all from him. "You've been calling?"

"You took a pretty long lunch."

"I wanted to tell you," she said slowly, trying to find an

easy way to break the bad news about the picture of she and Alec. "I was at . . ."

"I got another letter," he interrupted.

She paused for a second, at first not clear on what he'd said. Then it came to her in a wave of chills. "Another threat?"

"Yes, well if you want to call them that," he said flatly.

"What did it say?" She was frustrated by his tone of voice. It was as if it was nothing to him that someone was threatening his life.

"Factor,'" he read, "all this show is no good. Quit the race or face the consequence."

"That sounds like a threat to me," Hayden said, her heart racing. "How did you get it?"

"The lobby sent it up. They said a messenger brought it, but he didn't stay for a signature."

"Don't they have cameras at the desk?" Hayden asked, her mind racing a mile a minute. "Have them look over the cameras. When they spot him, check his uniform and call the company. We can find out who sent it."

"Hayden, we already went over all this. I don't want police involved. You can't get permission to access security tapes without police authorization. If the police get involved, it will get to the press and take over the campaign. This will all distract from my intentions."

"Cannon please," she pleaded. "I'm worried."

"Hayden, I'm hiring a bodyguard for you."

"For me? You have to get one for yourself. The threats are for you."

"I've talked to John about it. I know I asked you not to tell anyone, but he's my best friend and I know he won't say anything. He knows a company that offers very discreet protection. You won't even notice him. If anyone does notice, we'll say it's an extra precaution most people take when running for a high-profile political office. After all, that's all it is."

"We hope that's all it is. It's a good idea either way." She sighed, wondering if Cannon was really in danger? Was she? "We really need to find out who is behind all this."

"Do you think it's the same person who was trying to frame me in the papers?" His voice sounded cautious and uncertain.

"Yes I do, Cannon." She made sure to answer quick and firm, aware that he was testing her trust.

"So do I," he agreed calmly. "Let's let it go for now. We'll talk about it more when I get home."

Hayden left that conversation with conflicted emotions. All the more concerned that Cannon had received a threat, it hadn't gotten past her that by agreeing that the source of the rumors and the threats were the same person was some sort of progress on a personal level. That connection seemed more important to Hayden as each day with Cannon Factor went by.

When she arrived home that evening, Hayden wanted to be a source of comfort for Cannon, to ease the worries he tried so hard to hide, but she knew it wasn't a good idea. She didn't trust herself being so close to him and she could tell he felt the same. It was difficult enough being alone in the house with memories of their intimate encounters. She wanted Cannon and she knew he wanted her and despite the problems that could arise, Hayden couldn't hold back her desire to venture into the possibilities.

Only there was more to be worried about. She had come to believe that maybe his past, as unpleasant as it was to be reminded of it, was his past, but, she was still not quite sure. More importantly, the awkwardness of having begun a relationship under the guise of a lie, left little room for a feeling of rightness. Hayden wondered if that would eventually prove stronger than her feelings.

She was sure she would fall in love if they took the relationship any further. She wasn't sure she hadn't already. Apparently, Cannon understood the danger of rushing things between them. He also sensed her doubts. Doubts Hayden wished she could let go of.

She also had questions. For instance, why was Cannon so reluctant to find out who was behind the lies and now the threatening letters? Why was he so adamant about not involving the police? Hayden wished she knew more about this confusing man who was beginning to invade her every thought.

To avoid any questions from her mother, Hayden did her best to portray the happy, madly-in-love wife as she attended a small Evanston fund-raiser for Cannon's campaign with her mother and Tyler.

"Auntie Hayden, please don't let the ladies kiss me anymore." Tyler ran to Hayden, looking up at her with a lipstick-stained face.

"I'll try, precious." Hayden laughed and hugged the little boy. As she wiped the makeup from his chubby cheeks, she reflected with a full heart on how fond she had become of him in the short time she'd known him. She looked forward to spending time with him on his visits to the condo.

"Promise me!" He buried his small face in her arms.

"It would be easier if you weren't so adorable," Elise said with an affectionate smile on her face.

"We'll do what we can," Hayden said, hugging him even tighter.

"I'm surprised at how successful this evening has been." Elise glanced across the small room at the Orrington Omni Hotel in downtown Evanston.

"I want to thank you so much, Mama." Hayden was truly appreciative. She was surprised when her mother suggested she hold a little fund-raiser of her own with the women from her community center and church. It was very seldom Elise took the initiative in secular projects Hayden was involved in. Hayden jumped at the chance. She enjoyed spending time with her mother, especially now that they were talking to each other in a way they hadn't in the past. Hayden wasn't sure what had changed or why, but something had. Hayden wondered if it wasn't Elise who had changed, but herself. A lot had happened to her in the past year. The breakup with Alec, her father's heart attack, the Coverling account, and most of all, Cannon

Factor and everything his presence brought to her life. She realized she wasn't the same woman she had been a few months ago. Not at all.

"It was nothing really," Elise said, waving goodbye to a close friend. "All the women agree so much with Cannon's focus on the children. When I approached them about the fund-raiser, they were happy to oblige."

"Uncle Cannon likes kids," Tyler said, following a long yawn. He picked up one of the toys Hayden had brought along for him and began to play with it.

"He definitely likes this tired one." Hayden lightly pinched his little nose. "We better start wrapping this up. It's past Tyler's bedtime anyway."

"The room is clearing," Elise said. "We can all leave soon. I'm glad this has worked out. I felt it was the least I could do."

"What do you mean?" Hayden asked, noticing the obligated tone of her mother's voice.

"Alan called me last Friday," she said. "He offered me an extended sick leave of four more weeks."

"Paid?"

"At half the salary, but nonetheless."

"Mama, that's great!" Hayden reached over and squeezed her mother's arm in delight. It was definitely good news.

"I know you and Cannon have something to do with it." She smiled unassumingly.

"I knew about the first leave," Hayden admitted, "but I had no idea Alan would extend it. I guess he really does understand how important your loyalty to him has been." Hayden's heart sang with delight at the idea of Cannon doing this for her mother. He had probably never planned to tell her, but let her find out herself that he cared enough to remember her mother on his own. She was truly touched that he realized how important her family was to her. He really was a generous and caring man.

"I grilled him for several minutes as to his change of heart before he admitted he was encouraged by a mutual friend of

Cannon's and his. He wasn't angry. He said it made him realize how many people besides him understood how important I was.'' Elise smiled at her daughter. ''I'm not upset. I'm grateful. It made me realize something myself.''

''What was that?'' Hayden asked.

''That I'm very blessed to have such a loving and devoted daughter.'' Elise's face softened as she looked into her child's affectionate eyes. ''I don't show my appreciation enough.''

''Mama, you don't have to show anything,'' Hayden said, leaning closer. ''I know how you feel.''

''I hope you do.'' Elise wiped away a single, tender tear from her eyes. ''I hope you do, because I love you dearly, but I don't express it as well as I should. After Michael's death, I went from feeling intense grief to feeling sorry for myself. I didn't appreciate the fact that I still had a beautiful loving child to care for and receive love from. You and your father are the most precious things in this world to me. I just want you to know that I'm proud of you. You're a beautiful, intelligent, and devoted human being with a great career and a husband who could very well be the next senator from Illinois. I can see how happy you are. I couldn't hope for any more than that.''

With tears in both their eyes, the women stood up and hugged each other tightly as an entranced Tyler stood by. She could never begin to tell her mother how much her words meant to her. Her heart was overflowing with love. Over a decade of doubt since Michael's death had been erased in mere minutes.

''Don't mess up your makeup, dear.'' Elise kissed her daughter's soft tear-stained cheek tenderly, helping to wipe away her tears.

''You just don't know how happy you've made me,'' Hayden said as she regained her composure.

It amazed her, the power of words. Hearing Alec admit he should have asked her to join him in Atlanta and now her mother's loving words had cleared up so much confusion, doubt, and concern.

''I'm glad I can add to your happiness,'' Elise continued.

"I know how happy Cannon makes you. I see your eyes light up every time he's around. Marriage is wonderful isn't it?"

"Yes, Mama, it is." Guilt forced her to turn her head as she concentrated on Tyler's attentive gaze. "Yes, it is."

Maybe she did light up when Cannon was around. Hayden wasn't sure anymore what was acting and what was real, but she wouldn't worry about it now. Now she would share the joy she felt being here with her mother and knowing that one day she would be able to tell her the truth about everything. She just hoped when that time came her mother would understand how devoted a daughter she really was.

Back at home that night, Hayden watched as Cannon carefully put Tyler to sleep on the living room sofa. She was now occupying the room he usually slept in, but the boy didn't ask why that room was now locked. He was always asleep before Hayden headed off to bed. The other rooms in the condo had been turned into either an office or a workout room. Hayden felt a tug at her heart as she saw the care with which he gently laid the sleeping boy down and covered him with sheets that had pictures of puppies and kittens all over.

"I hope he behaved." Cannon turned to Hayden, with a tired smile.

To Hayden, Cannon looked like a gentle giant leaning against the sofa, watching over the small boy. His chest was broad and muscular underneath the aqua blue T-shirt, but his demeanor was tender and affectionate.

"He was perfect as usual." She felt the soothing desire within her in response to his seductive eyes sliding down her body.

"You know he has a crush on you." Cannon gently took her arm and led her down the hallway. She looked beautiful, her young body and natural features complimented by the casual feminine peach summer dress. Everything about her was what he'd always imagined was a woman.

"How do you know?" Hayden wasn't realizing the ease

with which she allowed him to guide her, still feeling a certain sense of sexual tautness that was now a norm in his presence.

"He told me in the car," he said. "On the way over here. He wanted to make sure it was okay with me."

"And what did you say?" She lifted her head to face him.

"I told him I'd have to think about it." He stopped, taking hold of her other arm and looking into her eyes. He loved the sweetness and honesty he saw in them. "I don't know if I can share you."

"Cannon." She admonished his compliment with a shy smile and whispered words. She was so close, but not anywhere near as nervous as she had been in the past. She wanted to be here. She suspected she always had, only now she knew. There wasn't any confusion about that. "I want to thank you."

"For what?" He never thought he could derive such pleasure from simply being this close to her.

"I know about my mother." She caught his compelling eyes with hers so he could see and believe her appreciation was from the heart. "You didn't have to. Our deal was for a six-week leave and Dr. Kent, but you went the extra mile."

"It's the least I could do," he said, feeling captivated by her gaze. "You've done so much for me."

She felt no apprehension as she slowly raised her hands to his head and brought it down to her uplifted face. She kissed him gently on his generous lips and felt a wanton warmth run through her. As he responded with pressure of his own, Hayden felt her head fill with thoughts of love, spring, colors, and the sun.

"See what I mean?" He spoke with a whisper as he lifted his head, wishing he could make love to her more than he had ever wished for anything.

"Yes I do," she responded with a smile. She had never in her life felt so comfortable and safe as she did with that kiss. She was falling in love with this man, this handsome man with such an arresting face and wickedly charming smile.

"I've never said no to my nephew, but I think I'll make an

exception over you.'' He walked backward toward his room, never taking an eye off of her sensuous, caring face.

"Good night, Cannon." She waved to him as if he was going far away. That was what it felt like as she knew anywhere other than her bed was farther than she'd like.

"Good night, Hayden." He gave her one last wink before turning and heading for his room. It was frustrating to leave her, but he knew it was right. He also knew there was hope and when that hope was fulfilled, it would be well worth the wait. His dreams would have to hold him for now.

As her eyes gave in to sleep late that night, the last picture Hayden saw was the gentle smile of the man she was falling in love with. He was so much: ambitious, caring, successful, and generous. All of his inner qualities were only complimented by his sexiness. He wanted her, Hayden knew. But did he want her forever or just for now? She didn't want to end up another first name only in his Rolodex, never to be mentioned again.

Chapter Ten

"I've drafted the release and Marcy should be E-mailing it to you directly as we speak." Hayden bit the tip of her pen anxiously, her mind on things other than work. "She'll be faxing it as well."

Spearheading an agreement allowing Coverling to display their diamonds in the Sak's Fifth Avenue Windows in New York and Chicago had been a difficult task. She had to do a great deal of maneuvering and appeasing. With everything else going on in her life, Hayden found the time to make everyone involved in the deal happy. Everyone at R&D was very proud of how well she was handling the project. She was pretty proud of herself, and seeing great avenues open up for Coverling as a result, and she wanted a press release out immediately. She knew the move would have a positive effect on Coverling stock as well as its public image.

"I'll have my secretary check the fax machine," said Mark Andre, president of Coverling. "What do you suggest next?"

"We must have the signed agreement before we release. I suggest we send a copy of our final draft to Sak's management for approval." She respected Mark for his intelligence, but felt he lacked the leadership his father had had when he made Coverling the Fortune 500 company it was today.

"It should be news by Friday?" he asked.

"Yes, you should have someone at Coverling available over the weekend to take any media calls."

"Where will you be this weekend, Hayden?"

"I'm traveling to Springfield with my husband. I'll leave a number where I can be reached." Hayden lifted her head as she thought she heard some noise down the hall. It sounded like arguing.

"A number would be helpful," Mark said.

"Mark, I have to go now," Hayden said quickly as the arguing came closer to her office. "Call me after you've read the release."

"I'm sure it will be perfect as all your work has been."

Maryann Holly stormed into the office just as Hayden placed the phone on the receiver. With a look of severe frustration covering her face, she headed straight for Hayden.

"What's going on here?" Hayden stood up, looking past Maryann toward the outside lobby.

"I'm sorry, Hayden." The voice came from around the corner as Turner Jefferson, an R&D account associate, entered the room. "Marcy wasn't here and I knew you wanted to be left . . ."

"Enough of this!" Maryann put a furious hand up to silence the young man, then turned back to Hayden. "We have to talk."

"I don't believe this behavior is at all necessary," Hayden said sternly.

"I could say the same about this behavior," Maryann responded adamantly as she threw a copy of today's *Chicago Sun Times* onto Hayden's desk. "Page C23 please."

Hayden took a deep breath as she spotted the picture of herself and Alec Gavin at Rosebud's restaurant. She should have realized that now that Cannon had announced his bid for the Senate seat, the larger city papers would become more interested. With everything that was going on with the campaign, the threats, and the Coverling account at work, she had forgotten about the lunch, never warning Cannon of the picture's possible appearance in a local paper. Cannon!

"Has Cannon seen this?" Hayden squeezed the paper in her hand.

"Of course he has." Maryann's tone was patronizing. "So has every subscriber to the *Times!* You know Cannon's popularity has spread to the mass media now that he's campaigning."

Hayden took a deep breath and turned to Turner who was still standing in the doorway. "Turner, you can go. Please close the door behind you."

"Alright, Hayden." He tossed an angry Maryann one last disgusted look before leaving the office.

"This is all explainable," Hayden said, scanning the paper. There was no attribution, only the picture with a short paragraph underneath. It mentioned her name in reference to being the health commissioner's wife and noted her having dinner with an unknown man.

"Things were going so well." Maryann folded her arms across her chest.

"Alec is my ex-boyfriend," Hayden continued, ignoring Maryann's hostile attitude. "You met him at the . . ."

"I know who he is and so does Cannon!"

"Cannon." Hayden picked up the phone and began dialing frantically. "I have to explain to him."

"He's not at the office. He left after seeing the photo. We were besieged with calls. Lee Sampson called three times."

"Oh no," she said in a choked whisper as she hung up the phone. "It was just lunch."

"You don't deserve him."

"What?" Hayden stepped back as Maryann gave her a wicked stare.

"There are thousands of women out there who would give anything to be Cannon's wife and devote their life to him, but not you. No, Mrs. Keeping-Her-Own-Last-Name has a career and goes out to lunch with single men."

"What women are you talking about Maryann?" Hayden

spoke in a knee-jerk reaction to the accusation. "Like you? Are you talking about yourself?"

Maryann suddenly became silent, a look of curiosity on her face. Hayden could tell she was wondering whether or not Cannon had told her about their misunderstanding months ago. Hayden would never admit to it.

"I'm sorry, Maryann." She turned away from the older woman. It wasn't Maryann's fault and Hayden knew that. "I didn't mean that."

"Well I meant every word I said." Maryann's voice was very calm and controlled. "Cannon will be the next senator from Illinois because he deserves it and is the best person for the position. I expect you as his wife and his public relations counselor to fix this fiasco you've caused and see that it doesn't happen again." With one last evil glare, Maryann stormed out of the office.

Maryann was wrong. If she only knew the whole story. Hayden was committed to Cannon's success and no longer because it was part of their deal. She was falling in love with Cannon and wanted him to be excel in everything. There was no way she could explain that to Maryann who obviously believed a woman's place was behind her man, especially if that man was Cannon Factor. Hayden believed a woman of the nineties could have a career and a certain level of independence while supporting the man she loved wholeheartedly. It was what she had planned to have for herself some day. She wondered if she could ever have a chance at that with Cannon.

Hayden sat defeated in her chair. She looked at the picture of Alec kissing her hand once more before tossing the entire paper into the trash can.

Hayden's stomach was churning and her head throbbing as she ran out of R&D's building. Her car was parked in the garage down the block, but it seemed a mile away. She had to get home. Everything, all the good that had been done could be destroyed because of her stupidity! It wasn't as if she didn't feel bad enough, when she heard her name being called by a woman running toward her. When she saw who it was, she wanted to turn and keep running, but she knew she couldn't. What was next? Another threat? Better yet, another warning?

Joanne Pearl looked like a runway model as she quickly strode across the street toward Hayden. She walked tall, with obvious self-esteem and assurance of her beauty. Her pastel peach minidress swayed with her and she moved in her high-heeled shoes as if they were gym shoes.

"Fancy meeting you here," Joanne said, not losing a step. Having practically run across the street, she wasn't the least bit out of breath. "I was just thinking of you."

"Don't tell me," Hayden said, unwelcoming chagrin on her face. She didn't care about manners right now. "Another warning."

"I've read the papers, hon." Joanne placed a bony hand on her agile hips and leaned back a bit. She quickly surveyed Hayden with a mocking smile. "It seems like Cannon's the one who needs to be warned. I guess birds of a feather . . ."

"Listen," Hayden started with a vehement tone, surprising herself. "I don't need this. That picture was misleading and I don't have to explain anything to bitter, gold-digging—"

"Not bitter, babe," Joanne interrupted her. "I care nothing for Cannon anymore."

"And I'm supposed to believed that?" Hayden asked.

"I've got my own man now," Joanne said. "Dr. William Jefferson Fox is chief surgeon at County General and he's ten times the man Cannon was.

"I'll bet he makes ten times the paycheck," Hayden said, not at all concerned with her brashness. "That's what really counts to you, right?"

"Listen"—Joanne leaned over, passing Hayden a threatening glance—"you say you don't have to explain anything to me? I don't have to explain anything to you."

"So," Hayden said, her curiosity urging her to take advantage of the opportunity, "can I expect that now that you have a new man, you'll stop this nonsense?"

Joanne's expression turned from sarcasm to concern. Her eyes blinked twice quickly and she took a step backward. Hayden swallowed hard as she realized she had struck a chord. Was it Joanne who was spreading the rumors and the sending the threats? Could it be that she was about to solve this mystery here and now?

"How did you know?" Joanne asked, her oval eyes widening in surprise.

"I just do," Hayden said, playing along. She had no idea what she was agreeing to, but she was determined to get an answer. "So?"

Joanne sighed, looking around as if to make sure no one was listening in. Her eyes shifted nervously before she turned to Hayden again. She took a deep breath and said, "Listen, I'm sorry. I know it was stupid and immature, but I was wronged and I felt he deserved it. It was no big deal."

"No big deal?" Hayden caught herself as her raised tone garnered a couple of stares from passersby. "How could you say it was no big deal? Cannon has been torn apart by this. He has lost sleep. Our lives have been turned upside down!"

"Over a couple of calls?" Joanne asked, her brows centering in utter confusion. "What is your problem? Who gives a damn?"

"Calls?" Hayden asked. What was she talking about? "What do you mean calls?"

"My phone calls." Joanne gasped in impatient disgust. "What is your problem?"

"Your phone calls?" Hayden thought she was in a mental maze. Was Joanne admitting to the rumors and threats or not?

"Yes," she said emphatically, mocking Hayden with a condescending smirk. "I made crank calls to Cannon's office and his condo. I only made a few. If you let it turn your lives upside down, then your lives are missing something."

"You're apologizing for crank calls?" Hayden felt her heart drop to the pit of her stomach. Could this be more disappointing! "Stupid, stupid crank calls."

"That's what you're talking about isn't it?" Joanne asked. "What in the hell were you talking about?"

"Nothing, Joanne." Hayden heaved a sigh in disgust. "Just . . . nothing."

"Whatever." She rolled her eyes and with a dramatic turn, strode away.

Hayden stood on the sidewalk for a moment, her mouth wide open. She stared ahead of her, but at nothing. She didn't notice the bewildered stares of people who walked by her. So close, but still nothing. When would this end, she wondered? When?

With a weak soul, Hayden bit her lower lip and continued toward the garage.

"It wasn't a good idea no matter how innocent," Cannon said in a harsh voice. His first thought upon seeing her had been to yell at the top of his lungs, wanting her in some way to understand how much and in how many ways she had hurt him. But the moment she looked into his eyes, he was reminded of his strong affection for her and the anger, although still there, was tempered.

"I know, Cannon." Hayden was surprised at how he maintained his composure as she explained herself out of the incriminating picture. His angry glare had met her at the door when she returned home and she immediately began to explain. He was unresponsive at first, but later began to listen and even talk to her, but in the raw tone he continued with now.

"I know you're busy at R&D, but I want you to get on fixing this first thing in the morning." Still in his work clothes, Cannon undid his Calvin Klein tie.

"I've already contacted the *Times*," Hayden said, "and they're running a retraction in tomorrow's paper. If you'll just tell me the names of the reporters who contacted your office, I can call . . ."

"Ask Maryann," he said, turning to leave the living room. "I don't want to discuss it anymore."

"Cannon, where are you going?" She followed him, deeply troubled by his anger.

"I'm going to the gym to work out." He didn't bother to look at her before walking to his room and slamming the door shut.

Hayden was forced to conquer the involuntary desire she had to go after him. She wanted so much to wipe away her mistake. If there was something she could say . . . could do . . . to make him feel better she would do it. She cursed herself for agreeing to lunch with Alec, thinking of how it could not only hurt Cannon's career, but turn back the progress he and Hayden had made in their budding relationship.

Turning on the television in the living room, her pride forced her to feign indifference as he strode past her, down the hallway and out the door. She couldn't bear to expose herself to him, not knowing if he still cared for her in any way. Grabbing a copy of *Medical Report,* one of several professional magazines Cannon subscribed to, she began flipping through the pages all the while cursing under her breath.

Not really paying attention, but merely turning page after page, Hayden was surprised as she noticed something peculiar. She called out to Cannon, having forgotten he was gone. Upon remembering she grabbed the magazine and crossed her fingers as she ran to Cannon's office. As hoped, the door was unlocked. In his anger he must have forgotten to lock the door as he usually did before leaving the house. Cautiously, she entered and headed for Cannon's desk. She remembered once seeing him place the threatening letters in the top drawer and, after a quick search, found them folded in the envelopes they came in.

She unfolded the first letter and then the second, laying them next to each other on the desk. As she sat in the large leather chair and studied them closer, she looked through several pages of the magazine. With the exception of a few letters, the print was the same! She had noticed because it was one of the most unusual print styles she had ever seen in a magazine, a mixture of calligraphy and script. It was meant as a joking reference to the terrible handwriting doctors were said to have. Although most letters in the threatening notes were cut individually and were of different sizes, the design style was exact.

This was a clue! Was it a coincidence that a magazine with this irregular type style would deal with the profession Cannon was a part of? She had never seen this magazine on the stands, so it's subscriber list must be small. Because of their encounter earlier that day, Hayden decided to rule out Maryann. She wouldn't have attacked Hayden so ruthlessly if she didn't truly want Cannon to be successful. Mavis and Joanne Pearl could have access to the magazine if they searched it out, but it seemed unlikely. Whoever was sending these threats subscribed to *Medical Report* magazine and was probably a doctor.

So again Hayden's thoughts went to Robert Marks. Her father had always taught her to follow her initial instincts and Robert Marks had been her first suspect. It made sense that he subscribed to the magazine and surely had the motive. He possibly had wanted to run for senator himself, but jealousy at Cannon's further success as commissioner was enough.

Gathering everything together, Hayden darted for the door. She would present this revelation to Cannon and he would forget all about Alec and everything else. The smile on her face was from ear to ear. A breakthrough at last, she thought. The possibilities were endless for her with Cannon. Who knew where their hearts would lead them?

As she opened the door, Hayden came to a sudden stop a second before running full force into Mavis and Tyler.

"Mavis! What are you doing here?" Almost out of instinct Hayden opened her arms for Tyler who jumped into them with a joyful yell.

"I need a babysitter. It's an emergency." Mavis walked past Hayden into the apartment. "The doorman let us up. He recognizes me. Where's Cannon?"

"Where is Candace?" Hayden asked.

"Grandma's at bingo!" Tyler squiggled and squirmed his way out of Hayden's arms and went on running around the condo in his usual frantic way.

Hayden expected Mr. Biggs, the tenant who lived below them to come up any minute to complain as he usually did every time Tyler was over.

"I have to meet someone at Water Tower Place in twenty-five minutes," Mavis said, looking at her watch. "Where is Cannon? His office?"

"He's working out," Hayden answered, wondering what this emergency was for. Was she meeting Sampson to tell him another lie? "Is there a problem?"

"No." Mavis turned to her. "Can you guys watch him? I'll pick him up before eleven." She seemed to notice Hayden's surprise at the time mentioned and said, "Don't give me any lectures. I get enough of those from Cannon."

"I'm not giving you a lecture Mavis. I was just wondering . . ."

"I have a date," Mavis said with a tone of sarcasm. "Is it alright with you if I have a life? Or, don't tell me, you think I should just be satisfied being a mother for the rest of my life."

"What is your problem, Mavis?" Hayden spoke with an angry voice, offended by her sister-in-law's eternally rude tone. "I haven't passed any judgment against you, yet you come here with this defensive attitude every time."

"Don't act like Cannon hasn't told you about me." Mavis placed her hands on her hips. She looked attractive in a two-piece peach summer outfit. A little makeup brightened her thin face. "Little Mavis, the mess up."

"Listen," Hayden said, checking for a moment to make sure Tyler wasn't within hearing distance. "I don't know why, but you seem to think Cannon disapproves of you or looks down on you, but—"

"Don't tell me what I think, Hayden." Mavis's tone was cool and unbroken. "I get enough of this crap from Cannon and Mom."

"What are you talking about? You're so quick to judge, it's unbelievable."

"You don't know what it's like, Hayden." Mavis looked

Hayden up and down quickly. "You're probably the apple of your parents' eyes. You're so perfect, always living up to their ideas for you. Never making a mistake. Never having to live up to someone like Cannon."

"That's not true," Hayden said as Mavis's words painfully touched her heart. "I spent most of my youth believing my brother Michael was my parents' favorite, especially my mother's. I spent my entire childhood trying to compete with him. I know exactly how you feel."

"That was different," she said, shaking her head. "That was when you were kids. I'm sorry about your brother's death, but it's different when it continues into your adult years."

"It hurts just as much." Hayden stepped closer to Mavis, noticing her words had reached her, softening her composure. "Seeing their attentive smiles at every little thing he did. It seemed like he was always introduced first, even though I was older. Everyone wanted to meet him. They were happy to meet cute little Hayden, but the son . . . well, the son was who they wanted to see."

Hayden sensed hesitation as well as recognition in Mavis's eyes as the other woman stared at her for a moment.

"I remember a family reunion when I was nine." Mavis leaned against the living room wall, her eyes staring straight ahead. "We were in Seattle and we met a lot of relatives from out West for the first time. I thought, here was my chance. Fresh new family. I would be so cute and they would love me, because they didn't know about Cannon and all the things he always did so perfectly."

"What happened?" Hayden asked, seeing a familiar pain in the other woman's eyes.

"All the same," she answered. "Just like you said. I was such a cute little girl, but Cannon, Cannon was the strong, smart son. He was going to make the family proud, carry on the Factor name and be a doctor like his famous daddy."

"It's not fair," Hayden said, "but you can't hate Cannon for that. If you feel Candace has slighted you in some way, you need to sit down with her and have a heartfelt, caring discussion. Cannon loves you so much and Tyler is the most important person in this world to him. It tears him apart when you lash out at him and express such strong disapproval of everything important to him.''

''I know it's not his fault.'' Mavis took a deep breath. ''I know he loves me. I guess that's why it's so easy to hurt him. It was always my way of getting someone back for the hurt I was feeling and I didn't think anyone else would care enough. Really, I'm proud of him, too, and it's funny because even though everyone always treated him better than me—''

''I know,'' Hayden interrupted with a nod, ''you never stopped loving your brother. Neither did I.''

Mavis's head was to the ground as she said, ''I'm prouder of him than anyone else and I adore him so much for what he's done for Tyler. I just don't know how to tell him.''

''You just did.''

Both women looked up to see Cannon step from the hallway into the living room. His face had a thoughtful, eager expression as he looked from Hayden to his sister.

''See how easy it is?'' Hayden felt tears well up in her throat as she watched Cannon step to his sister and hug her tightly.

''Stop it! Stop it!'' Mavis pushed her brother away, laughing and crying at the same time. She gently wiped her eyes. ''I have a date in fifteen minutes and my eyes are all red. He'll think I'm an alcoholic.''

''I'm sorry,'' Cannon said with a choked laugh of his own. ''I couldn't help myself.'' He looked around the apartment. ''Where's my boy?''

''He's running around here somewhere.'' Mavis checked her face in her pocket mirror. ''He just ate in the car on the way over here so you don't have to feed him anything.''

''Everything will be fine,'' Hayden told her. ''Go, or you'll be late. You have to find parking remember?''

''Thanks so much.'' Mavis waved behind her as she fled out the door. ''Bye.''

''You should be a family therapist instead of a public relations consultant,'' Cannon said, turning to Hayden. ''My mother and I have been trying to reach her forever and I think you've gotten more out of her than both of us combined.''

"Sometimes it doesn't matter how many people try to reach you,'' Hayden said reflectively. ''It takes someone who has gone through the same thing to get you to speak up.''

"Whatever it was, thanks.''

"Don't mention it.'' She passed him a quick wink. ''What happened to your workout?''

"Too many people in there.'' He shrugged. ''I'm used to going early in the A.M. I guess this isn't a good time to work out.''

"Uncle Cannon! Uncle Cannon!'' Tyler ran screaming through the living room and bounced off the sofa into Cannon's arms.

"Cannon.'' Hayden suddenly remembered her discovery. ''About the threats, I . . .''

"Hayden.'' He held up a hand to stop her from speaking more. ''Let's not talk about that now. There's a great feeling in this home right now because of Mavis, Tyler, and you. Let's enjoy that and let go of that business for a while.''

As Cannon headed for the living room with Tyler in his arms, Hayden glanced at the magazine in one hand and the threatening notes in the other. She made the decision to do as Cannon asked. This was important, but Hayden herself felt the warmth between them. The tug at her heart at feeling a part of Cannon's family, the security of feeling this place was her home, made her want to let go of the rumors and threats for now. She joined Cannon and Tyler on the sofa, wanting nothing but to enjoy this time.

The weekend came sooner than Hayden expected. Busy and happily distracted by how well she was getting along with Cannon, she put the magazine and the connections she had made with it and the letters in the back of her mind. She was still concerned, but there hadn't been one in more than a week and she was allowing herself to believe what Cannon had originally said. It was simply the ravings of a coward who had no intentions of following up or owning up to his words and would get bored and quit eventually. She had noticed the body-guard outside their condo building a couple of times. She recognized him the other day coming out of R&D's offices. She wasn't worried about safety. Instead, Hayden's thoughts were preoccupied with wonders of how she would handle sharing a hotel room in Springfield with Cannon.

For appearance's sake, they knew they couldn't get two rooms, just in case someone checked or paid a bellboy for information. So they got a suite, deciding that Cannon would sleep on the sofa and she would stay in the bedroom. It seemed innocent enough, but Hayden knew the growing attraction they felt for each other made it anything but innocent. She was beginning to dream about him at night and fantasize about him during the day. They talked more often now at home, eating dinner together almost every night. They talked of their child-hoods, what they wanted for their futures and their families. Hayden found out Cannon's favorite sport was skiing. He traveled to Vail, Colorado, every winter with friends. He loved the tender poems of Maya Angelou and taped reruns of *Good Times*. Hayden was coming to know Cannon from the inside out, learning to believe in him as a man and be attracted to more than his physical appearance. She was coming to love him, his dreams, and his plans to help the people of this state.

Cannon's physical attraction to Hayden had come to him like a lightening bolt the first time he'd seen her. The emotional attraction had taken longer, but he was fully aware it was here. He thought of her all the time. What would it be like if they were a real couple?

He looked forward to seeing her every day. Coming home to the condo took on a whole new meaning now. He anticipated her quick wit and sexy sarcasm. He deeply valued her judgment and opinion. Her kindness and loyalty were an inspiration to him. He could see she was coming to believe in him, trust him. It wouldn't be long now, he knew. As they checked into the hotel for the fund-raiser, he sensed the smoldering tension between them and wondered when she would be ready. He would wait, he had promised Hayden the wait would be well worth it.

Having arrived early Saturday they spent the day lunching with an old Morehouse friend of Cannon's and his wife, David and Danielle Banks. Both lawyers, the attractive African-American couple worked at the capitol building as legal advisors to the governor on civil rights issues. As they sat in the outdoor cafe on Main Street, Hayden enjoyed hearing some of the behind-the-scenes doings of the state government and listened attentively to their stories.

"It turns out," Danielle said, "this particular senator, who has been an outspoken opponent of furthering civil rights laws, didn't know one of his largest campaign contributors was a major civil rights organization."

"Why would they contribute to his campaign?" Hayden asked.

"I guess they don't want to appear partial," David said with a shrug. "Who knows?"

"When the local paper let this out," Danielle continued, "it was all over the news. Now, this senator is an advocate for what he calls *certain* civil rights."

"I'm telling you"—David leaned back in his seat and took a breath of fresh air—"that's not even a big story. Some of the stuff that goes on here . . . Cannon, are you sure you want to go to Washington, D.C.? It's got to be more of a mess there."

"That's why I want to go, Davey," Cannon said, "to do some good to combat the circus players."

"It must be exciting working here," Hayden said, turning to Danielle. "But also a little disheartening."

"It can be," Danielle agreed with a nod as she took her husband's hand in hers atop the table. "Only we're in it together. Keeps us going, working for the same cause. Our desire to see the visions of Dr. Martin Luther King protected and taken to that next level. I'm sure you feel it, too.''

"Yes," Cannon said as he wrapped an affectionate arm around Hayden. "Hayden has been a source of great comfort and encouragement to me throughout all of this."

"Cannon has enough desire for both of us." Hayden molded herself next to him, looking tenderly into his eyes.

"Only because of you," he added, returning her gaze. He meant every word.

It was moments before David cleared his throat. Both Hayden and Cannon realized they had blocked out the rest of the world and had been staring into each other's eyes for a few minutes.

"I can see you both have it," David said. "That love will get you through the disillusioned times. It'll get you through everything."

Hayden wondered, was that love in her eyes? She wasn't sure what her eyes were saying. She was only sure that she hadn't been faking anything for some time now.

After lunch, Cannon and Hayden went shopping in the small town area, enjoying the time alone with each other. As he firmly gripped her hand in his, Hayden felt comfortable talking about Michael's death and how it affected her family and herself.

"I'll never forget that night." She lowered her head as they walked together in the park. "It was very late and the sound of the doorbell ringing was so loud. I could hear Daddy cursing under his breath while he walked down the hallway to the door. He was sure it was a friend of mine or Michael's."

"It was the police, wasn't it?" Cannon asked, gripping her hand tighter.

"Yes." Hayden took a deep breath, fighting back the tears. "I heard my daddy give out this yell. I had never heard any sound so full of pain. At least not until I heard my mother's scream a few minutes later."

"Where were you?"

"I was in my bedroom, looking for a bathrobe. When I came out, I saw Mama holding onto Daddy, who could barely stand.

Then I saw the two police officers in the doorway. I asked what happened. They all looked at me. No one said anything. Then I knew. I can't tell you how I knew. I was only seventeen, but I knew my little brother was dead.''

''You poor kid.'' Cannon stopped and turned to look at her, lifting her chin with his finger. If he could, he would erase all the pain she had ever felt. ''You poor baby.''

She closed her eyes as he gently kissed her forehead and allowed his arms to envelop her in warmth and understanding. They stayed that way for a few minutes on the sidewalk. Hayden forgot they were outside, forgot there were dozens of people staring at them. She had just told Cannon about the most devastating event of her life and a peace had fallen over her. She wanted to stay in his arms forever.

''Let's sit down,'' Cannon said, as they separated.

She only nodded as she took his hand and let him guide her to a red sidewalk bench.

''Hayden, I can sympathize with you somewhat.'' He wiped a runaway tear from her cheek. ''I remember the day my father died. It's not the same really, because he'd had the cancer for some time and we knew he was going to pass. But the day he died, I was at my practice in Northbrook. I remember it so clearly. I was giving two-year-old Erin Brill an ear exam. Maryann knocked on the door and opened it. I looked at her and she lowered her eyes. I knew.''

''You loved him very much.'' She gently rubbed his cheek with her small hand, trailing his strong chin with her finger.

''He was a . . .'' Cannon shook his head in regret, not wanting to cover up after Hayden had been so truthful with him. ''I'm supposed to say he was a great guy and in many ways he was. But we're telling the truth now and in reality I have a lot of anger for him. Anger I know I shouldn't have.''

''Why do you have anger?'' Hayden asked. ''Why still?''

''He used to always tell me I had so much to carry on.'' Cannon sensed from the compassionate look on Hayden's face and the tender sound of her voice he could tell her anything. ''I had to be a doctor. I had to be a better doctor than anyone.

If I wasn't, I would just be remembered as the son of a doctor.
I tried to do everything right, but he always seemed so . . ."

"So what?" Hayden asked, sensing his hesitation.

"Satisfied," he said with resolve. "He was never elated,
never proud. Just satisfied. He was worse with Mavis. He never
expected anything of her and that's the only thing worse than
expecting too much."

"Is this why you strive for so much?" Hayden asked. "Why
you want so much?"

"Partly, yes," he answered. "Partly I want to be more than
he was, lift the handle a little higher, but that isn't all. I really
want to help people, I feel it in my heart."

"You have to want this for the right reasons Cannon. If
you're going to survive this. If you're going to make use of it,
you have to have it in your heart. It won't work if you're doing
it to get back at your dad."

"It's changed from that," he said, never taking his eyes from
her. Just talking to her made him feel better about something so
personal, which had bought him pain for years. "It used to be
revenge, but now that I've matured, I've tried to channel to a
more positive purpose. It's a desire for myself, but in a way
to make him proud. I've struggled to make it become that, but
I think I'm there."

"It wasn't all bad, was it?" Hayden asked. "You and your
father."

"In retrospect he was actually a very interesting guy." Cannon smiled with pride at all his father had accomplished. "I
didn't spend the time with him I should have after I became
an adult, I was so caught up in my bachelor life. Then he
passed, and all of the sudden I woke up and realized I was
responsible for this family now. Then a few months later, Mavis
told us she was pregnant, but the father had skipped town. Oh
well, you know everything since."

"Well, not everything." She gave him a cheerful smile,
hoping to brighten his spirits.

"Everything I want you to know." He shot her a playful wink and placed a strong, dark hand on her leg, loving the smooth touch of her skin and the sweet scent of her perfume as the wind blew it his way. "And I want you to know everything."

"I want to know everything about you Cannon and I want you to know everything about me." She placed her hand on his, her wedding ring reflecting off the brilliant sun.

They sat and watched the sky turn orange and purple, listening to the birds chirp and the wind blow. Hayden couldn't remember feeling so happy.

Returning to the hotel, they changed for the evening's event and arrived, hand in hand, in the main ballroom. The night turned out to be perfect, in Hayden's opinion. She met dozens of interesting people, some who had met the president of the United States in person. Cannon was his usual charming self. Never before involved so closely in a political campaign, Hayden was deeply affected by the fervor and intent of those around her, especially Cannon. The position of senator was a powerful one, allowing a person access to laws and committees that shape the lives of millions of men, women, and children in his or her state. Hayden had no doubt Cannon was perfect for the job and she continued to tell him so as they returned to the hotel room later that evening.

"Everyone is gone now," Cannon said. Falling onto the plush sofa, he opened a bottle of club soda from the refrigerator. "You can stop with the compliments."

"It's not a facade, Cannon." She searched through the minicooler for a snack and pulled out a Snicker's bar. Nice and cold like she liked them.

"I know, I was just joking." He motioned for her to sit next to him. He had never been so proud of her as he had been tonight. She was fantastic, dazzling the room, enchanting everyone in attendance with her beauty and intelligence.

"The more I hear about what people expect and want from their next senator, the more I know you're perfect for it." She sat on the edge of the sofa, too excited from the evening's success to calm down.

"At the risk of sounding conceited," he said, looking up at her with haughty eyes, "I'll agree with you wholeheartedly."

"You should." She flipped back the straying strands of hair that had fallen onto her face "Everyone is so excited about you. We all have faith in you."

"Right now, I don't care about anyone." He casually lifted himself from the sofa and walked to her. "Your faith in me is all I need to do anything."

A strong finger at her chin gently lifted her face to his. He searched her eyes, hoping to find feelings she was unable to decipher because she had never felt them before.

"Hayden." He spoke in a soft and gentle tone. "I realize now how right you were."

"What do you mean?" At that moment she was looking into his eyes, she believed she would do anything he wanted and knew he would do likewise for her.

"When you said this was a bad idea. Us getting married." He turned the lifted finger into a hand, cupping her soft round chin. "I had the wrong idea about marriage. I thought it could be made into whatever I wanted it to be. Whatever I needed at the moment."

"Nothing is ever that simple," she said, in a whisper.

"Not when it involves your heart. I was stupid to think it could work. I was stupid to think I could be so close to a beautiful, sexy, intelligent, and caring woman and not fall in love with her."

"Oh, Cannon." Hayden wanted to capture this moment and how she felt forever.

"Marriage isn't a business deal or an arrangement to be made for career goals." Cannon shook his head, smiling at how easily it came to him. The truth. His feelings. "Marriage is for love. I just want to know if you think we have a chance at a real marriage."

"Let me show you."

She raised her arms and held his head with her soft hands.

As she pulled his face to hers, he lifted her into the cradle of his arms.

Her heart fluttered wildly in her breast as his mouth covered hers hungrily. Her senses leaped to life as his tongue sent shivers of desire racing through her. What she had initially yearned for when he lifted her face to his became clearer with each of his slow drugging kisses. She felt like a feather as he lifted her body and carried her into the bedroom, his mouth never leaving hers. The passion, her body screamed, the passion was overwhelming.

Cannon felt on fire as he had every time he kissed Hayden. Only this time was different. This time there were no doubts, no insecurities; not for him. There was only love and raw need. This time, they would finish what they started. What they'd started months ago.

As he gently eased her down onto the bed, their lips briefly parted. Hayden's excitement and desire increased as she saw the fierceness in his eyes. She made her hips sway and move allowing him to slip the evening gown off her body. She was aroused to a frightening tilt as his eyes passionately raked her body with a hunger on his face she had never seen. A hunger that made her body beg to be devoured and delighted by him.

Supporting himself on his hands, he leaned down and softly kissed her forehead, her cheek and earlobe. She felt the blood pound in her brain and leap from her heart as he straddled her to unclothe himself. She reached to help him, but he pushed her hands away.

"No," he said in a deep husky breath. "I want you to lie there. I want to look at you. You're the most beautiful thing in this world."

As he removed the his tuxedo top and slid off the bed to do the same with his pants, Hayden begged him to hurry. If he didn't, she felt as if she would explode.

"Cannon." She spoke his name with urgency, holding her hand out to him.

Delighting in her desire, he quickly returned to her. She caressed his hard sleek body as he trailed her neck and chest with wet kisses. He begged his body for patience as he eased the lacy cup of her bra aside, taking one second to soak in her beautiful breasts, then fondled one, the light brown nipple marble hard. His tongue caressed the other with a fierce patience. Her back arched, breast surging at the intimacy of his mouth. Patience, he pleaded. Patience. He wanted to enjoy every sensuous inch of her perfect body and let her enjoy his.

His tongue made a path down her ribs to her flat stomach as he kissed her belly button. Hayden was sure she would lose her mind as he removed her satin panties and slowly parted her legs. He leaned in to gently bite the inner flesh of her smooth thighs and moved up to the center of her pleasure point. She let out a moan as his strong hands cupped her buttocks and arched her to greet him.

"Cannon, please. I can't take it." She ceased her begging as he lifted his head to look at her. She could see in his eyes his restraint was gone and she would have to wait no longer. He had finally lost all control as she had some time ago, and slowly slid his body over hers.

They both moaned as he entered her, the thrust slow and hard. She felt complete as his fullness made them one and his lips returned to hers. Flesh against flesh, man against woman. Hayden came to realize that nothing was as pure and sweet, yet as raw and hungry as a man and wife feeling love, sharing love, making love.

As she reached her peak, he joined with her and they both let out a yell. It was an exclamation of their love, their deep love for each other.

Panting, chests heaving, they lay next to each other in the bed. Savoring the erotic pleasure just shared, Hayden could only smile, feeling as if that smile stretched across her entire body. They were both exhausted by lovemaking that had been fervent and greedy.

He turned to her again, sweat on his brow, his face, his entire body. With a wicked smile he signaled his readiness to her and she slid her glistening brown body on top of his, ready as well to enter the realm of passion again. This time, able to take it slower and explore, to arouse and give each other pleasure, it was even better.

"Where did you get a crazy name like Hayden anyway?"

"What?" Hayden smacked Cannon on his back as he turned to reach for the drawer next to the bed.

"Hayden is the most unusual name I've ever heard." he turned to her again. "Tell me about it."

"You want to talk about names?"

"I guess so." He gave a childish wink.

"In that case," she said with a laugh, knowing he meant so because although they wanted to make love some more, they had run out of protection. "Hayden was my grandmother's name from my daddy's side. She was born on a farm in a haystack while my great-grandmother was working in the barn. Somewhere from that, the name Hayden was born. At least that's what I'm told."

"That's a little corny." He wrinkled his nose.

"Don't make fun of me," she said, forming an angry fist at the man she had just made love to three times. "What kind of name is Cannon?"

"Very simple," he responded with an easy smile. "When my mother gave birth, I shot right out. No pushing necessary.

"You were eager to get out and wreak havoc on the world."

"Sounds about right." He watched as she slid out of the bed, revealing her seductively naked body. He knew he would never tire of looking at it. "Where are you going?"

"To take a shower," she answered, reaching for the bathrobe on the chair. "Want to join me?"

"No thanks. I don't think I can move. You forget I'm a little older than you."

"A little? I'd say you were . . ."

"Watch it," he yelled, throwing a pillow at her.

As the hot water drained and massaged her tired body, Hayden glowed in the aftermath of lovemaking. She tried to ignore the little voice in her head that asked what came next and what about the doubts. She wouldn't allow anything to spoil the happy completeness she felt at the moment. She was in love and nothing could ever feel better than this.

Chapter Eleven

The long drive back to Chicago was a quiet one for the Factors. Hayden allowed everything that happened the night before to settle in her mind. She knew they had crossed the line, broken a barrier they could never return from. Although she had no regrets, she was a little scared. Everything was different and it wasn't just the added responsibilities and concerns that came with a sexual relationship. Hearts were at stake now. Hayden knew her own was in danger, for she had fallen in love the moment Cannon kissed her forehead with the gentleness of a brushing feather.

What was next? How would their daily life change? Did Cannon still doubt her trust? Did she still doubt it herself? It was all so complicated and left Hayden feeling as confused as ever. Only one thing was clear and it was that love alone wasn't enough to make this work.

"It's only five," Cannon said as they entered their condo building. "Do you want to go for dinner?"

"I'm tired." Hayden strengthened her grip around his trim waist. "I want to nap. Maybe later."

"You slept most of the way home."

''I'm not finished.'' She playfully patted his rear. ''We didn't get a lot of sleep last night, remember?''

''You've got a point there, Mrs. Factor,'' he said with a wink.

''Good afternoon Mr. and Mrs. Factor,'' Roger, the desk clerk, greeted them with a smile. ''How was your trip down state?''

''It was great, Roger,'' Hayden said, laughing to herself. If he only knew.

''I have your mail from Saturday here, sir.''

''Thank you.'' Cannon accepted the small stack held together by a rubberband. ''You have a nice evening, Roger.''

''Oh wait!'' Roger called to them as they headed for the elevator. ''This came for you as well.''

''What is it?'' Hayden turned and reached for the letter.

''I don't know. There's no stamp or return address.'' Roger scratched his head, frowning in confusion. ''It came yesterday.''

Hayden felt her pulse quicken as she knew exactly what it was. Ripping open the cream-colored envelope, she unfolded the letter.

RAISE ALL THE MONEY YOU WANT. WHO WILL SPEND IT WHEN YOU'RE DEAD?

''Cannon,'' Hayden screamed running to him. He had ignored Roger, continuing to elevator. ''Cannon, it's another threat.''

''What?'' Cannon grabbed the sheet of paper and read it, the fire of anger boiling in him. ''Damn it.'' He walked briskly to the front desk. ''Who sent this, Roger?''

''I'm not sure,'' he responded. ''As I told you last weekend, my niece was married yesterday so Davis took an extra day.''

''What did he say?'' Cannon anxiously gripped the edges of the sleek black and gray marbled desk Roger sat behind.

''I told 'em to be extra careful.'' Roger seemed a little nervous now. Hayden could tell because he was beginning to speak with a southern drawl. Cannon had told her he always did so when he became a little rattled. "I told 'em you wanted a little extra security. He said he already knew."

"Did Davis leave his post?" Hayden asked.

"No. He said he remembers a boy. He said the kid was about fourteen or so, but he couldn't see his face well, bein' covered in a rain coat and hat and all. It poured somethin' awful yesterday. Ruined the weddin'."

"He didn't even ask the kid who he was or who the letter was from?" Cannon was trying his best to control his anger.

"He said he tried to, but the kid ran out so quickly." Roger shook his head. "Davis couldn't go after him because old Ms. Harvey came in with all those dogs of hers and he said she was making such a mess. They were barkin' and yellin' and the McDonough kids were on their way out and the little one started crying cause he was afraid. He said it was crazy."

"Thank you, Roger," Hayden said, grabbing hold of Cannon and pulling him back toward the elevator. "Let's go upstairs, Cannon."

"That kid could have come from anywhere," Cannon said as they rode upstairs.

"I have to tell you something." Hayden regretfully remembered her discovery from last week. "You see the print on that letter?"

"What about the print? It's cut out from magazines."

"The same magazine," Hayden said. "With a few exceptions, which I assume are from advertisements, the style is exact, it's the same style as in *Medical Report*. You know, the magazine you receive?"

"How do you know?" He looked at her in surprise, then to the magazine. She was right!

"Last week I checked the other threats we've received, matching them with the magazine and they're all the same. I've never seen a magazine like it. I went to the Harold Washington Library the other day. They have every magazine imaginable. I looked at every one they had. No print was similar to this."

"When did you do all this?" His voice was strained as

he tried to comprehend her discoveries and the feelings of apprehension they gave him.

"Last week."

"Why didn't you say something?" He was almost yelling now as the elevator opened to the eleventh floor.

"I just did," she explained, confused at his suddenly exacerbated behavior. "I tried to tell you last week, but you didn't want to discuss it. I know, I should have said something anyway, but with the campaign and—"

"Should have?" He threw the door open and stormed inside. "At first I couldn't get you to stay out of this. Now, you find something out and you keep it from me? Exactly what is going on here, Hayden?"

"Why don't you tell me?" Hayden was certain he was accusing her of something, but she wasn't sure what. "I was just trying to . . . trying . . . Hell, I don't know. I don't know what to think or what to believe."

"So, we're back to that now?" Cannon asked. He paced the hallway, rubbing at his goatee. He didn't know what he was saying. The words were leaping from his head, uncensored to his mouth. These threats were coming to his home now!

"You don't believe me!"

"Not you, Cannon." Hayden followed him into the living room, her heart pounding. "I don't know whether or not to believe what I find is—"

"I don't want to hear anymore," Cannon said. He hated the way he felt right now. Confused and helpless. "You can go back and forth all you want, Hayden. I'm going to call Davis and find out what really is behind this."

Hayden stood speechless as he turned and walked away. It wasn't pride that kept her from going after him, it was a defeated heart. It lead her to fall onto the sofa, her mouth still wide open in disbelief. She blinked her eyes shut a few times, wondering if she had just imagined the whole scene. Biting her lip until it throbbed as hard as her pulse, she tried desperately to gather her thoughts and separate her mind from her heart. She knew things would be different, but she thought they would be better.

At least they had let their feelings for each other out, but apparently that wasn't enough. She knew he was being completely irrational and the words were angry words, but they came from a base somewhere and that base was mistrust and uncertainty.

Hayden stared into space, confused about her feelings, her life, and her future, now more than ever before.

"I told you this wouldn't work."

"Donna, you're not helping me one bit." Hayden's sense of humor was nonexistent as she sat across the table from her best friend. They were eating lunch together at a downtown cafe. She couldn't hide her sadness from Donna, and the moment they took their seats, she broke down, telling Donna everything. She told her about making love to Cannon as well as the threats.

"I know it doesn't help," Donna responded, her mouth full of french fries. "I just wanted to add that point. I know you, Hayden. You're a very good businesswoman, but you're not good enough to turn something as emotional as marriage into a business deal. I warned you about this and I warned you about falling for his charms."

Hayden picked at her turkey salad. "I tried to make sense of this, but it didn't work. The question now is, what do I do about it?"

"What do you feel, honey?"

"What do you mean, feel?" Hayden felt a million things right now. Love, fear, uncertainty, dread, mistrust, and anxiety.

"I mean you have to figure out how you feel and decide what to do from there."

"Oh, yes," Hayden said. "Follow your heart. I've heard that before. Doesn't that always get women in trouble?

"You couldn't be in any more trouble than you are right now," Donna said matter-of-factly. "You might as well try it. Doing things the other way hasn't worked so far."

"I love him." The words slipped from Hayden's tongue with ease and comfort. She couldn't remember ever feeling so sure about something she'd said. "I love his mind, his vision, and his heart. I love his body and the way he rubs his goatee when he's nervous."

"But?" Donna's brows rose in anticipation of more.

"It's a mixture of things," Hayden said with a sigh. "It's not that I think the rumors are true. I know the man he is now and I trust that man. It's just well, even though some questions I had about the past have been answered, some haven't. Is his past really in the past for good? What can make me believe I'm different than all those other women in his Rolodex? And what about his political dreams? Sometimes this desire he has to be senator . . . I wonder if he's changed for that. Will he be changed forever? And his need for this goal, I think it's more important than anything, including me. It makes me cautious about making him the most important thing in my life."

"Is that all?" Donna asked with a laugh.

"I don't know." Hayden sighed, wishing she could put all of her emotions into words. "What I'm really wondering is that deep down, we both know that this relationship was started under the guise of a lie. Can we build something real from that?"

Donna wiped her mouth with a napkin before saying, "You said you believed the articles were lies and the threats are real, right?"

"Yes, I do," Hayden said with conviction. "In my mind I'm sure of it, but Cannon seems to still see some doubts."

"He's scared because he loves you," Donna said. "He's scared because he's getting threats and doesn't know what to do about it. For a man, feeling helpless is worse than death. He's not being rational. You can't take anything he says seriously right now."

"So what do I do?" Hayden wondered if that meant not to take his confessions of love seriously either? It was too late for that to matter. She loved him now and his feelings for her couldn't change that.

"On the serious side, you've gotta get the police involved in this." Donna shook her head in disbelief. "I can't believe you're getting threats and you let that boy talk you into keeping it silent.''

"It's not like he's completely ignored it," Hayden said. "He's gotten us bodyguards and he and John are looking at Robert Marks, who I suspect is doing all of this. It's just Cannon and his dream. He wants to be a senator more than anything."

"If he loves you, Hayden, he'll want the two of you to be safe more than anything."

"I just need to find out who is doing this and put an end to it." Hayden crumbled her napkins in her fist. "I'm sure it's Robert Marks, but how can I prove that?"

"Don't worry about that," Donna said. "Give that problem to the cops. You need to concentrate on your relationship with Cannon."

"I am," Hayden said. "I love him and finding who's behind all this will prove that to him."

"Hayden, you prove that to him by showing him what's in your heart." Donna spoke in a soft, gentle voice. "You need to set him straight on that. It's okay. Sometimes men need a little direction when it comes to matters of the heart."

"I'm afraid, Donna." Hayden lowered her head. "It's not like we're just dating and if this doesn't get resolved, we go our separate ways. I'm legally married to this man. I've made love to this man."

"Three times," Donna added with a smile.

"Three times," Hayden repeated, managing a smile of her own. "Seriously. What about Dad? He's doing so well. Dr. Kent has worked wonders. He's even said its possible Dad can return to some form of teaching, like tutoring or counseling. Daddy's on the stars about that. What will become of that if Cannon turns away from me? Literally and emotionally."

"You and this man have a lot to talk about," Donna said, shaking her head. "You've fallen in love with a whirlwind of things going on around you. No matter what your intentions, you're going to continue to have problems if you don't focus on your relationship."

Hayden knew she was right, but she also knew that couldn't

be done until this issue of the threats was put aside. Her love for Cannon made her determined to make it work.

Hayden appreciated Donna's attempts at making her feel better with jokes and funny stories throughout their lunch, but their effect only went halfway. As they returned to work, what little laughter Hayden had expressed quickly ceased upon encountering a deeply concerned Marcy outside Hayden's office.

"What is it, Marcy?" Hayden, along with Donna, followed Marcy as she quietly summoned them into Hayden's office.

"Close the door." Marcy's young voice cracked.

"What's wrong?" Donna's eyes widened as she shut the door. "Say something. You're starting to scare me."

"I didn't want anyone else to hear," Marcy whispered. "Hayden, you know I open your mail unless it's from a personal friend or marked confidential, right?"

"Yes," Hayden said, remembering the agreement. It saved her a tremendous amount of time to have Marcy sift through the mail. She was able to eliminate junk and excess sales pitches as well as direct any résumés to the human resources department.

"I opened this." Marcy slowly brought her left hand from around her back and held out a sheet of paper to Hayden. "It came in the regular mail, but there's no return address."

Before Hayden could reach for it, Donna grabbed the slip of paper and began reading it out loud.

"Be a good wife," she read, "and tell Cannon to drop out. If not, you could be a widow."

Hayden covered her mouth in a gasp. The first two letters had frightened her, but now there was the one left while they were in Springfield and this one. This culprit was coming too close to home and was getting more and more graphic now.

"What is this about, Hayden?" Fear and concern was as apparent in Marcy's voice as it was on her face. "Is this why you told the front desk to check with you before letting anyone up?"

"Marcy, it's nothing really," Hayden lied, not wanting to

bring any more people into this tangled web. "I'm going to have to ask that you speak of this to no one right now."

"Are you in danger?" Her young eyes switched from Hayden to Donna, pleading for an honest answer.

"Marcy," Donna said calmly, placing a hand on each of the young girl's shoulders and guiding her toward the door. "It's not a big deal. Just some stupid coward. You aren't in any danger. Hayden and I will take care of everything. Just go back to work and don't say a word of this to anyone."

After Donna closed the door, Hayden let out a deep breath.

"I can't believe his life is being threatened." Hayden's stomach turned as the wretched words of the letter repeated themselves in her head. "He's not just some coward playing games. He's sending them to my job now! Directing them at me, too."

"You have a problem, girl," Donna said. "Cannon's success in Springfield was in all the papers. If this person is serious about him getting out of the race and he's reading about all the support Cannon's getting, he's probably getting real angry about now."

"What's going on with me and Cannon isn't important," Hayden said, despite the pain she felt in her heart at the rift between them. "Both of our lives are in danger and I'm going to find out from who."

"What can you do?" Donna asked, shaking her head in disbelief as she read the letter again. "Do you really think you're a match for some psycho?"

"I can only think of one thing to do right now." Hayden sat in her chair, rubbing her temples as she felt the onset of a tremendous headache. "I'm fairly positive the same person who was leaking those lies to the press is behind these threats."

"Why are you so sure?" Donna sat across from her with peaked interest. "These are two completely different types of approaches."

"I'm not sure," Hayden responded, shrugging her shoulders. "I have a feeling and that feeling is all I have to go on."

"A feeling is all you have?" Donna shook her head. "You

need more than that. This person is not trying to get caught. You need a clue, a link, a source.''

"I have one," Hayden said as an idea began forming in her mind. "The source. Lee Sampson's source."

"But you don't have that," Donna said. Noticing Hayden's determined stare, her suspicious frown returned. "What are you thinking?"

"I have to get that source," Hayden said with resolve.

"How?" Donna asked.

"I'm going to sneak into Sampson's office and find it." Hayden's face was full of strength, shining with a steadfast stare.

"You're going to break into the *Represent Chicago* offices?" Donna jumped from her seat, mouth open wide in amazement. "Are you crazy?"

"No, I can't do that." Hayden thought for a moment, letting her newfound determination inspire her. "I'm going over there now."

"What if he's there? How will you get him out of his office?"

"A distraction," Hayden said, giving Donna a mischievous smile and looking her up and down. "A beautiful distraction."

As she stood in the phone booth across the street from *Represent Chicago*'s headquarters, Hayden checked her watch. It was two fifteen and Sampson hadn't come out yet. As she gripped the large manilla envelope, full of bits of scrap paper, she felt nervous tension set in. Then she saw him.

In raggedy blue jeans and a blue and black plaid shirt, the little man exited the revolving doors to the building, looking both ways before crossing the street. Stomping out his cigarette butt, he headed up Michigan Avenue. Hayden only hoped Donna could keep his attention long enough.

Before leaving Hayden's office, Donna called Sampson, telling him she had some juicy news about a University of Chicago Medical School professor and one of her virile and young graduate students. Pretending she had a 4 P.M. flight leaving

O'Hare for Virginia, Donna got Sampson to agree to meet her at a downtown cafe right away. He seemed more than eager to hear more of the breaking story. Donna promised to keep him there until three at least. With what, Hayden had no idea, since the story was completely made up, but she trusted Donna's ability to improvise. So with forty-five minutes to do what she had to do, Hayden walked onto the fourth floor of the building with no specific plan in mind, but a composed courage and determination.

To her surprise, she was able to enter the offices and receive directions to Sampson's desk without anyone asking her for identification or purpose. She found that unusual with all the unfortunate events that happen these days, but wouldn't question her good fortune.

Sampson didn't have his own office, but fortunately for her, reporters were separated by cubicles. With newsroom chaos around her, Hayden crossed her fingers and walked directly to Sampson's high-walled cubicle, faking a confidence that would make anyone watching assume she belonged there, even if they'd never seen her before.

When she got there, she paused a moment, half expecting someone to walk up to her and ask her what she was doing there. No one came, and she felt a breath of relief escape her. She placed the manilla envelope on the air conditioning duct behind the desk and quickly went to work.

His desk was a complete mess. Hayden sorted through papers, scattered everywhere. She felt hurried as she saw no understandable order in the files on his desk, but warned herself to keep calm and think straight. She set her eyes to focus on anything with Cannon's name on it. Searching his drawers, she flipped through files labeled DISEASES, SEPARATE HOSPITAL CASES, and MEDICAL CLIPS. Just before letting nervous frustration get to her, she saw Sampson's expense reports, and beamed with hope.

Opening the folder, Hayden flipped through the pages recording calls for the past two months, finding the bill for March. Attached to a sheet marked CELLULAR was a copy of

Sampson's phone bill. The name FACTOR was in brackets attached to several records of calls to one number: 847-555-9876. It was an unrecognizable number to her.

As she quickly scribbled the number onto a piece of scrap paper and placed it in her pocket. Hayden considered quickly calling the number, but she knew she was short on time. Besides, she wanted to share this discovery with Cannon. Again returning the folder to the drawer, she closed it. She wasn't sure if this was the number of his source, but it had something to do with Cannon and it put Hayden ten steps ahead of where she'd been before. Glancing at her watch, Hayden noticed it was two forty-eight. She had taken enough chances today. She wasn't about to push the line. What she had would have to do for now.

"Can I help you?"

Hayden's stomach clenched tight as fear swept through her like a forest fire, but found the composure to slowly turn toward the voice as if it hadn't fazed her.

"Can I help you?" The young man repeated his question. Not looking a day over nineteen, he was dressed in a yellow and black Alpha Kappa Alpha T-shirt and shorts. The skin on his earth-brown-colored face creased as it contracted in an expression of confusion.

"Maybe you can," Hayden answered with a saccharine smile and a southern accent. "My name is Rayleen Stone and Lee Sampson was supposed to have a package for me. He told me to meet him here at two thirty but he is nowhere to be found."

"He received an emergency call a little while ago and had to run out," the boy said. "I'm sorry, he must have forgotten you."

"It looks like it." Hayden became more confident now that it appeared her facade was working. "I have to get back to work soon. My shift at the diner starts at three. What will I do?"

"I'll help you," he said, smiling as he stuck his chest out. "What did you say your name was?"

"Rayleen Stone." Hayden watched in amusement as the boy

searched around the desk. Pretending to be helpless had a certain effect on men, especially the younger ones. Helping a damsel in distress would make his day.

"Here we go." He picked up the manilla envelope from atop the air conditioning duct. "It's from Lee with your name on it."

"Oh, yes, this is it," Hayden said with pseudo-elation as she accepted the envelope she had purposefully placed there in anticipation of a situation such as this. She read the inscription aloud. "For Rayleen Stone." Just as she had written it.

"Thank you very much." Hayden gave the young boy a flirtatious wink.

"You're welcome," he said with a proud smile. "Anytime."

"You have a nice day now." Hayden threw him a quick wink before standing up and walking away. Outside of anyone's view, she quickly headed down the stairs and out of the building. Finally on the street, she let out a loud sigh before hailing a cab to the State Building. She hoped if Sampson ever became suspicious, the young man wouldn't get into too much trouble.

"You did what?" Cannon jumped from his seat, the chair sliding backward and hitting the wall. He couldn't believe what he was hearing.

When Hayden unexpectedly appeared in his doorway, he was overcome with affection for her, feeling the love in his heart just at the sight of her. He had felt such a fool for blowing up at her the other day, but wasn't sure what to say to make up for it. Sorry didn't seem satisfactory to him, making him certain it wouldn't be enough for Hayden. The truth was, he loved her dearly and hated himself for hurting her, putting her in danger, and making a mess of everything for the sake of his own selfish dream. What good would any accomplishments be without this enchanting woman in his life? This frustrating woman, he thought, as he sat and listened to her latest escapade.

"I know it wasn't too smart," Hayden said, "but . . ."

"Hayden, I can't believe you sneaked through his files." Cannon began pacing his office as he rubbed his goatee.

Hayden was incredibly excited, her adrenaline as high as a kite. She knew Cannon wouldn't be happy with her method, but she expected him to be happy about the result. If he only knew how hard it was for her to be this close to him, feeling the confusion between them and at the same time loving him with all her heart. She was setting it all aside to concentrate on helping him remove the obstacles to his dream. It was becoming her dream as well. Her heart wanted to yell at him for hurting her, for making her love him, but she wouldn't give in to her heart. Not yet at least.

"Will you stop that?" she asked in irritation at his constant rubbing.

"I can't help it," he said, shoving his hands into his pants pockets. "I always do it when I'm nervous."

"I know." Hayden extended the scrap of paper across the desk to him. "Aren't you excited? Here's the number."

"To what? Whose number is it?" He reached for the paper, wanting to look at it, but felt a certain sense of hesitation. He was afraid, he had to admit. It was hard, wanting to feel that, as a man, he should fear nothing. But he was afraid. More than anything, he was afraid of losing Hayden, but he was also afraid of finding out the truth behind these threats. He knew it could be someone close to him.

He knew he would have to follow up on it, for his sake as well as Hayden's. Would this be a final obstacle to his dreams? Would he be able to realize the old dreams he had been carrying with him? Would he be able to embark on the new dreams that he yearned for now that Hayden was in his life?

"You know whose number it could be." She reached for the phone and pushed it toward him. "That's why you're so nervous. Let's call it now. I'll bet you it's Robert Marks's home or office."

Cannon recaptured his chair and sat down. Taking a deep breath, he unfolded the small sheet of paper. He felt his heart drop, his mind explode, as he saw the number. It couldn't be true, he told himself.

"Where did you get this number?" He turned to her with sheer surprise and astonishment written all over his face.

"I told you where," Hayden said slowly. She watched with anxiety as his expression turned from surprise to confusion and then anger. "Next to the phone calls marked with your name."

"I can't believe this." he said, more to himself than anyone. "Hayden, this has to be a mistake."

"Why?" The anticipation was killing her as she leaned across the desk. He knew who it was, she was sure of it. He knew!

"I can't believe this." He looked to her, a distant pain in his eyes.

"Who is it?" She asked, seeing the pain in his eyes. "Is it Marks?"

"No, Hayden." His voice was calm and quiet as he lowered his head, holding on to the belief that this clue meant something else. It had to. "Marks's home and office are in Chicago. This number has a suburban area code. If you remember, I told you John and I were looking into him. We found out just a few days ago that the reason Marks's name was dropped for commissioner was because he was diagnosed with cancer. He chose to remove his name from consideration. He has nothing against me."

Hayden felt terrible guilt as she remembered her one encounter with Marks. She would have to apologize for her behavior.

"Then who is it?" she pleaded, now that the only suspect she had left was no longer one. "Please, Cannon. I can tell you know. Whose number is that?"

"You shouldn't have done this," he said, hearing the defeated sound in his voice. "You could have gotten in trouble doing something illegal."

"I had no choice," she said stubbornly.

"What do you mean?" His brows drew together in an agonized expression. What else was there? Could it get worse?

Hayden didn't know how else to tell him the bad news, so she said it like it was. "I got a threat at my office today."

"You what?" This time he yelled loud enough for anyone within a mile to hear him. His large hands gripped the edges of the desk as his eyes turned hard with fierce anger.

"It said I would be a widow if I didn't get you to drop out of the race. It was mailed to my office today." Hayden spoke with caution in response to Cannon's behavior. She could see he was terribly angry, and she didn't want him to do something stupid. "Let's calm down, Cannon, and think this through."

"Damn thinking it through. I've wasted enough time on this already!" Filled with a violent rage, Cannon leaped from his chair, grabbed his coat off the rack, and rushed out of the office. A line had been crossed by threatening the woman he loved.

"Cannon!" Hayden jumped up, running after him. He wasn't even running, but was quickly several strides ahead of her.

The elevator he was in closed just as she approached. In a panic, she hit the DOWN button several times before another opened. Ignoring the standing stares and open mouths of everyone around her, she jumped into the elevator. When she finally got down to the lobby, in all it's red and glass maze designs as well as the people bustling through, she couldn't find him. She looked around, calling Cannon's name out loud several times. No response came. Finally, Hayden decided to return to her office.

A gamut of emotions assailed her. She was excited that so much had been accomplished, angry that Cannon had deserted her, and confused at his suspicious behavior. She cursed herself for not remembering the phone number she had copied down. Back in her office she tried dozens of variations she remembered it to be, but nothing came of it. Realizing she couldn't do anything about it now, Hayden decided to first make sure everything was alright with Donna after her meeting with Sampson and then head home. If she couldn't prevent him from doing whatever it was he was going to do, at least she could be there for him afterward. Her love and support was what he needed now, no matter what.

Who had it been? she wondered. The look in Cannon's eyes, his anger and denial. Not only did he know who it was, but that person was close to him. Hayden was sure of that. Sampson had told her his source was reliable. She'd thought he was trying to divert her from his trail, but he didn't. Reliable indeed.

Feeling the onset of another headache, she knew she couldn't work any longer today. She tried calling Cannon's car phone, the condo, and his pager several times, but got no response. She left a message at home, begging him to talk to her before doing anything rash, even though she feared she was too late.

Chapter Twelve

After speaking with Donna, who proudly told her of a successful luncheon, ending with Sampson so confused he probably wouldn't bother to follow up, Hayden returned to her office to gather her things. She was angry Cannon hadn't shared what knowledge he had with her. She had done so with him, eagerly at that. Her hopes were that they would find out who was behind this disaster together and Cannon would see her efforts as an expression of her love for him.

No, it hadn't happened that way, but what bothered Hayden the most was when she'd told him about the threat she received. He was angry as she expected, knowing he cared for her, but that wasn't what she wanted. The threat had frightened her and she wanted, no needed, his comfort and consolation. She loved him with all her heart and wasn't sure she could stand to continue this arrangement if he decided his dream of being a senator took precedence over their love.

"Mrs. Factor?" Marcy's voice came over the intercom. "I know you said to take messages if it isn't Cannon, but there's a Jesse Dannell on line one for you and she's very insistent. She's a friend, right?"

The last thing Hayden was in the mood for was talking to Jesse, but knowing she could possibly know something about Cannon through John, she picked up the phone.

"Hello, Jesse," she said. "What can I do for you?"

"Your tupperware is here!" Jesse's squeaky high voice always sounded so cheerful.

"What?"

"Your tupperware, silly. You remember you ordered the picnic set at my party two weeks ago." Jesse paused, apparently awaiting a response. Not hearing one, she continued, "Well it's here."

"Oh, yeah. My picnic set." Hayden suddenly recalled the party.

"Are you going to come pick it up?" Jesse asked.

"I don't know, Jesse," Hayden said, not at all interested in driving into the north suburbs just as rush hour traffic was setting in. "It's really out of the way."

"You have to come. You know John and I are going to visit his father in New York on Saturday. I need to get all this stuff out beforehand."

"I can come next weekend." Hayden reached for her purse and car keys. All she could think of was getting to Cannon.

"No, you have to come tonight," Jesse said, apparently not giving up. "John hates this mess staying here. Besides, if you have the tupperware, you and Cannon can have a nice picnic this weekend. I think you need that."

"What do you mean by that?" Hayden was struck with curiosity as to why Jesse whispered her last sentence.

"I, uh, well you know John and Cannon are best friends."

"Cannon told him about our problems?"

"It's not important," Jesse said. "He just called that night you got back from Springfield. He was upset. John got upset, too."

"We all were upset, Jesse. Cannon's life had been threatened." Hayden was fuming inside, then remembered she'd confided in Donna. Cannon had that same right. "What else did he tell John? Did he tell him that I received another threat at my office?''

''You did?'' Jesse's voice reached a decimal higher than Hayden could ever remembering hearing. ''That's awful. No, Cannon hasn't talked to John since the night you both returned from downstate.''

''Can I speak to John?'' Hayden suddenly had a yearning to know what Cannon had said that night about her and his insane idea that she suspected him.

''Sorry, hon. He just got a call five minutes ago and ran out. He said he'd be right back. If you come by, he might be back by then.''

''I'm leaving right now.'' Hayden hung up the phone.

She wasn't looking forward to the drive during rush hour, but wanted to talk to John. Maybe he could give her some insight into Cannon's behavior and feelings. He was the most confusing man she'd ever known and, to the core of her heart, she wanted to know him from the inside out.

She knew she could also look in on Candace as well as see her parents which she hadn't done in a while.

''So I told John,'' Jesse went on to say, ''there is no way you're buying a new Jeep. You know how much those things cost?''

''Not really.'' Hayden sat on the Dannells' living room sofa, staring blankly at the woman who hadn't stopped talking since she arrived. It was six forty-five and there was no sign of John. Hayden had been tempted to leave for some time now, not sure she could take another second of Jesse's incessant talking. She was ready to beg for mercy.

''Thirty-seven thousand dollars.'' Jesse mouthed every syllable slowly. ''I just freaked out when I heard. And that's not even fully loaded.''

''That's a pretty penny.'' Hayden forced a smile, glancing at her watch. ''Jesse, I'm enjoying our talk, but I really have to get going. I wanted to stop by my folks and . . .''

"No . . . no . . . no. You have to stay." Jesse looked into Hayden's eyes with lonely desperation on her face. "I need someone to talk to."

"Alright." Hayden wasn't close to Jesse, but felt obligated to stay and listen to whatever problems the woman had. She couldn't help but feel sorry for her. She had no job and no children to look after. A maid cleaned their home and according to Cannon, Jesse never cooked or had any real hobbies. Hayden knew that, despite hosting the occasional tupperware party, Jesse wasn't involved in any community programs or organizations. With a husband who worked all day, including weekends, she was probably a very lonely and bored woman. "What's wrong Jesse?"

"I don't know." Jesse spoke with a sigh as her shoulders slumped. She leaned back as if exhausted from her own emotions. "I guess it's me. Or maybe it's John."

"Are you having problems?" Hayden was going to let Jesse be the one who brought up the money issue.

"John has changed." Jesse shrugged indecisively as her head turned to the left. She looked out the window at the blazing sunset. "Maybe I've changed. I don't know. Haven't you noticed?"

"Well, Jesse," Hayden said. "I haven't known him long enough to say that. Maybe you should ask Cannon this question."

"Cannon won't talk to me." Jesse frowned as she shook her head. "I mean he's a great guy, but he and John are like brothers. If John asked Cannon to keep a secret, Cannon wouldn't tell me if I begged."

"Do you think he's keeping secrets from you?" Hayden couldn't help but get emotional as thoughts of her confusion about Cannon's behavior came to mind. She never thought she'd have anything in common with Jesse Dannell, but she did.

"I see signs," Jesse said. "He's moody. He comes and goes at will. He locks himself in that office all the time. He's gotten so disorganized. I mean this is John Dannell. He's a neat freak.

He'd yell at me if I left one of my fashion magazines on the sofa instead of neatly closed on the coffee table. Now he leaves those darn medical magazines all over . . .''

Hayden watched in silence as Jesse tried to keep her emotions in check. Finally, she asked, ''When did this start, Jesse? Maybe if you can go back to when it started, you can get an idea of what brought this behavior on and work from there.''

''I guess . . . I guess this spring. We've been having money problems for a while, but early spring, like March or April, he started acting like this.''

A lightning bolt hit Hayden with the power of a thunderstorm and hurricane tied up in one. She knew she was crazy for her thoughts. Must be crazy. ''Since spring?'' she asked, piecing together a million thoughts in her mind, Hayden felt her brain's quick conflict with her heart. ''Things got worse since then?''

''Yes.'' Jesse's attention returned to the sunset. ''He's been like a different person since then.''

''Jesse?'' Hayden knew her idea was crazy. To even suggest such a thing. Only she couldn't help herself. She had to find out one way or another. ''You said something about medical magazines earlier? What did you mean by that?''

''Only that he's contradicting himself. He used to leave them at the office, but now he brings them all home. He leaves them laying around all day, then hauls them into his office. He makes me throw away my *Essence* and *Glamour* as soon as the next issue comes.''

''*Medical Report*,'' Hayden said. She felt her stomach begin to turn. She was wrong, she knew she must be. She had to be! Still she needed to find out. ''John gets *Medical Report* magazine, doesn't he?''

''I don't know what they're called.'' Jesse said, a hint of confusion appearing on her face as she seemed to notice Hayden's behavior changing. ''They're all the same.''

''I need to know, Jesse.'' Hayden clenched her hands into fists at her sides, her stomach in knots. ''I can't tell you why right now, but I need to know.''

''I can't tell you,'' she said. ''I don't pay attention to that.''

"Where's his office." Hayden leaped off the sofa. "I need to know."

"It's down the hall." Jesse stood up, her attention focused on Hayden and her peculiar behavior. "It's locked."

"Locked?" Hayden cursed under her breath. "Oh, Jesse. Tell me you have a key."

"I do, but . . ."

"Let's go." Hayden grabbed a bewildered Jesse's hand and lead her out of the living room and down the hallway of the Northbrook home.

"John has a fit when I . . ." Jesse reached for a string of keys on a high wooden Madison table. "Oh, what the heck."

Hayden rushed through the door as soon as Jesse undid the lock. The office was decorated in antique pine and wrought iron. The colors were a harsh white and pale beige. It was a cold and untouchable room, giving Hayden a sense of John she hadn't known. This room represented his current state of emotions. There was barely any cushion, no sofa, only sharp, tall chairs, a bare pine trestle table in a straight forward design. No pictures, nothing personal. Nothing soft. Hayden realized that John Dannell was an angry man, doing his best to void himself of feeling so he could do what he had to do.

Seating herself in the large black chair behind the desk, Hayden gathered several copies of *Medical Report* magazine, which were sprawled at will across the top. Jesse stood with a perplexed stare on her face as she watched Hayden run her hands over the magazines. Hayden looked up at her and could see the transformation in her eyes as she began to realize what Hayden had discovered. Hayden felt for her, but there was nothing she could do. The truth needed to be found out.

She held her breath as she flipped through one copy of the magazine and saw letters, even whole words cut out everywhere! Copy after copy. It was John! John had been threatening Cannon. But why? Hayden wondered. They were best friends. They loved each other.

"Jesse, when will he be home?" Hayden's voice relayed the desperation she felt.

''He never tells me anything anymore.'' Jesse said in a soft, quiet voice with separated words. ''Cannon called here for him this afternoon. I . . . I picked up the phone and Cannon sounded all flustered. I didn't pay attention.'' Her eyes fell closed as her head lowered pitifully to the ground. ''I never do. Oh, Hayden.''

Cannon knew! Of course, Hayden thought. He must have realized as soon as . . .

''Jesse, what's your phone number?'' Hayden quickly asked, trying to keep up with the thoughts racing through her mind. ''I just realized I don't really know it. Cannon has it set on speed dial at the house and on the car phone.''

''5-5-5-9-8-7-6.''

Hayden was certain that was the number she had found on Lee Sampson's phone report. She hadn't had time to memorize it before Cannon took it and left, but it came back to her after hearing it again. He realized it was John as soon as he saw the number which was why he had been so upset.

Hayden knew she had to get to Cannon. Not just to tell him she knew, but to comfort him. She knew it was tearing him apart to find out his best friend was behind this. Why?

''I have to get home Jesse,'' Hayden said, standing up from the chair. 'I hope you understand. I know you're probably more upset and confused than you've ever been, but at least you know the reason.''

''Hayden, I'm so sorry.'' Tears filled Jesse's eyes and quickly trickled down her cheeks. ''I'm so . . .''

''Don't apologize.'' Hayden reached over and hugged Jesse. ''You have to figure out what you're going to do now. I'm sorry, but I can't stay with you.''

''I understand.'' Jesse nodded as she wiped her cheeks with the back of her hand. ''Go to him.''

After a moment's hesitation and an affectionate nod, Hayden ran out of the office and out of the house. She had compassion for Jesse, wishing she didn't have to leave her alone at the worst possible time, but she had to get to her love. He needed her now more than ever and she needed to be with him the same.

Despite rush hour nearing its end for the day, it still took an eternity for her to get home. She was tempted to use her car phone, but no. She wanted to hold him when she told him she knew. She wanted Cannon to see her eyes when she told him she loved him and everything would be okay. Running to the front door, she barely had it open before she saw Cannon in the hallway. She headed for him with full steam.

"Cannon, it's John!" Arms open she hugged him tightly and felt his arms wrap around her. "I know it's John. I was at the house and I . . ."

"You saw the magazines in the office."

She knew that wasn't Cannon's voice and Hayden jumped with a start as she looked up and, from around the corner, stepped John Dannell.

Frightened and stunned, she grabbed hold of Cannon's arms and looked upward at his face. She saw a look of sadness and anger that made her heart ache.

"It's okay, baby." Cannon's voice was calm and soothing as he wrapped his strong arms around her. He would give anything to spare her this moment. He loved her so much, his own pain was secondary to hers. "I know and John knows we know."

"What are you doing here?" She spat the words out, turning to John with anger and anxiety raging within her.

"Hayden, I'm so very sorry." John, tired and haggard looking, reached out a sorrowful hand to Hayden, but pulled it back as she stepped away, clinging tighter to Cannon.

"You're sorry? You're sorry?" She shook her head in disbelief at his attempt at an apology. "You spread lies! You threatened his life! How could you John? You were supposed to be his best friend!"

"And he was supposed to be mine." Pain and anger seethed

through John's every word as he eyed her. "So why did he desert me?"

"That's enough, John." Cannon's voice was firm and direct. He had heard more than he could stand.

He had to pray for the strength to keep from strangling John while he sat and listened to him. Calling him over under the guise of needing to talk about his problems with Hayden, he'd hoped John could tell him the reason Sampson had contacted him was to dispute whomever was spreading the rumor. Or even something else. Any reason other than that John himself was the source. At the slightest hint of suspicion on Cannon's part John broke down in tears, confessing to everything. Cannon reached inside to find sympathy somewhere in all those years of friendship, but the thought of him threatening Hayden made him too angry. He tore into John with verbal assaults harsher than any physical blow could be.

"How could you say he deserted you?" Hayden asked, tears now coming down her face. "Why John? Why?"

"Tell her," Cannon said, after noticing John's shameful hesitation. He couldn't stand to hear it, but Hayden deserved an explanation after everything she had done to find out the truth.

"I needed Cannon to return to the practice," John said after a defeated sigh. He lowered his head in embarrassed humility as he continued. "It fell apart after he left. I just couldn't manage without him. Jesse and I could no longer live the lifestyle we'd grown accustomed to. It started with the rumors. I knew everyone was aware of Cannon's playboy past, so I thought it could be feasible. I also thought Cannon would get sick of caring and quit, so I leaked rumors about his moral character to the paper. I knew Sampson would never tell it was me. Then those rumors weren't working, so I thought to spread some about his job performance. I was sure Cannon couldn't tolerate that."

"So you gave Sampson the old picture of Cannon and that drug dealer Jackson." Hayden wiped away her tears, keeping her eyes on John and her arms around Cannon.

"Yes. I was cleaning out an old office." He laughed a pitied laugh for himself. "I was renting it out because I needed the money. I found the pictures and sent them. I told Sampson about the Bulls game with Mavis, the young girls he escorted to the cab at the hotel. I guess he got a little excited and started following Cannon himself. That's how he got the pictures of you at Cannon's office and at the Metropolitan Club. I told him when Cannon would be in Los Angeles and where we were staying. I had nothing to do with that picture of you and your ex-boyfriend that appeared in the *Times*."

"The rumors stopped when John and Jesse went on vacation." Cannon spoke after a long silence. He was still piecing things together for himself.

"Yes," John answered. "I was hoping it would be enough and that when we returned you would have decided to quit public life and return to the practice, bringing along your patients as well as the prestigious Factor name. That didn't happen. Nothing was working and then you went and got married. I knew it would be a lot harder than I planned."

"So you started the threats?" Hayden realized that John still didn't know the terms under which her and Cannon had married.

"I had no choice," he said in frustration, running a rugged hand over his head. "First you got married and then this senator thing started becoming a reality. I knew it was something you wanted, but so soon? I did what I had to. The threats were all I had left."

"You went too far period, but you really crossed the line when you sent a threat to Hayden." Cannon tightened his protective grip around his wife as he gave John a dangerously unforgiving stare. He never imagined John's resentment ran so deep, but now that he knew, it didn't matter. John had a serious problem. Hating him did no good.

"I know." John's eyes showed remorse as he looked from Hayden to Cannon. "From talking to you and being around the two of you I realized how much you really loved her. I thought that if I could scare her enough, she would convince you to drop out."

"Do you hear yourself, John?" Hayden asked. "Do you know how insane you sound?"

"Find out how you behave when everything is falling apart around you!" He heaved an angry, sad sigh.

"Get out, John." Cannon's voice was stern and forceful. He couldn't stand another minute.

"Cannon," John began, "I can never apologize enough."

"Shut up, John, and get out!" Cannon pointed harshly to the door and, without another word, John left.

Hayden clung to Cannon, allowing him to gently guide her to the living room sofa. As they sat, she leaned her head back and looked gently into his eyes. The mixture of sadness, anger, and warmth and comfort she saw emanating from them made her heart flutter.

"Are you going to be okay?" He gently caressed her arms and softly kissed her forehead. He wanted to kiss her every tear away.

"Don't worry about me," Hayden said, forcing a smile for his benefit. "John is your best friend. I can't imagine the pain you're feeling right now."

"I can't believe he did this." Cannon said, shaking his head. "Over the practice. An almost twenty-year friendship thrown away over wanting an expensive lifestyle. I don't understand."

"You never will." Hayden wrapped her arms around him. "He's completely lost his mind. Don't even try to understand."

"I let him go because I couldn't stand the sight of him, but I can't let him get away with this. I can't let him get away with causing this turmoil in our lives."

"You know you have some choices," she said comfortingly. "I know you're angry, as well you should be. I also know you still love your best friend despite what he's done. I take it you don't want to call the police."

"Could I do that to him?" Cannon turned to her with uncertainty in his eyes. "He's been my best friend forever and I'm not sure jail time is what he needs."

"I know. I know." Hayden gently kissed his rugged face, the rough bristles of his goatee brushing her lips. She wanted to kiss away the pain, loving him dearly. "I know you'll make the right decision and whatever that decision is, I'll be there for you."

"Hayden, I love you." Cannon took her face in his hands, cupping her chin. "I need you to know that. I've loved you from the first moment you walked into my office with all your spunk and aggressiveness. I knew then, no matter what, I would be with you. With your loyal heart and dangerous curiosity, I only wanted you to love me back, to trust me and believe in me. I let my desire to become senator mean more to me than anything, including us and that was a mistake. I put it before our safety and our love. Never, never again will I do that. Forget Washington, D.C. Forget it all. I'm going to concentrate all my time and effort on gaining your . . ."

"Cannon, you don't have to," Hayden said, putting her small index finger to his lips, her soul floating from his words. "I love you and I trust you more than I ever have anyone."

"Do you mean that?" A flicker of light and hope appeared in his eyes as her words erased his pain. "Please don't say these things because you feel sorry for me now. I couldn't bear it if you didn't mean it."

"I'm not," she said, speaking from her heart. "I was afraid. I had been hurt by Alec and I didn't want to get involved again. I was so attracted to you and I knew that wasn't a good thing since this was just business. I felt the only thing that could keep me from falling in love with you was to believe the worst of you, but it didn't work. I still fell in love with you and I love you now with all my heart. After our last argument, I was so afraid you would ask me to leave."

"Never, baby." He kissed her tear-stained cheek dozens of times, savoring the smell of her, the touch of her. "I wouldn't let you leave if you begged me." He laughed a choked laugh, the pain of John's confession still with him, but not stronger than his love. "You could do no wrong in my eyes, my love . . ."

"I knew you hadn't meant what you said." Hayden wrapped her arms around his neck, sliding as close to him as possible. She wished their bodies could fuse into one.

"No, I didn't," he said, "and I plan to spend the rest of our lives proving to you that I love you more than life itself."

A delightful shiver of wanting ran through her at the electricity of his touch as he brought her face to his and kissed her soft lips. The pressure brought her a pleasure that consumed her soul. It was a kiss of love, pure love, but also a release of emotions, both good and bad, over everything that had happened and what they would face in the future.

What would happen with John's confession and Cannon running for senator was uncertain, but both Hayden and Cannon knew one thing for sure. They had found the person they would spend the rest of their lives with.

Epilogue

"Cannon, where are you!" Hayden yelled as loud as she could. She was losing patience.

"I'm right here," he yelled back. As he rushed into the upstairs bedroom of their new Georgetown area townhouse, Cannon held out to his wife what she had sent him to the local store to get.

Hayden's eyes widened at the sight of chocolate chocolate chip ice cream in one of his hands and a caramel candy bar in the other.

"What took you so long?" She grabbed the food from him, hungrier than ever. Now in the eighth month of her pregnancy, Hayden found all she could do was eat.

"I couldn't help it," he said, slipping into the bed beside her. He relished the warmth of the body he still found sexier than any other woman's in the world. "There was a guy in the store from back home and he recognized me and had to stop me to explain all of his problems."

"Speaking of problems," Hayden said, "have you spoken to John?"

Ever since being elected senator in the November elections, Hayden knew Cannon had been bombarded constantly with calls and letters from people telling him what he needed to do for them. He swore to get on every one of their grievances and Hayden knew he meant it.

"Yes, I have." Cannon shook his head, still feeling a strong sense of disappointment over the situation. If it hadn't been for Hayden standing by his side through it all, he wasn't sure how he would have gotten over John's betrayal. "I feel sorry for him. He's still seeing a therapist and says he's improved, but Jesse's still going through with their divorce."

"That's too bad," Hayden said, biting into her candy bar. Cannon had promised John he wouldn't go to the police with what he had done if John would get psychiatric counseling. John had made great steps recently. Enough so that he and Cannon spoke on the phone a couple of times a month.

"It may be for the best. Jesse needs some time to find herself, develop a life of her own." Cannon snuggled closer to his hungry wife, placing a hand on her belly after kissing it. He couldn't bear to be apart from her. "Are you sure you want to take the train back to Chicago tomorrow? You can stay here a little longer."

"No," she said, kissing him on the forehead. "The doctor said it isn't safe for me to fly anymore so I have to go back now. I know this is where we live now and I'm sure one day I'll feel like this is my home. Only right now I still feel like my home is Chicago and I want to have our baby there. I want us to be with Mom, Dad, Candace, Donna, and everyone around." Hayden knew Elise would never forgive her if she wasn't there when the baby was born. Their parents, Candace especially, were almost more excited than Hayden and Cannon about the upcoming birth.

They had all been extremely disappointed, although understanding, when Cannon and Hayden sat them down to tell them all the truth about their marriage. It took some time before everyone accepted it, but the fact that Hayden and Cannon truly loved each other now helped. Mavis, becoming a different woman than she was before, had been the most supportive as they planned a very small and private second wedding ceremony to renew their vows.

Cannon and Hayden discussed their future and with Hayden's blessing, Cannon continued his bid for the senate. When he won the election, it became necessary for them to purchase a second home in the country's capitol. It had been difficult for Hayden to leave her full-time position at R&D, but she still worked with the company as a consultant, communicating mostly via the Internet on her home computer.

"All right," Cannon said. "But I'm going to have to stay here two more weeks for the last vote of this session of Congress, so you better not have this baby anytime soon."

"I promise." Hayden rubbed her large stomach, lovingly anticipating the birth of their baby. "I would never bring our child into the world without his daddy around. You just better be in Chicago in two weeks, because I don't know how much longer this little guy is going to stay in here."

"He'll wait for his daddy." Cannon stared at her stomach for a moment, love and excitement in his soft eyes. He'd never been so happy, so full of hope.

"Oh no, Cannon! This is awful." Hayden popped her husband on the head.

"What's wrong, honey?" Cannon asked, growing ever more nervous as the baby's date drew near. "What is it?"

"You didn't bring me a spoon." She held up the pint of ice cream. "How am I suppose to eat ice cream without a spoon?"

"Is that it?" He slid out from under the sheets, letting go a sigh of relief. "I'll go get it, but you have to say the magic words."

"Please, Senator," she said, blowing him a kiss and a sexy smile.

As he caught the kiss in his hand and smacked it to his cheek, he winked seductively at her.

Hayden felt the complete happiness as it blanketed her. She had made a sacrifice what seemed like a hundred years ago at the time, wishing for the day it would all end. Now, that sacrifice had reaped this blessing and she never wanted it to end. She wanted this to last forever and she knew it would.

Full of contentment beyond words, Hayden took another bite of her candy bar and laid back in her bed.

ABOUT THE AUTHOR

Angela Winters majored in Journalism at the University of Illinois at Urbana-Champaign, with double minors in Speech Communications and English. She is an executive search executive at a Chicago area firm. She lives in Evanston, Illinois with her nine-year-old cat, Jordan. She is a member of SinC, Sisters In Crime, an organization of female mystery and romantic suspense authors.

Look for these upcoming Arabesque titles:

April 1998

A PUBLIC AFFAIR by Margie Walker
OBSESSION by Gwynne Forster
CHERISH by Crystal Wilson Harris
REMEMBERANCE by Marcia King-Gamble

May 1998

LOVE EVERLASTING by Anna Larence
TWIST OF FATE by Loure Bussey
ROSES ARE READ by Sonia Seerani
BOUQUET, An Arabesque Mother's Day Collection

June 1998

MIRROR IMAGE by Shirley Hailstock
WORTH WAITING FOR by Roberta Gayle
HIDDEN BLESSINGS by Jacquelin Thomas
MAN OF THE HOUSE, An Arabesque Father's Day Collection

BOOK YOUR PLACE ON OUR WEBSITE AND MAKE THE ARABESQUE ROMANCE CONNECTION!

We've created a customized website just for our very special Arabesque readers, where you can get the inside scoop on everything that's going on with Arabesque romance novels.

When you come online, you'll have the exciting opportunity to:

- View covers of upcoming books
- Read sample chapters
- Learn about our future publishing schedule (listed by publication month *and author*)
- Find out when your favorite authors will be visiting a city near you
- Search for and order backlist books from our online catalog
- Check out author bios and background information
- Send e-mail to your favorite authors
- Meet the Kensington staff online
- Join us in weekly chats with authors, readers and other guests
- Get writing guidelines
- AND MUCH MORE!

**Visit our website at
http://www.arabesquebooks.com**

ENJOY THESE ARABESQUE FAVORITES!

FOREVER AFTER   (0-7860-0211-5, $4.99)
by Bette Ford

BODY AND SOUL   (0-7860-0160-7, $4.99)
by Felicia Mason

BETWEEN THE LINES   (0-7860-0267-0, $4.99)
by Angela Benson